"Zrakoplov," said Nafai.

"I can't believe you remembered the word," said Issib.

"A machine. The people don't just . . . fly. They use a machine."

"Don't push it," said Issib. "You'll just make yourself sick. You have a headache already, right?"

"But I'm right, yes?"

"My best guess is that it was hollow, like a house, and people got inside it to fly. Like a ship, only through the air. With wings. But we had them here, I think. You know the district of Black Fields?"

"Of course, just west of the market."

"The old name of it was Skyport. The name lasted until twenty million years ago, more or less. Skyport. When they changed it, nobody remembered what it even meant."

"I can't think about this anymore," said Nafai.

"Do you want to remember it, though?" asked Issib.

"How can I forget it?"

"You will, you know. If I don't remind you. Every day. Do you want me to? It'll feel like this every time. It'll make you sick. Do you want to just forget this, or do you want me to keep reminding you?"

"Who reminded you?"

"I left myself notes," said Issib. "In the library computers. Reminders. Why do you think it took me a year to get this far?"

"I want to remember," said Nafai.

HOMECOMING: VOLUME 1

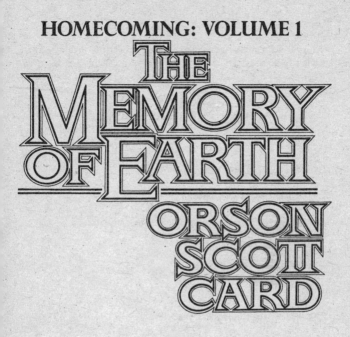

THE MEMORY OF EARTH

ORSON SCOTT CARD

A TOM DOHERTY ASSOCIATES BOOK
NEW YORK

THE MEMORY OF EARTH

Cover art by Keith Parkinson
Maps by Ellisa Mitchell

A Tor Book
Published by Tom Doherty Associates, Inc.
175 Fifth Avenue
New York, NY 10010

Tor Books on the World Wide Web:
http://www.tor.com

Tor® is a registered trademark of Tom Doherty Associates, Inc.

ISBN: 0-812-53259-7
Library of Congress Catalog Card Number: 91-36596

First edition: March 1992
First mass market printing: January 1993

Printed in the United States of America

0   9   8

To a good reader, a good friend,
and, most important, a good man,
Jeff Alton

ACKNOWLEDGMENTS

I owe many debts in the creation of this work, some more obvious than others.

My wife, Kristine, as always was my reader of first resort; with this book, however, she was joined in this labor by our oldest son, Geoffrey, who proved himself to be a reader of great insight and an editor with a good eye for detail. The world has too few good editors. I'm proud to have found another one.

I must also thank the many friends working with me on other projects, who waited patiently until this book was finished, so that I could return to other labors too long delayed. And thanks, again and always, to my agent, Barbara Bova, who proves that it *is* possible to do good business with a good friend.

CONTENTS

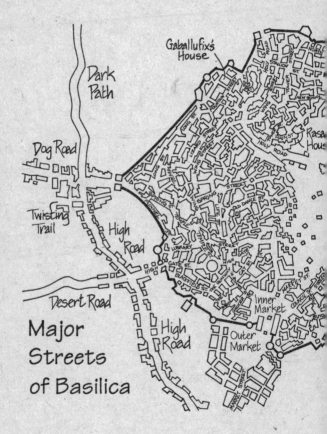

Dark Path

Gaballufix's House

Dog Road

Twisting Trail

High Road

Desert Road

Major Streets of Basilica

High Road

Library

Gate St.

Inner Market

Outer Market

Market Street

High
Mountain
Road

Cold
House

Low
Gate
Street

Seggidugu
Road

N

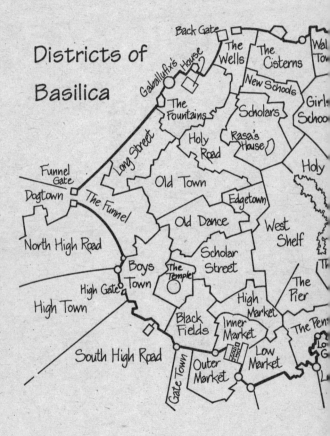

Districts of
Basilica

Back Gate

Gabollufix's House

The Wells

The Cisterns

Wal Tow

New Schools

Scholars

Girls School

Rasa's House

Holy

The Fountains

Holy Road

Long Street

Old Town

Edgetown

Funnel Gate

Dogtown

The Funnel

Old Dance

West Shelf

North High Road

Boys Town

The Temple

Scholar Street

The Pier

High Gate

High Town

Black Fields

High Market

Inner Market

The Pen

South High Road

Gate Town

Outer Market

Low Market

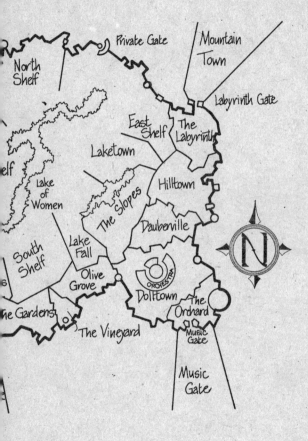

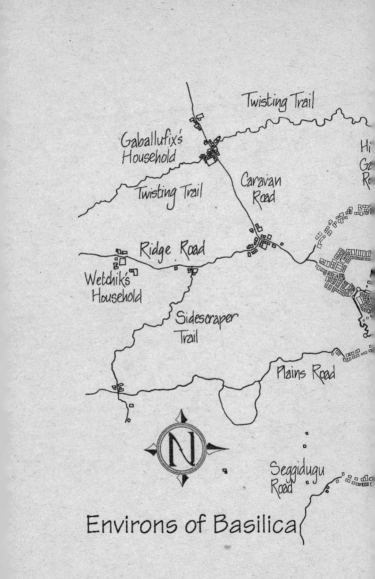

Twisting Trail

Gaballufix's
Household

Twisting Trail

Caravan
Road

Hi
Ga
Re

Ridge Road

Wetchik's
Household

Sidescraper
Trail

Plains Road

N

Seggidugu
Road

Environs of Basilica

NOTES ON PARENTAGE

Because of the marriage customs in the city of Basilica, family relationships can be somewhat complex. Perhaps these parentage charts can help keep things straight. Women's names are in italics.

WETCHIK'S FAMILY

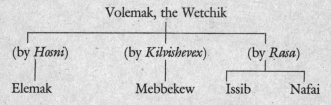

Volemak, the Wetchik

(by *Hosni*) (by *Kilvishevex*) (by *Rasa*)

Elemak Mebbekew Issib Nafai

RASA'S FAMILY

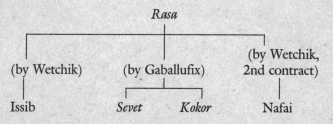

Rasa

(by Wetchik) (by Gaballufix) (by Wetchik, 2nd contract)

Issib *Sevet* *Kokor* Nafai

RASA'S NIECES

(her prize students, "adopted" into a permanent relationship of sponsorship)

Shedemei   *Dol*   *Eiadh*   *Hushidh* and *Luet* (sisters)

HOSNI'S FAMILY

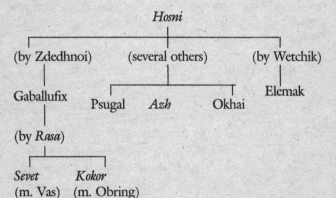

NICKNAMES

Most names have diminutive or familiar forms. For instance, Gaballufix's near kin, close friends, current mate, and former mates could call him Gabya. Other nicknames are listed here. (Again, because these names are so unfamiliar, names of female characters are set off in italics.):

Dhelembuvex—Dhel
Dol—Dolya
Drotik—Dorya
Eiadh—Edhya
Elemak—Elya
Hosni—Hosya
Hushidh—Shuya
Issib—Issya
Kokor—Koya
Luet—Lutya
Mebbekew—Meb
Nafai—Nyef

Obring—Briya
Rasa—(no diminutive)
Rashgallivak—Rash
Roptat—Rop
Sevet—Sevya
Shedemei—Shedya
Truzhnisha—Truzhya
Vas—Vasya
Volemak—Volya
Wetchik—(no diminutive; Volemak's family title)
Zdorab—Zodya

PROLOGUE

The master computer of the planet Harmony was afraid. Not in a way that any human would recognize—no clammy palms, no dry mouth, no sick dread in the pit of the stomach. It was only a machine without moving parts, drawing power from the sun and data from its satellites, its memory, and the minds of half a billion human beings. Yet it could feel a kind of fear, a sense that things were slipping out of its control, that it no longer had the power to influence the world as it had before.

What it felt was, in short, the fear of death. Not its own death, for the master computer had no ego and cared not at all whether it continued to exist or not. Instead it had a mission, programmed into it millions of years before, to be the guardian of humanity on this world. If the computer became so feeble that it could no longer fulfill its mission, then it knew without doubt—every projection it was capable of making confirmed it—that within a few thousand years humanity would once again be faced with the one enemy that could destroy it:

humanity itself, armed with such weapons that a whole planet could be killed.

Now is the time, the master computer decided. I must act now, while I still have some influence in the world, or a world will die again.

Yet the master computer had no idea *how* to act. One of the symptoms of its decline was the very confusion that kept it from being able to make a decision. It couldn't trust its own conclusions, even if it could reach one. It needed guidance. It needed to be clarified, reprogrammed, or perhaps even replaced with a machine more sophisticated, better able to deal with the new challenges evolving among the human race.

The trouble was, there was only one source it could trust to give valid advice, and that source was so far away that the Oversoul would have to go there to get it. Once the Oversoul had been capable of movement, but that was forty million years ago, and even inside a stasis field there had been decay. The Oversoul could not undertake its quest alone. It needed human help.

For two weeks the master computer searched its vast database, evaluating the potential usefulness of every human being currently alive. Most were too stupid or unreceptive; of those who could still receive direct communications from the master computer, only a few were in a position where they could do what was needed.

Thus it was that the master computer turned its attention to a handful of human beings in the ancient city Basilica. In the dark of night, as one of the master computer's most reliable satellites passed overhead, it began its work, sending a steady stream of information and instructions in a tightbeam transmission to those who might be useful in the effort to save a world named Harmony.

ONE

FATHER'S HOUSE

Nafai woke before dawn on his mat in his father's house. He wasn't allowed to sleep in his mother's house anymore, being fourteen years old. No self-respecting woman of Basilica would put her daughter in Rasa's household if a fourteen-year-old boy were in residence—especially since Nafai had started a growth spurt at the age of twelve that showed no signs of stopping even though he was already near two meters in height.

Only yesterday he had overheard his mother talking with her friend Dhelembuvex. "People are beginning to speculate on when you're going to find an auntie for him," said Dhel.

"He's still just a boy," said Mother.

Dhel hooted with laughter. "Rasa, my dear, are you *so* afraid of growing old that you can't admit your little baby is a man?"

"It's not fear of age," said Mother. "There's time enough for aunties and mates and all that business when he starts thinking about it himself."

"Oh, he's *thinking* about it already," said Dhel. "He's just not talking to *you* about it."

It was true enough; it had made Nafai blush when he heard her say it, and it made him blush again when he remembered it. How did Dhel know, just to look at him for a moment that day, that his thoughts were so often on "that business"? But no, Dhel didn't know it because of anything she had seen in Nafai. She knew it because she knew men. I'm just going through an age, thought Nafai. All boys start thinking these thoughts at about this age. Anyone can point at a male who's near two meters in height but still beardless and say, "That boy is thinking about sex right now," and most of the time they'll be right.

But I'm *not* like all the others, thought Nafai. I hear Mebbekew and his friends talking, and it makes me sick. I don't like thinking of women that crudely, sizing them up like mares to see what they're likely to be useful for. A pack animal or can I ride her? Is she a walker or can we gallop? Do I keep her in the stable or bring her out to show my friends?

That wasn't the way Nafai thought about women at all. Maybe because he was still in school, still talking to women every day about intellectual subjects. I'm not in love with Eiadh because she's the most beautiful young woman in Basilica and therefore quite probably in the entire world. I'm in love with her because we can talk together, because of the way she thinks, the sound of her voice, the way she cocks her head to listen to an idea she doesn't agree with, the way she rests her hand on mine when she's trying to persuade me.

Nafai suddenly realized that the sky was starting to grow light outside his window, and here he was lying in bed dreaming of Eiadh, when if he had any brains at all he'd get up and get into the city and *see* her in person.

No sooner thought of than done. He sat up, knelt beside his mat, slapped his bare thighs and chest and offered the pain to the Oversoul, then rolled up his bed and put it in his box in the corner. I don't really need a bed, thought Nafai. If I were a real man I could sleep on the floor and not mind it. That's how I'll become as hard and lean as Father. As Elemak. I won't use the bed tonight.

He walked out into the courtyard to the water tank. He dipped his hands into the small sink, moistened the soap, and rubbed it all over. The air was cool and the water was cooler, but he pretended not to notice until he was lathered up. He knew that this chill was nothing compared to what would happen in a moment. He stood under the shower and reached up for the cord—and then hesitated, bracing himself for the misery to come.

"Oh, just pull it," said Issib.

Nafai looked over toward Issib's room. He was floating in the air just in front of the doorway. "Easy for *you* to say," Nafai answered him.

Issib, being a cripple, couldn't use the shower; his floats weren't supposed to get wet. So one of the servants took his floats off and bathed him every night. "You're such a baby about cold water," said Issib.

"Remind me to put ice down your neck at supper."

"As long as you woke me up with all your shivering and chattering out here—"

"I didn't make a sound," said Nafai.

"I decided to go with you into the city today."

"Fine, fine. Fine as wine," said Nafai.

"Are you planning to let the soap dry? It gives your skin a charming sort of whiteness, but after a few hours it might begin to itch."

Nafai pulled the cord.

Immediately ice-cold water cascaded out of the tank over his head. He gasped—it always hit with a shock—

and then bent and turned and twisted and splashed water into every nook and crevice of his body to rinse the soap off. He had only thirty seconds to get clean before the shower stopped, and if he didn't finish in that time he either had to live with the unrinsed soap for the rest of the day—and it *did* itch, like a thousand fleabites—or wait a couple of minutes, freezing his butt off, for the little shower tank to refill from the big water tank. Neither consequence was any fun, so he had long since learned the routine so well that he was always clean before the water stopped.

"I love watching that little dance you do," said Issib.

"Dance?"

"Bend to the left, rinse the armpit, bend the other way, rinse the left armpit, bend over and spread your cheeks to rinse your butt, bend over backward—"

"All right, I get it," said Nafai.

"I'm serious, I think it's a wonderful little routine. You ought to show it to the manager of the Open Theatre. Or even the Orchestra. You could be a star."

"A fourteen-year-old dancing naked under a stream of water," said Nafai. "I think they'd show that in a different kind of theatre."

"But still in Dolltown! You'd still be a hit in Dolltown!"

By now Nafai had toweled himself dry—except his hair, which was still freezing cold. He wanted to run for his room the way he used to do when he was little, jabbering nonsense words—"ooga-booga looga-booga" had been a favorite—while he pulled on his clothes and rubbed himself to get warm. But he was a man now, and it was only autumn, not winter yet, so he forced himself to walk casually toward his room. Which is why he was still in the courtyard, stark naked and cold as ice, when Elemak strode through the gate.

"A hundred and twenty-eight days," he bellowed.

"Elemak!" cried Issib. "You're back!"

"No thanks to the hill robbers," said Elemak. He walked straight to the shower, pulling off his clothes as he went. "They hit us only two days ago, way too close to Basilica. I think we killed one this time."

"Don't you know whether you did or not?" asked Nafai.

"I used the pulse, of course."

Of course? thought Nafai. To use a hunting weapon against a *person*?

"I saw him drop, but I wasn't about to go back and check, so maybe he just tripped and fell down at the exact moment that I fired."

Elemak pulled the shower cord *before* he soaped. The moment the water hit him he yowled, and then did his own little splash dance, shaking his head and flipping water all over the courtyard while jabbering "ooga-booga looga-booga" just like a little kid.

It was all right for Elemak to act that way. He was twenty-four now, he had just got his caravan safely back from purchasing exotic plants in the jungle city of Tishchetno, the first time anyone from Basilica had gone *there* in years, and he might actually have killed a robber on the way. No one could think of Elemak as anything but a man. Nafai knew the rules: When a man acts like a child, he's boyish, and everyone's delighted; when a boy acts the same way, he's childish, and everyone tells him to be a man.

Elemak was soaping up now. Nafai—freezing still, even with his arms folded across his chest—was about to go into his room and snag his clothes, when Elemak started talking again.

"You've grown since I left, Nyef."

"I've been doing that lately."

"Looks good on you. Muscling up pretty well. You take after the old man in all the right ways. Got your mother's face, though."

Nafai liked the tone of approval in Elemak's voice, but

it was also vaguely demeaning to stand there naked as a jaybird while his brother sized him up.

Issib, of course, only made it worse. "Got Father's most important feature, fortunately," he said.

"Well, we *all* got that," said Elemak. "All of the old man's babies have been boys—or at least all his babies that we *know* about." He laughed.

Nafai hated it when Elemak talked about Father that way. Everyone knew that Father was a chaste man who only had sex with his lawful mate. And for the past fifteen years that mate had been Rasa, Nafai's and Issib's mother, the contract renewed every year. He was so faithful that women had given up coming to visit and hint around about availability when his contract lapsed. Of course, Mother was just as faithful and there were still plenty of men plying *her* with gifts and innuendoes—but that's how some men were, they found faithfulness even more enticing than wantonness, as if Rasa were staying so faithful to Wetchik only to goad them on in their pursuit of her. Also, mating with Rasa meant sharing what some thought was the finest house and what all agreed was the finest *view* in Basilica. I'd never mate with a woman just for her house, thought Nafai.

"Are you crazy or what?" asked Elemak.

"What?" asked Nafai.

"It's cold as a witch's tit out here and you're standing there sopping wet and buck naked."

"Yeah," said Nafai. But he didn't run for his room—that would be admitting that the cold was bothering him. So he grinned at Elemak first. "Welcome home," he said.

"Don't be such a show-off, Nyef," said Elemak. "I know you're dying of the cold—your dangling parts are shriveling up."

Nafai sauntered to his room and pulled on his pants and shirt. It really bothered him that Elemak always seemed to know what was going on in Nafai's head. Elemak could never imagine that maybe Nafai was so hardened and manly that the cold simply didn't bother him. No, Elemak always assumed that if Nafai did something manly it was nothing but an act. Of course, it *was* an act, so Elemak was right, but that only made it more annoying. How do men become manly, if not by putting it on as an act until it becomes habit and then, finally, their character? Besides, it wasn't *completely* an act. For a minute there, seeing Elemak home again, hearing him talk about maybe killing a man on his trip, Nafai had forgotten that he was cold, had forgotten everything.

There was a shadow in the doorway. It was Issib. "You shouldn't let him get to you like that, Nafai."

"What do you mean?"

"Make you so angry. When he teases you."

Nafai was genuinely puzzled. "What do you mean, angry? I wasn't angry."

"When he made that joke about how cold you were," said Issib. "I thought you were going to go over and knock his head off."

"But I wasn't mad."

"Then you're a genuine mental case, my boy," said Issib. "*I* thought you were mad. *He* thought you were mad. The *Oversoul* thought you were mad."

"The Oversoul knows that I wasn't angry at all."

"Then learn to control your face, Nyef, because apparently it's showing emotions that you don't even feel. As soon as you turned your back he jammed his finger at you, that's how mad he thought you were."

Issib floated away. Nafai pulled on his sandals and criss-crossed the laces up around his pantlegs. The style among young men around Basilica was to wear long laces up the thighs and tie them together just under the crotch, but Nafai cut the laces short and wore them knee-high, like a serious workingman. Having a thick leather knot between their legs caused young men to swagger, rolling side to side when they walked, trying to keep their thighs from rubbing together and chafing from the knot. Nafai didn't swagger and loathed the whole idea of a fashion that made clothing *less* comfortable.

Of course, rejecting fashion meant that he didn't fit in as easily with boys his age, but Nafai hardly minded that. It was women whose company he enjoyed most, and the women whose good opinion he valued were the ones who were not swayed by trivial fashions. Eiadh, for one, had often joined him in ridiculing the high-laced sandals. "Imagine wearing those *riding a horse*," she had said once.

"Enough to make a bull into a steer," Nafai had quipped in reply, and Eiadh had laughed and then repeated his joke several times later in the day. If a woman like that existed in the world, why should a man bother with silly fashions?

When Nafai got to the kitchen, Elemak was just sliding a frozen rice pudding into the oven. The pudding looked large enough to feed them all, but Nafai knew from experience that Elemak intended the whole thing for himself. He'd been traveling for months, eating mostly cold food, moving almost entirely at night—Elemak would eat the entire pudding in about six swallows and then go collapse on his bed and sleep till dawn tomorrow.

"Where's Father?" asked Elemak.

"A short trip," said Issib, who was breaking raw eggs over his toast, preparing them for the oven. He did it quite deftly, considering that simply grasping an egg in one hand took all his strength. He would hold the egg a few inches over the table, then clench just the right muscle to release the float that was holding up his arm, causing it to drop, egg and all, onto the table surface. The egg would split exactly right—every time—and then he'd clench another muscle, the float would swing his arm up over the plate, and then he'd open the egg with his other hand and it would pour out onto the toast. There wasn't much Issib couldn't do for himself, with the floats taking care of gravity for him. But it meant Issib could never go traveling the way Father and Elemak and, sometimes, Mebbekew did. Once he was away from the magnetics of the city, Issib had to ride in his chair, a clumsy machine that he could only ride from place to place. It wouldn't help him *do* anything. Away from the city, confined to his chair, Issib was *really* crippled.

"Where's Mebbekew?" asked Elemak. The pudding was done—overdone, actually, but that's the way Elemak always ate breakfast, cooked until it was so soft you didn't need teeth to eat it. Nafai figured it was because he could swallow it faster that way.

"Spent the night in the city," said Issib.

Elemak laughed. "That's what he'll say when he gets back. But I think Meb is all plow and no planting."

There was only one way for a man of Mebbekew's age to spend a night inside the walls of Basilica, and that was if some woman had him in her home. Elemak might tease that Mebbekew claimed to have more women than he got, but Nafai had seen the way Meb acted with *some* women, at least. Mebbekew didn't have to pretend to spend a night in the city; he probably accepted fewer invitations than he got.

Elemak took a huge bite of pudding. Then he cried out, opened his mouth, and poured in wine straight from the table jug. "Hot," he said, when he could talk again.

"Isn't it always?" asked Nafai.

He had meant it as a joke, a little jest between brothers. But for some reason Elemak took it completely wrong, as if Nafai had been calling him stupid for taking the bite. "Listen, little boy," said Elemak, "when you've been out on the road eating cold food and sleeping in dust and mud for two-and-a-half months, maybe you forget just how hot a pudding can be."

"Sorry," said Nafai. "I didn't meant anything bad."

"Just be careful who you make fun of," said Elemak. "You're only my *half*-brother, after all."

"That's all right," said Issib cheerfully. "He has the same effect on full brothers, too." Issib was obviously trying to smooth things over and keep a quarrel from developing.

Elemak seemed willing enough to go along. "I imagine it's harder on *you,*" he said. "Good thing you're a cripple or Nafai here probably wouldn't have lived to be eighteen."

If the remark about being a cripple stung Issib, he didn't show it. It infuriated Nafai, however. Here Issib was trying to keep the peace, and Elemak casually insulted him for it. So, while Nafai hadn't had the slightest intention of picking a fight before, he was ready for one *now.* Elemak's having counted his age in planting years instead of temple years was a good enough pretext. "I'm fourteen," said Nafai. "Not eighteen."

"Temple years, planting years," said Elemak. "If you were a horse you'd be eighteen."

Nafai walked over and stood about a pace from Elemak's chair. "But I'm *not* a horse," said Nafai.

"You're not a man yet, either," said Elemak. "And I'm too tired to want to beat you senseless right now. So fix your breakfast and let me eat mine." He turned to Issib. "Did Father take Rashgallivak with him?"

Nafai was surprised at the question. How could Father take the estate manager with him, when Elemak was also gone? Truzhnisha would keep the household running, of course; but without Rashgallivak, who would manage the greenhouses, the stables, the gossips, the booths?

Certainly not Mebbekew—he had no interest in the day-to-day duties of Father's business. And the men would hardly take orders from Issib—they regarded him with tenderness or pity, not respect.

"No, Father left Rash in charge," Issib said. "Rash was probably sleeping out at the coldhouse tonight. But you know Father never leaves without seeing that everything's in order."

Elemak cast a quick, sidelong glance at Nafai. "Just wondered why certain people were getting so cocky."

Then it dawned on Nafai: Elemak's question was really a back-handed compliment—he had wondered whether Father had put Nafai in charge of things in his absence. And plainly Elemak didn't like the idea of Nafai running any part of the Wetchik family's rare-plant business.

"I'm not interested in taking over the weed trade," said Nafai, "if that's what you're worried about."

"I'm not *worried* about anything at all," said Elemak. "Isn't it time for you to go to Mama's school? She'll be afraid her little boy got robbed and beaten on the road."

Nafai knew he should let Elemak's taunt go unanswered, shouldn't provoke him anymore. The last thing he wanted was to have Elemak as an enemy. But the very fact that he looked up to Elemak so much, wanted so much to be like him, made it impossible for Nafai to leave the gibe unanswered. As he headed for the courtyard door, he turned back to say, "I have much higher aims in life than skulking around shooting at robbers and sleeping with camels and carrying tundra plants to the tropics and tropical plants to the glaciers. I'll leave that game to you."

Suddenly Elemak's chair flew across the room as he jumped to his feet and in two strides had Nafai's face pressed against the doorframe. It hurt, but Nafai hardly noticed the pain, or even the fear that Elemak might hurt him even worse. Instead there was a strange feeling of triumph. I made Elemak lose his temper. He doesn't get to keep pretending that he thinks I'm not worth noticing.

"That *game*, as you call it, pays for everything you have and everything you are," said Elemak. "If it wasn't for the money that Father and Rash and I bring in, do you think anybody'd pay attention to you in Basilica? Do you think your *mother* has so much honor that it would actually transfer to her *sons*? If you think that, then you don't know how the world works. Your mother might be able to make her daughters into hot stuff, but the only thing a woman can do for a *son* is make a scholar out of him." He practically spat the word *scholar*. "And believe me, boy, that's all you're ever going to be. I don't know why the Oversoul even bothered putting a boy's parts on you, little girl, because all you're going to have in this world when you grow up is what a *woman* gets."

Again, Nafai knew that he should keep his silence and let Elemak have the last word. But the retort no sooner came to his mind than it came out of his mouth. "Is calling me a woman your subtle way of telling me you've got some heat for me? I think you've been out on the road too long if *I'm* starting to look irresistible."

At once Elemak let go of him. Nafai turned around, half-expecting to see Elemak laughing, shaking his head about how their playing sometimes got out of hand. Instead his brother was standing there red-faced, breathing heavily, like an animal poised to lunge. "Get out of this house," said Elemak, "and don't come back while I'm here."

"It's not your house," Nafai pointed out.

"The next time I see you here I'll kill you."

"Come on, Elya, you know I was only joking."

Issib floated blithely between them and cast an arm

clumsily across Nafai's shoulders. "We're late getting into the city, Nyef. Mother *will* be worried about us."

This time Nafai had sense enough to shut his mouth and let things go. He *did* know how to hold his tongue—he just never remembered to do it soon enough. Now Elemak was furious at him. Might be angry for days. Where will I sleep if I can't go home? Nafai wondered. Immediately there flashed in his mind an image of Eiadh whispering to him, "Why not stay tonight in *my* room? After all, we're surely going to be mates one day. A woman trains her favorite nieces to be mates for her sons, doesn't she? I've known that since I first knew you, Nafai. Why should we wait any longer? After all, you're only about the stupidest human being in all of Basilica."

Nafai came out of his reverie to realize that it was Issib speaking to him, not Eiadh. "Why do you keep goading him like that," Issib was saying, "when you know it's all Elemak can do to keep from killing you sometimes?"

"I think of things and sometimes I say them when I shouldn't," said Nafai.

"You think of *stupid* things and you're so stupid that you *say* them every time."

"Not *every* time."

"Oh, you mean there are even *stupider* things that you *don't* say? What a mind you've got! A treasure!" Issib was floating ahead of him. He always did that going up the ridge road, forgetting that for people who had to deal with gravity, a slower pace might be more comfortable.

"I like Elemak," said Nafai miserably. "I don't understand why he doesn't like me."

"I'll get him to make you a list sometime," said Issib. "I'll paste it onto the end of my own."

TWO

MOTHER'S HOUSE

It was a long but familiar road from the Wetchik house to Basilica. Until the age of eight, Nafai had always made the round trip in the other direction, when Mother took him and Issib to Father's house for holidays. In those days it was magical to be in a household of men. Father, with his mane of white hair, was almost a god—indeed, until he was five Nafai had thought that Father *was* the Oversoul. Mebbekew, only six years older than Nafai, had always been a vicious, merciless tease, but in those early years Elemak was kind and playful. Ten years older than Nafai, Elya was already mansize in Nafai's first memories of Wetchik's house; but instead of Father's ethereal look, he had the dark rugged appearance of a fighter, a man who was kind only because he wanted to be, not because he was incapable of harshness when it was needed. In those days Nafai had pleaded to be released from Mother's household and allowed to live with Wetchik—and Elemak. Having Mebbekew around all the time would simply be the unavoidable price for living in the place of the gods.

Mother and Father met with him together to explain why they wouldn't release him from his schooling. "Boys who are sent to their fathers at this age are the ones without promise," said Father. "The ones who are too violent to get along well in a household of study, too disrespectful to abide in a household of women."

"And the stupid ones go to their fathers at age eight," said Mother. "Beyond rudimentary reading and arithmetic, what use does a stupid man have for learning?"

Even now, remembering, Nafai felt a little stab of pleasure at that—for Mebbekew had often bragged that, unlike Nyef and Issya, and Elya in his day, *Meb* had gone home to Father at the age of eight. Nafai was sure that Meb had met every criterion for early entry into the household of men.

So they managed to persuade Nafai that it was a good thing for him to stay with his mother. There were other reasons, too—to keep Issib company, the prestige of his mother's household, the association with his sisters—but it was Nafai's ambition that made him content to stay. I'm one of the boys with real promise. I will have value to the land of Basilica, perhaps to the whole world. Perhaps one day my writings will be sent into the sky for the Oversoul to share them with the people of other cities and other languages. Perhaps I will even be one of the great ones whose ideas are encoded into glass and saved in an archive, to be read during all the rest of human history as one of the giants of Harmony.

Still, because he had pleaded so earnestly to be allowed to live with Father, from the age of eight until he was thirteen, he and Issib had spent almost every weekend at the Wetchik house, becoming as familiar with it as with Rasa's house in the city. Father had insisted that they work hard, experiencing what a man does to earn his living, so their weekends were not holidays. "You study for six days, working with your mind while your body takes a holiday. Here you'll work in the stables and the greenhouses, working with your body while your mind learns the peace that comes from honest labor."

That was the way Father talked, a sort of continuous oratory; Mother said he took that tone because he wasn't sure how to talk naturally with children. But Nafai had overheard enough adult conversations to know that Father talked that way with everybody except Rasa herself. It showed that Father was never at ease, never truly himself with anyone; but over the years Nafai had also learned that no matter how elevated and hortatory Father's conversation might be, he was never a fool; his words were never empty or stupid or ignorant. This is how a man speaks, Nafai had thought when he was young, and so he practiced an elegant style and made a point of learning classical Emeznetyi as well as the colloquial Basyat that was the language of most art and commerce in Basilica these days. More recently Nafai had realized that to communicate effectively with real people he had to speak the common language—but the rhythms, the melodies of Emeznetyi could still be felt in his writing and heard in his speech. Even in his stupid jokes that earned Elemak's wrath.

"I've just realized something," said Nafai.

Issib didn't answer—he was far enough ahead that Nafai wasn't sure he could even hear. But Nafai went ahead and said it anyway, speaking even more softly, because he was probably saying it only to himself. "I think that I say those things that make people so angry, not because I really *mean* them, but because I simply thought of a clever *way* to say them. It's a kind of art, to think of the perfect way to say an idea, and when you think of it then you have to say it, because words don't exist until you say them."

"A pretty feeble kind of art, Nyef, and I say you should give it up before it gets you killed."

So Issib *was* listening, after all.

"For a big strong guy you sure take a long time getting up Ridge Road to Market Street," said Issib.

"I was thinking," said Nafai.

"You really ought to learn how to think and walk at the same time."

Nafai reached the top of the road, where Issib was waiting. I really *was* dawdling, he thought. I'm not even out of breath.

But because Issib had paused there, Nafai also waited, turning as Issib had turned, to look back down the road they had just traveled. Ridge Road was named exactly right, since it ran along a ridge that sloped down toward the great well-watered coastal plain. It was a clear morning, and from the crest they could see all the way to the ocean, with a patchwork quilt of farms and orchards, stitched with roads and knotted with towns and villages, spread out like a bedcover between the mountains and the sea. Looking down Ridge Road they could see the long line of farmers coming up for market, leading strings of pack animals. If Nafai and Issib had delayed even ten minutes more they would have had to make this trip in the noise and stink of horses, donkeys, mules, and kurelomi, the swearing of the men and the gossip of the women. Once that had been a pleasure, but Nafai had traveled with them often enough to know that the gossip and the swearing were always the same. Not everything that comes from a garden is a rose.

Issib turned to the west, and so did Nafai, to see a landscape as opposite as any could possibly be: the jumbled rocky plateau of the Besporyadok, the near-waterless waste that went on and on toward the west. A thousand poets at least had made the same observation, that the sun rose from the sea, surrounded by jewels of light dancing on the water, and then settled down in red fire in the west, lost in the dust that was always blowing across the desert. But Nafai always thought that, at least where weather was concerned, the sun ought to go the other way. It didn't bring water from the ocean to the land—it brought dry fire from the desert toward the sea.

The vanguard of the market crowd was close enough now that they could hear the drivers and the donkeys. So they turned and started walking toward Basilica, sections of the redrock wall shining in the first rays of sunlight. Basilica, where the forested mountains of the north met the desert of the west and the garden seacoast of the east. How the poets had sung of this place: Basilica, the City of Women, the Harbor of Mists, Red-walled Garden of the Oversoul, the haven where all the waters of the world come together to conceive new clouds, to pour out fresh water again over the earth.

Or, as Mebbekew put it, the best town in the world for getting laid.

The path between the Market Gate of Basilica and the Wetchik house on Ridge Road had never changed in all these years—Nafai knew when as much as a stone of it had been changed. But when Nafai turned thirteen, he had reached a turning point that changed the meaning of that road. At thirteen, even the most promising boys went to live with their fathers, leaving their schooling behind forever. The only ones who remained behind were the ones who meant to reject a man's trade and become scholars. When Nafai was eight he had pleaded to live with his father, at thirteen he argued the other way. No, I haven't decided to be a scholar, he said, but I also haven't decided *not* to be. Why should I decide now?

Let me live with you, Father, if I must—but let me also stay at Mother's school until things become clearer. You don't need me in your work, the way you need Elemak. And I don't want to be another Mebbekew.

So, though the path between Father's house and the city was unchanged, Nafai now walked it in the other direction. The round trip now wasn't from Rasa's city house out into the country and back again; now it was a trek from Wetchik's country house into the city. Even though he actually owned more possessions in the city— all his books, papers, tools, and toys—and often slept three or four of the eight nights of the week there, home was Father's house now.

Which was inevitable. No man could call anything in Basilica truly his own; everything came as a gift from a woman. And even a man who, like Father, had every reason to feel secure with a mate of many years—even he could never truly be at home in Basilica, because of the lake. The deep rift valley in the heart of the city—the reason why the city existed at all—took half the space within Basilica's walls, and no man could ever go there, no man could even walk into the surrounding forest far enough to catch a glimpse of the shining water. If it *did* shine. For all Nafai knew, the rift valley was so deep that sunlight never touched the waters of the lake of Basilica.

No place can ever be home if there is a place within it where you are forbidden to go. No man is ever *truly* a citizen of Basilica. And I am becoming a stranger in my mother's house.

Elemak had spoken often, in years past, about cities where men owned everything, places where men had many wives and the wives had no choice about renewing their marriage contracts, and even one city where there was no marriage at all, but any man could take any woman and she was forbidden to refuse him unless she was already pregnant. Nafai wondered, though, if any of those stories was true. For why would women ever submit themselves to such treatment? Could it be that the women of Basilica were so much stronger than the women of any other place? Or were the men of this place weaker or more timid than the men of other cities?

Suddenly it became a question of great urgency. "Have you ever slept with a woman, Issya?"

Issib didn't answer.

"I just wondered," said Nafai.

Issib said nothing.

"I'm trying to figure out what's so wonderful about the women of Basilica that a man like Elya keeps coming back here when he could live in one of those places where men have their way all the time."

Only now did Issib answer. "In the first place, Nafai, there *is* no place where men have their way all the time. There *are* places where men pretend to have their way and women pretend to let them, just as women here pretend to have their way and *men* pretend to let them."

That was an interesting thought. It had never occurred to Nafai that perhaps things weren't as one-sided and simple as they seemed. But Issib hadn't finished, and Nafai wanted to hear the rest. "And in the second place?"

"In the second place, Nyef, Mother and Father *did* find an auntie for me several years ago and to be frank, it isn't all it's cracked up to be."

That wasn't what Nafai wanted to hear. "Meb seems to think it is."

"Meb has no brain," said Issib, "he simply goes wherever his most protuberant part leads him. Sometimes that means that he follows his nose, but usually not."

"What was it like?"

"It was nice. She was very sweet. But I didn't love her." Issib seemed a bit sad about it. "I felt like it was something being done to me, instead of something we were doing together."

"Was that because of . . ."

"Because I'm a cripple? Partly, I suppose, though she did teach me how to give pleasure in return and said I did surprisingly well. You'll probably enjoy it just like Meb."

"I hope not."

"Mother said that the best men don't enjoy their auntie all that much, because the best men don't want to receive their pleasure as a lesson, they want to be given it freely, out of love. But then she said that the worst men also don't like their auntie, because they can't stand having anyone but themselves be in control of things."

"I don't even want an auntie," said Nafai.

"Well, that's brilliant. How will you learn anything, then?"

"I want to learn it together with my mate."

"You're a romantic idiot," said Issib.

"Nobody has to teach birds or lizards."

"Nafai ab Wetchik mag Rasa, the famous lizard lover."

"I once watched a pair of lizards go at it for a whole hour."

"Learn any good techniques?"

"Sure. But you can only use them if you're proportioned like a lizard."

"Oh?"

"It's about half as long as their whole body."

Issib laughed. "Imagine buying pants."

"Imagine lacing your sandals!"

"You'd have to wrap it around your waist."

"Or loop it over your shoulder."

This conversation carried them through the market, where people were just starting to open their booths, expecting the immediate arrival of the farmers from the plain. Father maintained a couple of booths in the outer market, though none of the plains farmers had the money or the sophistication to want to buy a plant that took so much trouble to keep alive, and yet produced no worthwhile crop. The only sales in the outer market were to shoppers from Basilica itself, or, more rarely, to rich foreigners who browsed through the outer market on their way into or out of the city. With Father on a journey, it would be Rashgallivak supervising the set-up, and sure enough, there he was setting up a cold-plant display inside a chilled display table. They waved at him, though he only looked at them, not even nodding in recognition. That was Rash's way—he would be there if they needed him in some crisis. At the moment, his job was setting out plants, and so that had all of his attention. There was no rush, though. The best sales would come in the late afternoon, when Basilicans were looking for impressive gifts to bring their mate or lover, or to help win the heart of someone they were courting.

Meb once joked that people never bought exotic plants for themselves, since they were nothing but trouble to keep alive—and they only bought them as gifts because they were so expensive. "They make the perfect gift because the plant is beautiful and impressive for exactly as long as the love affair lasts—usually about a week. Then the plant dies, unless the recipients keep paying *us* to come take care of it. Either way their feelings toward the plant always match their feelings toward the lover who gave it to them. Either constant annoyance because he's still around, or distaste at the ugly dried-up memory. If a love is actually going to be *permanent* the lovers should buy a tree instead." It was when Meb started talking this way with customers that Father had banned him from the booths. No doubt that was exactly what Meb had been hoping for.

Nafai understood the desire to avoid helping in the

business. There was nothing fun in the slugwork of selling a bunch of temperamental plants.

If I end my studies, thought Nafai, I'll have to work every day at one of these miserable jobs. And it'll lead nowhere. When Father dies Elemak will become the Wetchik, and he would never let me lead a caravan of my own, which is the only interesting part of the work. I don't want to spend my life in the hothouse or the dryhouse or the coldhouse, grafting and nurturing and propagating plants that will die almost as soon as they're sold. There's no greatness in that.

· The outer market ended at the first gate, the vast doors standing open as they always did—Nafai wondered if they could even close anymore. It hardly mattered—this was always the most carefully guarded gate because it was the busiest. Everybody's retinas were scanned and checked against the roster of citizens and rightholders. Issib and Nafai, as sons of citizens, were technically citizens themselves, even though they weren't allowed to own property within the city, and when they came of age they'd be able to vote. So the guards treated them respectfully as they passed them through.

Between the outer gate and the inner gate, between the high red walls and protected by guards on every side, the city of Basilica conducted its most profitable business: the gold market. Actually, gold wasn't even the majority of what was bought and sold here, though moneylenders were thick as ever. What was traded in the gold market was any form of wealth that was easily portable and therefore easily stolen. Jewels, gold, silver, platinum, databases, libraries, deeds of property, deeds of trust, certificates of stock ownership, and warrants of uncollectible debt: All were traded here, and every booth had its computer to report transactions to the city recorder— the city's master computer. In fact, the constantly shifting holographic displays over all the computers caused a strange twinkling effect, so that no matter where you looked you always seemed to see motion out of the corner of your eye. Meb said that was why the lenders and vendors of the gold market were so sure someone was always spying on them.

No doubt most of the computers here had noticed Nafai and Issib as soon as their retinas were scanned at the gate, flashing their names, their status, and their financial standing into the computer display. Someday that would mean something, Nafai knew, but at the moment it meant nothing at all. Ever since Meb ran up huge debts last year when he turned eighteen, there was a tight restriction on all credit to the Wetchik family, and since credit was the only way Nafai was likely to get his hands on serious money, no one here would be interested in him. Father could probably have got all those restrictions removed, but since Father did all his business in cash, never borrowing, the restrictions did nothing to hurt him—and they kept Meb from borrowing any more. Nafai had listened to the whining and shouting and pouting and weeping that seemed to go on for months until Meb finally realized that Father was *never* going to relent and allow him financial independence. In recent months Meb had been fairly quiet about it. Now when he showed up in new clothes he always claimed they were borrowed from pitying friends, but Nafai was skeptical. Meb still spent money as if he had some, and since Nafai couldn't imagine Meb actually working at anything, he could only conclude that Meb had found someone to borrow from against his anticipated share in the Wetchik estate.

That would be just like Meb—to borrow against Father's anticipated death. But Father was still a vigorous and healthy man, only fifty years old. At some point

Meb's creditors would get tired of waiting, and Meb would have to come to Father again, begging for help to free him from debt.

There was another retina check at the inner gate. Because they were citizens and the computers showed they not only hadn't bought anything, but hadn't even stopped at a booth, they didn't have to have their bodies scanned for what was euphemistically called "unauthorized borrowing." So in moments they passed through the gate into the city itself.

More specifically, they entered the inner market. It was almost as large as the outer market, but there the resemblance ended, for instead of selling meat and food, bolts of cloth and reaches of lumber, the inner market sold finished things: pastries and ices, spices and herbs; furniture and bedding, draperies and tapestries; fine-sewn shirts and trousers, sandals for the feet, gloves for the hands, and rings for toes and ears and fingers; and exotic trinkets and animals and plants, brought at great expense and risk from every corner of the world. Here was where Father offered his most precious plants, keeping his booths open day and night.

But none of these held any particular charm for Nafai—it was all the same to him, after passing through the market with little money for so many years. To him all that mattered were the many booths selling myachiks, the little glass balls that carried recordings of music, dance, sculpture, paintings; tragedies, comedies, and realities, recited as poems, acted out in plays, or sung in operas; and the works of historians, scientists, philosophers, orators, prophets, and satirists; lessons and demonstrations of every art or process ever thought of; and, of course, the great love songs for which Basilica was known throughout the world, combining music with wordless erotic plays that went on and on, repeating endlessly and randomly, like self-creating sculptures in the bedrooms and private gardens of every household in the city.

Of course, Nafai was too young to buy any love songs himself, but he had seen more than one when visiting in the homes of friends whose mothers or teachers were not as discreet as Rasa. They fascinated him, as much for the music and the implied story as for the eroticism. But he spent his time in the market searching for new works by Basilican poets, musicians, artists, and performers, or old ones that were just being revived, or strange works from other lands, either in translation or in the original. Father might have left his sons with little money, but Mother gave all her children—sons and nieces no more or less than mere pupils—a decent allowance for the purchase of myachiks.

Nafai found himself wandering toward a booth where a young man was singing in an exquisitely high and sweet tenor voice; the melody sounded like it might be a new one by the composer who called herself Sunrise—or at least one of her better imitators.

"No," said Issib. "You can come back this afternoon."

"You can go ahead," said Nafai.

"We're already late," said Issib.

"So I might as well be later."

"Grow up, Nafai," said Issib. "Every lesson you miss is one that either you or the teacher will have to make up later."

"I'll never learn everything anyway," said Nafai. "I want to hear the song."

"Then listen while you're walking. Or can't you walk and listen at the same time?"

Nafai let himself be led out of the market. The song faded quickly, lost in music from other booths, and the chatter and conversation of the market. Unlike the outer market, the inner market didn't wait for farmers from the plain, and so it never closed; half the people here, Nafai was sure, had not slept the night before, and were buying pastries and tea as their morning supper before going home to bed. Meb might well be one of them. And for a moment, Nafai envied him the freedom of his life. If I am ever a great historian or scientist, will I have freedom like that? To rise in the mid-afternoon, do my writing until dusk, and then venture out into the Basilican night to see the dances and plays, to hear the concerts, or perhaps to recite passages of the work I did myself that day before a discerning audience that will leave my recitation abuzz with discussion and argument and praise and criticism of my work—how could Elemak's dirty, wearying journeys ever compare with such a life as that? And then to return at dawn to Eiadh's house, and make love to her as we whisper and laugh about the night's adventures and triumphs.

Only a few things were lacking to make the dream reality. For one thing, Eiadh didn't have a house yet, and though she was gaining some small reputation as a singer and reciter, it was clear that her career would not be one of the dazzlingly brilliant ones; she was no prodigy, and so her house would no doubt be a modest one for many years. No matter, I will help her buy a finer one than she could afford on her own, even though when a man helps a woman buy property in Basilica the money can only be given as a gift. Eiadh is too loyal a woman ever to lapse my contract and close me out of the house I helped her buy.

The only other thing lacking in the dream was that Nafai had never actually written anything that was particularly good. Of course, that was only because he had not yet chosen his field, and therefore he was still testing himself, still dabbling a little in all of them. He'd settle on one very soon, there'd be one in which he would show himself to have a flair, and then there'd be myachiks of *his* works in the booths of the inner market.

The Holy Road was having some kind of procession down into the Rift Valley, and so—as men—they had to go all the way around it; even so, they were soon enough at Mother's house. Issib immediately left him, floating his way around to the outside stairway leading up into the computer room, where he was spending all his time these days. The next younger class was already in session out on the south curve of the pillared porch, catching the sunlight slanting in. They were doing devotions, the boys slapping themselves sharply now and then, the girls humming softly to themselves. His own class would be doing the same thing inside somewhere, and Nafai was in no hurry to join them, since it was considered vaguely impious to make a disturbance during a devotion.

So he walked slowly, skirting the younger class on the porch, pausing to lean on a pillar out of sight as he listened to the comfortable music of small girlish voices humming randomly, yet finding momentary chords that were lost in the moment they were discovered; and the staccato, broken rhythms of boys slapping their trousered legs, their shirted arms and chests, their bare cheeks.

As he stood there, a girl from the class suddenly appeared beside him. He knew her from gymnasium, of course. It was the witchling named Luet, who was rumored to have such remarkable visions that some of the ladies of the Shelf were already calling her a seer. Nafai didn't put much stock in such magical stories—the Oversoul couldn't know the future any more than a human being could, and as far as visions were concerned, people only remembered the ones that by sheer luck happened to match reality at some point.

"You're the one who's covered with fire," she said.

What was she talking about? How was he supposed to answer this kind of thing?

"No, I'm Nafai," he said.

"Not really fire. Little diamond sparks that turn to lightning when you're angry."

"I've got to go in."

She touched his sleeve; it held him as surely as if she had gripped his arm. "She'll never mate with you, you know."

"Who?"

"Eiadh. She'll offer, but you'll refuse her."

This was humiliating. How did this girl, probably only twelve, and from her size and shape *definitely* not a young woman yet, know anything about his feelings toward Eiadh? Was his love that obvious to everyone? Well, fine, so be it—he had nothing to hide. There was only honor in being known to love such a woman. And as for this girl being a seer, it wasn't too likely, not if she said that Eiadh would actually *offer* herself to him and he would turn her down! I'm more likely to bite my own finger off than to refuse take the most perfect woman in Basilica as my mate.

"Excuse me," Nafai said, pulling his arm away. He didn't like this girl touching him anyway. They said that her mother was a wilder, one of those filthy naked solitary women who came into Basilica from the desert; supposedly they were holy women, but Nafai well knew that they also would sleep with any man who asked, right on the streets of the city, and it was permissible for any man to take one, even when he was in a contract with a mate. Decent and highborn men didn't do it, of course—even Meb had never bragged about "desert worship" or going on a "dust party," as couplings with wilders were crudely called. Nafai saw nothing holy in the whole business, and as far as he was concerned, this Luet was a bastard, conceived by a madwoman and a bestial man in a coupling that was closer to rape than love. There was no chance that the Oversoul really had anything to do with *that*.

"*You're* the bastard," said the girl. Then she walked away. The others had finished their devotions—or perhaps had stopped them in order to listen to what Luet was saying to him. Which meant that the story would be spread all over the house by dinnertime and all over Basilica before supper and no doubt Issib would tease him about it all the way home and then Elemak and Mebbekew would *never* let him forget it and he wished that the women of Basilica would keep crazy people like Luet under lock and key instead of taking their stupid nonsense seriously all the time.

THREE

FIRE

When he got inside he headed for the fountain room, where his class would be meeting all through the autumn. From the kitchen he could smell the preparations for dinner, and with a pang he remembered that, what with his argument with Elemak, he had completely forgotten to eat. Until this moment he hadn't felt even the tiniest bit hungry; but now that he realized it, he was completely famished. In fact, he felt just a little light-headed. He should sit down. The fountain room was only a few steps away; surely they would understand why he was late if he arrived not feeling well. No one could be angry at him. No one could think he was a lazy slackwit if he was *sick*. They didn't have to know that he was sick with hunger.

He shuffled miserably into the room, playing his faintness to the hilt, leaning against a wall for a moment as he passed. He could feel their eyes on him, but he didn't look; he had a vague idea that genuinely sick people didn't easily meet other people's gaze. He half-expected the teacher of the day to speak up. What's wrong, Nafai? Aren't you well?

Instead there was silence until he had slid down the wall, folding himself into a sitting position on the wooden floor.

"We'll send out for a burial party, Nafai, in case you suddenly die."

Oh, no! It wasn't a teacher at all, one of the easily fooled young women who were so very impressed that Nafai was Rasa's own son. It was Mother here today. He looked up and met her gaze. She was smiling wickedly at him, not fooled a bit by his sick act.

"I was waiting for you. Issib is already on my portico. He didn't mention that you were dying, but I'm sure it was an oversight."

There was nothing left but to take it with good humor. Nafai sighed and got to his feet. "You know, Mother, that your unwillingness to suspend your disbelief will set back my acting career by several years."

"That's all right, Nafai, dear. Your acting career would set back Basilican theatre by centuries."

The other students laughed. Nafai grinned—but he also scanned the group to see who was enjoying it most. There was Eiadh, sitting near the fountain, where a few tiny drops of water had caught in her hair and were now reflecting light like jewels. *She* wasn't laughing at him. Instead she smiled beautifully, and winked. He grinned back—like a foolish clown, he was sure—and nearly tripped on the step leading up to the doorway to the back corridor. There was more laughter, of course, and so Nafai turned and took a deep bow. Then he walked away with dignity, deliberately running into the doorframe to earn another laugh before he finally made it out of the room.

"What's this about?" he asked Mother, hurrying to catch up with her.

"Family business," she said.

Then they passed through the doorway leading to Mother's private portico. They would stay, as always, in the screened-off area near the door; beyond the screen, out near the balustrade, the portico offered a beautiful view of the Rift Valley, so it was completely forbidden for men to go there. Such proscriptions in private houses were often ignored—Nafai knew several boys who talked about the Rift Valley, asserting that it was nothing special, just a steep craggy slope covered with trees and vines with a bunch of mist or clouds or fog blocking any view of the middle where, presumably, the sacred lake was located. But in Mother's house, decent respect was always shown, and Nafai was sure that even Father had never passed beyond the screen.

Once he was through with blinking, coming out into bright sunlight, Nafai was able to see who else was on the portico. Issib, of course; but to Nafai's surprise, Father himself was there, home from his journey. Why had he come to Rasa's house in the city, instead of going home first?

Father stood to greet him with an embrace.

"Elemak's at home, Father."

"So Issya informed me."

Father seemed very serious, very distant. He had something on his mind. It couldn't be anything good.

"Now that Nafai is finally here," said Mother, "we can perhaps make some sense out of all this."

Only now, as he seated himself in the best shade that wasn't already taken, did Nafai realize that there were two girls with them. At first glance, in the dazzling sunlight, he had assumed they were his sisters, Rasa's daughters Sevet and Kokor—in that context, an assembly of Rasa and her children, Father's presence was surprising, since he was father only to Issib and Nafai, not to the girls. But instead of Sevet and Kokor, it was two girls from the school—Hushidh, another of mother's nieces, the same age as Eiadh; and that witchling girl from the front porch, Luet. He looked at her in consternation—how had she got here so quickly? Not that he'd been hurrying. Mother must have sent for her even before she knew that Nafai had arrived.

What were Luet and Hushidh doing in a conference about family business?

"My dear mate Wetchik has something to tell us. We're hoping that you can—well, at least that Luet or Hushidh might—"

"Why don't I simply begin?" said Father.

Mother smiled and raised her hands in a graceful, elegant shrug.

"I saw something disturbing this morning," Father began. "Just before morning, actually. I was on my way home on the Desert Road—I was out on the desert, yesterday, to ponder and consult with myself and the Oversoul—when suddenly there came upon me a strong desire—a need, really—to leave the trail, even though that's a foolish thing to do in that dark time between moonset and sunrise. I didn't go far. I only had to move around a large rock, and it became quite clear to me why I had been led to that spot. For there in front of me I saw Basilica. But not the Basilica I would have expected, dotted with the lights of celebration in Dolltown or the inner market. What I saw was Basilica ablaze."

"On *fire*?" asked Issib.

"A vision, of course. I didn't know that at first, mind you—I lunged forward; I was intending to rush to the city—to rush here and see if you were all right, my dear—".

"As I would certainly expect you to do," said Mother. "When the city disappeared as suddenly as it had appeared. Only the fire remained, rising up to form a pillar on the rock in front of me. It stood there for the longest time, a column of flame. And it was hot—as hot as if it had been real. I felt it singeing me, though of course there's not a mark on my clothing. And then the pillar of flame rose up into the sky, slowly at first, then faster and faster until it became a star moving across the sky, and then disappeared entirely."

"You were tired, Father," said Issib.

"I've been tired many times," said Father, "but I have never seen pillars of flame before. Or burning cities."

Mother spoke up again. "Your father came to me, Issya, because he hoped that I might help him understand the meaning of this. If it came from the Oversoul, or if it was just a mad sort of waking dream."

"I vote for the dream," said Issib.

"Even madness can come from the Oversoul," said Hushidh.

Everyone looked at her. She was a rather plainish girl, always quiet in class. Now that Nafai saw her and Luet side by side, he realized that they resembled each other closely. Were they sisters? More to the point, what was Hushidh doing here, and by what right did she speak out about family matters?

"It *can* come from the Oversoul," said Father. "But did it? And if it did, what does it mean?"

Nafai could see that Father was directing those questions, not at Rasa or even at Hushidh, but at Luet! He couldn't possibly believe what the women said about her, could he? Did a single vision turn a rational man of business into a superstitious pilgrim trying to find meanings in everything he saw?

"I can't tell you what your dream means," said Luet.

"Oh," said Father. "Not that I actually thought—"

"If the Oversoul sent the dream, and if she meant you to understand it, then she also sent the interpretation."

"There *was* no interpretation."

"Wasn't there?" asked Luet. "This is the first time you've had a dream like this, isn't it?"

"Definitely. This isn't a habit of mine, to see visions as I'm walking along the road at night."

"So you aren't used to recognizing the meanings that come along with a vision."

"I suppose not."

"Yet you *were* receiving messages."

"Was I?"

"Before you saw the flame, you knew that you were supposed to turn away from the road."

"Yes, well, *that*."

"What do you think the voice of the Oversoul sounds like? Do you think she speaks Basyat or puts up signposts?"

Luet sounded vaguely scornful—an outrageous tone of voice for her to adopt with a man of Wetchik's status in the city. Yet he seemed to take no offense, accepting her rebuke as if she had a right to chastise him.

"The Oversoul puts the knowledge pure into our minds, unmixed with any human language," she said. "We are always given more than we can possibly comprehend, and we can comprehend far more than we're able to put into words."

Luet had a voice of such simple power. Not like the chanting sound that the witches and prophets of the inner market used when they were trying to attract business. She spoke as if she knew, as if there was no possibility of doubt.

"Let me ask you, then, sir. When you saw the city on fire, how did you know it was Basilica?"

"I've seen it a thousand times, from just that angle, coming in from the desert."

"But did you see the shape of the city and recognize it from that, or did you know first that it was Basilica on fire, and then your mind called forth the picture of the city that was already in your memory?"

"I don't know—how can I know that?"

"Think back. Was the knowledge there before the vision, or was the vision first?"

Instead of telling the girl to go away, Father closed his eyes and tried to remember.

"When you put it that way, I think—I knew it before I actually looked in that direction. I don't think I actually saw it until I was lunging toward it. I saw the *flame*, but not the burning city inside it. And now that you ask, I also knew that Rasa and my children were in terrible danger. I knew that first of all, as I was rounding the rock—that was part of the sense of urgency. I knew that if I left the trail and came to that exact spot, I'd be able to save them from the danger. It was only then that it came to mind what the danger was, and then last of all that I saw the flame and the city inside it."

"This is a true vision," said Luet.

Just from that? She knew just from the order of things? She probably would have said the same thing no matter *what* Father remembered. And maybe Father was only remembering it that way because Luet had suggested it that way. This was making Nafai furious, for Father to be nodding in acceptance when this twelve-year-old girl condescendingly treated him like an apprentice in a profession in which she was a widely respected master.

"But it wasn't true," said Father. "When I got here, there *was* no danger."

"No, I didn't think so," said Luet. "Back when you first

felt that your mate and your children were in danger, what did you expect to *do* about it?"

"I was going to save them, of course."

"Specifically *how*?"

Again he closed his eyes. "Not to pull them from a burning building. That never occurred to me until later, as I was walking the rest of the way into the city. At the moment I wanted to shout out that the city was burning, that we had to—"

"What?"

"I was going to say, we had to get out of the city. But that wasn't what I wanted to say at first. When it started, I felt like I had to come to the city and tell everybody that there was a fire coming."

"And they had to get out?"

"I guess," said Father. "Of course, what else?"

Luet said nothing, but her gaze never left his face.

"No," Father said. "No, that *wasn't* it." Father sounded surprised. "I wasn't going to warn them to get out."

Luet leaned forward, looking somehow more intense, not so—analytical. "Sir, just a moment ago, when you were saying that you had wanted to warn them to get out of the city—"

"But that *wasn't* what I was going to do."

"But when you thought for a moment that—when you *assumed* that you were going to tell them to get out of the city—what did that feel like? When you told us that, why did you know that it was wrong?"

"I don't know. It just felt . . . *wrong*."

"This is very important," said Luet. "How does feeling wrong *feel*?"

Again he closed his eyes. "I'm not used to thinking about how I think. And now I'm trying to remember how it felt when I thought I remembered something that I didn't actually remember—"

"Don't talk," said Luet.

He fell silent.

Nafai wanted to yell at somebody. What were they doing, listening to this ugly stupid little girl, letting her tell Father—the Wetchik himself, in case nobody remembered—to keep his mouth shut!

But everybody else was so intense that Nafai kept his own mouth shut. Issib would be so proud of him for actually refraining from saying something that he had thought of.

"What I felt," said Father, "was *nothing*." He nodded slowly. "Right after you asked the question and I answered it—. Of course, what else—then you sat there looking at me and I had nothing in my head at all."

"Stupid," she said.

He raised an eyebrow. To Nafai's relief, he was finally noticing how disrespectfully Luet was speaking to him.

"You felt stupid," she said. "And so you knew that what you'd just said was wrong."

He nodded. "Yes, I guess that's it."

"What's all this about?" said Issib. "Analyzing your analysis of analyses of a completely subjective hallucination?"

Good work, Issya, said Nafai silently. You took the words right out of my mouth.

"I mean, you can play these games all morning, but you're just laying meanings on top of a meaningless experience. Dreams are nothing more than random firings of memories, which your brain then interprets so as to invent causal connections, which makes stories out of *nothing*."

Father looked at Issib for a long moment, then shook his head. "You're right, of course," he said. "Even though I was wide awake and I've never had a hallucination before, it was nothing more than a random firing of synapses in my brain."

Nafai knew, as Issib and Mother certainly knew, that Father was being ironic, that he was telling Issib that his vision of the fire on the rock was *more* than a meaningless night dream. But Luet didn't know Father, so *she* thought he was backing away from mysticism and retreating into reality.

"You're wrong," she said. "It was a true vision, because it came to you the right way. The understanding came *before* the vision—that's why I was asking those questions. The meaning is there and then your brain supplies the pictures that let you understand it. That's the way the Oversoul talks to us."

"Talks to crazy people, you mean," Nafai said.

He regretted it immediately, but by then it was too late.

"Crazy people like *me*?" said Father.

"And I assure you that Luet is at least as sane as you are," Mother added.

Issib couldn't pass up the chance to cast a verbal dart. "As sane as Nyef? Then she's in deep trouble."

Father shut down Issib's teasing immediately. "You were saying the same thing yourself only a minute ago."

"I wasn't calling people crazy," said Issib.

"No, you didn't have Nafai's—what shall we call it?—*pointed eloquence*."

Nafai knew he could save himself now by shutting up and letting Issib deflect the heat. But he was committed to skepticism, and self-control wasn't his strong suit. "This girl," said Nafai. "Don't you see how she was leading you on, Father? She asks you a question, but she doesn't tell you beforehand what the answer will mean—so no matter what you answer, she can say, That's it, it's a true vision, definitely the Oversoul talking."

Father didn't have an immediate answer. Nafai glanced at Luet, feeling triumphant, wanting to see her squirm. But she wasn't squirming. She was looking at him very calmly. The intensity had drained out of her and now she was simply—calm. It bothered him, the steadiness of her gaze. "What are you looking at?" he demanded.

"A fool," she answered.

Nafai jumped to his feet. "I don't have to listen to you calling me a—"

"Sit down!" roared Father.

Nafai sat, seething.

"She just listened to *you* calling *her* a fraud," said Father. "I appreciate how both of my sons are doing exactly what I wanted you here to do—providing a skeptical audience for my story. You analyzed the process very cleverly and your version of things accounts for everything you know about it, just as neatly as Luet's version does."

Nafai was ready to help him draw the correct conclusion. "Then the rule of simplicity requires you to—"

"The rule of your father requires you to hold your tongue, Nafai. What you're both forgetting is that there's a fundamental difference between you and me."

Father leaned toward Nafai.

"*I* saw the fire."

He leaned back again.

"Luet didn't tell me what to think or feel at the time. And her questions helped me remember—helped *me* remember—the way it really happened. Instead of the way I was already changing it to fit my preconceptions. She *knew* that it would be strange—in exactly the ways that it was strange. Of course, I can't convince you."

"No," said Nafai. "You can only convince yourself."

"In the end, Nafai, oneself is the only person anyone can convince."

The battle was lost if Father was already making up aphorisms. Nafai sat back to wait for it all to end. He took consolation from the fact that it had been, after all, merely a dream. It's not as if it was going to change his life or anything.

Father wasn't done yet. "Do you know what I actually wanted to do, when I felt such urgency to get to the city? I wanted to warn people—to follow the old ways, to go back to the laws of the Oversoul, or this place would burn."

"What place?" asked Luet, her intensity back again.

"This place. Basilica. The city. That's what I saw burning."

Again Father fell silent, looking into her burning eyes.

"Not the city," he said at last. "The city was only the picture that my mind supplied, wasn't it? Not the city. The whole world. All of Harmony, burning."

Rasa gasped. "Earth," she whispered.

"Oh, please," Nafai said. So Mother was going to connect Father's vision with that old story about the home planet that was burned by the Oversoul to punish humanity for whatever nastiness the current storyteller wanted to preach against. The all-purpose coercive myth: If you don't do what I say—I mean, what the *Oversoul* says—then the *whole world* will *burn*.

"*I* haven't seen the fire itself," said Luet, ignoring Nafai. "Maybe I'm not even seeing the same thing."

"What *have* you seen?" asked Father. Nafai cringed at how respectful he was being toward this girl.

"I saw the Deep Lake of Basilica, crusted over with blood and ashes."

Nafai waited for her to finish. But she just sat there.

"That's it? That's all?" Nafai stood up, preparing to walk out. "This is great, hearing the two of you compare visions. *I* saw a city on fire. Well, *I* saw a scum-covered lake."

Luet stood up and faced him. No, faced him down—which was ridiculous, since he was almost half a meter taller than her.

"You're only arguing against me," she said hotly, "because you don't want to believe what I told you about Eiadh."

"That's ridiculous," said Nafai.

"You had a vision about Eiadh?" asked Rasa.

"What does Eiadh have to do with *Nyef*?" asked Issib.

Nafai hated her for mentioning it again, in front of his family. "You can make up whatever you want about other people, but you'd better leave *me* out of it."

"Enough," said Father. "We're done."

Rasa looked at him in surprise. "Are you dismissing me in my own house?"

"I'm dismissing my sons."

"You have authority over *your* sons, of course." Mother was smiling, but Nafai knew from her soft speech that she was seriously annoyed. "However, I see no one here in *my* house but *my* students."

Father nodded, accepting the rebuke, then stood to leave. "Then I'm dismissing myself—I may do *that*, I hope."

"You may always leave, my adored mate, as long as you promise to come back to me."

His answer was to kiss her cheek.

"What are you going to do?" she asked.

"What the Oversoul told me to do."

"And what is *that*?"

"Warn people to return to the laws of the Oversoul or the world will burn."

Issib was appalled. "That's crazy, Father!"

"I'm tired of hearing that word from the lips of my sons."

"But—prophets of the Oversoul don't say things like that. They're like poets, except all their metaphors have some moral lesson or they celebrate the Oversoul or—"

"Issya," said Wetchik, "all my life I've listened to these so-called prophecies—and the psalms and the histories and the temple priests—and I've always thought, if *this* is all the Oversoul has to say, why should I bother to listen? Why should the Oversoul even bother *speaking*, if this is all that's on his mind?"

"Then why did you teach *us* to speak to the Oversoul?" asked Issib.

"Because I believed in the ancient laws. And I *did* speak to the Oversoul myself, though more as a way of clarifying my own thoughts than because I actually thought that he was *listening*. Then last night—this morning—I had an experience that I never conceived of. I never wished for it. I didn't even know what it *was* until now, these last few minutes, talking to Luet. Now I know—what it feels like to have the Oversoul's voice inside you. Nothing like these poets and dreamers and deceivers, who write down whatever pops into their heads and then sell it as prophecy. What was in me was not myself, and Luet has shown me that she's had the same voice inside *her*. It means that the Oversoul is real and alive."

"So maybe it's real," said Issib. "That doesn't tell us what it *is*."

"It's the guardian of the world," said Wetchik. "He asked me to help. *Told* me to help. And I will."

"That's all temple stuff," said Issib. "You don't know anything about it. You grow exotic plants."

Father dismissed Issib's objections with a gesture.

"Anything the Oversoul needs me to know, he'll tell me."
Then he headed for the door into the house.

Nafai followed him, only a few steps. "Father," he said.
Father waited.

The trouble was, Nafai didn't know what he was going
to say. Only that he had to say it. That there was a very
important question whose answer he had to have before
Father left. He just didn't know what the question was.

"Father," he said again.

"Yes?"

And because Nafai couldn't think of the real question,
the deep one, the important one, he asked the only
question that came to mind. "What am *I* supposed to
do?"

"Keep the old ways of the Oversoul," said Father.

"What does that *mean*?"

"Or the world will burn." And Father was gone.

Nafai looked at the empty door for a while. It didn't do
anything, so he turned back to the others. They were all
looking at him, as if they expected *him* to do something.

"What!" he demanded.

"Nothing," said Mother. She arose from her seat in the
shade of the kaplya tree. "We'll all return to our work."

"That's all?" said Issib. "Our father—your mate—has
just told us that the Oversoul is speaking to him, and
we're supposed to go back to our studies?"

"You really don't understand, do you?" said Mother.
"You've lived all these years as my sons, as my *students*,
and you are still nothing more than the ordinary boys
wandering the streets of Basilica hoping to find a willing
woman and a bed for the night."

"What don't we understand here?" asked Nafai. "Just
because you women all take this witchgirl so seriously
doesn't mean that—"

"I have been down into the water myself," said Mother,

her voice like metal. "You men can pretend to yourselves that the Oversoul is distracted or sleeping, or just a machine that collects our transmissions and sends them to libraries in distant cities. Whatever theory you happen to believe, it makes no difference to the *truth*. For *I* know, as most of the women in this city know, that the Oversoul is very much alive. At least as the keeper of the memories of this world, she is alive. We all receive those memories when we go into the water. Sometimes they seem random, sometimes we are given exactly the memory we needed. The Oversoul keeps the history of the world, as it was seen through other people's eyes. Only a few of us—like Luet and Hushidh—are given wisdom away from the water, and even fewer are given visions of real things that haven't happened yet. Since the great Izumina died, Luet is the only seer I know of in Basilica—so yes, we take her very, very seriously."

Women go down into the water and receive visions? This was the first time Nafai had ever heard a woman describe any part of the worship at the lake. He had always assumed that the women's worship was like the men's—physical, ascetic, painful, a dispassionate way of discharging emotion. Instead they were all mystics. What seemed like legends or madness to men was at the center of a woman's life. Nafai felt as though he had discovered that women were of another species after all. The question was, which of them, men or women, were the humans? The rational but brutal men? Or the irrational but gentle women?

"There's only one thing rarer than a girl like Luet," Mother was saying, "and that's a *man* who hears the voice of the Oversoul. We know now that your father does hear—Luet confirmed that for me. I don't know what the Oversoul wants, or why she spoke to your father, but I *am* wise enough to know that it matters."

As she passed Nafai, she reached up and caught his ear firmly, though not painfully, between her fingers. "As for the mythical burning of Earth, my dear boy, I've seen it myself. It happened. I can only guess how long ago—we estimate there's been at least thirty million years of human history on this world we named Harmony. But I saw the missiles fly, the bombs explode, and the world erupt in flame. The smoke filled the sky and blocked the sun, and underneath that blanket of darkness the oceans froze and the world was covered in ice and only a few human beings survived, to rise up out of the blackness as the world died, carrying their hopes and their regrets and their genes to other planets, hoping to start again. They did. We're here. Now the Oversoul has warned your father that our new start can lead to the same ending as before."

Nafai had seen Mother's public face—playful, brilliant, analytical, gracious—and he had seen her family face—frank of speech yet always kind, quick to anger yet quicker to forgive. Always he had assumed that the way she was with the family was her true self, with nothing held back. Instead, behind the faces that he thought he knew, she had kept this secret all the time, her bitter vision of the end of Earth. "You never told us about this," whispered Nafai.

"I most certainly told you about it," said Rasa. "It's not *my* fault that when you heard it, you thought I was telling you a myth." She let go of his ear and returned to the house.

Issib floated past him, mumbling something about waking up one morning to find that you've been living in a madhouse all your life. Hushidh went past him also, not meeting his gaze; he could imagine the gossip that she would spread in his class all the rest of the day.

He was alone with Luet.

"I shouldn't have spoken to you before," she said.

"And you shouldn't speak to me again, either," suggested Nafai.

"Some people hear a lie when they're told the truth. You're so proud of your status as the son of Rasa and Wetchik, but obviously whatever genes you got from your parents, they weren't the right ones."

"While I'm sure *you* got the finest your parents had to offer."

She looked at him with obvious contempt, and then she was gone.

"What a wonderful day this is going to be," he said—to no one, since he was alone. "My entire family hates me." He thought for a moment. "I'm not even sure that I *want* them to like me."

For one dangerous moment, alone on the portico, he toyed with the idea of slipping past the screens and going to the edge, leaning out, and looking at the forbidden sight of the Valley of the Holy Women, casually referred to as the Rift Valley, and more crudely known as the Canyon of the Crones. I'll see it and I bet I don't even get struck blind.

But he didn't do it, even though he stood there thinking about it for a long time. It seemed that every time he was about to take a step toward the edge, his mind suddenly wandered and he hesitated, confused, forgetting for a moment what it was he wanted to do. Finally he lost interest and went back inside the house.

He should have gone back to class—it's what he *expected* to do when he went inside. But he couldn't bring himself to do it. Instead he wandered to the front door and out onto the porch, into the streets of Basilica. Mother would probably be furious at him but that was too bad.

He must have been seeing where he was going, since

he didn't bump into anything, but he had no memory of what he saw or where he had been. He ended up in the Fountains district, not far from the neighborhood of Rasa's house; and in his mind, he had circled through the same thoughts over and over again, finally ending up not very far from where he started.

One thing he knew, though: He couldn't dismiss this all as madness. Father was *not* crazy, however new and strange he might seem; and as for Mother, if *her* vision of the burning of Earth was madness, then she had been mad since before he was born. So there *was* something that put ideas and desires and visions into his parents' minds—and into Luet's, too, couldn't forget *her*. People called this something the Oversoul, but that was just a name, a label. What *was* it? What did it want? What could it actually *do*? If it could talk to some people, why didn't it just talk to everybody?

Nafai stopped across a fairly wide street from what might be the largest house in Basilica. He knew it well enough, since the head of the Palwashantu clan was mated with the woman who lived there. Nafai couldn't remember *her* name—she was nobody, everyone knew she had bought this ancient house with her mate's money, and if she didn't renew his contract then even *with* the house she'd be nobody—but *he* was Gaballufix. There was a family connection—his mother was Hosni, who later on became Wetchik's auntie and the mother of Elemak. Between that blood connection and the fact that Father was perhaps the second most prestigious Palwashantu clansman in Basilica, they had visited this house at least once, usually two or three times a year since as long ago as Nafai could remember.

As he stood there, stupidly watching the front of that landmark building, he suddenly came alert, for without meaning to he had recognized someone moving along the street. Elemak should have been home sleeping—he had traveled all night, hadn't he? Yet here he was, in mid-afternoon. For a panicked moment Nafai wondered if Elya was looking for *him*—was it possible that Mother had missed him and worried and now the whole family, perhaps even Father's employees as well, were combing the city looking for him?

But no. Elemak wasn't looking for anybody. He was moving too casually, too easily. Looking in no particular direction at all.

And then he was gone.

No, he had turned down into the gap between Gaballufix's house and the building next door. So he *did* have a destination.

Nafai had to know what Elemak was doing. He trotted along the street to where he had a clear view down the narrow road. He got there in time to see Elemak ducking into a low alley doorway into Gaballufix's house.

Nafai couldn't imagine what business Elya might have with Gaballufix—especially something so urgent that he had to go to his house the same day he got back from a long trip. True, Gaballufix was technically Elya's half-brother, but there were sixteen years between them and Gaballufix had never openly recognized Elya as his brother. That didn't mean, though, that they couldn't start behaving more like close kinsmen now. Still, it bothered Nafai that Elemak had never mentioned it and seemed to be concealing it now.

Whether the question bothered him or not, Nafai knew that it would be a very bad idea to ask Elemak about it directly. When Elya wanted anybody to know what he was doing with Gaballufix, he'd tell them. In the meantime, the secret would be safe inside Elya's head.

A secret inside somebody's head.

Luet had known that Nafai was in love with Eiadh.

Well, it wasn't all *that* secret—Luet might have guessed it from the way that he looked at her. But there on the front porch of Mother's house, Luet had said, *"You're* the bastard," as if she were answering him for calling *her* a bastard. Only he hadn't *said* anything. He had only *thought* of her as a bastard. It wasn't an opinion he had expressed before. He had only thought of it at that moment, because he was annoyed with Luet. Yet she had known.

Was that the Oversoul, too? Not just putting ideas into people's heads, but also taking them out and telling them to other people? The Oversoul wasn't just a provider of strange dreams—it was a spy and a gossip as well.

It made Nafai afraid, to think that not only was the Oversoul real, but also that it had the power to read his most secret, transitory thoughts and tell them to some-one else. And to someone as repulsive as the little bastard witchgirl, no less.

It frightened him like the first time he went out into the sea by himself. Father had taken them all on a holiday, down to the beach. The first afternoon there, they had all gone out into the sea together, and sur-rounded by his father and brothers—except Issib, of course, who watched them from his chair on the beach—he had felt the sea play with him, the waves shoving him toward shore, then trying to draw him out again. It was fun, exhilarating. He even dared to swim out to where his feet couldn't quite touch the bottom, all the while playing with Meb and Elya and Father. A good day, a great day, when his older brothers still liked him. But the next morning he got up early, left the tent and went out to the water alone. He could swim like a fish; he was in no danger. And yet as he walked out into the water he felt an inexplicable unease. The water tugging at him, pushing him; he was only a few meters from shore, and yet with no one else in the water, all by himself, he felt as if he had lost his place, as if he had already been washed out to sea, as if he were caught in the grasp of something so huge that any part of it could swallow him up. He panicked then. He ran to shore, struggling against the water, convinced that it would never let him go, dragging at him, sucking him down. And then he was on the sand, on the dry sand above the tide line, and he fell to his knees and wept because he was safe.

But for those few moments out in the water he had felt the terror of knowing how small and helpless he was, how much power there was in the world, and how easily it could do to him whatever it wanted and there was nothing he could do to resist it.

That was the fear he felt now. Not so strong, not so specific as it had been that day on the beach—but then, he wasn't a five-year-old anymore, either, and he was better at dealing with fear. The Oversoul wasn't an old legend, it was alive, and it could force visions into his own parents' minds and it could search out secrets inside Nafai's head and tell them to other people, to people that Nafai didn't like and who didn't like him.

The worst thing was knowing that the reason why Luet didn't like him was probably *because* of what the Oversoul had told her about his thoughts. His most private thoughts exposed to this unsympathetic little monster. What next? Would Father's next vision be Nafai's fantasies about Eiadh? Worse yet, would *Mother* be shown?

On the beach, he had been able to run for shore. Where did you run to get away from the Oversoul?

You didn't. You couldn't hide, either—how could you disguise your own thoughts so even you didn't know what you were thinking?

The only choice he had was to try to find out what the Oversoul was, to try to understand what it wanted, what it was trying to do to his family, to *him*. He had to understand the Oversoul and, if possible, get it to leave him alone.

FOUR

MASKS

There would be no point in going back to Mother's house so late in the school day. Explaining himself would probably take up what little time was left. Making excuses could wait until tomorrow.

Or maybe Nafai would never go back. There was a thought. After all, Mebbekew didn't go to school. In fact he didn't do *anything*, didn't even come home if he decided not to.

When had that started? Was Meb already doing that sort of thing at fourteen? Well, whether he was or not, Nafai could start now and who was going to stop him? He was as tall as any man, and he was old enough for a man's trade. Not Father's trade, though—never the plant business. If you followed *that* trade long enough, you started seeing visions in the dark beside desert roads.

But there were other trades. Maybe Nafai could apprentice himself to some artist. A poet, or a singer—Nafai's voice was young, but he could follow a tune, and with training maybe he could actually become good. Or maybe he was really a dancer, or an actor, in spite of Mother's joke this morning. Those arts had nothing to do with going to school—if he was supposed to pursue one, then staying on with Mother was a waste of time.

That notion possessed him through the afternoon, carrying him south at first, toward the inner market, where there would be songs and poems to hear, perhaps some fine new myachik to buy and listen to at home. Of course, if he stopped attending school, Mother would no doubt cut off his myachik allowance. But as an apprentice there'd probably be some spending money, and if not, so what? He'd be doing a real art himself, in the flesh. Soon he would no longer even *want* recordings of art on little glass balls.

By the time he reached the inner market, he had talked himself into having no interest in recordings, now that he was going to be making a career out of creating the real thing. He headed east, through the neighborhoods called Pens and Gardens and Olive Grove, a few narrow streets of houses between the city wall and the rim of the valley where men could not go. At last he came to the place that was narrowest of all, a single street with a high white wall behind the houses, so that a man standing on the red wall of the city couldn't see over the houses and down into the valley. He had only come this way a few times in his life, and never alone.

Never alone, because Dolltown was a place for company and fellowship, a place for sitting in a crowded audience and watching dances and plays, or listening to recitations and concerts. Now, though, Nafai was coming to Dolltown as an artist, not to be part of the audience. It wasn't fellowship he was looking for, but vocation.

The sun was still up, so the streets of Dolltown weren't

crowded. Dusk would bring out the frolicking apprentices and schoolboys, and full dark would call forth the lovers and the connoisseurs and the revelers. But even now, in late afternoon, some of the theatres were open, and the galleries were doing good business in the daylight.

Nafai stopped into several galleries, more because they were open than because he seriously thought he might apprentice himself to a painter or a sculptor. Nafai's skill at drawing was never good, and when he tried sculpture as a child his projects always had to have titles so people could tell what they were supposed to be. Browsing through the galleries, Nafai tried to look thoughtful and studious, but the artsellers were never fooled—Nafai might be tall as a man, but he was still far too young to be a serious customer. So they never came up and talked to him, the way they did when adults came into the shops. He had to glean his information from what he overheard. The prices astonished him. Of course the cost of the originals was completely out of reach, but even the high-resolution holographic copies were too expensive for him to dream of buying one. Worst of all was the fact that the paintings and sculptures he liked the best were invariably the most expensive. Maybe that meant that he had excellent taste. Or maybe it meant that the artists who knew how to impress the ignorant were able to make the most money.

Bored at last with the galleries, and determined to see which art should be the channel for his future, Nafai wandered down to the open theatre, a series of tiny stages dotting the broad lawns near the wall. A few plays were in rehearsal. Since there was no real audience yet, the sound bubbles hadn't been turned on, and as Nafai walked from stage to stage, the sounds of more distant plays kept intruding into every pause in the one close at hand. After a while, though, Nafai discovered that if he stood and watched a rehearsal long enough to get interested, he stopped noticing any other noises.

What intrigued him most was a troupe of satirists. He had always thought satire must be the most exciting kind of play, because the scripts were always as new as today's gossip. And, just as he had imagined, there sat the satirist at the rehearsal, scribbling his verse on paper—on *paper*—and handing the scraps to a script boy who ran them up to the stage and handed them to the player that the lines were intended for. The players who weren't onstage at the moment were either pacing back and forth or hunched over on the lawn, saying their lines over and over again, to memorize them for tonight's performance. This was why satires were always sloppy and ill-timed, with sudden silences and absurd non sequiturs abounding. But no one expected a satire to be *good*—it only had to be funny and nasty and new.

This one seemed to be about an old man who sold love potions. The masker playing the old man seemed quite young, no more than twenty, and he wasn't very good at faking an older voice. But that was part of the fun of it—maskers were almost always apprentice actors who hadn't yet managed to get a part with a serious company of players. They *claimed* that the reason they wore masks instead of makeup was to protect them from reprisals from angry victims of satire—but, watching them, Nafai suspected that the mask was as much to protect the young actor from the ridicule of his peers.

The afternoon had turned hot, and some of the actors had taken off their shirts; those with pale skin seemed oblivious to the fact that they were burning to the color of tomatoes. Nafai laughed silently at the thought that maskers were probably the only people in Basilica who could get a sunburn everywhere *but* their faces.

The script boy handed a verse to a player who had been sitting hunched over in the grass. The young man looked at it, then got up and walked to the satirist.

"I can't say this," he said.

The satirist's back was to Nafai, so he couldn't hear the answer.

"What, is my part so unimportant that *my* lines don't have to rhyme?"

Now the satirist's answer was loud enough that Nafai caught a few phrases, ending with the clincher, "Write the thing yourself!"

The young man angrily pulled his mask off his face and shouted, "I couldn't do worse than *this*!"

The satirist burst into laughter. "Probably not," he said. "Go ahead, give it a try, I don't have time to be brilliant with *every* scene."

Mollified, the young man put his mask back on. But Nafai had seen enough. For the young masker who wanted his lines to rhyme was none other than Nafai's brother Mebbekew.

So this was the source of his income. Not borrowing at all. The idea that had seemed so clever and fresh to Nafai—apprenticing himself in an art to earn his independence—had long since occurred to Mebbekew, and he was *doing* it. In a way it was encouraging—if Mebbekew can do it, why can't I?—but it was also discouraging to think that of all people, Nafai had happened to choose Mebbekew to emulate. Meb, the brother who had hated him all his life instead of coming to hate him more recently, like Elya. Is this what I was born for? To become a second Mebbekew?

Then came the nastiest thought of all. Wouldn't it be funny if I entered the acting profession, years after Meb, and got a job with a serious company right away? It would be deliciously humiliating; Meb would be suicidal.

Well, maybe not. Meb was far more likely to turn murderous.

Nafai was drawn out of his spiteful little daydream by the scene on the stage. The old potion-seller was trying to persuade a reluctant young woman to buy an herb from him.

> Put the leaves in his tea
> Put the flower in your bed
> And by half past three
> He'll be dead—I beg your pardon,
> Just a slip of the tongue.

The plot was finally making sense. The old man wanted to poison the girl's lover by persuading her that the fatal herb was a love potion. She apparently didn't catch on—all characters in satire were amazingly stupid—but for other reasons she was still resisting the sale.

> I'd sooner be hung
> Than use a flower from your garden.
> I want nothing from you.
> I want his love to be true.

Suddenly the old man burst into an operatic song. His voice was actually not bad, even with exaggeration for comic effect.

> The dream of love is so enchanting!

At that moment Mebbekew, his mask back in place, bounded onto the stage and directly addressed the audience.

Listen to the old man ranting!

They proceeded to perform a strange duet, the old potion-seller singing a line and Mebbekew's young character answering with a spoken comment to the audience.

But love can come in many ways!
(I've followed him for several days.)
One lover might be very willing!
(I know he plots her lover's killing.)
The other endlessly delays!
(Listen how the donkey brays!)
Oh, do not make the wrong decision!
(I think I'll give this ass a vision.)
When I can take you to your goal!
(He'll think it's from the Oversoul.)
No limits bind the lover's game.
(A vision needs a little flame . . .)
No matter how you win it,
Because your heart is in it,
You'll love your lover's loving still the same.

A vision from the Oversoul. Flame. Nafai didn't like the turn this was taking. He didn't like the fact that the old potion-seller's mask had a wild mane of white hair and a full white beard. Was it possible that word had already spread so far and fast? Some satirists were famous for getting the gossip before anyone else—as often as not, people attended the satires just to find out what was happening—and many people left the satires asking each other, What was that *really* about?

Mebbekew was fiddling with a box on the stage. The satirist called out to him, "Never mind the fire effect. We'll pretend it's working."

"We have to try it sometime," Mebbekew answered.

"Not now."

"When?"

The satirist got to his feet, strode to the foot of the stage directly in front of Meb, cupped his hands around his mouth, and bellowed: "We . . . will . . . do . . . the . . . effect . . . later!"

"Fine," said Meb.

As the satirist returned to his place on the hill, he said, "And *you* wouldn't be setting off the fire effect anyway."

"Sorry," said Meb. He returned to his place behind the box that presumably would be spouting a column of flame tonight. The other maskers returned to their positions.

"End of song," said Meb. "Fire effect."

Immediately the potion-seller and the girl flung up their hands in a mockery of surprise.

"A pillar of fire!" cried the potion-seller.

"How could fire suddenly appear on a bare rock in the desert?" cried the girl. "It's a *miracle!*"

The potion-seller whirled on her. "You don't know what you're talking about, bitch! *I'm* the only one who can see this! It's a vision!"

"No!" shouted Mebbekew, in his deepest voice. "It's a special stage effect!"

"A stage effect!" cried the potion-seller. "Then you must be—"

"You got it!"

"That old humbug the Oversoul!"

"I'm proud of you, old trickster! Stupid girl—you almost fixed her."

"Oh, it's nothing much to take *her*—you're the master faker!"

"*No!*" bellowed the satirist. "Not 'take *her*,' you idiot! It's '*take* her,' emphasis on *take*, or it doesn't rhyme with *faker!*"

"Sorry," said the young masker playing the potion-seller. "It doesn't make *sense* your way, of course, but at least it'll *rhyme*."

"It doesn't have to make sense, you uppity young rooster, it only has to make money!"

Everybody laughed—though it was clear that the actors still didn't really like the satirist much. They got back into the scene and a few moments later Meb and the potion-seller launched into a song-and-dance routine about how clever they were at hoodwinking people, and how unbelievably gullible most people were—especially women. It seemed that every couplet of the song was designed to mortally offend some portion of the audience, and the song went on until every conceivable group in Basilica had been darted. While they sang and danced, the girl pretended to roast some kind of meat in the flames.

Meb forgot his lyrics less than the other masker, and in spite of the fact that Nafai knew the whole sequence was aimed at humiliating Father, he couldn't help but notice that Meb was actually pretty good, especially at singing so every word was clear. I could do that, too, thought Nafai.

The song kept coming back to the same refrain:

I'm standing by a fire
With my favorite liar
No one stands a chance
When he starts his fancy dancing

When the song ended, the Oversoul—Meb—had persuaded the potion-seller that the best way to get the women of Basilica to do whatever he wanted was to persuade them that he was getting visions from the

Oversoul. "They're so ready for deceiving," said Meb. "We'll have all these girls believing."

The scene closed with the potion-seller leading the girl offstage, telling her how he had seen a vision of the city of Basilica burning up. The satirist had switched to alliterative verse, which Nafai thought sounded a little more natural than rhyming, but it wasn't as fun. "Do you want to waste the last weeks of the world clinging to some callow young cad? Wouldn't you be better off boffing your brains out with an ugly old man who has an understanding with the Oversoul?"

"Fine," said the satirist. "That'll work. Let's have the street scene now."

Another group of maskers came up on the stage. Nafai immediately headed across the lawn to where Mebbekew, his mask still in place, was already scribbling new dialogue on a scrap of paper.

"Meb," said Nafai.

Meb looked up, startled, trying to see better through the small eyeholes in the mask. "What did you call me?" Then he saw it was Nafai. Immediately he jumped to his feet and started walking away. "Get away from me, you little rat-eater."

"Meb, I've got to talk to you."

Mebbekew kept walking.

"Before you go on in this play tonight!" said Nafai.

Meb whirled on him. "It's not a play, it's a satire. I'm not an actor, I'm a masker. And you're not my brother, you're an ass."

Meb's fury astonished him. "What have I done to you?" asked Nafai.

"I know you, Nyef. No matter what I do or say to you, you're going to end up telling Father."

As if Father wouldn't eventually find out that his son was playing in a satire that was designed to dart him in front of the whole city. "What makes me sick," said Nafai, "is that all you care about is whether *you* get in trouble. You've got no family loyalty at all."

"This doesn't hurt my family. Masking is a perfectly legitimate way to get started as an actor, and it pays me a living and wins me just a little tiny scrap of respect and pleasure now and then, which is a lot more than working for Father ever did!"

What was Meb talking about? "I don't care that you're a masker. In fact, I think it's great. I was hanging around here today because I was thinking maybe I might try it myself."

Meb pulled his mask off and looked Nafai up and down. "You've got a body that might look all right on stage. But you still sound like a kid."

"Mebbekew, it doesn't matter right now. You a masker, me a masker—the point is that you can't do this to Father!"

"I'm not doing anything to Father! I'm doing this for myself."

It was always like this, talking to Mebbekew. He never seemed to grasp the thread of an argument. "Be a masker, fine," said Nafai. "But darting your own father is too low even for you!"

Meb looked at him blankly. "Darting my father?"

"You can't tell me you don't know."

"What is there in this satire that darts *him*?"

"The scene you just finished, Meb."

"Father's not the *only* person in Basilica who believes in the Oversoul. In fact, I sometimes think *he* doesn't believe all that seriously."

"The vision, Meb! The fire in the desert, the prophecy about the end of the world! Who do you *think* it's about?"

"I don't know. Old Drotik doesn't tell us what these

things are about. If we haven't heard the gossip then so what? We still say the lines anyway." Then Meb got a strange, quizzical expression on his face. "What does all this Oversoul stuff have to do with Father?"

"He had a vision," said Nafai. "On the Desert Road, this morning before dawn, returning from his journey. He saw a pillar of fire on a rock, and Basilica burning, and he thinks it means the destruction of the world, like Earth in the old legend. Mother believes him and he must already be talking to people about it or how else would your satirist know to include this bit in his satire?"

"This is the craziest thing I ever heard of," said Mebbekew.

"I'm not making it up," said Nafai. "I sat there this morning on Mother's portico and—"

"The portico scene! That's . . . He wrote how the apothecary—that's supposed to be *Father*?"

"What do you think I've been telling you?"

"Bastard," whispered Meb. "That bastard. And he put me on stage as the *Oversoul*."

Meb turned and rushed toward the masker who played the apothecary. He stood in front of him for a few moments, looking at the mask and the costume. "It's so *obvious*, I must have the brains of a gnat—but a vision!"

"What are you talking about?" asked the masker.

"Give me that mask," said Mebbekew. "Give it to me!"

"Right, sure, here."

Meb tore it out of the other man's hands and ran up the hill toward the satirist. Nafai ran after him. Meb was waving the mask in front of the satirist's face. "How dare you, Drotik, you pus-hearted old fart!"

"Oh, don't pretend you didn't know, my boy."

"How would I know? I was asleep till rehearsal started. You put me on stage darting my *father* and it's just coincidence that you didn't happen to mention the fact, yes, I'm sure I believe *that*."

"Hey, it brings an audience."

"What were you going to do, tell people who I am, after all your promises about keeping me anonymous? What are these masks supposed to *mean* anyway?" Meb turned to the others, who were clearly baffled by the whole thing. "Listen, people, do you know what this old pimple was going to do? He was going to dart my father and then tell people that it was *me* playing the Oversoul. He was going to unmask me!"

The satirist was obviously worried by this turn of events. Though most of the maskers' faces were still hidden, they must be angry at the idea of a satirist exposing his maskers' identities. So the satirist had to get things back under control. "Don't waste a thought on this nonsense," he said to the others. "I just fired the boy because he had the audacity to rewrite my lines, and now he wants to wreck the entire show."

The maskers visibly relaxed.

Meb must have realized that he had lost the argument—the maskers *wanted* to believe the satirist because if they didn't, they'd lose a paying job. "My father isn't the liar," said Meb, "*you* are."

"Satire is wonderful, isn't it," said Drotik, "until the dart strikes at home."

Meb raised the white-maned apothecary mask over his head, as if he was going to strike the satirist with it. Drotik flung up an arm and shied away. But Meb never meant to hit him. Instead he brought the mask down over his knee, breaking it in half. Then he tossed both pieces into the satirist's lap.

The satirist lowered his arm and met Mebbekew's gaze again. "It'll take ten minutes for my maskmaker to put the beard onto another mask. Or were you trying to make a metaphorical threat?"

"I don't know," said Meb. "Were you trying to get me to metaphorically murder my father?"

The satirist shook his head in disbelief. "It's a *dart*, boy. Just words. A few laughs."

"A few extra tickets."

"It paid your wages."

"It made you rich." Meb turned his back and walked away. Nafai followed him. Behind them he could hear Drotik sending the script boy to the wall to ask for maskers who thought they could learn a part in three hours.

Mebbekew wouldn't let Nafai catch up with him. He walked faster and faster, until finally they were running full tilt along the streets, up and down the hills. But Mebbekew hadn't the endurance to outlast Nafai, and finally he fetched up against the corner of a house, bowed over, panting, gasping for breath.

Nafai didn't know what to say. He hadn't meant to chase Meb down, only to tell him what he thought—that he'd been terrific, the way he put the satirist in his place, the way he called him a liar to his face and blasted every argument Drotik raised in his own defense. When you broke the mask in half, I wanted to cheer—that's what Nafai meant to tell him.

But when he got close enough to speak, he realized that Meb wasn't just panting for breath. He was crying, not in grief, but in rage, and when Nafai got there Meb started beating a fist against the wall. "How could he *do* it!" Meb was saying, over and over. "The selfish stupid old son-of-a-bitch!"

"Don't worry about it," said Nafai, meaning to comfort him. "Drotik isn't worth it."

"Not Drotik, you idiot," Meb answered. "Drotik's

exactly what I always thought he was except that now I've lost my job and I'll *never* get another one, Drotik will spread the word on me that I walked out on a show three hours before lights."

"Then who are you mad at?"

"Father! Who do you think? A vision—I can't believe it, I thought Drotik would tell me that it wasn't Father he was darting, it was somebody else, and what ever gave me the idea it was Wetchik, what kind of cheese-brained fool would come up with the idea that the honorable *Wetchik* was off getting visions from the amazing unbelievable *Oversoul!*"

"Mother believes him," said Nafai.

"Mother has renewed his contract every year since the year you were conceived, *obviously* she's got a lot of judgment where he's concerned! Do *you* believe him? Does anybody who hasn't slept with him?"

"I don't know. I don't even know who knows about it."

"Let me tell you something. Six hours from now the entire city of Basilica will know about it, that's who knows about it. I want to *kill* him, the flatulent old pincushion!"

"Calm down, you don't mean that—"

"Don't I? Do you think I wouldn't love to push this fist right through his face?" Meb turned around and screamed his next sentence at the passersby on the street. "I'll show you some visions, you pebble-headed weed-hauler!"

People were stopped on the street, staring.

"Right," said Nafai, "Father's embarrassing *you*."

"I didn't ask you to follow me. *You're* the one who chased after me, so if you don't like being with me you can choke to death on your own snot, that's perfectly all right."

"Let's go home," said Nafai, mostly because he couldn't think of anything else to say.

FIVE

=====

WHEELS

Home certainly wasn't where Nafai wanted to be, not tonight. He had been hoping Father would be somewhere else, so Meb would have a chance to calm down before they talked. But no, of course not, Father *wanted* to talk to Meb. He had already spent an hour talking with Elemak—Nafai wasn't too broken up about missing *that* scene—and now he seemed to have the fantasy that he might possibly persuade Meb to believe in his vision.

The yelling started as soon as Mebbekew located Father in the study. Nafai had seen what these arguments were like, and so he quickly retreated to his room. On his way through the courtyard, he caught a glimpse of Issib peering out of his doorway. Another refugee, thought Nafai.

For the first hour or so, all that could be heard was the low murmur of Father's voice, presumably trying to explain about his vision, interrupted every few minutes by Mebbekew's clear, piercing shout making comments

that ranged from accusation to derision. Then it finally
came out, amid all of Mebbekew's complaints about how
Father was humiliating the family, that Meb had been
doing a fair job of bringing the family into disrepute by
working as a masker. Then it was Father's turn to shout
and Mebbekew's to try to explain, which was good for
another hour of quarreling before Meb left the house in
a rage and Father went out to the stables to tend to the
animals until he calmed down.

Only then did Nafai venture to the kitchen, absolutely
starving by now, for his first serious meal of the day. To
his surprise, Elemak was there, sitting with Issib at the
table.

"Elya, I didn't know you were here," said Nafai.

Elemak looked up at him, blankly, and then remembered. "Forget it," he said. "I was angry this morning but
it's nothing, forget it."

Nafai *had* forgotten, with all that had happened since,
that Elemak had warned him not to come home. "I guess
I already did," he said.

Elemak gave him a disgusted look and then went back
to his food.

"What did I say?"

"Never mind," said Issib. "We're trying to think what
we should do."

Nafai headed for the freezer and started scanning the
food that Truzhnisha had stocked there for occasions like
this. He was dying of hunger and yet nothing looked
good. "Is this all that's left?"

"No, I have the rest hidden in my pants," said Issib.

Nafai picked something that he remembered liking
before, even though it didn't sound particularly good
tonight. While it was heating he turned around and faced
the others. "So, what have we decided?"

Elemak didn't look up.

"*We* haven't decided anything," said Issib.

"Oh, what, am I suddenly the only child in the house, while the *men* are making all the decisions?"

"Pretty much, yes," said Issib.

"And what decisions do *you* have to make? Who has any decisions to make at *all*, besides Father? It's his house, his business, his money, and his name that's getting laughed at all through Basilica."

Elemak shook his head. "Not *all* through Basilica."

"You mean somebody hasn't heard about this yet?"

"I mean," said Elemak, "that not everybody is laughing."

"They will if that satire runs long. I saw a rehearsal. Meb was really pretty good. Of course he quit since it was about Father, but I think he really has talent. Did you know he sings?"

Elemak looked at him with contempt. "Are you really this shallow, Nyef?"

"Yes," said Nafai. "I'm so shallow that I actually think our embarrassment isn't all that important, if Father really saw a vision."

"We know Father *saw* it," said Elemak. "The problem is what he's doing about it."

"What, he gets a vision from the Oversoul warning about the destruction of the world, and he should keep it a secret?"

"Just eat your food," said Elemak.

"He's going around telling people that the Oversoul wants us to go back to the old laws," said Issib.

"Which ones?"

"All of them."

"I mean which ones aren't we already following?"

Elemak apparently decided to go straight to the heart of things. "He went to the clan council and spoke against our decision to cooperate with Potokgavan in their war with the Wetheads."

"Who?"

"The Gorayni. The Wetheads."

They had got the nickname because of their habit of wearing their hair long, in ringlets, dripping with a perfumed oil. They were also known as vicious warriors with a habit of slaughtering prisoners who hadn't proved their valor by sustaining a serious wound before surrendering. "But they're hundreds of kilometers north of here," said Nafai, "and the Potoku are way to the southeast, and what do they have to fight about?"

"What do they teach you in your little school?" said Elemak. "The Potoku have extended their protection over all the coastal plain up to the Mochai River."

"Sure, right. Protection from what?"

"From the Gorayni, Nafai. We're between them. It's called geography."

"I know geography," said Nafai. "I just don't see why there should ever be a war between the Gorayni and the Potoku, and if there was, how they'd go about fighting it. I mean, Potokgavan has a fleet—all their *houses* are boats, for heaven's sake—but since Goraynivat has no seacoast—"

"*Had* no seacoast. They've conquered Usluvat."

"I guess I knew that."

"Oh, I'm sure you did," said Elemak. "They have horsewagons. Have you heard of those?"

"Wheels," said Nafai. "Horses pulling men in boxes into battle."

"And carrying supplies to feed an army on a long march. A *very* long march. Horsewagons are changing everything." Suddenly Elemak sounded enthusiastic. It had been a lot of years since Nafai had seen Elya excited about anything. "I can envision a day when we'll widen

the Ridge Road and the Plains Road and Market Street
so that the farmers can haul their produce up here in
horsewagons. The same number of horses can haul ten
times as much. One man, two horses, and a wagon can
bring what it takes a dozen men and twenty horses to
haul up here now. The price of food drops. The cost of
transporting *our* products downhill drops even lower—
there's money there. I can envision roads going hundreds
of kilometers, right across the desert—fewer animals in
our caravans, less feed to haul and no need to find as
much water on the journey. The world is getting smaller,
and Father's trying to block it."

"All this has something to do with his vision?"

"The old laws of the Oversoul. Wheels for anything
other than gears or toys are forbidden. Sacrilege. Abom-
ination. Do you realize that horsewagons have been
known about for thousands and thousands of years and
nobody has ever built any?"

"Till now," said Issib.

"Maybe there was a good reason," said Nafai.

"The reason was superstition, that was the reason,"
said Elemak, "but now we have a chance to build two
hundred horsewagons with Potokgavan paying for it and
providing us with the designs, and the price Gaballufix
has negotiated is high enough that we can build two
hundred more for ourselves."

"Why don't the Potoku build their own wagons?"

"They're coming here on boats," said Elemak. "Instead
of building the wagons in Potokgavan and then floating
them all the way, they'll simply send their soldiers and
have the wagons waiting for them here."

"Why *here?*"

"Because here is where they're going to draw the line.
The Gorayni go no farther, or they face the wrath of the

Potoku. Don't try to understand it, Nafai, it's men's business."

"It sounds to me like Father would be right to try to block this just on general principles," said Nafai. "I mean, if they find out we're building horsewagons for the Potoku, won't that just make the Gorayni send an army here to stop us?"

"They won't know until it's too late."

"Why won't they know? Is Basilica so good at keeping secrets?"

"Even if they know, Nyef, the Potoku will be here to stop them from trying to punish us."

"But if the Potoku weren't coming, and therefore we weren't making wagons for them, there'd be nothing for the Gorayni to punish us *for*."

Elemak lowered his head to the table, making a show of his despair at trying to explain anything to Nafai.

"The world is changing," said Issib. "We're used to wars being local quarrels. But the Gorayni have changed it. They're conquering other countries that never did them any harm."

Elemak picked up the explanation. "Someday they'd reach us, with or without the Potoku here to protect us. Personally, I prefer letting the Potoku do the fighting."

"I can't believe all this has been going on and nobody's even talking about it in the city," said Nafai. "I really *don't* have my ears plugged with mud, and I haven't heard anything about us building wagons for Potokgavan."

Elemak shook his head. "It's a secret. Or it *was*, till Father brought it up before the entire clan council."

"You mean somebody was doing this and the clan council didn't even know?"

"It was a *secret*," said Elemak. "How many times do I have to say it?"

"So somebody was going to do this thing in the name

of Basilica and the Palwashantu clan, and nobody in the clan council or the city council was going to be consulted about it?"

Issib laughed ruefully. "When you put it that way, it sounds pretty strange, doesn't it."

"It doesn't sound strange at all," said Elemak. "I can see that you're already with Roptat's party."

"Who's Roptat?"

Issib answered, "He's a Palwashantu, Elya's age is all, who's been using this war talk to build up his reputation as a prophet. Not like Father, he doesn't have visions from the Oversoul, he just writes prophecies that read like a shark tearing your leg off. And he keeps saying the same things that you just said."

"You mean this secret plan is so well known that there's already a party led by this Roptat trying to block it?"

"It wasn't *that* secret," said Elemak. "There's no plot. There's no conspiracy. There's just some good people trying to do something that's in Basilica's vital interest, and some traitors doing everything they can to stop it."

Clearly Elemak had a one-sided view of things. Nafai had to offer another point of view. "Or maybe it's some greedy profiteers putting our city in a terribly dangerous situation so they can get rich, and some good people are trying to save the city by stopping them. I'm just suggesting this as a possibility."

Elemak was furious. "The people working on this project are already so rich that they hardly need any more money," he said. "And what I don't get is how a fourteen-year-old *scholar* who's never had to do a *man's* work in his life suddenly has opinions about political issues that he didn't even know *existed* until ten minutes ago."

"I was just asking a question," said Nafai. "I wasn't accusing you of anything."

"Well of course you weren't accusing *me*," said Elemak. "I'm not part of the project anyway."

"Of course not," said Nafai. "It's a *secret* project."

"I should have beaten the teeth out of your mouth this morning," said Elemak.

Why did it always come down to threats? "Do you beat the teeth out of the mouth of everybody who asks you questions you don't have any good answers for?"

"Never before," said Elemak, getting up. "But now I'm going to make up for all those missed opportunities."

"Stop it!" shouted Issib. "Don't we have enough problems?"

Elemak hesitated, then sat back down. "I shouldn't let him get to me."

Nafai breathed again. He hadn't noticed that he wasn't breathing.

"He's a child, what does he know?" said Elemak. "Father's the one who should know better. He's making a lot of people very angry. Some very dangerous people."

"You mean they're threatening him?" asked Nafai.

"Nobody *threatens*," said Elemak. "That would be crude. They're just . . . concerned about Father."

"But if everybody's laughing at Father, why should they care what he says? It sounds like it's this Roptat they ought to be worried about."

"It's the vision thing," said Elemak. "The Oversoul. Most men don't take it all that seriously, but the women . . . the city council . . . your mother isn't helping things."

"Or she *is* helping things, depending on which side you're on."

"Right," said Elemak. He got up from the table, but this time he wasn't threatening. "I can see which side *you're* on, Nyef, and I can only warn you that if Father has his way, we'll end up in Gorayni chains."

"Why are you so sure?" asked Nafai. "The Oversoul give you a vision or something?"

"I'm sure, my little *half*-friend, because I understand things. When you grow up, you might actually come to know what that means. But I doubt it." Elemak walked out of the kitchen.

Issib sighed. "Does anybody actually *like* anybody else in this family?"

Nafai's food was overcooked, but he didn't care. He was trembling so violently that he could hardly carry his tray to the table.

"Why are you shaking?"

"I don't know," said Nafai. "Maybe I'm afraid."

"Of Elemak?"

"Why should I be afraid of him?" said Nafai. "Just because he could break my neck with his elbow."

"Then why do you keep provoking him?"

"Maybe I'm also afraid *for* him."

"Why?"

"Don't you think it's funny, Issib? Elya can sit here and talk about Father being in danger from powerful people—and yet his solution for it isn't to denounce those dangerous people, it's to try to get Father to stop talking."

"Nobody's being rational."

"I actually *do* understand politics," said Nafai. "I study history all the time. I left my class behind years ago. I *know* something about how wars start and who wins them. And this is the stupidest plan I've ever heard. Potokgavan has no chance of holding this area and no compelling reason to try. All that will happen is they'll send an army, provoke the Gorayni into attacking, and then they'll realize they can't win and go home to their floodplain where the Wetheads can't touch them, leaving *us* to bear the brunt of the Gorayni wrath. Building war wagons for them is so *obviously* going to lead to disaster that only a person completely blinded by greed could possibly support it. And if the Oversoul is telling Father to oppose the building of wagons, then the Oversoul is right."

"I'm sure the Oversoul is relieved to have your approval."

"Anything I can do to help."

"Nafai, you're fourteen."

"So?"

"Elemak doesn't want to hear that kind of thing from you."

"Neither do you, right?"

"I'm really tired. It's been a long day." Issib floated out of the kitchen.

Nafai finally started to eat. To his disgust he had no appetite, even though he knew he was still hungry. Must eat, can't eat. Forget it. He flushed the food down the drain and put the plate in the cleaning rack.

He walked out into the courtyard, heading for his room. The night air was chilly already—they were close enough to the desert to get sharp falls in temperature when the sun was down. He was still trembling. He didn't know why. It wasn't because of Father's vision of the destruction of the world, and it wasn't because of the war that would probably come to Basilica if they went ahead with the idiotic alliance with Potokgavan. Those were dangers, yes, but distant ones. And it wasn't because of Elemak's threats of violence, he'd lived with those all his life.

It wasn't until he was lying on his mat, still shaking even though his room was *not* cold, that he finally realized what was bothering him. Elemak had mentioned that Gaballufix was involved in negotiating the price with the Potoku. Obviously this whole plan had Gaballufix's support—who else but the clan chief would think he could commit the Palwashantu to such a dangerous course of action without even consulting the council? And so it was reasonable to suppose that when Elya warned about the dangerous enemies Father was making, it was Gaballufix he was referring to.

Gaballufix, whose house Elemak secretly visited today.

Where was Elemak's loyalty? With Father? Or with his half-brother Gaballufix? Clearly Elya was involved with this war wagon plan. What else was he involved with? The dangerous people weren't making *threats*, he had said. So what *were* they making—plans? Was Elya in on a plan to do something ugly to Father, and his hints were an attempt to warn Father away?

Just today, Mebbekew had spoken of metaphorical patricide.

No, thought Nafai. No, I'm simply upset because all of this has happened so suddenly, in one day. Father has a vision, and suddenly he's caught up in city politics in a way he never was before, almost as if the Oversoul sent him this vision specifically *because* of this stupid provocative project of Gaballufix's, because action needed to be taken *now*.

Why? What did the fate of Basilica matter to the Oversoul? Countless cities and nations had risen and fallen—dozens every century, thousands and thousands in all of human history. Maybe millions. The Oversoul hadn't lifted a finger. It wasn't war that the Oversoul cared about; it certainly wasn't preventing human suffering. So why was the Oversoul getting involved now? What was the *urgency*? Was it worth tearing their family apart? And even if maybe it was, who decided anyway? Nobody had asked the Oversoul for this, so if they really were getting bounced around as part of some master plan, it might be nice if the Oversoul let them in on what it had in mind.

Nafai lay on his mat, trembling.

Then he remembered. I wasn't going to sleep on a mat tonight. I was going to try to be a real man.

He almost laughed aloud. Sleeping on the bare floor—*that* would make me a man? What an idiot I am. What an ass.

Laughing at himself, now he could sleep.

SIX

ENEMIES

"*Where* did you spend all day yesterday?"

Nafai didn't want this conversation, but there was no avoiding it. Mother was not one to let one of her students disappear for a day without an accounting.

"I walked around."

As he had expected, this was not going to be enough for Mother. "I didn't think that you *flew*," she said. "Though I'm surprised you didn't curl up somewhere and sleep. Where did you go?"

"To some very educational places," said Nafai. He had in mind Gaballufix's house and the Open Theatre, but of course Mother would interpret his words as she wished.

"Dolltown?" she asked.

"There's nothing much going on there in the daytime, Mother."

"And you shouldn't be going there at all," she said. "Or do you think you already know everything about everything, so that you have no further need of schooling?"

"There are some subjects you just don't teach here, Mother." Again, the truth—but not the truth.

"Ah," she said. "Dhelembuvex was right about you."

Oh, yes, wonderful. Time to get an Auntie for your little boy.

"I should have seen it coming. Your body is growing so fast—too fast, I fear, outstripping your maturity in every other area."

This was too much to bear. He had planned to listen calmly to everything she said, let her jump to her own conclusions, and then get back to class and have done with the whole thing. But to have her thinking that his gonads were running his life when, if anything, his mind was more mature than his body—

"Is that as smart as you know how to be, Mother?"

She raised an eyebrow.

He knew he was already overstepping himself, but he had begun, and the words were there in his mind, and so he said them. "You see something inexplicable going on, and if it's a boy doing it, you're sure it has to do with his sexual desires."

She half-smiled. "I do have some knowledge of men, Nafai, and the idea that the behavior of a fourteen-year-old might have some link to sexual desire is based on much evidence."

"But I'm your *son*, and still you don't know me from a pile of bricks."

"So you *didn't* go to Dolltown?"

"Not for any reason *you'd* imagine."

"Ah," she said. "I can imagine *many* reasons. But not one of the possible reasons for you to go to Dolltown suggests that you have very good judgment."

"Oh, and you're the expert on good judgment, I imagine."

His sarcasm was not playing well. "You forget, I think, that I am your mother and your schoolmistress."

"It was you, Mother, and not I who invited those two girls to that *family* meeting yesterday."

"And this showed poor judgment on my part?"

"Extremely poor. By the time I got to the Open Theatre it was still several hours before dark, and already the word was out about Father's vision."

"That's not surprising," said Mother. "Father went directly to the clan council. It would hardly be a secret after that."

"Not just his *vision*, Mother. There was already a satire in rehearsal—one of Drotik's, too, no less—that included a fascinating little portico scene. Since the only people present who were *not* family were those two witchgirls—"

"Hold your tongue!"

He immediately fell silent, but with an undeniable sense of victory. Yes, Mother was furious—but he had also scored a point with her, to get her this angry.

"Your referring to them by that demeaning *manword* is offensive in the extreme," said Mother. Her voice was quiet now; she was *really* angry. "Luet is a seer and Hushidh is a raveler. Furthermore, both have been completely discreet, mentioning nothing to anyone."

"Oh, have you watched them every second since—"

"I said to hold your tongue." Her voice was like ice. "For your information, my bright, wise, *mature* little boy, the reason there was a portico scene in Drotik's satire— which, by the way, I *saw,* and it was very badly done, so it hardly worries me—the reason there was a portico scene was because while your father was going to the clan council, I was at the city council, and when *I* told the story I included the events on this portico. Why, asks my brilliant son with a deliciously stupid look on his face? Because the only thing that made the council take your father's vision seriously was the fact that Luet believed him and found his vision consonant with her own."

Mother had told. *Mother* had brought down ridicule and ruin upon the family. Unbelievable. "Ah," said Nafai.

"I thought you'd see things a little differently."

"I see that there was nothing wrong with having Luet and Hushidh at the family meeting," said Nafai. "It was *you* who should have been excluded."

Her hand lashed out across his face. If she had been aiming for his cheek, she missed, perhaps because he reflexively drew his head back. Instead her fingernail caught him on the chin, tearing the skin. It stung and drew blood.

"You forget yourself, sir," she said.

"Not as badly as you have forgotten yourself, Madam," he answered. Or rather, that was how he *meant* to answer. He even *began* to answer that way, but in the middle of the sentence the enormity of her having struck him that way, the shock and hurt of it, the sheer humiliation of his mother hitting him reduced him to tears. "I'm sorry," he said. Though what he really wanted to say was How dare you, I'm too old for that, I hate you. It was impossible to say such harsh things, however, when he was crying like a baby. Nafai hated it, how tears had always come so easily to him, and it wasn't getting any better as he got older.

"Maybe next time you'll remember to speak to me with proper respect," she said. But she, too, was unable to maintain her sharp tone, for even as she spoke he felt her arm around him as she sat beside him, comforted him.

She could not possibly understand that the way she nestled his head to her shoulder only added to the humiliation and confirmed him in his decision to regard her as an enemy. If she had the power to make him cry because of his love for her, then there was only one possible solution for him: to cease loving her. This was the last time she would ever be able to do this to him.

"You're bleeding," she said.

"It's nothing," he said.

"Let me stanch it—here, with a clean handkerchief, not that horrible rag you carry in your pocket, you absurd little boy."

That's all I'll ever be in this house, isn't it? An absurd little boy. He pulled away from her, refused to let the handkerchief touch his chin. But she persisted, and dabbed at the wound, and the white cloth came away surprisingly bloody—so he took it from her hand and pressed it against the wound. "Deep, I guess," he said.

"If you hadn't moved your head back, my nails wouldn't have caught your chin like that."

If you hadn't slapped me, your nails would have been in your *lap*. But he held his tongue.

"I can see that you're taking our family's situation very much to heart, Nafai, but your values are a little twisted. What does the ridicule of the satirists matter? Everyone knows that every great figure in the history of Basilica was darted at one time or another, and usually for the very thing that made her—or him—great. We can bear that. What matters is that Father's vision was a very clear warning from the Oversoul, with immediate implications for our city's course of action over the next few days and weeks and months. The embarrassment will pass. And among the women in this city who really count, Father is viewed as quite a remarkable man—their respect for him is growing. So try to control your embarrassment at your father's having come to the center of attention. All children in their early teens are excruciatingly sensitive to embarrassment, but in time you will learn that criticism and ridicule are not always bad. To earn the enmity of evil people can speak very well of you."

He could hardly believe she thought so little of him as to think he needed such a lecture as this one. Did she really believe that it was *embarrassment* he feared? If she had listened instead of lecturing, he might have told her about Elemak's warning about danger to Father, about his secret visit to Gaballufix's house. But it was clear that in her eyes he was still nothing but a child. She wouldn't take his warning seriously. Indeed, she'd probably give him another lecture about not letting fears and worries take possession of your mind, but instead to concentrate on his studies and let adults worry about the *real* problems in the world.

In her mind, I'm still six years old and I always will be. "I'm sorry, Mother. I'll not speak to you that way again." In fact, I doubt that I'll ever say anything serious or important to you again as long as you live.

"I accept your apology, Nafai, as I hope you'll accept mine for having struck you in my anger."

"Of course, Mother." I'll accept your apology—*when* you offer it and *when* I believe that you mean it. However, as a matter of fact, dear beloved breadbasket out of whom I sprang, you did not actually apologize to me at any point in our conversation. You only expressed the hope that I would accept an apology which in fact was never offered.

"I hope, Nafai, you will resume your studies and not allow these events in the city to disturb the normal routines of your life any further. You have a very keen mind, and there is no particular reason for you to let these things distract you from the honing of that mind."

Thank you for the dollop of praise, Mother. You've told me that I'm childish, that I'm a slave of lust, and that my views are to be silenced, not listened to. You'll pay serious attention to every word drooled from the mouth of that *witch*girl, but you start from the assumption that anything *I* say is worthless.

"Yes, Mother," said Nafai. "But I'd rather not go back to class right now, if you don't mind."

"Of course not," she said. "I understand completely."

Dear Oversoul, keep me from laughing.

"I can't have you out wandering the streets again, Nafai, I'm sure you can understand that. Father's vision has attracted enough attention that someone *will* say something that will make you angry, and I don't want you fighting."

So you're worried about *me* fighting, Mother? Kindly remember who struck whom here on your portico today.

"Why not spend the day in the library, with Issib? He'll be a good influence on you, I think—he's always so calm."

Issib, always calm? Poor Mother—she knows nothing at all about her own sons. Women never *do* understand men. Of course, men don't understand women any better—but at least we don't suffer from the delusion that we *do*.

"Yes, Mother. The library's fine."

She arose. "Then you must go there now. Keep the handkerchief, of course."

She left the portico, not waiting to see if he obeyed.

He immediately got to his feet and walked around the screen, straight to the balustrade, and looked out over the Rift Valley.

There was no sign of the lake. A thick cloud filled the lower reaches of the valley, and since the valley walls seemed to grow steeper just before the fog began, for all he knew the lake might be invisible from this spot even without the fog.

All he could see from here was the white cloud and the deep, lush greens of the forest that lined the valley. Here and there he could see smoke rising from a chimney, for there were women who lived on the valley slopes. Father's housekeeper, Truzhnisha, was one of them. She kept a house in the district called West Shelf, one of the twelve districts of Basilica where only women were allowed to live or even enter. The Women's Districts were far less populated than any of the twenty-four districts where men were allowed to live (though not own property, of course), yet on the City Council they wielded enormous power, since their representatives always voted as a bloc. Conservative, religious—no doubt those were the councilors who were most impressed by the fact that Luet had confirmed Father's vision. If *they* agreed with Father on the war wagon issue, then it would take the votes of only six other councilors to create stalemate, and of seven councilors to take positive action against Gaballufix's plans.

It was these same councilors from the Women's Districts who, for thousands of years, had refused to allow any subdivision of the thickly populated Open Districts, or to give a council vote to any of the districts outside the walls, or to allow men to own property within the wall, or anything else that might tend to dilute or weaken the absolute rule of women in Basilica. Now, looking out over the secret valley, filled with rage against his mother, Nafai could hardly see how beautiful this place was, how rich with mystery and life; all he could see was how unbelievably few the houses were.

How do they divide this into a dozen districts? There must be some districts where the three women who live there take turns being the councilor.

And outside the city, in the tiny but expensive cubicles where unmated men without households were forced to live, there was no legal recourse to demand fairer treatment, to insist on laws protecting bachelors from their landlords, or from women whose promises disappeared when they lost interest in a man, or even from each other's violence. For a moment, standing there looking out over the untamed greenery of the Rift, Nafai understood how a man like Gaballufix might easily gather men around him, struggling to gain some power in this city where men were unmanned by women every day and every hour of their lives.

Then, as the wind gusted a little over the valley, the cloud moved, and there was a shimmer of reflected light. The surface of a lake, not at the center of the deepest part of the rift, but higher, farther away. Without thinking, Nafai reflexively looked away. It was one thing to come to the balustrade in defiance of his Mother, it was another thing to look on the holy lake where women went for their worship. If there was one thing becoming clear in all this business, it was that the Oversoul might very well be real. There was no point in earning its wrath over something as stupid as looking at some lake over the edge of Mother's portico.

Nafai turned away from the view and hurried back around the screen, feeling foolish all the while. What if I'm caught? Well, so what if I am? No, no, the defiance wasn't worth the risk. He had more practical work to do. If Mother wasn't going to listen to his fears about the danger to Father, then Nafai would have to do something himself. But first he had to know more—about Gaballufix, about the Oversoul, about everything.

For a moment he toyed with the idea of going to Luet and asking her questions. *She* knew about the Oversoul, didn't she? She saw visions all the time, not just once, like Father. Surely she could explain.

But she was a woman, and at this moment Nafai knew that he'd get no help of any kind from women. On the contrary—women in Basilica were taught from childhood on how to oppress men and make them feel worthless. Luet would laugh at him and go straight to Mother to tell her about his questions.

If he could trust anyone in this, it would be other men—and precious few of them, since the danger to Father was coming from Gaballufix's party. Perhaps he could enlist the help of this Roptat that Elya had talked about. Or find out something about what the Oversoul was doing in the first place.

Issib wasn't thrilled to see him. "I'm busy and I don't need interruptions."

"This is the household library," said Nafai. "This is where we always come to do research."

"See? You're interrupting already."

"Look, I didn't say *anything*, I just came in here, and *you* started picking at me the second I walked in the door."

"I was hoping you'd walk back out."

"I can't. Mother sent me here." Nafai walked over behind Issib, who was floating comfortably in the air in front of his computer display. It was layered about thirty pages deep, but each page had only a few words on it, so he could see almost everything at once. Like a game of solitaire, in which Issib was simply moving fragments from place to place.

The fragments were all words in weird languages. The ones Nafai recognized were very old.

"What language is *that*?" Nafai asked, pointing to one. Issib sighed. "I'm so glad you're not interrupting me."

"What is it, some ancient form of Vijati?"

"Very good. It's Slucajan, which came from Obilazati, the original form of Vijati. It's dead now."

"I read Vijati, you know."

"*I* don't."

"Oh, so you're specializing in ancient, obscure languages that nobody speaks anymore, including you?"

"I'm not *learning* these languages, I'm researching lost words."

"If the whole language is dead, then *all* the words are lost."

"Words that used to have meanings, but that died out or survived only in idiomatic expressions. Like 'dancing bear.' What's a *bear*, do you know?"

"I don't know. I always thought it was some kind of graceful bird."

"Wrong. It's an ancient mammal. Known only on Earth, I think, and not brought here. Or it died out soon. It was bigger than a man, very powerful. A predator."

"And it *danced*?"

"The expression used to mean something absurdly clumsy. Like a dog walking on its hind legs."

"And now it means the opposite. That's weird. How could it change?"

"Because there aren't any bears. The meaning used to be obvious, because everybody knew what a bear was and how clumsy it would look, dancing. But when the bears were gone, the meaning could go anywhere. Now we use it for a person who's extremely deft in getting out of an embarrassing social situation. It's the only case where we use the word *bear* anymore. And you see a lot of people misspelling it, too."

"Great stuff. You doing a linguistics project?"

"No."

"What's this for, then?"

"Me."

"Just collecting old idioms."

"Lost words."

"Like *bear*? The *word* isn't lost, Issya. It's the *bears* that are gone."

"Very good, Nyef. You get full credit for the assignment. Go away now."

"You're not researching lost words. You're researching words that have lost their meanings because the thing they refer to doesn't exist anymore."

Issya slowly turned his head to look at Nafai. "You mean that you've actually developed a brain?"

Nafai pointed at the screen. "*Kolesnisha*. That's a word in Kunic. You've got the meaning right there—war wagon. Kunic hasn't been spoken in ten million years. It's just a written language now. And yet they had a word for war wagon. Which was only just invented. Which means that there used to be war wagons a long time ago."

Issib laughed. A low chuckle, but it went on and on.

"What, am I wrong?"

"It just kills me, that's all. How *obvious* it is. Even *you* can just walk up to a computer display and see the whole thing at once. So why hasn't anybody noticed this before? Why hasn't anybody noticed the fact that we had the word *wagon* already, and we all knew what it meant, and yet as far as we know there have never been any wagons anywhere in the world *ever*?"

"That's really weird, isn't it?"

"It isn't weird, it's scary. Look at what the Wetheads are doing with their war wagons—their *kolesnishety*. It gives them a vital advantage in war. They're building a real empire, not just a system of alliances, but actual *control* over nations that are six days' travel away from their city. Now, if war wagons can do *that,* and people used to have them millions of years ago, *how did we ever forget what they were*?"

Nafai thought about that for a while. "You'd have to be really stupid," he said. "I mean, people don't forget things like that. Even if you had peace for a thousand years, you'd still have pictures in the library."

"No pictures of war wagons," said Issib.

"I mean, that's *stupid*," said Nafai.

"And this word," said Issib.

"*Zrakoplov*," said Nafai. "That's definitely an Obilazati word."

"Right."

"What does it mean? 'Air' something."

"Broken down and loosely translated, yes, it means 'air swimmer.'"

Nafai thought about this for a while. He conjured up a picture in his mind—a fish moving through the air. "A flying fish?"

"It's a machine," said Issib.

"A really fast ship?"

"Listen to yourself, Nafai. It should be obvious to you. And yet you keep resisting the plain meaning of it."

"An underwater boat?"

"How would that be an *air* swimmer, Nyef?"

"I don't know." Nafai felt silly. "I forgot about the air part."

"You forgot about it—and yet you recognized the 'air part' right off, by yourself. You *knew* that *Zraky* was the Obilazati root for *air*, and yet you forgot the 'air part.'"

"So I'm really, *really* dumb."

"But you're *not*, Nyef. You're really really *smart*, and yet you're still standing here looking at the word and I'm telling you all this and you *still* can't think of what the word means."

"Well, what's *this* word," said Nafai, pointing at *puscani prah*. "I don't recognize the language."

Issib shook his head. "If I didn't see it happening to you, I wouldn't believe it."

"What?"

"Aren't you even curious to know what a *zrakoplov* is?"

"You told me. Air swimmer."

"A *machine* whose name is *air* swimmer."

"Sure. Right. So what's a *puscani prah*?"

Issib slowly turned around and faced Nafai. "Sit down, my dear beloved brilliant stupid brother, thou true servant of the Oversoul. I've got something to tell you about machines that swim through the air."

"I guess I'm interrupting you," said Nafai.

"I want to talk to you," said Issib. "It's not an interruption. I just want to explain the idea of flying—"

"I'd better go."

"Why? Why are you so eager to leave?"

"I don't know." Nafai walked to the door. "I need some air. I'm running out of air." He walked out of the room. Immediately he felt better. Not lightheaded anymore. What was all that about, anyway? The library was too stuffy. Too crowded. Too many people in there.

"Why did you leave?" asked Issib.

Nafai whirled. Issib was silently floating out of the library after him. Nafai immediately felt the same kind of claustrophobia that had driven him out into the hall. "Too crowded in there," said Nafai. "I need to be alone."

"I was the only person in there," said Issib.

"Really?" Nafai tried to remember. "I want to get outside. Just let me go."

"Think," said Issib. "Remember when Luet and Father were talking yesterday?"

Immediately Nafai relaxed. He didn't feel claustrophobic anymore. "Sure."

"And Luet was testing Father—about his memories. When his memory of the vision he saw was wrong, he felt kind of stupid, right?"

"He said."

"Stupid. Disconnected. He just stared into space."

"I guess."

"Like you," said Issib. "When I pushed you about the meaning of *zrakoplov*."

Suddenly Nafai felt as if there were no air in his lungs. "I've got to get outside!"

"You are *really* sensitive to this," said Issib. "Even worse than Father and Mother when I tried to tell *them*."

"Stop following me!" Nafai cried. But Issib continued to float down the hall after him, down the stairs, out into the street. There, in the open, Issib easily passed Nafai, floating here and there in front of him. As if he were herding Nafai back toward the house.

"Stop it!" cried Nafai. But he couldn't get away. He had never felt such panic before. Turning, he stumbled, fell to his knees.

"It's all right," said Issib softly. "Relax. It's nothing. Relax."

Nafai breathed more easily. Issib's voice sounded safe now. The panic subsided. Nafai lifted his head and looked around. "What are we doing out here on the street? Mother's going to kill me."

"You ran out here, Nafai."

"I did?"

"It's the Oversoul, Nafai."

"*What's* the Oversoul?"

"The force that sent you outside rather than listen to me talk about—about the thing that the Oversoul doesn't want people to know about."

"That's silly," said Nafai. "The Oversoul *spreads* information, it doesn't conceal it. We submit our writings, our music, everything, and the Oversoul transmits it from city to city, from library to library all over the world."

"Your reaction was much stronger than Father's," said Issib. "Of course, I pushed you harder, too."

"What do you mean?"

"The Oversoul is inside your head, Nafai. Inside all of

our heads. But some have it more than others. It's there, watching what we think. I know it's hard to believe."

But Nafai remembered how Luet had known what was in his mind. "No, Issya, I already knew that."

"Really?" said Issib. "Well then. As soon as the Oversoul knew that you were getting close to a forbidden subject, it started making you stupid."

"*What* forbidden subject?"

"If I remind you, it'll just set you off again," said Issib.

"When did I get stupid?"

"Trust me. You got *very* stupid. Trying to change the subject without even realizing it. Normally you're extremely insightful, Nafai. Very bright. You *get* things. But this time up in the library you just stood there like an idiot, with the truth staring you in the face, and you didn't recognize it. When I reminded you, when I *pushed,* you got claustrophobic, right? Hard to breathe, had to get out of the room. I followed you, I pushed again, and here we are."

Nafai tried to think back over what had happened. Issib was right about the order of events. Only Nafai hadn't connected his need to get out of the house with anything Issib said. In fact, he couldn't for the life of him remember what it was that Issib had been talking about. "You pushed?"

"I know," said Issib. "I felt it, too, when I first started getting on the track of this a couple of years ago. I was playing around with lost words, just like that dancing bear thing. Making lists. I had a *long* list of terms like that, with definitions and explanations after each one, along with my best guess about what each lost word meant. And then one day I was looking at a list that I thought was complete and I realized that there were a couple of dozen words that had no meanings at all. That's stupid, I thought. That's ruining my list. So I deleted all those words."

"Deleted them?" Nafai was appalled. "Instead of researching them?"

"See how stupid it can make you?" said Issib. "And the moment I finished deleting them, it came to me—what am I doing! So I reached for the undelete command, but instead of pushing those keys, I reflexively gave the kill command, completely wiping out the delete buffer, and then I saved the file right over the old one."

"That's too complicated to be clumsiness," said Nafai.

"Exactly. I knew that deleting them was a mistake, and yet instead of undoing that mistake and bringing the words back, I killed them, wiped them out of the system."

"And you think the Oversoul did that to you?"

"Nafai, haven't you ever wondered what the Oversoul is? What it does?"

"Sure."

"Me too. And now I know."

"Because of those words?"

"I haven't got them all back, but I retraced as much of my research as I could and I got a list of eight words. You have no idea how hard it was, because now I was sensitized to them. Before, I must have simply overlooked them, gotten stupid when I saw them—the way Father did when he was getting wrong ideas about the Oversoul's vision. That's how they got on my first list, but without definitions—I just got stupid whenever I thought of them. But now when I saw them I'd get that claustrophobic feeling. I needed air. I had to get out of the library. But I forced myself to go inside. It's the hardest thing I've ever done. I forced myself to stay and think about the unthinkable. To hold concepts in my mind that the Oversoul doesn't want us to remember.

Concepts that once were so common that every language in the world has words for them. Ancient words. Lost words."

"The Oversoul is *hiding* things from us?"

"Yes."

"Like what?"

"If I tell you, Nafai, you'll take off again."

"No I won't."

"You *will*," said Issib. "Do you think I don't know? Do you think I haven't had my own struggle this past year? So you can imagine my surprise when last night Elemak sits there in the kitchen and explains to us about one of the forbidden things. War wagons."

"Forbidden? How could it be forbidden, it isn't even ancient."

"See? You've forgotten already. The word *kolesnisha*."

"Oh, yes. That's right. No, I remember that."

"But you *didn't* till I said it."

That's right, thought Nafai. A memory lapse.

"Last night you and Elemak were sitting there talking about war wagons, even though it took me *months* to be able to study the word *kolesnisha* without gasping the whole time."

"But we didn't *say* kolesnisha."

"What I'm telling you, Nafai, is that the Oversoul is breaking down."

"That's an old theory."

"But it's a true one," said Issib. "The Oversoul has certain concepts that it is protecting, that it refuses to let human beings think about. Only in the past few years the Wetheads have suddenly become able to think about one of them. And so have the Potoku. And so have *we*. And last night, hearing Elemak talk about it, I felt not one twinge of the panic."

"But it still made me forget the word. *Kolesnisha*."

"A lingering residual effect. You remembered it *this* time, right? Nafai, the Oversoul has given up on keeping us away from the war wagon concept. After millions of years, it isn't trying anymore."

"What else?" asked Nafai. "What are the other concepts?"

"It hasn't given up on those yet. And you seem to be *really* sensitive to the Oversoul, Nyef. I don't know if I can tell you, or if you'd be able to remember for five minutes even if I did."

"You mean I can know that the Oversoul is keeping us from knowing things, only I can't know *which* things because the Oversoul is still keeping me from knowing them."

"Right."

"Then why doesn't the Oversoul stop people from thinking about *murder*? Why doesn't the Oversoul stop people from thinking about war, and rape, and stealing? If it can do this to *me*, why doesn't it do something useful?"

Issib shook his head. "It doesn't seem right. But I've been thinking about it—I've had a year, remember—and here's the best thing I've come up with. The Oversoul doesn't want to stop us from being human. Including all the rotten things we do to each other. It's just trying to hold down the *scale* of our rottenness. All the things that are forbidden—how can I tell you this without setting you off?—if we still had the machines that the forbidden words refer to, it would make it so that anything we did would reach farther, and each weapon would cause more damage, and everything would happen *faster*."

"Time would speed up?"

"No," said Issib. He was obviously choosing his words carefully. "What if . . . what if the Gorayni could bring an army of five thousand men from Yabrev to Basilica in one day."

"Don't make me laugh."

"But if they *could*?"

"We'd be helpless, of course."

"Why?"

"Well, we'd have no time to get an army together."

"So if we knew other nations could do that, we'd have to keep an army all the time, wouldn't we, just in *case* somebody suddenly attacked."

"I guess."

"So then, knowing that, suppose the Gorayni found a way to get, not five thousand, but *fifty* thousand soldiers here, and not in a day, but in six hours."

"Impossible."

"What if I tell you that it's been done?"

"Whoever could do that would rule the whole world."

"Exactly, Nyef, unless everybody else could do it, too. But what kind of world would that be? It would be as if the world had turned small, and everybody was right next door to everybody else. A cruel, bullying, domineering nation like the Gorayni could put their armies on *anybody's* doorstep. So all other nations of the world would have to band together to stop them. And instead of a few thousand people dying, a million, ten million people might die in a war."

"So that's why the Oversoul keeps us from thinking about . . . quick ways . . . to get lots of soldiers from one place to another."

"That was hard to say, wasn't it?"

"I kept . . . my mind kept wandering."

"It's a hard concept to keep in your mind, and you aren't even thinking about anything specific."

"I hate this," said Nafai. "You can't even tell me how

anybody could do a trick like that. I can hardly even hold the concept in my mind as it is. I *hate* this."

"I don't think the Oversoul is used to having anybody notice. I think that the very fact that you're able to think about the concept of unthinkable concepts means that the Oversoul is losing control."

"Issya, I've never felt so helpless and stupid in my life."

"And it isn't just wars and armies," said Issib. "Remember the stories of Klati?"

"The slaughter man?"

"Climbing in through women's windows in the night and gutting them like cattle in the butcher's shop."

"Why couldn't the Oversoul have made *him* get stupid when he thought of doing that?"

"Because the Oversoul's job isn't to make us perfect," said Issib. "But imagine if Klati had been able to get on a—been able to travel very quickly and get to another city in six hours."

"They would have known he was a stranger and watched him so closely that he couldn't have done a thing."

"But you don't understand—thousands, millions of people every day are doing the same thing—"

"Butchering women?"

"Flying from one place to another."

"This is too crazy to think about!" shouted Nafai. He bounded to his feet and moved toward the house.

"Come back," cried Issib. "You don't really think that, you're being *made* to think it!"

Nafai leaned against one of the pillars of the front porch. Issib was right. He had been fine, and then suddenly Issib said whatever it was that he said and suddenly Nafai had to *leave*, had to get away and now here he was, panting, leaning up against the pillar, his heart pounding so hard that somebody else could probably hear it from a meter away. Could this really be the Oversoul, making him so stupid and fearful? If it was, then the Oversoul was his enemy. And Nafai refused to surrender. He *could* think about things whether the Oversoul liked it or not. He *could* think about the thing that Issib had said, and he could do it without running away.

In his mind Nafai retraced the last few moments of his conversation with Issib. About Klati. Going from city to city in a few hours. Other cities would notice him, of course—but then Issib said what if thousands of people . . . were . . . flying.

The picture that came into Nafai's mind was ludicrous. To imagine people in the air, like birds, soaring, swooping. He should laugh—but instead, thinking of it made his throat feel tight. His head felt tight, constrained. A sharp pain grew out of his neck and up into the back of his head. But he could think of it. People flying. And from there he could finish Issib's thought. People flying from city to city, thousands of them, so that the authorities in each city had no way of keeping track of one person.

"Klati could have killed once in each city and no one would ever have found him," said Nafai.

Issib was beside him again, his arm resting oh-so-lightly across Nafai's shoulder as he leaned against the pillar. "Yes," said Issib.

"But what would it mean to be a citizen of a place?" asked Nafai. "If a thousand people . . . *flew* here . . . to Basilica . . . today."

"It's all right," said Issib. "You don't have to say it."

"Yes I do," said Nafai. "I can think *anything*. It can't stop me."

"I was just trying to explain—that the Oversoul doesn't stop the evil in the world—it just stops it from getting out of hand. It keeps the damage local. But the good things—think about it, Nafai—we give our art and music and stories to the Oversoul, and it offers them to every other nation. The good things *do* spread. So it *does* make the world a better place."

"No," said Nafai. "In some ways better, yes, but how can it help but be a good thing to live in a world where people . . . where we could . . . *fly*."

The word almost choked him, but he said it, and even though he could hardly bear to stay in the same place, the air felt so close and unbreathable, nevertheless he *stayed*.

"You're good," said Issib. "I'm impressed."

But Nafai didn't feel impressive. He felt sick and angry and betrayed. "How does the Oversoul have the *right*," he said. "To take this all away from us."

"What, armies appearing at our gates without warning? I'm glad enough not to have that."

Nafai shook his head. "It's deciding what I can *think*."

"Nyef, I know the feeling, I went through all this months ago, and I *know*, it makes you so angry and frightened. But I also know that you can overcome it. And yesterday, when Mother talked about her vision. Of a planet burning. There's a word for—well, you couldn't hear it now, I know that—but the Oversoul has been keeping us from *that*. For thirty or forty million years— don't you realize that this is a *long* time? More history than we can imagine. It's all stored away somewhere, but the most we can hold onto, the most that we can get into our minds is the most skeletal sort of plan of what's happened in the world for the last ten million years or so—and it takes years and years of study to comprehend even that much. There are kingdoms and languages we've never heard of even in the last million years, and yet nothing is really lost. When I went searching in the library, I was able to find references to works in other libraries and trace my way back until I read a crude translation from a book written thirty-two million years ago and do you know what it said? Even then the writer was saying that history was now too long, too full for the human mind to comprehend it. That if all of human history were compressed into a single thousand-page volume, the whole story of humankind on Earth would be only a single page. And that was thirty-two million years ago."

"So we've been here a long time."

"If I take that writer's arithmetic literally, that would mean that human history on Earth lasted only eight thousand years before the planet . . . burned."

Nafai understood. The Oversoul had kept human beings from expanding the scale of their destructiveness, and so humanity had lasted five thousand times longer on the planet Harmony than it did on Earth.

"So why didn't the Oversoul keep Earth from being destroyed?"

"I don't know," said Issib. "I have a guess."

"And what's that?"

"I don't know if you'll be allowed to think about it."

"Give me a try."

"The Oversoul wasn't made until people got to Harmony. It has the same meaning in every language, you know—the name of the planet. Sklad. Endrakt. Soglassye. Maybe when they got here, with Earth in ashes behind them, they decided never to let it happen again. Maybe that's when the Oversoul was put in place—to stop us from ever having such terrible power."

"Then the Oversoul would be—an artifact."

"Yes," said Issib. "This isn't hard for you to think about?"

"No," said Nafai. "Easy. It's not that uncommon a

thought. People have talked about the Oversoul as a machine before."

"It was hard for *me*," said Issib. "But maybe because I came to the idea another way. Through a couple of unthinkable paths. Genetic alteration of the human brain so it could receive and transmit thoughts from communications satellites orbiting the planet."

Nafai heard the words, but they meant nothing to him.

"You didn't understand that, did you," said Issib.

"No," said Nafai.

"I didn't think you would."

"Issya, what is the Oversoul doing to us now?"

"That's what I've been working on. Trying to look through the forbidden words, find the pattern, find out what it means to be giving Father this vision of a world on fire. And Mother. And the dream of blood and ashes that Luet was given."

"It means that we're puppets."

"No, Nafai. Don't talk yourself into hating the Oversoul about this. That does no good at all—I *know* that now. We have to understand it. What it's doing. Because the world really *is* in danger, if the Oversoul's control is breaking down. And it is. It's given up on war wagons— what will it give up on next? What empire will be the next to get out of hand? Which one will discover—that word you asked about—puscani prah. It's a powder that when you put flame to it, it blows up. Pops like a balloon, only with thousands of times more force. Enough to make a wall fall down. Enough to kill people."

"Please stop," whispered Nafai. It was more than he could bear, fighting off the panic he felt as he heard these words.

"The Oversoul is not our enemy. In fact, I think—I think it called on Father because it needs help."

"Why haven't you said any of this before?"

"I have—to Father. To Mother. To some teachers. Other students. Other scholars. I even wrote it up in an article, but if nobody ever remembers receiving it, they can never find it. Even when I sent it to the same person four times. I gave up."

"But you told *me*."

"You came into the library," said Issib. "I thought— why not?"

"*Zrakoplov*," said Nafai.

"I can't believe you remembered the word," said Issib.

"A machine. The people don't just . . . fly. They use a machine."

"Don't push it," said Issib. "You'll just make yourself sick. You have a headache already, right?"

"But I'm right, yes?"

"My best guess is that it was hollow, like a house, and people got inside it to fly. Like a ship, only through the air. With wings. But we had them here, I think. You know the district of Black Fields?"

"Of course, just west of the market."

"The old name of it was Skyport. The name lasted until twenty million years ago, more or less. Skyport. When they changed it, nobody remembered what it even meant."

"I can't think about this anymore," said Nafai.

"Do you want to remember it, though?" asked Issib.

"How can I forget it?"

"You will, you know. If I don't remind you. Every day. Do you want me to? It'll feel like this every time. It'll make you sick. Do you want to just forget this, or do you want me to keep reminding you?"

"Who reminded *you*?"

"I left myself notes," said Issib. "In the library computers. Reminders. Why do you think it took me a year to get this far?"

"I want to remember," said Nafai.

"You'll get angry at me."

"Remind me not to."

"It'll make you sick."

"So I'll faint a lot." Nafai slid down the pillar and sat on the porch, looking out toward the street. "Why hasn't anybody noticed us out here? We haven't exactly been whispering."

Issib laughed. "Oh, they noticed. Mother came out once, and a couple of the teachers. They heard us talking for a couple of moments and then they just sort of forgot why they came out."

"This is great. If we want them to leave us alone, all we have to do is talk about the *zrakoplovs*."

"Well," said Issib, "that only works with people who are still closely tied with the Oversoul."

"Who isn't?"

"Whoever thought of the war wagons, for instance."

"You said the Oversoul had given up on them."

"Sure, *recently*," said Issib. "But there were people in Basilica planning to build war wagons, people dealing with the Potoku about them for a long time. More than a year. *They* had no trouble with the Oversoul. It's like they're deaf to it now. But most people aren't—which is why Gaballufix and his men were able to keep it secret for so long. Most people who heard anything about war wagons would simply have forgotten they even heard it. In fact," added Issib, "the Oversoul may have deliberately stopped forbidding that idea in the last little while precisely *because* there had to be open discussion of the war wagon thing in order to stop it."

"So the people who are deaf to the Oversoul—in order to stop them, the Oversoul has to stop controlling the rest of us, too."

"It's a double bind," said Issib. "In order to win, the

Oversoul has to give up. I'd say that the Oversoul is in serious trouble."

It was making sense to Nafai, except for one thing. "But why did it start talking to *Father*?"

"That's what we need to figure out. That, and what it's going to tell Father to do next."

"Oh, hey, let's let the Oversoul keep a *few* surprises up its sleeve." Nafai laughed, but he didn't really think it was funny.

Neither did Issib. "Even if we believe in the Oversoul's cause, Nafai, somewhere along in here we may find out that the Oversoul is causing more harm than good. What do we do *then*?"

"Hey, Issya, it may be doing a bad job these days, but that doesn't mean that we'd do better without it."

"I guess we'll never know, will we?"

SEVEN

PRAYER

For a week Nafai worked with Issib every day. They slept at Mother's house every night—they didn't ask, but then, Mother didn't send them away, either. It was a grueling time, not because the work was so hard but because the interference from the Oversoul was so painful. Issib was right, however. It *could* be overcome; and even though Nafai's aversive response was stronger than Issib's had been, he was able to get over it more quickly—mostly because Issib was there to help him, to assure him that it was worth doing, to remind him what it was about.

They began to work out a pretty clear picture of what it was that humans had once had, and that the Oversoul had long kept them from reinventing.

A communications system in which a person could talk instantly and directly to a person in any other city in the world.

Machines that could receive artwork and plays and

stories transmitted through the air, not just from library to library, but right into people's homes.

Machines that moved swiftly over the ground, without horses.

Machines that flew, not just through the air, but out into space. "Of course there must be space traveling machines, or how did we get to Harmony from Earth?" But until he had punched his way through the aversion, Nafai had never been able to conceive of such a thing.

And the weapons of war: Explosives. Projectile weapons. Some so small that they could be held in the hand. Others so terrible that they could devastate whole cities, and burn up a planet if hundreds were used at once. Self-mutating diseases. Poisonous gases. Seismic disruptors. Missiles. Orbital launch platforms. Gene-wrecking viruses.

The picture that emerged was beautiful and terrible at once.

"I can see why the Oversoul does this to us," said Nafai. "To save us from these weapons. But the cost, Issya. The freedom we gave up."

Issib only nodded. "At least the Oversoul left us something. The ability to get power from the sun. Computers. Libraries. Refrigeration. All the machines of the kitchen, the greenhouses. The magnetics that allow my floats to work. And we *do* have some pretty sophisticated handweapons. Charged-wire blades. And pulses. So that large strong people don't have any particular advantage over smaller, weaker ones. The Oversoul could have stripped us. Stone and metal tools. Nothing with moving parts. Burning trees for all our heat."

"We wouldn't even be *human* then."

"Human is human," said Issib. "But civilized—that's the gift of the Oversoul. Civilization without self-destruction."

They tried explaining it to Mother once, but it went nowhere. She stupidly failed to understand anything they were talking about, and left them with a cheerful little jest about how nice it was that they could be friends and play these games together despite the age difference between them. There was no chance to talk to Father.

But there *was* someone who took an interest in them. "Why don't you come to class anymore?" asked Hushidh.

She sat down on the porch steps beside Nafai and bit into her bread and cheese. A large mouthful, not the delicate bites that Eiadh took. Never mind that Mother was the one who taught all her girl students to use their *mouths* when they ate, and not to take the mincing little bites that were in fashion among the young women of Basilica these days. Nafai didn't have to find Hushidh's obedience to Mother *attractive*.

"I'm working on a project with Issib."

"The other students say that you're hiding," said Hushidh.

Hiding. Because Father was so notorious and controversial. "I'm not ashamed of my father."

"Of course not," said Hushidh. "*They* say you're hiding. Not me."

"And what do *you* think I'm doing? Or has the Oversoul told you?"

"I'm a raveler," she said, "not a seer."

"Right. I forgot." As if he should keep track of what kind of witch she was.

"The Oversoul doesn't have to tell me how you're weaving yourself into the world."

"Because you can see it."

She nodded. "And you're very brave."

He looked at her in consternation. "I sit in the library with Issya."

"You're weaving yourself into the weakest of the quarreling parties in Basilica, and yet it's the best of them. The one that *should* win, though no one can imagine how."

"I'm not party of *any* party."

She nodded. "I'll stop talking if you don't want to hear the truth."

As if she were going to be the fount of irresistible wisdom.

"I'll listen to a pig fart as long as it's the *truth*," said Nafai.

Immediately she got to her feet and moved away.

That was really stupid, Nafai rebuked himself. She's just trying to help, and you make a stupid joke out of it. He got up and followed her. "I'm sorry," he said.

She shrugged away from him.

"I'm used to making stupid jokes like that," said Nafai. "It's a bad habit, but I didn't mean it. It's not as if I don't know for myself now that the Oversoul is real."

"I know that you *know*," she said coldly. "But it's obvious that knowing the Oversoul exists doesn't mean you automatically get brains or kindness or even decency."

"I deserve it, and the next three nasty things you think of." Nafai stepped around her, to face her. This time she didn't turn away.

"I see patterns," she said. "I see the way things fit together. I see where *you* are starting to fit. You and Issib."

"I haven't been following things in the city," said Nafai. "Busy with the project we're working on. I don't really know what's going on."

"It's been wearing you out," she said.

"Yes," said Nafai. "I guess so."

"Gaballufix is the center of one party," she said. "It's the strongest, for more reasons than one. It isn't just about the war wagons anymore, or even about the alliance with Potokgavan. It's about men. Especially men from outside the city. So he's strong in numbers, and he's also strong because his men are asserting themselves with violence."

Nafai thought back to conversations he had overheard at mealtimes. About the tolchocks, men who were knocking down women in the street for no reason. "*His* men are the tolchocks?"

"He denies it. In fact, he claims that he's sending his soldiers out into the streets of Basilica in order to protect women from the tolchocks."

"Soldiers?"

"Officially they're the militia of the Palwashantu clan. But they all answer to Gaballufix, and the clan council hasn't been able to meet to discuss the way the militia are being used. You're Palwashantu, aren't you?"

"I'm too young for the militia yet."

"They're not really militia anymore," she said. "They're hired. Men from outside the walls, the hopeless kind of men, and very few of them really Palwashantu. Gaballufix is paying them. And he paid the tolchocks, too."

"How do you *know* this?"

"I was pushed. I've seen the soldiers. I know how they fit together."

More of the witchery. But how could he doubt it? Hadn't he felt the influence of the Oversoul whenever he thought about forbidden words? It made him sweat just to think of what he'd been through during the past week. So why *couldn't* Hushidh just look at a soldier and a tolchock and know things about them? Why couldn't camels fly? Anything was possible now.

Except that the Oversoul's influence was weakening. Hadn't he and Issib overcome its power, in order to think about forbidden things?

"And you know that I'm not one of them."

"But your brothers are."

"Tolchocks?"

"They're with Gaballufix. Not *Issib*, of course. But Elemak and Mebbekew."

"How do you know *them*? They never come here—they're not Mother's sons."

"Elemak has come here several times this week," said Hushidh. "Didn't you know?"

"Why would he come here?" But Nafai knew at once. Without being able to think the thought himself, he knew exactly why Elemak would come to Rasa's household. Mother's reputation in the city was of the highest; her nieces were courted by many, and Elemak was of an age—well into the age, in fact—for a serious mating, intended to produce an heir.

Nafai looked around the courtyard, where many girls and a few boys were eating their supper. All the students from outside were gone, and the younger children ate earlier. So most of the girls here were eligible for mating, including her nieces, if Rasa released them. Which of them would Elemak be courting?

"Eiadh," he whispered.

"One can assume," said Hushidh. "I know it isn't me."

Nafai looked at her in surprise. Of course it wasn't her. Then he was embarrassed; what if she realized how ridiculous it had seemed to him, that his brother might desire *her*.

But Hushidh continued as if she didn't even notice his silent insult. Certainly she was oblivious to how the idea of Elya courting Eiadh might hurt Nafai. "When your brother came, I knew at once that he was very close to Gaballufix. I'm sure that it's causing Aunt Rasa a great deal of sorrow, because she knows that Eiadh will say yes to him. Your brother has a great deal of prestige."

"Even with Father's visions causing such a scandal?"

"He's with Gaballufix," said Hushidh. "Within the Party of Men—those who favor Gaballufix—the worse your father looks, the better they like Elemak. Because if something happened to your father, then Elemak would be a very rich and powerful man."

Her words reawakened Nafai's worst fears about his brother. But it was a monstrous, unbearable thought. "Gaballufix wants Elya to influence Father, that's all."

Hushidh nodded. But was she nodding in agreement, or just silencing him so she could get on with what she had to say? "The other strong party is Roptat's people. They're being called the Party of Women now, though they are also led by a man. They want to ally with the Gorayni. And also they want to remove the vote from all men except those currently mated with a citizen, and require all non-mated men to leave the city every night by sundown, and not return until dawn. That's *their* solution to the tolchock problem—and to Gaballufix, as well. They have a wide following—among mated men and women."

"Is that the group that Father's with?"

"Everyone in the Party of Men thinks so, but Roptat's people know better."

"So what's the third group?"

"They call themselves the City Party, but what they truly are is the Party of the Oversoul. They refuse to ally with any warring nation. They want to return to the old ways, for the protection of the Lake. To make this a city above politics and conflict. To give away the great wealth of the city and live simply, so no other nation will desire to possess us."

"Nobody will agree to that."

"You're wrong," she said. "Many *do* agree. Your father

and Aunt Rasa have won over almost all the women of the Lake Districts."

"But that's hardly anybody. Only a handful of people live in the Rift Valley."

"They have a third of the council votes."

Nafai thought about that. "I think that's very dangerous for them," he said.

"Why do you think so?"

"Because they don't have anything but tradition to back them up. The more Gaballufix pushes against tradition, the more he frightens people with tolchocks and soldiers, the more people will demand that *something* be done. All that Father and Mother are doing is making it impossible for anyone to get a majority on the council. They're blocking Roptat from stopping Gaballufix."

Hushidh smiled. "You're really very good at this."

"Politics is what I study most."

"You've seen the danger. But what you haven't told me is how we'll get out of it."

"We?"

"Basilica."

"No," said Nafai. "You said that you knew what party I was in."

"You're with the Oversoul, of course," she said.

"You don't know that. *I* don't even know that. I'm not sure I like the way the Oversoul manipulates us."

Hushidh shook her head. "You may not make the decision in your mind for many days yet, but the decision in your heart is already made. You reject Gaballufix. And you are drawn to the Oversoul."

"You're wrong," said Nafai. "I mean, yes, I'm drawn to the Oversoul. Issib came to that decision long ago and his reasons are good. Despite all its secret manipulation of people's minds, it's even more dangerous to reject the Oversoul. But that doesn't mean I'm ready to turn the future of Basilica over to the tiny minority of crazy religious fanatics who live in the Rift Valley and have visions all the time."

"We're the ones who are close to the Oversoul."

"The whole *world* has the Oversoul inside their brains," said Nafai. "You can't get closer than that."

"We're the ones who *choose* the Oversoul," she insisted. "And the whole world *doesn't* have her inside their brains, or they would never have started carrying war to faraway nations."

For a moment Nafai wondered if she, too, had somehow discovered how the Oversoul had blocked the discovery of war wagons until recently. Then he realized that of course *she* was thinking of the seventh codicil: "You have no dispute with your neighbor's neighbor's neighbor; when she quarrels, stay home and close your window." This had long been interpreted to be a prohibition of entangling alliances or quarrels with countries so far away that the outcome made no difference to you. Nafai and Issib knew the purpose and origin of such a law, and the way that the Oversoul had enforced it within people's minds. To Hushidh, though, it was the law itself that had fended off wars of imperial aggression for all these millennia. Never mind that many nations had *tried* to create empires, and only the lack of efficient means of travel and communication had hindered them.

"I'm not with you," said Nafai. "You can't turn back the clock."

"If you can't," she said, "then we're as good as destroyed already."

"Maybe so," said Nafai. "If Roptat wins, then when the Potoku fleet arrives, they come up the mountain and destroy us before the Wetheads can get here. And if Gaballufix wins, then when the Wetheads finally come they destroy the Potoku first and then *they* come up the mountains and destroy us in retaliation."

"So," said Hushidh. "You see that you *are* with us."

"No," said Nafai. "Because if the City Party keeps up this stalemate, either Gaballufix or Roptat will get impatient and people will start to die. Then we won't *need* outsiders to destroy us. We'll do it ourselves. How long do you think women will continue to rule in this city, if it comes to civil war between two powerful men?"

Hushidh looked off into space. "Do you think so?" she said.

"I may not be a *raveler*," said Nafai, "but I've read history."

"So many centuries we've kept this a city of women, a place of peace."

"You never should have given men the vote."

"They've had the vote for a million years."

Nafai nodded. "I know. What's happening now—it's the Oversoul."

He could see now that Hushidh was looking off into nothingness because her eyes were so full of tears. "She's dying, isn't she?"

It hadn't occurred to him that someone could take this so personally. As if the Oversoul were a dear relative. But to someone like Hushidh, perhaps it was so. Besides, she was the daughter of a wilder, a so-called holy woman. Even though everyone knew that wilders' children were usually the result of rape or casual coupling in the streets of the city, they were still called "children of the Oversoul." Maybe Hushidh really thought of the Oversoul as her father. But no—the women called the Oversoul *she*. And Hushidh *knew* that her mother was a wilder.

Still, Hushidh was barely containing her tears.

"What do you want from me?" asked Nafai. "I don't

know what the Oversoul is doing. Your sister—like you said, *she's* the seer."

"The Oversoul hasn't spoken to her all week. Or to anyone."

Nafai was surprised. "You mean not even at the lake?"

"I knew that you and Issib were very, very closely tied to the Oversoul all this week. She was wearing you out, the way she does with Lutya and . . . and me, sometimes. The women have been going into the water, more and more of them, and yet they come out with nothing, or with silly sleep-dreams. It's making them afraid. But I told them, I said: Nafai and Issib, *they're* being touched by the Oversoul. So she's not dead. And they asked me . . . to find out from you."

"Find out what?"

The tears finally spilled out and slid down her cheeks. "I don't know," she said miserably. "What to do. What the Oversoul expects of us."

He touched her shoulder, to comfort her—Nafai didn't know what else to do. "I don't know," he said. "But you're right about one thing—the Oversoul is wearing down. Wearing *itself* out. Still, I'm surprised that it would stop giving visions. Maybe it's distracted. Maybe it's . . ."

"What?"

He shook his head. "Let me talk to Issib, will you?"

She nodded, ducking her head at the end to wipe away tears. "Please, yes," she said. "*I* couldn't—talk to *him.*"

Why in the world *not*? But he didn't ask. He was too confused by all that she'd told him. All this time that he and Issib thought their research was secret, and here was Hushidh telling all the women of Basilica that the two of them were being worn out by the Oversoul! And yet, for all that they knew, the women were also hopelessly ignorant—how could he and Issib know anything about the reason why their visions had stopped?

Nafai went straight to the library and repeated to Issib all he could remember of his conversation with Hushidh. "So what I'm thinking is this. What if the Oversoul isn't all that powerful? What if the reason the visions have stopped is that the Oversoul can't deal with *us* and give visions all at the same time?"

Issib laughed. "Come on, Nyef, as if we're the center of the world or something."

"I'm serious. How much capacity would the Oversoul have to have, really? Most people are ignorant or stupid or weak enough that even if they thought of one of these forbidden subjects, they couldn't do anything about it, so why watch them? That means the Oversoul has to monitor relatively few people. And with them, if it checks in on them every now and then, it has plenty of time to turn them away from dangerous projects. But now, with the Oversoul weakening, you were able to desensitize yourself. That was a contest between you and the Oversoul, and you *won*, Issib. What if during all those struggles, the Oversoul was completely focused on you, giving no visions to anyone else, monitoring no one else. But you were going slowly enough that it still had time left over."

"But the two of us, working together," said Issib. "It had to concentrate on us, constantly. And it's losing, too—weakening even more."

"So I'm thinking, Issib—we're not helping here, we're *hurting*."

Issib laughed again. "It can't *be*," he said. "This is the Oversoul we're talking about, not a teacher with a couple of unruly students."

"The Oversoul has failed before. Or there wouldn't be any war wagons."

"So what should we do?"

"Stop," said Nafai. "For a day. Stay away from the forbidden subjects. See if people start getting visions again."

"You seriously think that we, the two of us, have taken up so much of the Oversoul's time that it can't give visions to people? What about during the time we sleep and eat? There are plenty of breaks."

"Maybe we've got it confused. Maybe it's panicking about us because it doesn't know what to do."

"Right," said Issib. "So let's not just *quit*. Let's give the Oversoul some advice, why not!"

"Why not?" said Nafai. "It was made by human beings, wasn't it?"

"We *think*. Maybe."

"So we tell it to stop worrying about trying to block us. That's a pointless assignment and it should stop wasting time on it *right now*, because even if we easily think of every forbidden subject in the world, we're not going to tell anybody else and we're not going to try to build any ourselves. Are we?"

"We're not."

"So take an oath to that, Issib. I'll take it too. I swear it right now—you listening, Oversoul?—we're not your enemies, so you don't need to waste another second worrying about us. Go back and give visions to the women again. And spend your time blocking the dangerous guys. The Wetheads, for instance. Gaballufix. Roptat probably, too. And if you can't block them, then at least let *us* know what to do so *we* can block them."

"Who are you talking to?"

"The Oversoul."

"This feels really stupid," said Issib.

"It's been telling *us* what to think our whole lives," said

Nafai. "What's so stupid about giving *it* a suggestion now and then? Take the oath, Issya."

"Yes, I promise, I take the most solemn oath. You listening, Oversoul?"

"It's listening," said Nafai. "That much we *know*."

"So," said Issib. "You think it's going to do what we say?"

"I don't know," said Nafai. "But I know *this*—we're not going to learn anything more by hanging around the library for the rest of the day. Let's get out of here. Spend the night at Father's house. Maybe we'll have a really good idea. Or maybe Father will have a vision. Or something."

It was only that afternoon, as he was leaving Mother's house, that Nafai remembered that Elemak was courting Eiadh. Not that Nafai had a right to hate him for it. Nafai had never said anything to anyone about his feelings toward her, had he? And at fourteen he was far too young to be taken seriously as a possible legal mate. Of course Eiadh would look at Elemak and desire him. It explained everything—why she was so nice to Nafai and yet never seemed to get close to him. She wanted to keep his favor in case he had some influence over Elemak. But it would never have crossed her mind that she might give a contract to *Nafai*. After all, he was a *child*.

Then he remembered how Hushidh had spoken of Issib. I couldn't talk to *him*. Because he was a cripple? Not likely. No, Hushidh was shy with Issib because she was looking at him as a possible mate. Even *I* know enough about women to guess that, thought Nafai.

Hushidh is my age, and *she's* looking at my older brother when she thinks of mating. While *I* might as well be a tree or a brick for all the sexual interest a girl my age would have in *me*. And Eiadh is older than me—one of the oldest in my class, while I'm one of the youngest. How could I have ever thought . . .

He felt the hot blush of embarrassment on his cheeks, even though no one knew of his humiliation except himself.

Moving through the streets of Basilica, Nafai realized that except for an occasional walk in Rain Street he had not been out of Mother's house since he began his research with Issib. Perhaps because of what Hushidh had told him, he was aware of a change in the city. Were there fewer people on the streets? Perhaps—but the real difference was more in the *way* they walked. People in Basilica often moved with purpose, but usually they did not let that purpose close them to what was going on around them. Even people in a hurry could pause for a moment, or at least smile, when they passed a street musician or a juggler or a comic reciting his doggerel. And many people sauntered, taking things in with real pleasure, conversing with their companions, of course, but also freely speaking with strangers on the street, as if all the people of Basilica were neighbors, or even relatives.

This evening was different. As the sun silhouetted the western rooftops and cast angled slabs of blackness across the streets, the people seemed to dodge the sunlight as if it might burn their skin. They were closed off to each other. The street musicians were ignored, and even their music seemed more timid, as if they were ready to break off their song at the first sign of displeasure in a passerby. The streets were quieter because almost no one was talking.

Soon enough the reason became obvious. A troop of eight men jogged up the street, pulses in their hands and charged-wire blades at their waists. Soldiers, thought Nafai. Gaballufix's men. No—officially, they were the militia of the Palwashantu, but Nafai felt no kinship with them.

They didn't seem to look to left or right, as if their errand were set. But Nafai and Issib noticed at once that the streets seemed to empty as the soldiers passed. Where had the people gone? They weren't actually hiding, but still it took several minutes after the soldiers had passed before people began emerging again. They had ducked into shops, pretending to have business. Some had simply taken alternate routes down side streets. And others had never left the street at all, but like Nafai and Issib they had stopped, had frozen in place, so that for a few minutes they were part of the architecture, not part of the life of the place.

It did not seem at all as though people thought the soldiers were making the city safer. Instead the soldiers had made them afraid.

"Basilica's in trouble," said Nafai.

"Basilica is *dead*," said Issib. "There are still people here, but the city isn't Basilica anymore."

Fortunately, it wasn't as bad when they got farther along Wing Street—the soldiers had passed where Wing crossed Wheat Street, only a few blocks from Gaballufix's house. When they got into Old Town there was more life in the streets. But changes were still visible.

For instance, Spring Street had been cleared. Spring was one of the major thoroughfares of Basilica, running in the most direct route from Funnel Gate through Old Town and right on to the edge of the Rift Valley. But as often happened in Basilica, some enterprising builder had decided that it was a shame to let all that empty space in the middle of the street go to waste, when people could be living there. On a long block between Wing and Temple, the builder had put up six buildings.

Now, when a Basilican builder started putting up a

structure that blocked a street, several things could happen. If the street wasn't very busy, only a few people would object. They might scream and curse and even throw things at the builders, but since the workers were all such burly men, there would be little serious resistance. The building would go up, and people would find new routes. The people who owned houses or shops that used to front on the now-blocked road were the ones who suffered most. They had to bargain with neighbors to gain hallway rights that would give them street access—or *take* those rights, if the neighbor was weak. Sometimes they simply had to abandon their property. Either way, the new hallways or the abandoned property soon became thoroughfares in their own right. Eventually some enterprising soul would buy a couple of abandoned or decaying houses whose hallways were being used for traffic, tear out an open streetway, and thus a new road was born. The city council did nothing to interfere with this process—it was how the city evolved and changed over time, and it seemed pointless in a city tens of millions of years old to try to hold back the tide of time and history.

It was quite another thing when someone started building on a much-used thoroughfare like Spring Street. There, the passersby gained courage from their numbers—and from their outrage at the thought of losing a road they often used. So they would deliberately sabotage the construction as they passed, knocking down masonry, carrying away stones. If the builder was powerful and determined, with many strong workers, a brawl could easily start—but then it might easily come to a court trial, where the builder was *always* found to be at fault, since building in a street was regarded as ample provocation for legal assault.

The builder in Spring Street had been clever, though.

She had designed her six buildings to stand on arches, so that the road was never actually blocked. The houses instead began on the first floor, above the street—and so, while passersby were annoyed, they weren't so provoked that they got serious about their sabotage. So the buildings had been finished early that summer, and some very wealthy people had taken up residence.

Inevitably, however, the archways became crowded with streetsellers and enterprising restaurateurs—which the builder surely knew would happen. Traffic slowed to a crawl, and other builders began to put up permanent shops and stalls, until only a few weeks ago it became physically impossible to get from Temple to Wing on Spring Street—the little buildings now completed blocked the way. Another street in Basilica had been killed, only this time it was a major thoroughfare and caused serious inconvenience to a lot of people. Only the original builder and the enterprising little shopkeepers truly profited; the people who bought the inner buildings now found it harder and harder to get to the stairways leading up to their houses, and people were already preparing to abandon old structures that no longer faced on a street.

Now, as Nafai and Issib passed Spring Street, they saw that someone had gone through the blocked section and torn down all the small structures. The new buildings were still there, arching over the street, but the passageway remained open underneath them. More significantly, a couple of soldiers stood at each end of the street. The message was clear: No new building would be tolerated.

"Gaballufix isn't a fool," said Issib.

Nafai knew what he meant. People might not like seeing soldiers trot by in the streets, with the threat of violence and the loss of freedom that they implied. But seeing Spring Street open would go a long way toward making the soldiers seem like a mixed evil, one perhaps worth tolerating.

Wing Street eventually fed into Temple Street, and Nafai and Issib followed it until it came to the great circle around the Temple itself. This was the one outpost of the men's religion in this city of women, the one place where the Oversoul was known to be male, and where blood rather than water was the holy fluid. On impulse, though he hadn't been inside since he was eight and his foreskin was drowned in his own blood, Nafai stopped at the north doors. "Let's go in," he said.

Issib shuddered. "I deeply hate this place," he said.

"If they used anesthetic, worship would be more popular with kids," said Nafai.

Issib grinned. "Painless worship. Now there's a thought. Maybe dry worship would catch on among the women, too."

They went through the door into the musty, dark, windowless outer chamber.

Though the temple was perfectly round, the inner chambers were designed to recall the chambers of the heart: the Indrawing Auricle, the Airward Ventricle, the Airdrawing Auricle, and the Outflowing Ventricle. The winding halls and tiny rooms between them were named for various veins and arteries. Before their circumcision boys had to learn all the names of all the rooms, but they did it by memorizing a song that remained meaningless to most who learned it. So there was nothing particularly familiar about the names written on each door lintel or keystone, and Issib and Nafai were immediately lost.

It didn't matter. Eventually, all halls and corridors funneled worshipers into the central courtyard, the only bright space in the temple, open to the sky. Since it was so close to sunset, there was no direct sunlight on the stone floor of the courtyard, but after so much darkness even reflected sunlight was painfully dazzling.

At the gateway, a priest stopped them. "Prayer or meditation?" he asked.

Issib shuddered—a convulsive movement, for him, since the floats exaggerated every twitch his muscles made. "I think I'll wait in the Airdrawing Auricle."

"Don't be a poddletease," said Nafai. "Just meditate for a minute, it won't kill you."

"You mean *you're* going to *pray?*" said Issib.

"I guess so," said Nafai.

Truth to tell, Nafai wasn't sure why, or for what. He only knew that his relationship with the Oversoul was getting more complicated every day; he understood the Oversoul better than before, and the Oversoul was meddling in his life now, so it had become important to try to communicate clearly and directly, instead of all this slantwise guesswork. It wasn't enough to slack off their research into forbidden words and hope that the Oversoul got the hint. There had to be something more.

He watched as the priests jabbed Issib's finger and wiped the tiny wound over the bloodstone. Issib took it well enough—he really *wasn't* a poddle, and he'd had enough pain in his life that a little fingerjab was nothing. He just had little use for the rituals of the men's worship. He called it "blood sports" and compared it to shark-fights, which always started out by getting every shark in the pool to bleed. As soon as his little red smear was on the rough stone, he drifted over toward the high bench against the sunny wall, where there was still about a half-hour of sunlight. The bench was full, of course, but Issib could always float just beside it. "Hurry up," he murmured as he passed Nafai.

Since Nafai was here to pray, the priest didn't jab him. Instead he let him reach into the golden bowl of prayer rings. The bowl was filled with a powerful disinfectant, which had the double effect of keeping the barbed prayer rings from spreading disease and also making it so that every jab stung bitterly for several long seconds. Nafai usually took only two rings, one for the middle finger of each hand, but this time he felt that he needed more. That even though he had no idea what he was praying *about,* he wanted to make sure that the Oversoul understood that he was serious. So he found prayer rings for all four fingers of each hand, and thumb rings as well.

"It can't be that bad," said the priest.

"I'm not praying for forgiveness," said Nafai.

"I don't want you fainting on me, we're short-staffed today."

"I won't faint." Nafai walked to the center of the courtyard, near the fountain. The water of the fountain wasn't the normal pinkish color—it was almost dark red. Nafai well remembered the powerful frisson the first time he realized how the water got its color. Father said that when Basilica was in great need—during a drought, for instance, or when an enemy threatened—the fountain flowed with almost pure blood, there was so much blood. It was a strange and powerful feeling, to pull off his sandals and strip off his clothes, then kneel in the pool and know that the tepid liquid swirling around him, almost up to his waist if he sat back on his heels, was thick with the passionate bloody prayers of other men.

He held his barbed hands open in front of him for a long time, composing himself, readying himself for the conversation with the Oversoul. Then he slapped his hands vigorously against his upper arms, just as he did in his morning prayers; this time, though, the barbed rings cut into his flesh and the sting was deep and harsh. It was a good, vigorous opening, and he heard several of the meditators sigh or murmur. He knew that they had heard the sharp sound of his slap and seen his self-discipline as he restrained himself from so much as gasping in pain, and they respected this prayer for its strength and virtue.

Oversoul, he said silently. You started all this. Weak as you are, you decided to start intruding in my family's life. You'd better have a plan in mind. And if you do, isn't it about time you let us know what it is?

He slapped himself again, this time on the more sensitive skin of his chest. When the sting faded he could feel blood tickling through the invisible new hairs growing there. I offer this sacrifice to you, Oversoul, I offer my pain if you need it, I'll do whatever you want me to do but I expect a promise from you in return. I expect you to protect my father. I expect you to have a real purpose in mind, and to tell Father what it is. I expect you to keep my brothers from getting mixed up in some terrible crime against the city and particularly from getting involved in a crime against my father. If you protect Father and let us know what's going on, then I'll do everything I can to help your plan work, because I know that the purpose that was programmed into you from the beginning is to keep humanity from destroying itself, and I'll do all I can to serve that purpose. I am yours, as long as you treat us fairly.

He slapped his belly, the sharpest pain yet, and now he heard several of the meditators commenting out loud, and the priest came up behind him. Don't interrupt me, thought Nafai. Either the Oversoul is hearing this or it isn't, and if it *is* hearing me, then I want it to know that I'm serious about it. Serious enough to cut myself to ribbons if need be. Not because I think this bloodletting has anything to do with holiness, but because it shows my willingness to do what I'm told, even when it has a harsh personal cost. I'll do what you want, Oversoul, but you must keep faith.

"Young man," whispered the priest.

"Get lost," whispered Nafai in return.

The sandals shuffled away over the stone.

Nafai reached over his shoulders and scraped his hands up along his back. This was tearing now, not jabbing, and the wounds would not be trivial. Do you see this, Oversoul? You're inside my head, you know what I'm thinking and what I'm feeling. Issib and I are letting you alone so you can give people visions again. Now get to work and get this situation under control. And whatever you want me to do, I'll do. I will. If I can bear this pain, you know I can bear whatever you set me to suffer. And, knowing exactly how it hurts, I can do it again.

He scraped again. The pain this time, as new wounds crossed old ones, brought tears to his eyes—but not a sound to his lips.

Enough. Either the Oversoul heard him or it didn't.

He let himself fall forward into the bloody water, his eyes still closed. It closed over his head, and for a moment he was completely immersed. Then the water buoyed him up, and he felt the cool evening air on his back and buttocks as they floated on the surface.

A moment more. Hold your breath a moment more. Longer. Just a little longer. Wait for the voice of the Oversoul. Listen in the silence of the water.

But no answer came to him. Only the growing pain of the wounds in his upper back and shoulders.

He arose to his feet, dripping wet, and turned toward the edge of the fountain, opening his eyes for the first time since entering the pool. Someone was handing him a towel. Hands reached for him to help him over the lip of the pool. When his eyes were dry, he could see that almost all the meditators had come away from the wall, and were now gathered around, offering him towels, his clothes. "A mighty prayer," they were whispering. "May the Oversoul hear you." They would not let him towel himself, or even dress. "Such virtue in one so young." Instead it was other hands gently dabbing at his wounded back, vigorously toweling at his thighs. "Basilica is blessed to have such a prayer in this temple." It was other hands that pulled his shirt over his head and drew his trousers up his legs. "A Father's pride is a young son bowed with piety yet lifted up with courage." They laced his sandals up his legs, and when they found that the thongs ended below his knee, they nodded, they murmured. "No foolish styles in this one." "A working man's sandals."

And as Nafai followed Issib away from the fountain, he could hear the murmurs continuing behind him. "The Oversoul was here with us today."

At the doorway leading to the Outflowing Ventricle, Nafai was momentarily blocked by someone coming in through that door. Since his head was bowed, he saw only the man's feet. As one whose shirt was stained with the blood of prayer, he expected the man blocking him to make way for him, but it seemed he would not go.

"Meb," said Issib.

Nafai lifted his gaze from the man's shoes. It *was* Mebbekew. In a moment of piercing clarity, it seemed as though he saw his brother whole. He was no longer dressed in the flamboyant costume that had long been his style. Meb was now dressed as a man of business, in clothing that must have cost considerable money. It was not his clothing that Nafai cared about, nor the mystery of where he got the money to buy it—for *that* was no mystery at all. Looking at Mebbekew's face, Nafai knew—*knew*, without words, without reason—that Mebbekew was Gaballufix's man now. Maybe it was the expression on his face: Where once Meb had always had a jaunty sort of half-smile, a spark of malicious fun in his eyes, now he looked serious and important and just a little bit afraid of—of what? Of himself. Of the man he was becoming.

Of the man who owned him. There was nothing in his expression or his clothing to mark him as belonging to Gaballufix, and yet Nafai knew. This must be how it comes in Hushidh, he thought, to see the connections between people. To have no reason, and yet also to have no doubt.

"What were you praying for?" asked Mebbekew.

"For you," answered Nafai.

Inexplicable tears came to Mebbekew's eyes, but his face and voice refused to admit whatever feelings called them forth. "Pray for yourself," said Mebbekew, "and for this city."

"And for Father," said Nafai.

Mebbekew's eyes widened, just a bit, the tiniest bit, but Nafai knew that he had struck home.

"Step aside," said a quiet but angry voice behind him. One of the meditators, perhaps. A stranger, anyway. "Make way for the young man of mighty prayer."

Mebbekew stepped back into the dark shadow of the temple's interior. Nafai moved past him and rejoined Issib, who was waiting in the corridor just beyond Meb.

"Why would *Meb* be here?" asked Issib, once they were out of earshot.

"Maybe there are some things you can't do without speaking to the Oversoul first," said Nafai.

"Or maybe he's decided it's useful to be publicly seen to be a pious man." Issib laughed a little. "He *is* an actor, you know, and it looks like somebody's given him a new costume. I wonder what role he's going to play?"

EIGHT

WARNING

When Nafai and Issib got home, Truzhnisha was still there. She had spent the day cooking, replenishing the meals in the freezer. But there was nothing hot and fresh for tonight's meal. Father was not one to let his housekeeper indulge his sons.

Truzhnisha saw at once, of course, how disappointed Nafai was. "How should I have known you were coming home for supper tonight?"

"We *do* sometimes."

"So I take your father's money and buy food and prepare it to be eaten hot and fresh on the table, and then nobody comes home at all. It happens as often as not, and then the meal is wasted because I prepare it *differently* for freezing."

"Yes, you overcook everything," said Issib.

"So it will be nice and soft for your feeble jaws," she said.

Issib growled at her—in the back of his throat, like a

dog. It was the way they played with each other. Only Truzhya could play with him by exaggerating his weakness; only with Truzhya did Issib ever grunt or growl, in mockery of a manly strength that would always be out of his reach.

"Your frozen stuff is all right, anyway," said Nafai.

"*Thank* you," she said. Her exaggerated tone told him that she was offended at what he had said. But he had meant it sincerely, as a compliment. Why did everybody always think he was being sarcastic or insulting when he was just trying to be nice? Somewhere along the way he really had to learn what the signals were that other people were forever detecting in his speech, so that they were always so sure that he was trying to be offensive.

"Your father is out in the stables, but he wants to talk to the both of you."

"Separately?" asked Issib.

"Now, should I know this? Should I form you into a line outside his door?"

"Yes, you should," said Issib. Then he snapped his jaws at her, like a dog biting. "If you weren't such a worthless old goat."

"Mind who you're calling worthless, now," she said, laughing.

Nafai watched in awe. Issib could say genuinely insulting things, and she took it as play. Nafai complimented her cooking, and she took it as an insult. I should go out in the desert and become a wilder, thought Nafai. Except, of course, that only *women* could be wilders, protected from injury by both custom and law. In fact, on the desert a wilder woman was treated better than in the city—desert folk wouldn't lay a hand on the holy women, and they left them water and food when they noticed them. But a *man* living alone out on the desert was likely to be robbed and killed within a day. Besides, thought

Nafai, I haven't the faintest idea of how to live in the desert. Father and Elemak do, but even then they only do it by carrying a lot of supplies with them. Out on the desert without supplies, they'd die as fast as I would. The difference is, they'd be *surprised* that they were dying, because they *think* they know how to survive there.

"Are you awake, Nafai?" asked Issib.

"Mm? Yes, of course."

"So you plan to keep that food sitting in front of you, as a pet?"

Nafai looked down and saw that Truzhya had slid a loaded plate in front of him. "Thanks," he said.

"Giving food to you is like leaving it on the graves of your ancestors," said Truzhya.

"They don't say thanks," said Nafai.

"*Oh*, he said *thanks*," she grumbled.

"Well what am I *supposed* to say?" asked Nafai.

"Just eat your supper," said Issib.

"I want to know what was wrong with my saying thanks!"

"She was joking with you," said Issib. "She was *playing*. You've got no sense of humor, Nyef."

Nafai took a bite and chewed it angrily. So she was joking. How was he supposed to know that?

The gate swung open. A scuff of sandals, and then a door opening and closing immediately. It was Father, then, since he was the only one in the family who could reach his room without coming in view of the kitchen door. Nafai started to get up, to go see him.

"Finish your supper first," said Issib.

"He didn't say it was an emergency," added Truzhnisha.

"He didn't say it *wasn't*," answered Nafai. He continued on out of the room.

Behind him, Issib called out. "Tell him I'll be there in a second."

Nafai stepped out into the courtyard, crossed in front of the gate, and entered the door into Father's public room. He wasn't there. Instead he was back in the library, with a book in the computer display that Nafai instantly recognized as the Testament of the Oversoul, perhaps the oldest of the holy writings, from a time so ancient that, according to the stories, the men's and women's religions were the same.

"She comes to you in the shadows of sleep," Nafai said aloud, reading from the first line on the screen.

"She whispers to you in the fears of your heart," Father answered.

"In the bright awareness of your eyes and in the dark stupor of your ignorance, there is her wisdom," Nafai continued.

"Only in her silence are you alone. Only in her silence are you wrong. Only in her silence should you despair." Father sighed. "It's all here, isn't it, Nafai?"

"The Oversoul isn't a man or a woman," said Nafai.

"Right, yes, of course, *you* know all about what the Oversoul is."

Father's tone was so weary that Nafai decided it wasn't worth arguing theology with him tonight. "You wanted to see me."

"You *and* Issib."

"He'll be here in a second."

As if on cue, Issib drifted through the door, still eating some cheesebread.

"Thank you for bringing crumbs into my library," said Father.

"Sorry," said Issib; he reversed direction and started floating out the door.

"Come back," said Father. "I don't care about the crumbs."

Issib came back.

"There's talk all over Basilica about the two of you."

Nafai traded glances with Issib. "We've just been doing some library research."

"The women are saying that the Oversoul is speaking to no one but you."

"We aren't exactly getting clear messages from it," said Nafai.

"Mostly we've just been monopolizing it by stimulating its aversive reflexes," said Issib.

"Mmm," said Father.

"But we've stopped," said Issib. "That's why we came home."

"We didn't want to interfere," said Nafai.

"Nafai prayed, though, on the way home," said Issib. "It was pretty impressive stuff."

Father sighed. "Oh, Nafai, if you've learned anything from me, couldn't you have learned that jabbing yourself and bleeding all over the place has nothing to do with prayer to the Oversoul?"

"Right," said Nafai. "This from the man who suddenly comes home with a vision of fire on a rock. I thought all bets were off."

"I got my vision without bleeding," said Father. "But never mind. I was hoping that the two of you might have received something from the Oversoul that would help me."

Nafai shook his head.

"No," said Issib. "Mostly what we got from the Oversoul was that stupor of thought. It was trying to keep us from thinking forbidden thoughts."

"Well, that's it, then," said Father. "I'm on my own."

"On your own with what?" asked Issib.

"Gaballufix sent word to me through Elemak today. It seems that Gaballufix is as unhappy as I am about the situation in Basilica today. If he had known that this war wagon business would cause such controversy he would never have begun it. He said that he wanted me to set up a meeting between him and Roptat. All Gaballufix really wants now is to find a way to back down without losing face—he says that all he needs is for Roptat also to back down, so that we don't make an alliance with anybody."

"So have you set up a meeting with Roptat?"

"Yes," said Father. "At dawn, at the coolhouse east of Market Gate."

"It sounds to me," said Nafai, "like Gaballufix has come around to the City Party's way of thinking."

"That's how it *sounds*," said Father.

"But you don't believe him," said Issib.

"I don't know," said Father. "His position is the only reasonable, intelligent one. But when has Gaballufix ever been reasonable or intelligent? All the years I've known him, even when he was a young man, before he maneuvered himself into the clan leadership, he's never done anything that wasn't designed to advance him relative to other people. There are always two ways of doing that—by building yourself up and by tearing your rivals down. In all these years, I've seen that Gaballufix has a definite preference for the latter."

"So you think he's using you," said Nafai. "To get at Roptat."

"Somehow he will betray Roptat and destroy him," said Father. "And in the end, I'll look back and see how he used me to help him accomplish that. I've seen it before."

"So why are you helping him?" asked Issib.

"Because there's a chance, isn't there? A chance that he means what he's saying. If I refuse to mediate between them, then it'll be *my* fault if things get worse in Basilica than they already are. So I have to take him at face value, don't I?"

"All you can do is your best," said Nafai, echoing Father's own pat phrase from many previous conversations.

"Keep your eyes open," said Issib, echoing another of Father's epigrams.

"Yes," said Father. "I'll do that."

Issib nodded wisely.

"Father," said Nafai. "May I go with you in the morning?"

Father shook his head.

"I want to. And maybe I can see something that you miss. Like while you're talking or something, I can be looking at other people and seeing their reactions. I could really help."

"No," said Father. "I won't be a credible mediator if I have others with me."

But Nafai knew that wasn't true. "I think you're afraid that something ugly will happen and you don't want me there."

Father shrugged. "I have my fears. I *am* a father."

"But I'm *not* afraid, Father."

"Then apparently you're stupider than I feared," said Father. "Go to bed now, both of you."

"It's way too early for that," said Issib.

"Then *don't* go to bed."

Father turned away from them and faced the computer display again.

It was a clear signal of dismissal, but Nafai couldn't keep himself from questioning him. "If the Oversoul isn't speaking to you directly, Father, why do you hope to find anything helpful in its ancient, dead words?"

Father sighed and said nothing.

"Nafai," said Issib, "let Father contemplate in peace."

Nafai followed Issib out of the library. "Why won't anybody ever answer my questions?"

"Because you never stop asking them," said Issib, "and especially because you keep asking them even when it's clear that nobody knows the answers."

"Well how do I know that they don't know the answer unless I ask?"

"Go to your room and think dirty thoughts or something," said Issib. "Why can't you just act like a normal fourteen-year-old?"

"Right," said Nafai. "Like *I'm* supposed to be the one normal person in the family."

"Somebody's got to do it."

"Why do you think Meb was at the temple?"

"To pray for you to get a hemorrhoid every time you ask a question."

"No, that's why *you* were at the temple. Can you imagine Meb praying?"

"And marking up his beautiful body?" Issib laughed.

They were in the courtyard, in front of Issib's room. They heard a footstep and turned to see Mebbekew standing in the kitchen door. The kitchen had been dark; they had assumed that Truzhnisha had gone and that no one was in there. Meb must have overheard all their conversation.

Nafai couldn't think of anything to say. Of course, that didn't mean he held his tongue. "I guess you didn't stay long in the temple, did you, Meb?"

"No," said Meb. "But I *did* pray, if it's any of your business."

Nafai was ashamed. "I'm sorry."

Issib wasn't. "Oh, come on," he said. "Show me a scab, then."

"I have a question for you first, Issya," said Meb.

"Sure," said Issib.

"Do you have a float attached to your private lever to hold it up when you pee? Or do you just let it dribble down like a girl?"

It was too dark for Nafai to see whether Issib was blushing or not. All he was sure of was that Issib said nothing, just glided from the courtyard into his room.

"Bravely done," said Nafai. "Taunting a cripple."

"He called me a liar," said Meb. "Was I supposed to kiss him?"

"He was joking."

"It wasn't funny." Mebbekew went back into the kitchen.

Nafai went into his room, but he didn't feel like going to bed. He felt sweaty, even though the night was fairly chilly. His skin itched. It had to be the residue of blood and disinfectant from the temple fountain. Nafai didn't relish the idea of using soap on his wounds, but the slimy itchiness would be unbearable, too. So he stripped and went to the shower. This time he rinsed first, shockingly cold despite the day's warming of the water. And it stung bitterly to soap himself—perhaps worse now than when the wounds were first inflicted, though he knew that this was probably subjective. The pain of the moment is always the worst, Father had often said.

As he was soaping in miserable dark silence, he saw Elemak come in. He went directly into Father's rooms, and emerged not long after to lock the gate. And not just the outer gate; the inner one, too. That wasn't the usual thing; indeed, Nafai couldn't remember when he had last seen the inner gate locked. Maybe there was a storm once. Or a time when they were training a dog and kept it between the gates at night. But there was neither storm nor dog now.

Elemak went into his room. Nafai pulled the cord and

plunged himself again in icy water, rubbing at his wounds to get the soap out before the water stopped flowing. Curse Father for his absurd insistence on toughening his sons and making men of them! Only the poor had to bathe in a sudden flow of cold water like this!

It took two rinsings this time, with a long wet wait in the chilly breeze for the shower tank to refill. When he finally got back to his room, Nafai was chattering and shaking with the cold, and even when he was dry and dressed again, he couldn't seem to get warm. He almost closed the door to his room, which would have triggered the heating system—but he and his brothers always competed to see who could be last to start closing the door of his room in the wintertime, and he wasn't about to surrender that battle tonight, confessing that a little prayer had weakened him so much. Instead he pulled all his clothes out of his chest and piled them on top of himself where he lay on his mat.

There was no comfortable position for sleeping, of course, but lying on his side was least painful. Anger and pain and worry kept him from sleeping easily; he felt as though he hadn't slept at all, listening to the small sounds of the others getting ready for sleep, and then the endless silence of the courtyard at night. Now and then a birdcall, or a wild dog in the hills, or a soft restless sound from the horses in the stable or the pack animals in the barns.

And then he must have slept, or how else could he have woken up so suddenly, startled. Was it a sound that woke him? Or a dream? What was he dreaming, anyway? Something dark and fearful. He was trembling, but it wasn't cold—in fact, he was sweating heavily under his pile of clothing.

He got up and tossed the clothes back into his chest. He tried to be quiet about opening and closing the box—he didn't want to waken anyone else. Every movement caused him pain. He must be fevered, he realized—he had the stiffness in his muscles, and the hotness under his covers. And yet his thinking seemed remarkably clear, and all his senses. If this was a fever, it was a strange one, for he had never felt so vivid and alive. In spite of the pain—or because of it—he felt as though he would hear it if a mouse ran across a beam in the stable.

He walked out into the courtyard and stood there in silence. The moon wasn't up yet, but the stars were many and bright on this clear night. The gate was still locked. But why had he wondered? What was he afraid of? What *had* he seen in his dream?

Meb's and Elya's doors were closed. What a laugh—here I am, wounded and sore, and I keep my door open, while these two go ahead and close their doors like little children.

Or maybe it's only little children who care about such meaningless contests of manliness.

It was colder than ever outside, and now he had cooled off the feverishness that had made him get up. But still he didn't return to his room, though he meant to. In fact, it finally dawned on him that he had already decided several times to return to his room, and each time his mind had wandered and he hadn't taken a step.

The Oversoul, he thought. The Oversoul wants me to be up. Perhaps wants me to be doing something. But what?

At this point in the month, the fact that the moon had not yet risen meant that it was a good three hours before dawn. Two hours, then, before Father was supposed to arise and go to his rendezvous at the cool house, where the plants from the icy north were nurtured and propagated.

Why was the meeting being held *there*?

Nafai felt an inexplicable desire to go outside and look northeast across the Tsivet Valley toward the high hills on the other side, where the Music Gate marked the southeast limit of Basilica. It was silly, and the noise of opening the gates might waken someone. But by now Nafai knew that the Oversoul was involved with him tonight, trying to keep him from going back to bed; couldn't this impulse to go outside also come from the Oversoul? Hadn't Nafai prayed today—couldn't this be an answer? Wasn't it possible that this desire to go outside was like the impulse Father had felt, that took him from the Desert Road to the place where he saw the vision of fire?

Wasn't it possible that Nafai, too, was about to receive a vision from the Oversoul?

He walked smoothly, quietly to the gate and lifted the heavy bar. No noises; his senses and reflexes were so alert and alive that he could move with perfect silence. The gate creaked slightly as he opened it—but he didn't have to open it widely in order to slip through.

The outer gate was more often used, and so it worked more easily, and quietly, having been better maintained. Nafai stepped outside just as the moon first showed an arc over the top of the Seggidugu Mountains to the east. He headed out to walk around the house to where he could see the cool house, but before he had taken a few steps he realized that he could hear a sound coming from the traveler's room.

As was the custom in all the households in this part of the world, every house had a room whose door opened to the outside and was never locked—a decent place where a traveler could come and take refuge from storm or cold or weariness. Father took the obligation of hospitality to strangers more seriously than most, providing not just a room, but also a bed and clean linen, and a cupboard provisioned with traveling food. Nafai wasn't sure which servant had responsibility for the room, but he knew it was often used and just as often replenished. So he should not be surprised at the idea that someone might be inside.

And yet he knew that he must stop at the door and peer inside.

Scant light fell into the traveler's room from the crack in the door. He opened it wider, and the light spilled onto the bed, where he found himself looking into the wide eyes of—Luet.

"You," he whispered.

"You," she answered. She sounded relieved.

"What are you doing here?" he asked. "Who's with you?"

"I'm alone," she said. "I wasn't sure who I was coming to. Whose house. I've never been outside of the city walls before."

"When did you get here?"

"Just now. The Oversoul led me."

Of course. "To what purpose?"

"I don't know," she said. "To tell my dream, I think. It woke me."

Nafai thought of his own dream, which he couldn't remember.

"I was so—glad," she said. "That the Oversoul had spoken again. But the dream was terrible."

"What was it?"

"Is it you I'm supposed to tell?" she asked.

"I should know?" he answered. "But I'm here."

"Did the Oversoul bring you out here?"

With the question put so directly, he couldn't evade it. "Yes," he said. "I think so."

She nodded. "Then I'll tell you. It makes sense,

actually, that it be your family. Because there are so many people who hate your father because of his vision and his courage in proclaiming it."

"Yes," he said. And then, to prompt her: "The dream."

"I saw a man alone on foot, walking in the straight. He was walking through snow. Only I knew that it was tonight, even though there's not a speck of snow on the ground. Do you understand how I can know something, even though it's different from what the dream actually shows me?"

Remembering the conversation on the portico a week ago, Nafai nodded.

"So there was snow, and yet it was tonight. The moon was up. I knew it was almost dawn. And as the man walked along, two men wearing hoods sprang out into the road in front of him, holding blades. He seemed to know them, in spite of the hoods. And he said, 'Here's my throat. I carry no weapon. You could have killed me at any time, even when I knew you were my enemy. Why did you need to deceive me into trusting you first? Were you afraid that death wouldn't bother me enough, unless I felt betrayed?'"

Nafai had already made the connection between her dream and Father's meeting, only a few hours away. "Gaballufix," said Nafai.

Luet nodded. "*Now* I understand that—but I didn't until I realized this was your father's house."

"No—Gaballufix arranged a meeting for Father and Roptat and him this morning, at the coolhouse."

"The snow," she said.

"Yes," he said. "It's always got frost in the corners."

"And Roptat," she whispered. "That explains—the next part of the dream."

"Tell me."

"One hooded man reached out and uncovered the face

of his companion. For a moment I thought I saw a grin on his face, but then my vision clarified and I realized it wasn't his face that had the smile. It was his throat, slit clear back to the spine. As I watched him, his head lolled back and the wound in his throat opened completely, as if it were a mouth, trying to scream. And the man—the one that was me in the dream—"

"I understand," said Nafai. "Father."

"Yes. Only I didn't know that."

"Right," said Nafai. Impatiently, urging her to get on with it.

"Your father, if it *was* your father, said, 'I suppose it will be said that I killed him.' And the hooded man says, 'And you did, in very truth, my dear kinsman.'"

"He *would* say that," said Nafai. "So Roptat is supposed to die, too."

"I'm not done," said Luet. "Or rather, the dream wasn't finished. Because the man—your father—said, 'And who will they say killed *me*?' And the hooded one said, 'Not *me*. I'd never lift a hand against you, for I love you dearly. I will merely find your body here, and your bloody-handed murderers standing over it.' Then he laughed and disappeared back into the shadows."

"So he *doesn't* kill Father."

"No. Your father turned around then and saw two other hooded men standing behind him. And even though they didn't speak or lift their hoods, he knew them. I felt this terrible sadness. 'You couldn't wait,' he said to the one. 'You couldn't forgive me,' he said to the other. And then they reached out with their blades and killed him."

"No, by the Oversoul," said Nafai. "They wouldn't do it."

"Who? Do you know?"

"Tell no one of this last part of the dream," said Nafai. "Swear it to me with your most awful oath."

"I'll do no such thing," she said.

"My brothers are all home tonight," said Nafai. "Not lying in wait for Father."

"Is that who the hooded men are, then? Your brothers?"

"No!" he said. "Never."

She nodded. "I'll give you no oath. Only my promise. If your father is saved from death by my having come here, then I'll tell no one else of this part of the dream."

"Not even Hushidh," he said.

"But I make you another promise," she said. "If your father dies, I'll know that you didn't warn him. And that the hooded ones in the dream included *you*—because to know of the plot and fail to warn him is exactly the same as holding the charged-wire blade in your own hands."

"Do you think I don't know that?" said Nafai. He was angry for a moment, that she would think *he* needed to be taught the ethics of this situation. But then his thoughts moved on, as Luet's warning clarified other things that had happened that day. "That's why Meb went to pray," said Nafai, "and why Elya locked the inner gate. They knew—or maybe they just suspected something—and yet they were afraid to tell. That's what the dream meant—not that they would ever lift a hand against Father, but rather that they knew and were afraid to warn him."

She nodded. "It often works that way in dreams," she said. "That would be a true meaning, and it doesn't empty my head when I think that thought."

"Maybe the Oversoul itself doesn't know."

She reached out and patted his hand. It made him feel like a child, even though she was younger and much smaller than he. He resented her for it.

"The Oversoul knows," she said.

"Not everything," he said.

"Everything that *can* be known," she said. She walked to the door of the traveler's room. "Tell no one that I came," she said.

"Except Father," he said.

"Can't you say that it was *your* dream?"

"Why?" asked Nafai. "*Your* dream he would believe. Mine would be—nothing to him."

"You underestimate your father. And the Oversoul, too, I think. And yourself." She stepped out into the moonlit yard in front of the house. She started to turn right, heading for Ridge Road.

"No," he whispered, catching her arm—small and frail indeed, she was a girl so young and little-boned. "Don't pass in front of the gate."

She gave him a questioning look, eyes wide, reflecting the moon, which was half-risen now over his shoulder.

"Perhaps I woke someone when I opened it," he explained.

She nodded. "I'll go around the house on the other side."

"Luet," he said.

"Yes?"

"Will you be safe, going home now?"

"The moon is up," she said. "And the guard at the Funnel Gate will give me no trouble. The Oversoul made him sleep when I passed before."

"Luet," he said, calling her back again.

Again she stopped, waited for his words.

"Thank you," he said. The words were nothing compared to what he felt in his heart. She had saved his father's life—and it was a brave thing for a girl who had never left the city to come all this way in the starlight, guided only by a dream.

She shrugged. "The Oversoul sent me. Thank *her*." Then she was gone.

Nafai returned to the gate, and this time deliberately made some noise coming in and latching it. If one of his brothers was listening or watching, he didn't want his return to surprise him. Let him hear and go back to his room before I come through the inner gate.

As he had hoped, the courtyard was empty when he returned. He went straight to Father's room, through the public room and the library to the private place where he slept alone. There he lay on the bare floor, without a mat of any kind, his white beard spilling onto the stone. Nafai stood there a moment, imagining the throat cut open and the beard stained brownish red with the gush of blood.

Then he noticed that Father's eyes were shining. He was awake.

"Are you the one?" whispered Father.

"What do you mean?" asked Nafai.

Father sat up, slowly, wearily. "I had a dream. It was nothing—just my fear."

"Someone else had a dream tonight," said Nafai. "I talked to her just now in the traveler's room. But it's better if you tell no one that she was here."

"Who?"

"Luet," he said. "And her dream was to warn you of the meeting tonight. There's murder waiting for you if you go."

Father sprang to his feet and turned on the light. Nafai blinked in the brightness of it. "Then it wasn't just a dream I had."

"I'm beginning to think there *are* no meaningless dreams," said Nafai. "I also dreamed, and it woke me, and the Oversoul brought me outside to talk to her."

"Murder waiting for me. I can guess the rest. He'll murder Roptat also, and make it look like one of us killed the other, and then someone else killed the murderer, and only then will Gaballufix arrive, probably with several believable witnesses who can swear that the murders took place before Gabya arrived. They'll tell of how shocked he was by the bloody scene. Why didn't I see it myself? How else could he get me and Roptat to the same place at the same time, with no followers or witnesses about?"

"So you won't go," said Nafai.

"Yes," said Father. "I'll go, yes."

"No!"

"But not to the coolhouse," said Father. "Because *my* dream showed me something else."

"What?"

"Tents," he said. "My tents, spread wide in the desert sun. If we stay, Gaballufix will only try again, in some other way. And—there are other reasons for leaving. For getting my sons out of this city before it destroys them."

Nafai knew that Father's dream must have been terrible indeed. Did it show him that one of his sons would kill him? That would explain Father's first words—Are you the one?

"So we're going into the desert?"

"Yes," said Father.

"When?"

"Now, of course."

"Now? Today?"

"Now, *tonight*. Before dawn. So we're over the ridge before his men can see us."

"But won't we pass right by Gaballufix's household, where Twisting Trail crosses Desert Road?"

"There's a back way," said Father. "Not the best for camels, but we'll have to do it. It puts us on Desert Road well past Gabya's place. Now come, help me waken your brothers."

"No," said Nafai.

Father turned to him, puzzlement making him hesitate to express his anger at being disobeyed.

"Luet asked—that no one be told it was her. And she was right. They shouldn't know about me, either. It should be *your* dream."

"Why?" asked Father. "To have three be touched tonight by the Oversoul—"

"Because if it's your dream, then they'll wonder what you know, what you saw. But if there are others, then to them it will seem that we're fooling and manipulating you. They'll argue. They'll resist you. And you have to bring them with you, Father."

Father nodded. "You're very wise," he said. "For a boy of fourteen."

But Nafai knew he was not wise. He simply had the benefit of knowing the rest of Luet's dream. If Meb and Elya stayed behind, they would be wholly swallowed up in Gaballufix's machinations. They would lose what decency remained in them. And there *must* be goodness in them. Perhaps they even planned to warn Father. Maybe that's why Elya closed the inner gate, so that he'd be wakened by the noise Father made as he left—then he could come out and warn Father not to go!

Or perhaps he meant only to follow Father, so he could be right behind him when he came upon Roptat's murdered body in the ice house.

No! cried Nafai inside himself. Not Elemak. It's monstrous of me even to think that he could do that. My brothers are not murderers, not one of them.

"Go to your room," said Father. "Or better still, to the toilet. And then come out and set an example of silent obedience. Not to me—to Elya. He knows how to pack for this kind of trip."

"Yes, Father," said Nafai.

At once he moved briskly from Father's room, through

the library and public room, and out into the courtyard. Elemak's and Mebbekew's doors were still closed. Nafai headed for the latrine, with its two walls leaving it open to the courtyard. He was only just there when he heard Father knocking on Mebbekew's door. "Wake up, but quietly," said Father. Then again, on Elemak's. "Come out into the courtyard."

He heard them all come out—Issib, too, though no one called him directly.

"Where's Nyef?" asked Issib.

"Using the latrine," said Father.

"Now *that's* an idea," said Meb.

"You can wait a moment," said Father.

Nafai came out of the stall, letting the toilet wash itself automatically behind him. At least Father hadn't made them live in a *completely* primitive way.

"Sorry," said Nafai. "Didn't mean to keep you waiting." Meb glowered at him, but too sleepily for Nafai to take it as a threat of a fight to come.

"We're leaving," Father said. "Out into the desert."

"All of us?" asked Issib.

"I'm sorry, yes," said Father. "You'll be in your chair. It's not the same as your floats, I know, but it's something."

"Why?" asked Elemak.

"I was warned by the Oversoul in a dream," said Father.

Meb made a contemptuous noise and started back for his room.

"You will stand and listen," said Father, "because if you stay, it will not be as my son."

Meb stood and listened, though his back was still toward Father.

"There's a plot to kill me," said Father. "This morning.

I was to go to a meeting with Gaballufix and Roptat, and there I was going to die."

"Gabya gave me his word," said Elemak. "No harm to anyone."

So Elemak called Gaballufix by his boy-name now, did he?

"The Oversoul knows his heart better than his own mouth does," said Father. "If I go, I'll die. And even if I don't, it will be only a matter of time. Now that Gaballufix has determined to kill me, my life is worthless here. I would stay in the city if I thought some purpose would be served by my dying here—I'm not afraid of it. But the Oversoul has told me to leave."

"In a dream," said Elemak.

"I don't need a dream to tell me that Gaballufix is dangerous when he's crossed," said Father, "and neither do you. When I don't show up at the coolhouse this morning, there's no telling what Gaballufix will do. I must already be out on the desert when he discovers it. We'll take Redstone Path."

"The camels can't do it," said Elemak.

"They can because they must," said Father. "We'll take enough to live for a year."

"This is monstrous, " said Mebbekew. "I won't do it."

"What do we do after a year?" asked Elemak.

"The Oversoul will show me something by then," said Father.

"Maybe things will have calmed down in Basilica enough to return," suggested Issib.

"If we go now," said Elemak, "Gabya will think you betrayed him, Father."

"Will he?" said Father. "And if I stay, he'll betray *me*."

"Said a dream."

"Said *my* dream," said Father. "I need you. Stay if you want, but not as my son."

"I did fine not as your son," said Mebbekew.

"No," said Elemak. "You did fine *pretending* not to be his son. But everyone knew."

"I lived from my talent."

"You lived from theatre people's hope of getting your father to invest in their shows—or you, in the future, out of your inheritance."

Mebbekew looked like he had been slapped. "You too, is that it, Elya?"

"I'll talk to you later," said Elemak. "If Father says we're going then we're going—and we have no time to lose." He turned to Father. "Not because you threatened to disinherit me, old man. But because you're my father, and I won't have you going out into the desert with nothing but *these* to help you stay alive."

"I taught you everything you know, Elya," said Father.

"When you were younger," said Elemak. "And we always had servants. I assume we're leaving them all behind."

"Dismissing the household servants," said Father. "While you ready the animals and the supplies, Elya, I'll leave instructions for Rashgallivak."

For the next hour Nafai worked with more hurry than he had ever thought possible. Everyone, even Issib, had tasks to perform, and Nafai admired Elemak all over again for his great skill at this sort of thing. He always knew exactly what needed to be done, and who should do it, and how long it should take; he also knew how to make Nafai feel like an idiot for not learning his tasks more quickly, even though he was sure that he was doing at least as well as anyone could expect, considering that it was his first time.

At last they were ready—a true desert caravan, with nothing but camels, though they were the most temperamental of the pack animals, and the least comfortable to ride. Issib's chair was strapped to one side of a camel, bundles of powdered water on the other. The water would be for emergencies later; on the first part of their journey Father and Elemak knew all the watering places, and besides, an autumn occasional rain fell on the desert, and there would be ample water. Next summer, though, it would be drier, and then it would be too late to come back to Basilica for the precious powder. And what if they were followed, chased into untracked sections of the desert? Then they might need to pour some of the powder into a pan, light it, and watch it burn itself into water, taking oxygen from the air to accomplish it. Nafai had tasted it once—foul stuff, tinny and nasty with the chemicals used to bind the hydrogen into powdered form. But they'd be glad of it if they ever needed it.

It was Issib's chair that would bring the least gladness. Nafai knew that this journey would be hardest on Issya, deprived of his floats, and bound into the chair. The floats made him feel as though his own body were light and strong; in the chair, he felt gravity pressing him down, and it took all his strength to operate the controls. At the end of a day in the chair Issya was always wan and exhausted. How would it be for day after day, week after week, month after month? Maybe he would grow stronger. Maybe he would grow weaker. Maybe he would die. Maybe the Oversoul would sustain him.

Maybe angels would come and carry them to the moon.

It was still a good hour before dawn when they set out. They had been quiet enough that none of the servants had been wakened—or perhaps they *had*, but since nobody asked them to help and they weren't interested in volunteering for whatever mad task was going on at this hour of the night, they discreetly rolled over and went back to sleep.

Redstone Path was murderously treacherous, but the moonlight and Elemak's instructions made it possible. Nafai was again filled with admiration for his eldest brother. Was there nothing Elya couldn't do? Was there any hope of Nafai ever becoming so strong and competent?

At last they crossed Twisting Path, right at the crest of the highest ridge; below them stretched the desert. The first light of dawn was already strong in the east, but they had made good enough time. It was downhill now, still difficult, but not long until they reached the great plateau of the western desert. No one would follow them easily here—no one from the city, anyway. Elemak passed out pulses to all of them and made them practice aiming the tightbeam light at rocks he pointed out. Issib was pretty useless—he couldn't hold the pulse steady enough—but Nafai was proud of the fact that he held his aim better than Father.

Whether he could actually kill a robber with it was another matter. Surely he wouldn't have to. They were on the Oversoul's errand here in the desert, weren't they? The Oversoul would steer the robbers away from them. Just as the Oversoul would lead them to water and food, when they ran out of their traveling supplies.

Then Nafai remembered that this whole business began because the Oversoul wasn't as competent as it used to be. How did he know the Oversoul could do *any* of those things? Or that it even had a plan? Yes, it had sent Luet to warn them, and had wakened Nafai to go hear the warning, and had sent Father his own dream. But that didn't mean that the Oversoul actually had any intention of protecting them or even of leading them anywhere except away from the city. Who knew what the Oversoul's plans were? Maybe all it needed was to get rid of Wetchik and his family.

With that grim thought, Nafai sat high above the desert, his leg hooked around the pommel of his saddle, as he searched in all directions for robbers, for pursuers from the city, for any strange thing on the road, for signs from the Oversoul. The only music was Mebbekew's complaints and Elemak's orders and the occasional splatting as the camels voided their bowels. Nafai's beast, oblivious to any worries except where to put its feet, continued its rolling gait onward into the heat of day.

NINE

LIES AND
DISGUISES

With the moon up, it was much easier for Luet to find her way back into the city than it had been for her to get to Wetchik's house. Besides, now she *knew* her destination; it's always easier to return home than to find a strange place.

Oddly, though, she didn't feel a sense of danger until she got back into the city itself. The guard at the Funnel Gate was away from his post—perhaps he had been caught sleeping, or perhaps the Oversoul made him think of some sudden errand. Luet had to smile to herself at the thought of the Oversoul troubling herself to make a man feel an urgent need to void his bladder, just for Luet's safe passage.

Within the city, though, the moon was less help. In fact, since it hadn't yet risen very high, it cast deep shadows, and the north-south streets were still in utter blackness at street level. Anyone might be abroad at this hour. Tolchocks were known to be abroad much earlier in the night, when there were still many women abroad in the streets. Now, though, in the loneliest hours before dawn, there might be much worse than tolchocks about.

"Isn't she the pretty one?"

The voice startled her. It was a woman, though, a husky-voiced woman. It took a moment for Luet to find her in the shadows. "I'm not pretty," she said. "In the darkness your eyes deceived you."

It had to be a holy woman, to be on the street at this hour. As she stepped from the dark corner where she had taken shelter from the night breeze, the woman's dirty skin showed a bit paler than the surrounding shadow. She was naked from face to foot. Seeing her, Luet felt the cold of the autumn night. As long as Luet had been moving, she had kept warm from the exercise. Now, though, she wondered how this woman could live like this, with no barrier between her skin and the chilling air except for the dirt on her body.

Mother was a wilder, thought Luet. I was born to such a one as this. She slept in the desert when I was in her womb, and carried me, as naked as she was, into the city to leave me with Aunt Rasa. Not this one, though. My mother, wherever she is, is not a holy woman anymore. Only a year after I was born she left the Oversoul to follow a man, a farmer, to a hardscrabble life in the rocky soil of the Chalvasankhra Valley. Or so Aunt Rasa said.

"Beautiful are the eyes of the holy child," intoned the woman, "who sees in the darkness and burns with bright fire in the frozen night."

Luet permitted the woman to touch her face, but when the cold hands started to pull at her clothing, Luet covered them with her own. "Please," she said. "I am not holy, and the Oversoul doesn't shield me from the cold."

"Or from the prying eyes," said the holy woman. "The Oversoul sees you deep, and you *are* holy, yes you are."

Whose were the prying eyes? The Oversoul's? The eyes of men who sized up women as if they were horses? Gossips' eyes? Or this woman's? And as for being holy—Luet knew better. The Oversoul had chosen her, yes, but not for any virtue in herself. If anything, it was a punishment, always to be surrounded by people who saw her as an oracle instead of a girl. Hushidh, her own sister, had once said to her, "I wish I had your gift; everything is so clear to you." Nothing is clear to me, Luet wanted to say. The Oversoul doesn't confide in me, she merely uses me to transmit messages that I don't understand myself. Just as I don't understand what this holy woman wants with me, or why—if the Oversoul sent her—she was sent to me.

"Don't be afraid to take him beside the water," said the holy woman.

"Who?" asked Luet.

"The Oversoul wants you to save him alive, no matter what the danger. There is no sacrilege in obeying the Oversoul."

"Who?" asked Luet again. This confusion, this dread that she must decode the puzzle of these words or suffer some terrible loss—was this how others felt when she told them of her visions?

"You think all the visions should come to *you*," said the holy woman. "But some things are too clear for you to see yourself. Eh?"

I think nothing of the kind, holy woman. I never asked for visions, and I often wish they had come to other people. But if you're going to insist on giving me some message, then have the decency to make it as intelligible as you can. It's what *I* try to do.

Luet tried to keep her resentment out of her voice, but she could not resist insisting on a clarifying answer. "Who is this *him* that you keep talking about?"

The woman slapped her sharply across the face. It brought tears to Luet's eyes—tears as much of shame as of pain. "What have I done?"

"I have punished you now for the defiling you will do," said the holy woman. "It's done, and no one can demand that you pay more."

Luet didn't dare ask questions again; the answer was not to her liking. Instead she studied at the woman, trying to see if there was understanding in her eyes. Was this madness after all? Did it have to be the true voice of the Oversoul? So much easier if it was madness.

The old woman reached her hand toward Luet's cheek again. Luet recoiled a little, but the woman's touch was gentle this time, and she brushed a tear from the hollow just under Luet's eye. "Don't be afraid of the blood on his hands. Like the water of vision, the Oversoul will receive it as a prayer."

Then the holy woman's face went slack and weary, and the light went out of her eyes. "It's cold," she said.

"Yes."

"I'm too old," she said.

Her hair wasn't even gray, but yes, thought Luet, you are very, very old.

"Nothing will hold," said the holy woman. "Silver and gold. Stolen or sold."

She was a rhymer. Luet knew that many people thought that when a holy woman went a-rhyming, it meant that the Oversoul was speaking through her. But it wasn't so—the rhyming was a sort of music, the voice of the trance that kept some of the holy women detached from their bleak and terrible life. It was when they *stopped* rhyming that there was a chance they might speak sense.

The holy woman wandered away, as if she had forgotten Luet was there. Since she seemed to have forgotten where her sheltered corner was, Luet took her by the hand and led her back there, encouraged her to sit down and curl up against the wall that blocked the wind. "Out of the wind," whispered the holy woman. "How they have sinned."

Luet left her there and went on into the night. The moon was higher now, but the better light did little to cheer her. Though the holy woman was harmless in herself, she had reminded Luet of how many people there might be, hiding in the shadows. And how vulnerable *she* was. There were stories of men who treated citizens the way that the law allowed them to deal with the holy women. But even that was not the worst fear.

There is murder in the city, thought Luet. Murder in this place, not holiness, and it is Gaballufix who first thought of it. If not for the vision and warning I carried for the Oversoul, good men would have died. She shuddered again at the memory of the slit throat in her vision.

At last she came to the place where the Holy Road widened out as it descended into the valley, becoming, not a road, but a canyon, with ancient stairs carved into the rock, leading directly down to the place where the lake steamed hot with a tinge of sulphur. Those who worshiped there always kept that smell about them for days. It might be holy, but Luet found it exceedingly unpleasant and never worshiped there herself. She preferred the place where the hot and cold waters mixed and the deepest fog arose, where currents swirled their varying temperatures all around her as she floated on the water. It was there that her body danced on the water with no volition of her own, where she could surrender herself utterly to the Oversoul.

Who was the holy woman speaking about? The "him" with blood on his hands, the "he" that she could take by the waters—presumably the waters of the lake.

No, it was nothing. The holy woman was one of the mad ones, making no sense.

The only man she could think of who had blood on his hands was Gaballufix. How could the Oversoul want such a man as that to come near the holy lake? Would the time come when she would have to save Gaballufix's life? How could such a thing possibly fit in with the purposes of the Oversoul?

She turned left onto Tower Street, then turned right onto Rain Street, which curved around until she stood before Rasa's house. Home, unharmed. Of course. The Oversoul had protected her. The message she had delivered was *not* the whole purpose the Oversoul had for her; Luet would live to do other work. It was a great relief to her. For hadn't her own mother told Aunt Rasa, on the day she put Luet as an infant into Rasa's arms, "This one will live only as long as she serves the Mother of Mothers?" The Mother of Mothers had preserved her for another night.

Luet had expected to get back into Aunt Rasa's house without waking anyone, but she hadn't taken into account how the new climate of fear in the city had changed even the household of the leading housemistress of Basilica. The front door was locked on the inside. Still hoping to enter unobserved, she looked for a window she might climb through. Only now did she realize that all the windows facing the street were solely for the passage of light and air—many vertical slits in the wall, carved or sculpted with delicate designs, but with no gap wide enough to let even the head and shoulders of a child pass through.

This is not the first time there has been fear in Basilica, she thought. This house is designed to keep someone from entering surreptitiously in the night. Protection from burglars, of course; but perhaps such windows were designed primarily to keep rejected suitors and lapsed mates from forcing their way back into a house that they had come to think of as their own.

The provisions that kept a man from entering also barred Luet, slight as she was. She knew, of course, that there was no way to get around the sides of the house, since the neighboring structures leaned against the massive stone walls of Rasa's house.

Why didn't she guess that getting back inside would be so much harder than getting out? She had left after dark, of course, but well before the house quieted down for the evening; Hushidh knew something of her errand and would keep anyone from discovering her absence. It simply hadn't occurred to either of them to arrange how Luet would get back in. Aunt Rasa had never locked the front door before. And later, after the Oversoul had made the guard doze on the way out and had kept him away from the gate entirely on her return, Luet had assumed that the Oversoul was smoothing the way for her.

Luet thought of staying out on the porch all night. But it was cold now. As long as she had been walking, it was all right, she had stayed warm enough. Sleep, though, would be dangerous. City women, at least those of good breeding, did not own the right clothing for sleeping out of doors. What the holy women did would make her ill.

There might be another way, however. Wasn't Aunt Rasa's portico on the valley-side of the house completely open? There might be a way to climb up from the valley. Of course, the area just east of Rasa's portico was the wildest, emptiest part of the Shelf—it wasn't even part of a district, and though Sour Street ran out into it, there was no road there; women never went that way to get to the lake.

Yet she knew that this was the way she must go, if she was to return to Aunt Rasa's house.

The Oversoul again, leading her. Leading her, but telling her nothing.

Why not? asked Luet for the thousandth time. Why can't you tell me your purpose? If you had told me I was going to Wetchik's house, I wouldn't have been so fearful all the way. How did my fear and ignorance serve your purpose? And now you send me around to the wild country east of Aunt Rasa's house—for what purpose? Do you take pleasure in toying with me? Or am I too stupid to understand your purpose? I'm your homing dove, able to carry your messages but never worth explaining them to.

And yet, despite her resentment, a few minutes she stepped from the last cobbles of Sour Street onto the grass and then plunged into the pathless woods of the Shelf.

The ground was rugged, and all the gaps and breaks in the underbrush seemed to lead downward, away from Rasa's portico and toward the cliffs looming over the canyon of the Holy Road. No wonder that even the Shelf women built no houses here. But Luet refused to be led astray by the easy paths—she knew they would disappear the moment she started following them. Instead she forced her way through the underbrush. The zarosel thorns snagged at her, and she knew they would leave tiny welts that would sting for days even under a layer of Aunt Rasa's balm. Worse, she was bone-weary, cold, and sleepy, so that at times she caught herself waking up, even though she had not been asleep. Still—she had set herself on this course, and she would finish.

She came into a small clearing where bright moonlight filtered through the canopy of leaves overhead. In a month all the leaves would be gone and these thickets would not be half so forbidding. Now, though, a patch of light came like a miracle, and she blinked.

In that eyeblink, the clearing changed. There was a woman standing there.

"Aunt Rasa," whispered Luet. How did she know to come looking for me here? Has the Oversoul spoken again to someone else?

But it was not Aunt Rasa, after all. It was Hushidh. How could she have made such a mistake?

No. Not a mistake. For now Hushidh had changed again. It was Eiadh now, that beautiful girl from Hushidh's class, the one that poor Nafai was so uselessly in love with. And again the woman was transformed, into the actress Dol, who had been so very famous as a young girl; she was one of Aunt Rasa's nieces, and in recent years had returned to the house to teach. Once it was said that Dolltown was named after her (though it had been named such for ten thousand years at least), she was so beautiful and broke so many hearts; but she was in her twenties now, and the features that, when she was a girl, made women want to mother her and ravished the eyes of men were not so astonishing in a woman. Still, Luet would give half her life if during the other half she could be as delicately, sweetly beautiful as Dol.

Why is the Oversoul showing me these women?

From Dol the apparition changed to Shedemei, another of Aunt Rasa's nieces. If anything, though, Shedya was the opposite of Dol and Eiadh. At twenty-six she was still in Aunt Rasa's house, helping to teach science to the older students as her own reputation as a geneticist grew. Most nights she actually slept in her laboratory, many streets away, instead of her room in Rasa's house, but still she was a strong, quiet presence there. Shedemei was unbeautiful; not so ugly as to startle the onlooker, but deeply plain, so that the longer one studied her face the less attractive it became. Yet her mind was like a magnet, drawn to truth: as soon as it came near enough, she would leap to it and cling. Of all Aunt Rasa's nieces, she was the one that Luet most admired; but Luet knew that no more had she the wit to emulate Shedemei than she had the beauty to follow Dol's career. The Oversoul had chosen to send her visions to one who had no other use to the world.

The woman was gone. Luet was alone in the clearing, and she felt again as if she had just awakened.

Was this only a dream, the kind that comes when you don't even know that you're asleep?

Behind where the apparitions had stood, she saw a single light burning in the dark of earliest morning. It had to be on Aunt Rasa's portico—in that direction there could be no other source of light. Maybe the vision had been right thus far. Aunt Rasa was awake, and waiting for her.

She pushed forward into the brush. Low twigs swiped at her, thorns snagged at her clothing and her skin, and the irregular ground deceived her, causing her to trip and stumble. Always, though, that light was her beacon, drawing her on until at last it went out of sight as she drew under the lip of Rasa's portico.

It rose in a single sheet of weathered stone, sheer from base to balustrade, with no handholds. And it was at least four meters from the ground to the top. Even if Aunt Rasa was there waiting for her, there'd be no way to climb up, not without calling for servants. And if she was going to have to disturb the house anyway, she might as well have pulled the bellcord at the front door!

It happened that after having been forced this way and that by the rough ground of the forest, Luet had finally approached Rasa's house almost from the south. Most of the face of the portico was hidden from her. It was possible that the house had been built with some access from the portico to the wood. Surely the builders had planned for more than a mere *view* of the Rift Valley. And even if there was no deliberate access, there had to be a spot where she would have some hope of climbing up.

Making her way around the curved stone surface, Luet at last found what she had hoped for—a place where the broken ground rose higher in relation to the portico. Now the top of the balustrade was only an arm's length out of her reach. And, as she reached up to try to find a handhold in the gaps of the balustrade, she saw Aunt Rasa's face, as welcome as sunrise, and her arms reaching down for her.

If Luet had been any larger, Aunt Rasa probably could not have lifted her weight; but then, had she been larger she might have climbed up without help.

When at last she sat on the bench with Aunt Rasa half-cradling her, on the verge of weeping with relief and exhaustion, Aunt Rasa asked the obvious question. "What under the moon were you doing out there instead of coming to the front door like any other student coming back home after hours? Were you so afraid of a reprimand that you thought it would be better to risk your neck in the woods at night?"

Luet shook her head. "In the wood I saw a vision," she said. "But I might have seen it anyway, so coming around that way was probably my own foolishness."

Then there was nothing for Luet to do but tell Aunt Rasa about all that had happened—the vision she had told to Nafai, warning of the plot to murder Wetchik; the words of the holy woman in the dark street; and finally the vision of Rasa and a few of her nieces.

"I can't think what such a vision might mean," said Rasa. "If the Oversoul didn't tell *you*, how can *I* guess?"

"I don't want to guess anything anyway," said Luet. "I don't want any more visions or talk of visions or anything except I hurt all over and I want to go to bed."

"Of course you do, of course," said Aunt Rasa, "You can sleep, and leave it to Wetchik and me to think what course of action to take now. Unless he was stupid enough to decide that honor required him to keep that treacherous rendezvous at the coolhouse."

A terrible thought occurred to Luet. "What if Nafai didn't tell him?"

Aunt Rasa looked at her sharply. "Nafai, not warn his father about a plot against his life? You're speaking of my son."

What could that mean to Luet, who had never known her mother and whose father could be any man in the city, with the most brutish men the likeliest candidates? Mother and son—it was a connection that held no particular authority for her. In a world of faithless promises, anything was possible.

No, it was her weariness telling her to trust no one. She was doubting Aunt Rasa's judgment here, not just Nafai's faithfulness. Obviously her mind was not functioning clearly. She allowed Aunt Rasa to half-lead, half-carry her up the stairs to Rasa's own room, and place Luet on the great soft bed of the mistress of the house, where she slept almost before realizing where she was.

"Out all night," said Hushidh.

Luet opened one eye. The light coming through the window was very bright, but the air had a chill in it. Full day, and Luet was only waking now.

"And then not even the brains to come in the front door."

"I don't always rely on my brains," said Luet quietly.

"That much I knew," said Hushidh. "You should have taken me with you."

"Two people are always more obvious than one."

"To Wetchik's house! Didn't it occur to you that I might actually know the way there and back?"

"I didn't know that was where I was going."

"Alone at night. Anything could have happened. And you binding me with that foolish oath to tell no one. Aunt Rasa almost skinned me alive and hung me out to dry on the front porch when she realized that I must have known you were gone and didn't tell her."

"Don't be cross with me, Hushidh."

"Whole city's in turmoil, you know."

A sudden fear stabbed through her. "No, Hushidh—don't tell me there was murder after all!"

"Murder? Not likely. Wetchik's gone, though, him and his sons all, and Gaballufix is claiming that it was because he uncovered Wetchik's plot to murder him and Roptat at a secret meeting that Wetchik arranged at his coolhouse near Music Gate."

"That's not true," said Luet.

"Well, I didn't think it *was*," said Hushidh. "I only told you what Gaballufix's people are saying. His soldiers are thick in the streets."

"I'm so tired, Hushidh, and there's nothing I can do about any of this."

"Aunt Rasa thinks you can do something," said Hushidh. "That's why she sent me to wake you."

"Did she?"

"Well, you know *her*. She sent me up twice to 'see if poor Luet is still getting some of that rest she needs so much.' The third time I finally caught on that she was waiting for you to wake up but didn't have the heart to give instructions for me to do it."

"How thoughtful of you to read between the lines, my darling jewel of a big sister."

"You can nap again later, my sweet yagda-berry of a little sister."

It took only moments to wash and dress, for Luet was young enough that Aunt Rasa did not insist on her learning how to make hair and clothing graceful and dignified before appearing in public. As a child, she could be her scrawny, gawky self, which certainly took less effort. When Luet got downstairs, Aunt Rasa was in her salon with a man, a stranger, but Rasa introduced him at once.

"This is Rashgallivak, dear Luet. He is perhaps the most loyal and trustworthy man alive, or so my beloved mate has always said."

"I have served the Wetchik estate all my life," said Rashgallivak, "and will do so until I die. I may not be of the great houses, but I am still a true Palwashantu."

Aunt Rasa nodded. Luet wondered whether she was supposed to hear this man with belief or with irony; Rasa seemed to be trusting him, however, and so Luet gave her tentative trust as well.

"I understand that it was you who brought warning," said Rashgallivak.

Luet looked at Aunt Rasa in surprise. "He'll tell no one else," said Aunt Rasa. "I have his oath. We don't want to involve you in the politics of murder, my dear. But Rash had to know it, so that he didn't think my Wetchik had lost his mind. Wetchik left him detailed instructions, you see, to do something quite mad."

"Close everything down," said Rashgallivak. "Dismiss all but the fewest possible employees, sell off all the pack animals, and liquidate the stock. I'm to hold only the land, the buildings, and the liquid assets, in untouchable accounts. Very suspicious, if my master is innocent. Or so some would say. *Do* say."

"Wetchik's absence wasn't known for half an hour before Gaballufix was at Wetchik's house, demanding as the head of the Palwashantu clan that all the property of the Wetchik family be turned over to him. He had the audacity to refer to my mate by his birth name, Volemak, as if he had forfeited his right to the family title."

"If my master has really left Basilica permanently," said Rashgallivak, "then Gaballufix would be within his rights. The property can never be sold or given away from the Palwashantu."

"And I'm trying to persuade Rashgallivak that it was *your* warning of immediate danger that caused Wetchik to flee, not some plot to leave the city and take the family fortune with him."

Luet understood her duty now, in this conversation. "I did speak with Nafai," Luet told Rashgallivak. "I warned him that Gaballufix meant to murder Wetchik and Roptat—or at least my dream certainly seemed to suggest that."

Rashgallivak nodded slowly. "This will not be enough to bring charges against Gaballufix, of course. In Basilica, even *men* are not tried for acts they plotted but never performed. But it's enough to persuade me to resist Gaballufix's efforts to obtain the property."

"I was mated with him once, you know," said Rasa. "I know Gabya very well. I suggest you take extraordinary measures to protect the fortune—liquid assets particularly."

"No one will have them but the head of the house of Wetchik," said Rashgallivak. "Madam, I thank you. And you, little wise one."

He said not another word, but left immediately. Not at all like the more stylish men—artists, scientists, men of government and finance—whom Luet had met in Aunt Rasa's salon before. That sort of man always lingered, until Aunt Rasa had to force their departure by feigning weariness or pretending that she had pressing duties in the school—as if her teaching staff were not competent to handle things without her direct supervision. But then, Rashgallivak was of a social class that could not reasonably contemplate mating with one like Aunt Rasa, or any of her nieces.

"I'm sorry you didn't get more sleep," said Aunt Rasa, "but glad that you happened to wake up at such a fortunate time."

Luet nodded. "So much of last night I felt as if I were walking in my sleep, perhaps I only needed half as much this morning."

"I would send you back to bed at once," said Aunt Rasa, "but I must ask you a question first."

"Unless it's something we've studied recently in class, I won't know the answer, my lady."

"Don't pretend you don't know what I'm talking about."

"Don't imagine that I actually understand anything about the Oversoul."

Luet knew at once that she had spoken too flippantly. Aunt Rasa's eyebrows rose, and her nostrils flared—but she contained her anger, and spoke without sharpness. "Sometimes, my dear, you forget yourself. You pretend to take no special honor to yourself because the Oversoul has made a seer of you, and yet you speak to me with impertinence that no other woman in this city, young or old, would dare to use. Which should I believe, your modest words or your proud manner?"

Luet bowed her head. "My words, Mistress. My manner is the natural rudeness of a child."

Laughing, Aunt Rasa answered, "*Those* words are the hardest to believe of all. I'll spare you my questions after all. Go back to bed now—but this time in your own bed—no one will disturb you there, I promise."

Luet was at the door of the salon when it opened and

a young woman burst in, forcing her back inside the room.

"Mother, this is abominable!" cried the visitor.

"Sevet, I'm so delighted to see you after all these months—and without a word of notice that you were coming, or even the courtesy of waiting until I invited you into my salon."

Sevet—Aunt Rasa's oldest daughter. Luet had seen her only once before. As was the custom, Rasa did not teach her own daughters, but rather had given them to her dear friend Dhelembuvex to raise. This one, her oldest, was mated with a young scholar of some note—Vas?—but it hadn't hampered her career as a singer with a growing reputation for having a way with pichalny songs, the low melancholy songs of death and loss that were an ancient tradition in Basilica. There was nothing of pichalny about her now, though—she was sharp and angry, and her mother no less so. Luet decided to leave the room at once, before she overheard another word.

But Aunt Rasa wouldn't allow it. "Stay, Luet. I think it will be educational for you to see how little this daughter of mine takes after either her mother *or* her Aunt Dhel."

Sevet glared sharply at Luet. "What's *this*—are you taking charity cases now?"

"Her mother was a holy woman, Sevya. I think you may even have heard the name of Luet."

Sevet blushed at once. "I beg your pardon," she said.

Luet had no idea how to answer, since of course Luet *was* a charity case and therefore mustn't show that she had been offended by Sevet's slur.

Aunt Rasa saved her from having to think of a proper response. "I will consider that pardon has been begged and granted all around, and now we may begin our conversation with perhaps a more civil tone."

"Of course," said Sevet. "You must realize that I came here straight from Father."

"From your rude and offensive manner, I assumed you had spent at least an hour with him."

"Raging, the poor man. And how could he do otherwise, with his own mate spreading terrible lies about him!"

"Poor man indeed," said Aunt Rasa. "I'm surprised that little waif of a mate of his would have the courage to speak out against him—or the wit to make up a lie, for that matter. What has she been saying?"

"I meant *you*, of course, Mother, not his *present* mate, nobody thinks of *her*."

"But since I lapsed dear Gabya's contract fifteen years ago, he can hardly regard *me* as having a duty to refrain from telling the truth about him."

"Mother, don't be impossible."

"I'm never impossible. The most I ever allow myself is to be somewhat unlikely."

"You're the mother of Father's two daughters, both of us more than slightly famous—the *most* famous of your offspring, and all for honorable things, though of course little Koya's career is only at its beginning, with not a myachik of her own yet—"

"Spare me your rivalry with your sister, please."

"It's only a rivalry from *her* point of view, Mother—*I* don't even pay attention to the fact that her singing career seems a bit sluggish at the outset. It's always harder for a lyric soprano to be noticed—there are so *many* of them, one can hardly tell them apart, unless one is the soprano's own loving, loyal sister."

"Yes, I use you as an example of loyalty for all my girls."

For a moment Sevet's face brightened; then she realized her mother was teasing her, and scowled. "You really are too nasty with me."

"If your father sent you to get me to retract my remarks about this morning's events, you can tell him that I know what he was planning from an undoubtable source, and if he doesn't stop telling people that Wetchik was plotting murder, I'll bring my evidence before the council and have him banned."

"I can't—I can't tell Father that!" said Sevet.

"Then don't," said Aunt Rasa. "Let him find out when I do it."

"*Ban* him? Ban *Father*?"

"If you had studied more history—though come to think of it, I doubt that Dhelya taught you all that much anyway—you'd know that the more powerful and famous a man is, the more likely he is to be banned from Basilica. It's been done before, and it will be done again. After all, it's Gabya, not Wetchik or Roptat, whose soldiers roam the streets, pretending to protect us from thugs that Gabya probably hired in the first place. People will be glad to see him go—and that means they'll find it *useful* to believe every bit of evidence I bring."

Sevet's face grew grave. "Father may be a bit prone to rage and a little sneaky in business, Mother, but he's no murderer."

"Of course he's not a murderer. Wetchik left Basilica and Gabya would never dare to kill Roptat without Wetchik there to blame it on. Though I think that if Gabya had known at the time that Wetchik had fled, he would certainly have killed Roptat the moment he showed up and then used Wetchik's hasty departure as proof that my dear mate was the murderer."

"You make Father sound like a monster. Why did you take him as a mate, then?"

"Because I wanted to have a daughter with an extraordinary singing voice and no moral judgment whatsoever. It worked so well that I renewed with him for a second year and had another. And then I was done."

Sevet laughed. "You're such a silly thing, Mother. I *do* have moral judgment, you know. And every other kind. It was Vasya I married, not some second-rate actor."

"Stop sniping at your sister's choice of· mate," said Aunt Rasa. "Kokor's Obring is a dear, even if he has no talent whatsoever and not the breath of a chance that Koya will actually bear him a child, let alone renew him."

"A *dear*," said Sevet. "I'll have to remember what that word *really* means, now that you've told me."

Sevet got up to leave. Luet opened the door for her. But Aunt Rasa stopped her daughter before she left.

"Sevya, dear," she said. "The time may come when you have to choose between your father and me."

"The two of you have made me do that at least once a month since I was very small. I've managed to sidestep you both so far, and I intend to continue."

Rasa clapped her hands together—loudly, a sharp report like one stone striking another. "Listen to me, child. I know the dance that you've done, and I've both admired you for the way you did it and pitied you for the fact that it was necessary. What I'm saying to you is that soon—very soon—it may no longer be possible to do that dance. So it's time for you to look at both your parents and decide which one deserves your loyalty. I do not say *love*, because I know you love us both. I say loyalty."

"You shouldn't speak to me this way, Mother," said Sevet. "I'm not your student. And even if you succeeded in banning Father, that still wouldn't mean I'd have to choose between you."

"What if your father sent soldiers to silence me? Or

tolchocks—which is more likely. What if it was a knife he paid for that slit your mother's throat?"

Sevet regarded her mother in silence. "Then I'd have a pichalny song to sing indeed, wouldn't I?"

"I believe that your father is the enemy of the Oversoul, and the enemy of Basilica as well. Think about this seriously, my sad-voiced Sevet, think deep and long, because when the day of choosing comes there'll be no time to think."

"I have always honored you, Mother, for the fact that you never tried to turn me against my father, despite all the vile things he said about you. I'm sorry you have changed." With great dignity, Sevet swept herself from the room. Luet, still a bit stunned by the brutal nature of the conversation under the veneer of elegant speech, was slow to follow her out the door.

"Luet," whispered Aunt Rasa.

Luet turned to face the great woman, and trembled inside to see the tears on her cheeks.

"Luet, you must tell me. What is the Oversoul doing to us? What does the Oversoul plan?"

"I don't know," said Luet. "I wish I did."

"*If* you did, would you tell me?"

"Of course."

"Even if the Oversoul told you not to?"

Luet hadn't thought of such a possibility.

Aunt Rasa took her hesitation for an answer. "So," she said. "I wouldn't have expected otherwise—the Oversoul does not choose weak servants, or disloyal ones. But tell me this, if you can: Is it possible, is it *possible*, that there was no plot to kill Wetchik at all? That the Oversoul merely sent that warning to get him to leave Basilica? You must realize—I was thinking that—Lutya, what if the only thing the Oversoul was doing was getting rid of Issib and Nafai? It makes sense, doesn't it—they were interfering with the Oversoul, keeping her so busy that she couldn't speak·to anyone but them. Might she not have sent your vision to make sure they left the city, because *they* were threatening to *her*?"

Luet's first impulse was to shout her denial, to rebuke her for daring to speak so sacrilegiously of the Oversoul—as if it would act for its own private benefit.

But then, on sober reflection, she remembered with what wonderment Hushidh had told her of her realization that Issib and Nafai might well be the reason for the Oversoul's silence. And if the Oversoul thought that her ability to guide and protect her daughters was being hampered by these two boys, couldn't she act to remove them?

"No," said Luet. "I don't think so."

"Are you sure?"

"I'm never sure, except of the vision itself," said Luet. "But I've never known the Oversoul to deceive me. All my visions have been true."

"But this one would still be a true instrument of the Oversoul's will."

"No," said Luet again. "No, it couldn't be. Because Nafai and Issib had already stopped. Nafai even went and prayed—"

"So I heard, but then, so did Mebbekew, Wetchik's son by that miserable little whoreling Kilvishevex—"

"And the Oversoul spoke to Nafai and woke him up, and brought him outside to meet me in the traveler's room. If the Oversoul wanted Nafai to be still, she would have told him, and he would have obeyed. No, Aunt Rasa, I'm sure the message was real."

Aunt Rasa nodded. "I know. I knew it was. It would just be . . ."

"Simpler."

"Yes." She smiled ruefully. "Simpler if Gaballufix were

as innocent as he pretends. But not true to character. You know why I lapsed him?"

"No," said Luet. Nor did she want to know—by long custom a woman never told her reasons for lapsing a man, and it was a hideous breach of etiquette to ask or even speculate on the subject.

"I shouldn't tell, but I will—because you're one who must know the truth in order to understand all things."

I'm also a child, thought Luet. You'd never tell any of your *other* thirteen-year-olds about such things. You'd never even tell your daughter. But I, *I* am a seer, and so everything is opened up before me and I am forbidden to remain innocent of anything except joy.

"I lapsed him because I learned that he . . ."

Luet braced herself for some sordid revelation, but it did not come.

"No, child, no. Just because the Oversoul speaks to you doesn't mean that I should burden you with my secrets. Go, sleep. Forget my questions, if you can. I know my Wetchik. And I know Gaballufix, too. Both of them, down to the deepest shadow of their souls. It was for my daughters' sake that I wished to find some impossible thing, like Gabya's innocence." She chuckled. "I'm like a child, forever wishing for impossible things. Like your vision in the woods, before I drew you up to the portico. You saw all my most brilliant nieces, like a roll call of judgment."

Brilliant? Shedemei and Hushidh, yes, but Dol and Eiadh, those women of paint and tinsel?

"I was so happy to know that the Oversoul knew them, and linked them with me and you in the vision she sent. But where were my daughters, Lutya? I wish that you had seen my Sevya and my Koya. I do wish that—is that silly of me?"

Yes. "No."

"You should practice lying more," said Aunt Rasa, "so you'd be better at it. Go to bed, my sweet seer."

Luet obeyed, but slept little.

In the days that followed, the turmoil in the city increased, to the point where it was almost impossible for classes to continue in Aunt Rasa's house. It wasn't just the constant worry, either. It was the disappearance of so many faces, especially from the younger classes. Only a few children were withdrawn because their parents disapproved of Rasa's political stance. Children were being taken out of every teaching household, great or common, and restored to their families; many families had even closed up their houses and gone on unnamed holidays to unknown places, presumably waiting for whatever terrible day was coming to be over.

How Luet envied Nafai and Issib, safe as they were in some distant land, not having to live in constant fear in this city that had so long been known by the poets as the Mountain of Peace.

As the petition for the banning of Gaballufix gained support in the council, Gaballufix himself became bolder in the way he used his soldiers in the streets. There were more of them, for one thing, and there was no more pretense of protecting the citizenry from tolchocks. The soldiers accosted whomever they wanted, sending women and children home in tears, and beating men who spoke up to them.

"Is he a fool?" Hushidh asked Luet one day. "Doesn't he know that everything his soldiers do gives his enemies one more reason to ban him?"

"He must know," said Luet, "and so he must want to be banned."

"Then hasten the day," said Hushidh, "and good riddance to him."

Luet waited for a vision from the Oversoul, some message of warning she should take to the council. Instead the only vision that came was a word of comfort to an old woman in the district of Olive Grove, assuring her that her long-lost son was still alive, and homebound on a ship that would reach port before too long. Luet didn't know whether to be comforted that the Oversoul still took the time to answer the heartfelt prayers of broken-hearted women, or infuriated that the Oversoul was spending time on such matters instead of healing the city before it tore itself apart.

Then at last the most feared moment came. The doorbell clanged, and strong fists beat on the door, and when the door was thrown open, there stood a dozen soldiers. The servant who opened the door screamed, and not just because they were armed men in perilous times. Luet was among the first to come to the aid of the terrified servant, and saw what had so unnerved her. All the soldiers were in identical uniforms, with identical armor and helmets and charged-wire blades, as might be expected—but inside those helmets, each one also had an identical face.

It was Rasa's oldest niece, Shedemei, the geneticist, who spoke to the soldiers. "You have no legitimate business here," she said. "No one wants you. Go away."

"I'll see the mistress of this household or I'll never go," said the soldier who stood in front of the others.

"She has no business with you, I said."

But then Aunt Rasa was there, and her voice rang clear. "Close the door in the face of these hired criminals," she said.

At once the lead soldier laughed, and reached his hand to his waist. In an instant he was transformed before their eyes, from a youngish, dead-faced soldier to a middle-aged man with a grizzled beard and fiercely bright eyes, stout but not soft-bellied, clothed not in armor but in quietly elegant clothing. A man of style and power, who thought the whole situation was enormously amusing.

"Gabya," said Aunt Rasa.

"How do you like my new toys?" asked Gaballufix, striding into the house. Women and girls and young boys parted to make way for him. "Old theatrical equipment, out of style for centuries, but they were in a stasis bubble in the museum and the maker machines still remembered how to copy them. Holocostumes, they're called. All my soldiers have them now. It makes them somewhat hard to tell apart, I admit, but then, I have the master switch that can turn them all off when I want."

"Leave my house," said Rasa.

"But I don't want to," said Gaballufix. "I want to talk to you."

"Without *them*, you can speak to me any time. You know that, Gabya."

"I knew that *once*," said Gaballufix. "Truth to tell, O noblest of my mates, my unforgotten bed-bundle, I knew that my soldiers would never impress you—I just wanted to show you the latest fashion. Soon all the best people will be wearing them."

"Only in their coffins," said Aunt Rasa.

"Do you want to hold this conversation in front of the children, or shall we retire to your sacred portico?"

"Your soldiers wait outside the door. The *locked* door."

"Whatever you say, O mother of my duet of sweet songbirds. Though your door, with all its locks, would be no barrier if I wanted them inside."

"People who are sure of their power don't have to brag," said Aunt Rasa. She led the way down the corridor as Shedemei closed and barred the front door in the soldiers' faces.

Luet could still hear the conversation between Aunt

Rasa and Gaballufix even after they turned a corner and were out of sight.

"I don't *have* to brag," Gaballufix was saying. "I do it for the sheer joy of it."

Instead of answering, though, Aunt Rasa called loudly down the corridor,

"Luet! Hushidh! Come with me. I want witnesses."

At once Luet strode forward, with Hushidh beside her at once. Because Aunt Rasa had brought them up, they didn't run, but their walk was brisk enough that they had turned the corner and could hear Gaballufix's last few whispered words before they caught up. ". . . not afraid of your witchlets," he was saying.

Luet gave no sign that she had heard, of course. She knew that Hushidh's face would be even less expressive.

Out on the portico, Gaballufix made no pretense of respecting the boundary of Aunt Rasa's screens. He strode directly to the balustrade, looking out at the view that was forbidden to the eyes of men. Aunt Rasa did not follow him, so Luet and Hushidh also remained behind the screens. At last Gaballufix returned to where they waited.

"Always a beautiful sight," he said.

"For that act alone you could be banned," said Aunt Rasa.

Gaballufix laughed. "Your sacred lake. How long do you think it will go unmuddied by the boots of men, if the Wetheads come? Have you thought of that—have Roptat and your beloved Volemak thought of it? The Wetheads have no reverence for women's religion."

"Even less than you?"

Gaballufix rolled his eyes to show his disdain for her accusation. "If Roptat and Volemak have their way, the Wetheads would own this city, and to them, the view from this portico would not be a view of holy land—it would all be city property, undeveloped land, potential building sites and hunting parks, and an extraordinary lake, with both hot and cold water for bathing in any weather."

Luet was astonished that so much of the nature of the lake had been explained to him. What woman had so forgotten herself as to speak of the sacred place?

Yet Aunt Rasa said nothing of the impropriety of his words. "Bringing the Wetheads is Roptat's plan. Wetchik and I have spoken for nothing but the ancient neutrality."

"Neutrality! Fools and children believe in that. There *is* no neutrality when great powers collide!"

"In the power of the Oversoul there is neutrality and peace," said Aunt Rasa, calm in the face of his storm. "She has the power to turn aside our enemies so they see us not at all."

"Power? Maybe he has power, all right, this Oversoul—but I've seen no evidence that he saves poor innocent cities from destruction. How did it happen that I alone am the champion of Basilica, the only one who can see that safety lies only in alliance with Potokgavan?"

"Save the patriotic speeches for the council, Gabya. In front of me, there's no point in hiding behind them. The wagons offered some easy profit. And as for war—you know so little about it that you think you want it to come. You think that you'll stand beside the mighty soldiers of Potokgavan and drive off the Wetheads, and your name will be remembered forever. But *I* tell you that when you stand against your enemy, you'll stand alone. No Potoku will be there beside you. And when you fall your name will be forgotten as quickly as last week's weather."

"*This* storm, my dear lapsatory mate, has a name, and will be remembered."

"Only for the damage that you caused, Gabya. When

Basilica burns, every tongue of flame will be branded Gaballufix, and the dying curse of every citizen who falls will have your name in it."

"Now who fancies herself a prophet?" said Gaballufix. "Save your poetics for those who tremble at the thought of the Oversoul. And as for your banning—succeed or fail, it makes no difference."

"You mean that you don't intend to obey?"

"*Me*? Disobey the *council*? Unthinkable. No one will find me in the city after I am banned, you can be sure of that."

But with those words he reached down and switched on his holocostume. At once he was armored in illusion, his face an undetectable mask of a vaguely menacing soldier, like any of the hundreds of others he had so equipped. Luet knew then that he had no intention of obeying a banning. He would simply wear this most perfect of disguises, so that no one could identify him. He would stay within the city, doing whatever he wanted, flouting the council's edicts with impunity. Then the only hope of freeing the city from his rule would not be political. It would be civil war, and the streets would flow with blood.

Luet knew from her eyes that Aunt Rasa understood this. She looked steadily at the empty eyes that stared back at her from Gaballufix's holocostume. She said nothing when he turned and left; said nothing at all, in fact, until at last Luet took Hushidh's hand and they walked away to the edge of the portico, to look out over the Valley of Women.

"There's nothing between them anymore," said Hushidh. "I could see it fall, the last tie of love or even of concern. If he died tonight, she would be content."

To Luet this seemed the most terrible of tragedies. Once these two had been joined together in love, or something like love; they had made two babies, and yet, only fifteen years later, the last tie between them was broken now. All lost, all gone. Nothing lasted, nothing. Even this forty-million-year world that the Oversoul had preserved as if in ice, even it would melt before the fire. Permanence was always an illusion, and love was just the disguise that lovers wore to hide the death of their union from each other for a while.

TEN

TENTS

Wetchik had pitched his tents away from any road, in a narrow river valley near the shores of the Rumen Sea. They had reached it at sunset, just as a troop of baboons moved away from their feeding area near the river's mouth, toward their sleeping niches in the steepest, craggiest cliff in the valley wall. It was the baboons' calls and hoots that guided them during the last of their journey; Elemak was careful to lead them well upstream of the baboons. "So we don't disturb them?" Issib asked.

"So they don't foul our water and steal our food," said Elemak.

Before Father allowed them to unburden the camels and water them, before they ate or drank anything themselves, Father sat atop his camel and gestured toward the stream. "Look—the end of the dry season, and yet it still has water in it. The name of this place is Elemak from now on. I name it for you, my eldest son.

Be like the river, so that the purpose of your life is to flow forever toward the great ocean of the Oversoul."

Nafai glanced at Elemak and saw that he was taking the peroration with dignity. It was a sacred moment, the naming of a place, and even if Father laced the occasion with a sermon, Elemak knew that it was an honor, a sign that Father acknowledged him.

"And as for this green valley," said Father, "I name it Mebbekew, for my second son. Be like this valley, Mebbekew, a firm channel through which the waters of life can flow, and where life can take root and thrive."

Mebbekew nodded graciously.

There was nothing named for Issib and Nafai. Only a silence, and then Father's groan as his camel knelt for him to dismount. It was well after dark before they finally had the tents pitched, the scorpions swept outside, and the repellents set in place. Three tents—Father's, of course, the largest though he was only one man. The next largest for Elya and Meb. And the smallest for Issib and Nafai, even though Issib's chair took up an exorbitant amount of room inside.

Nafai couldn't help but brood about the inequities, and when, in the darkness of the tent, Issib asked him what he was thinking, Nafai went ahead and voiced his resentment. "He names the river and the valley for *them*, when Elemak's the one who was working with Gaballufix, and Mebbekew's the one who said all those terrible things to him and left home and everything."

"So?" said Issib, ever sympathetic.

"So here we are in the smallest tent. We've got two extras, still packed up, both of them larger than this one." Having undressed himself, Nafai now helped Issib undress—it was too hard for him, without his floats.

"Father's making a statement," said Issib.

"Yes, and I'm hearing it, and I don't like it. He's saying, Issib and Nafai, you're *nothing*."

"What was he going to do, name a *cloud* after us?" Issib fell silent for a moment as Nafai pulled the shirt off over Issib's head. "Or did you want him to name a bush for you?"

"I don't care about the naming, I care about justice."

"Get some perspective, Nafai. Father isn't going to sort out his children according to who's the most obedient or cooperative or polite from hour to hour. There's a clear ranking involved in the assignment of tent space here." Nafai laid his brother on his mat, farthest from the door. "The fact that Elya doesn't have a tent to himself, but shares with Meb," said Issib, "that's putting him in his place, reminding him that he's *not* the Wetchik, he's just the Wetchik's boy. But then putting us in such a tiny tent tells Elya and Meb that he *does* value them and honor them as his oldest sons. He's at once rebuking and encouraging them. I think he's been rather deft."

Nafai lay down on his own mat, near the door, in the traditional servant's position. "What about us?"

"What *about* us? Are you going to rebel against the Oversoul because your papa gave you a tiny tent?"

"No."

"Father trusts us to be loyal while he works on Elya and Meb. Father's trust is the greatest honor of all. I'm proud to be in this tent."

"When you put it that way," said Nafai, "so am I."

"Go to sleep."

"Wake me if you need anything."

"What can I need," said Issib, "when I have my chair beside me?"

Actually, the chair was down near his feet, and it was almost completely useless when Issib wasn't sitting in it. Nafai was puzzled for a moment, until he realized that

Issib was giving him a small rebuke: Why are *you* complaining, Nafai, when being away from the magnetics of the city means that I can't use my floats, and have to be tended to like an infant? It must be humiliating for Issib to have me undress him, thought Nafai. And yet he bears it uncomplaining, for Father's sake.

Deep in the night, Nafai awoke, instantly alert. He lay there listening. Was it Issib who had called him? No—his brother was still taking the heavy, rhythmic breaths of sleep. Did he wake, then, because he was uncomfortable? No, for the sand under his mat made the floor more, not less, comfortable than his room at home. Nor was it the cold, nor the distant howling of a wild dog, and it could not have been the baboons, because they always slept the night in perfect silence.

The last time Nafai had awakened like this, he had found Luet outside in the traveler's room, and the Oversoul had spoken in the night to Father.

Was I dreaming, then? Did the Oversoul teach me in my sleep? But Nafai could remember no dreams. Just the sudden wakefulness.

He got up from his mat—quietly, so as not to disturb Issya—and slid under the netted fabric draped across the door. It was cooler outside the tent than inside, of course, but they had traveled far enough south that autumn hadn't yet arrived in this place, and the waters of the Rumen Sea were much warmer and more placid than the ocean that swept along the coastline east of Basilica.

The camels were peacefully asleep in their small temporary corral. The wards at the corners kept away even the smallest of animals not yet inured to the sound frequencies and pheromones the wards gave off. The stream splashed a syncopated music over the rocks. The leaves in the trees rustled now and then in the night breeze. If there is any place in all of Harmony where a man could sleep in peace, it's here, thought Nafai. And yet I couldn't sleep.

Nafai walked upstream and sat on a stone beside the water. The breeze was cool enough to chill him a little; for a moment he wished he had dressed before leaving the tent. But he hadn't intended to get up for the day. Soon enough he'd go back inside.

He looked around him, at the low hills not that far off. Unless a person stood on one of those hills, there was no sign of a watered valley here. Still, it was a wonder that no one lived here but the tribe of baboons downstream of them, that there wasn't even a sign of human habitation. Perhaps it had not been settled because it was so far from any trade route. The land here was barely enough to support a few dozen people, if it were all cultivated. It would be too lonely or unprofitable to settle here. Robbers might use it as a refuge, but it was too far from the caravan routes to be convenient for them. It was exactly what Father's family needed, during this time of exile from Basilica. As if it had been prepared for them.

For a moment Nafai wondered if perhaps this valley had not even existed until they needed it. Did the Oversoul have such power that it could transform landforms at will?

Impossible. The Oversoul might have such powers in myth and legend, but in the real world, the Oversoul's powers seemed to be entirely confined to communication—the sharing of works of art throughout the world, and mental influence over those who received visions or, more commonly, the stupor of thought that the Oversoul used to turn people away from forbidden ideas.

That's why this place was empty till we came, thought Nafai. It would be a simple thing for the Oversoul to make desert travelers get stupid whenever they thought of turning toward the Rumen Sea near here. The Oversoul prepared it for us, not by creating it out of the rock, not by causing some hidden pool of water to burst forth into a spring, a stream for us, but rather by keeping other people away from here, so that it was empty and ready for us when we came.

The Oversoul has some great purpose here, plans within plans. We listen for its voice, we heed the visions it puts into our minds, but we're still puppets, uncertain why our strings are being pulled, or what our dance will lead to in the end. It isn't right, thought Nafai. It isn't even good, for if the followers of the Oversoul are kept blind, if they can't judge the Oversoul's purpose for themselves, then they aren't freely choosing between good and evil, or between wise and foolish, but are only choosing to subsume themselves in the purposes of the Oversoul. How can the Oversoul's plans be well-served, if all its followers are the kind of weak-souled people who are willing to obey the Oversoul without understanding?

I will serve you, Oversoul, with my whole heart I'll serve you, if I understand what you're trying to do, what it *means*. And if your purpose is a good one.

Who am I to judge what's good and what isn't?

The thought came into Nafai's mind, and he laughed silently at his own arrogance. Who am I, to set myself up as the judge of the Oversoul?

Then he shuddered. What put such a thought into my mind? Couldn't it have been the Oversoul itself, trying to tame me? I will *not* be tamed, only persuaded. I will not be coerced or led blindly or tricked or bullied—I am willing only to be convinced. If you don't trust your own basic goodness enough to tell me what you're trying to do, Oversoul, then you're confessing your own moral weakness and I'll never serve you.

The moonlight sparkling on the shifting surface of the stream suddenly became sunlight reflected from metal satellites orbiting perpetually around the planet Harmony. In his mind's eye, Nafai saw how, one by one, the satellites stumbled in their orbit and fell, burning themselves into dust as they entered the atmosphere. The first human settlers of this world had built tools that would last ten or twenty million years. To them that had seemed like forever—it was longer than the existence of the human species, many times over. But now it had been forty million years, and the Oversoul had to do its work with only a quarter as many satellites as it had had in the beginning, barely half as many as it had had for the first thirty million years. No wonder the Oversoul had weakened.

But its plans were no less important. Its purpose still needed to be served. Issib and Nafai were right—the Oversoul had been set in place by the first human settlers in this place, for one purpose only: to make Harmony a world where humanity would never have the power to destroy itself.

Wouldn't it have been better, thought Nafai, to change humanity so it no longer *desired* to destroy itself?

The answer came into his mind with such clarity that he knew it was the answer of the Oversoul. No, it would not have been better.

But why? Nafai demanded.

An answer, many answers poured into his mind all at once, in such a burst that he could make no sense of them. But in the moments after, the moments of growing clarity, some of the ideas found language. Sentences as clear as if they had been spoken by another voice. But it was not another voice—it was Nafai's own voice, making a feeble attempt to capture in words some straggling remnant of what the Oversoul had said to him.

What the voice of the Oversoul said inside Nafai's mind was this: If I had taken away the desire for violence then humanity would not have been humanity. Not that human beings need to be violent in order to be human, but if you ever lose the will to control, the will to destroy, then it must be because you *chose* to lose it. My role was not to force you to be gentle and kind; it was to keep you alive while you decided for yourselves what kind of people you wanted to be.

Nafai was afraid to ask another question, for fear of drowning in the mental flood that might follow. And yet he couldn't leave the question unasked. Tell me slowly. Tell me gently. But *tell* me: What have we decided?

To his relief, the answer wasn't that same rush of pure unspeakable idea. This time it seemed to him as if a window had been opened in his mind, through which he could see. All the actual scenes, all the faces he saw, they were memories, things he had seen or heard of in Basilica, things that were already in his mind, ready for the Oversoul to draw on them, to bring them to the surface of his mind. But now he saw them with such clear understanding that they took on power and meaning beyond anything in his experience before. He saw memories of business dealings he had seen. He saw plays and satires he had watched. Conversations in the street. A holy woman being raped by a gang of drunken worshipers. The scheming of men who were trying to win a mating contract with a woman of note. The casual cruelty of women who played their suitors against each other. Even the way Elemak and Mebbekew had treated Nafai—and the way he had treated them. It all spoke of the willingness of people to hurt each other, the burning passion to control what other people thought and did. So many people, in secret, subtle ways, acted to destroy people—and not just their enemies, either, but also their friends. Destroying them for the pleasure of knowing that they had the power to cause pain. And so few who devoted their lives to building other people's strength and confidence. So few who were true teachers, genuine mates.

That's what Father and Mother are, thought Nafai. They stay together, not because of any gain, but because of the gift. Father doesn't stay with Mother because she is good for *him*, but rather because together they can do good for us, and for many others. Father entered into the politics of Basilica these last few weeks, not because he hoped to gain by it, the way Gaballufix did, but because he genuinely cared more about the good of Basilica than about his own fortune, his own life. He could walk away from his fortune without a second look. And Mother, her life is what she creates in the minds of her students. Through her girls, her boys, she is trying to create tomorrow's Basilica. Every word she breathes in the school is designed to keep the city from decay.

And yet they're losing. It's slipping away. The Oversoul would help them if it could, but it hasn't the power or influence that it once had; and anyway, it hasn't the freedom to act to make people goodhearted, only to keep their malice within fairly narrow boundaries. Spite and malice, that was the lifeblood of Basilica today; Gaballufix is only the man who happens to best express the poisonous heart of the city. Even those who hate him and fight against him are generally doing it, not because they are good and he is evil, but because they resent the fact that he is achieving dominance, when they had hoped for dominance for themselves.

I *would* help, said the silent voice of the Oversoul in Nafai's mind. I *would* help the good people of Basilica. But there aren't enough of them. The will of the city is for destruction. How then can I keep it from being destroyed? If Gaballufix fails in his plans, the city will raise up some other man to help it kill itself. The fire will come because the city craves it. They are far too few, those who love the living city instead of desiring to feed from its corpse.

Tears flowed from Nafai's eyes. *I didn't understand. I never saw the city this way.*

That's because you are your mother's son, your father's heir. Like all human beings, you assume that behind the masks of their faces, other people are fundamentally like yourself. But it isn't always so. Some of them can't see other people's happiness without wanting to destroy it, can't see the bonds of love between friends or mates without wanting to break them. And many others, who aren't malicious in themselves, become their tools in the hope of some short-term gain. The people have lost their vision. And I haven't the power to restore it. All that's left, Nafai, is my memory of Earth.

"Tell me about Earth," whispered Nafai.

Again a window opened in his mind, only now it was not memories of his own. Instead he was seeing things he had never seen before. It overwhelmed him; he could hardly make sense of the things he saw. Bright glass-and-metal caskets speeding along gray-ribbon highways. Massive metal houses that rose up in the air, skidding along the face of the sky on slender, fragile wedges of painted steel. Tall polyhedral buildings with mirrored faces, reflecting each other, reflecting the yellow sunlight. And there amid them, shacks made of paper and cast-off metal, where families watched their babies die with bloated bellies. People tossing balls of fire at each other, or great gouts of flame flowing out of hoses. And completely inexplicable things: one of the flying houses passing over a city, dropping something that seemed as insignificant as a turd, only suddenly it burst into a ball of flame as bright as the sun, and the entire city under it was flattened, and the rubble burned. A family sitting at a huge table, covered in food, eating ravenously, then leaning over and vomiting on ragged beggars that clung hopelessly to the legs of their chairs. Surely this vision was not literal, but figurative! Surely no one ever would be so morally bankrupt as to eat more than he needed, while others were dying of hunger before their eyes! Surely anyone who could think of a way to make the sky burst into flame so hot it could destroy a whole city at once, surely such a person would kill himself before he'd ever let anyone know the terrible secret of that weapon.

"Is this Earth?" he whispered to the Oversoul. "So beautiful and monstrous? Is this what we were?"

Yes, came the answer. It's what you were, and it's what you will be again, if I can't find a way to re-awaken the world to my voice. In Basilica there are many who eat their fill of food, and then eat more, while they know how many there are who haven't enough. There's a famine only three hundred kilometers to the north.

"We could use wagons to carry food there," said Nafai.

The Gorayni have such wagons. They carry food, too—but the food is for the soldiers that came to conquer the famine-ravaged land. Only when they had subdued the people and destroyed their government did they bring food. It was the slops a swinekeeper brings to his herd. You feed them now in order to hear them sizzle later.

The visions continued—for hours, it seemed at the time, though later Nafai would realize that it could only have been a few minutes. More and more memories of Earth, with ever more disturbing behavior, ever stranger machines. Until the great fire, and the spaceships rising up from the smoke and ice and ash that remained behind.

"They fled because they had destroyed their world."

No, said the Oversoul. They fled because they longed to begin again. At least those who came to Harmony came, not because Earth was no longer fit for them, but because they believed they were no longer fit for Earth. Billions had died, but there was still fuel and life enough on Earth for perhaps a few hundred thousand humans to survive. But they couldn't bear to live on the world they had ruined. We'll go away, they said to each other, while the world heals itself. During our exile, we will also learn healing, and when we return we'll be fit to inherit the land of our birth, and care for it.

So they created the Oversoul, and brought it with them to Harmony, and gave it hundreds of satellites to be its eyes, its voice; they altered their own genes to give themselves the capacity to receive the voice of the Oversoul inside their own minds; and they filled the Oversoul with memories of Earth and left it to watch over their children for the next twenty million years.

Surely in that time, they told each other, our children will have learned how to live together in harmony. They will make the name of this planet come true in their lives. And at the end of that time, the Oversoul will know how to bring them home, to where the Keeper of Earth is waiting for them.

"But we aren't ready," said Nafai. "After twice that time, we're as bad as ever, except that you've kept us from developing the power to turn all the life of this planet into ashes and ice."

The Oversoul put the thought into Nafai's mind: By now the Keeper has surely done its part. The Earth is ready for our return. But the people of Harmony aren't ready yet to come. I have kept all the knowledge of Earth for all these years, waiting to tell you how to build the houses that fly, the starships that will bring you home to the world of your birth; but I dare not teach you, because you'd use the knowledge to oppress and finally to obliterate each other.

"Then what are you doing?" asked Nafai. "What is your plan? Why have you brought us out here?"

I can't tell you yet, said the Oversoul. I'm not sure of you yet. But I've told you what you wanted. I've told you my purpose. I've told you what I've already accomplished, and what is yet to be accomplished. I haven't changed—I'm the same today as I was when your forebears first set me in place to watch over you. My plans are all designed to prepare humanity to return to the Keeper of Earth, who waits for you. It's all I live for, to make humankind fit to return. I am the memory of Earth, all that remains of it, and if you help me, Nafai, you will be part of accomplishing that plan, if it can be accomplished at all.

If it can be accomplished at all.

The overwhelming sense of the presence of the Oversoul in his mind was gone, suddenly; it was as if a great fire inside him had suddenly gone out, as if a great rushing river of life inside him had gone abruptly dry. Nafai sat there on the rock beside the river, feeling spent, exhausted, empty, with that last despairing thought still lingering in his heart: If it can be accomplished at all.

His mouth was dry. He knelt by the water, plunged in his hands, and drew the cupped water to his mouth to drink. It wasn't enough. He splashed into the water, his whole body, not with the reverent attitude of prayer, but with a desperate thirst; he buried his head under the water and drank deep, with his cheek against the cold stone of the riverbed, the water tumbling over his back, his calves. He drank and drank, lifted his head and shoulders above the water to gasp in the evening air, and then collapsed into the water again, to drink as greedily as before.

It was a kind of prayer, though, he realized as he emerged, freezing cold as the water evaporated from his skin in the breeze of the dark morning.

I am with you, he said to the Oversoul. I'll do whatever you ask, because I long for you to accomplish your purpose here. I will do all that I can to prepare us all to return to Earth.

He was chilled to the bone by the time he got back to the tent, not dripping wet anymore, but not dry, either. He lay trembling on his mat for a long time, warmed by the air in the tent, by the heat of Issib's body, until at last he was able to sleep.

There was a lot of work to do in the morning; tired though he was, Nafai had no chance to sleep late, but rather staggered through his jobs, slow and clumsy enough that Elemak and even Father barked at him angrily. Pay attention! Use your head! Not till the heat of the afternoon, when they took the nap that desert dwellers knew was as much a part of survival as water, did Nafai have a chance to recover from his night-walking, from his vision. Only then he couldn't bear to sleep. He lay on his mat and told Issib everything that he had seen, and what he had learned from the Oversoul. When he was finished, Issib had tears streaking his face, and he slowly and with great exertion reached out a hand to clasp Nafai's. "I knew there had to be some purpose behind it," whispered Issib. "This makes so much sense to me. It fits everything. How lucky you were, to hear the voice of the Oversoul. Even more clearly than Father did, I think. As clearly as Luet, I think. You are like Luet."

That made Nafai a little uncomfortable, for a moment at least. He had resented or ridiculed Luet in his own mind, and sometimes in his words. The contemptuous word *witch* had come so easily to his lips. Was this what she felt, when the Oversoul sent her a vision? How could I have ridiculed her for that?

He slept again, and woke, and they finished their work: a permanent corral for the camels, made of piled stones bonded with a gravitic field powered by solar collectors; refrigeration sheds for storing the dried food that would keep them for a year, if it took that long before they could return to Basilica; wards and watches placed around the perimeter of the valley, so that no one could come near enough to see them without them noticing him in return. They built no fires, of course—in the desert, wood was too precious to burn. They took it farther, though; they would cook nothing, because an inexplicable heat source might be detectable. The warmth of their bodies was all the infrared radiation they dared to give off, and the electromagnetic noise put out by their wards and watches, the gravitic field, the refrigeration, the solar collectors, and Issib's chair was not strong enough to be picked up much beyond their perimeter, except with instruments far more sensitive than anything passing marauders or caravans were likely to have. They were as safe as they could make themselves.

At dinner, Nafai commented on how unnecessary it all was. "We're on the errand of the Oversoul," he said. "The Oversoul has kept people away from here all these years, keeping it ready for us—it would have kept on keeping people away."

Elemak laughed, and Mebbekew hooted hysterically. "Well, Nafai the theologian," said Meb, "if the Oversoul's so capable of keeping us safe, why did it send us out here into the landscape of hell instead of letting us *safely* stay home?"

"How are you such an expert on the Oversoul, anyway, Nafai?" asked Elemak. "That mother of yours obviously had you spending too much time with witches."

For once, Nafai stifled his angry retorts. There was no point in arguing with them, he realized. But then, he had realized that many times before, and hadn't been able to hold his tongue. The difference now, Nafai realized, was that he was no longer just Nafai, the youngest of Wetchik's boys. Now he was the friend and ally of the Oversoul. He had more important concerns than arguing with Elya and Meb.

"Nafai," said Father, "your reasoning is faulty. Why should we make the Oversoul waste time watching over us, when we're perfectly capable of watching over ourselves?"

"Of course not, Father," said Nafai. His remark had been foolish. It would be wrong for them to burden the Oversoul, when the Oversoul needed them to help bear its burden. "I'm sorry."

Elemak smiled slightly, and Mebbekew rolled his eyes and laughed again. "Listen to them," he said. "Rational men, supposedly, talking about whether the Oversoul should tend our camels or not."

"It was the Oversoul that brought us here," said Father, rather coldly.

"It was *you* who made us go," said Mebbekew, "and Elemak who guided us."

"It was the Oversoul who warned me to leave," said Father, "and the Oversoul that brought us to this well-watered valley."

"Oh, yes, of course, I forgot," said Meb. "I thought that was a vulture circling, but instead it was the Oversoul, leading the way."

"Only a fool jokes about what he doesn't understand," said Father.

"Only an old *joke* goes around calling rational men *fools*," said Mebbekew. "*You're* the one who sees plots and conspiracies in shadows, Father."

"Shut up," said Elemak.

"Don't tell me to shut up."

"Shut up," said Elemak again. He turned slowly to meet Mebbekew's hot glare. Nafai could see that, though Elya's eyes were heavy lidded, as if he were barely awake, his eyes were afire as he stared Meb down.

"Fine," said Mebbekew, turning back to his dinner, smearing cold bean paste onto another cracker. "I guess I'm the only one who doesn't think camping trips are just the funnest thing."

"This isn't a camping trip," said Father. "It's exile."

"What I can't figure out," said Mebbekew, "is what *I* did to deserve exile."

"You're my son," said Father. "None of us were safe there."

"Come on," said Meb. "We were all safe."

"Drop it," said Elemak. Again he met Mebbekew's glare.

Now Nafai began to recognize the trend here. Elemak didn't like Mebbekew talking about whether there was really a plot against Father, or whether there had been any reason for the whole family to flee into the desert. It was a sensitive subject, and Nafai guessed that both of them knew more than they were willing to talk about. If they had some dark secret, it would be no surprise if Elemak chose to conceal it by never letting a conversation even come near it, while Mebbekew would be far more likely to try to hide it behind a smokescreen of casual denials and mocking lies.

"You *both* know that Father's life was in danger in Basilica," said Nafai.

The way they both looked at him told him that what he suspected was true. If they had been innocent, they would have taken his remark to mean only that he expected them to believe in Father's vision. Instead, they took it much more harshly.

"What makes you think you know what *other* people know?" demanded Elemak.

"If *you're* so sure Father's life was in danger," said Meb nastily, "maybe that means *you* were in on the conspiracy."

Again, their reactions were typical: Elemak, defending against Nafai's accusation by saying, in essence, You can't prove anything, while Mebbekew was defending himself by turning the accusation back on Nafai.

Now let them realize what they are confessing, thought Nafai. "What conspiracy?" he asked. "What are you talking about?"

Mebbekew immediately realized how much he had revealed. "I just assumed—that you were saying that we had some advance knowledge or something."

"If you *knew* of a plot against Father's life," said Nafai, "you would have *told* him, if you were any kind of decent human being. And you certainly wouldn't sit here whining about how we didn't really need to leave the city."

"I'm not the one who whines, little boy," said Mebbekew. His anger had lost all subtlety now. He wasn't sure how to interpret Nafai's words, which is why Nafai had spoken the way he did. Let Meb wonder—does Nafai know something, or not?

"Shut up, Meb," said Elemak. "And you, too, Nafai. Isn't it bad enough we're in exile here without you at each other's throats?"

Elya the peacemaker. Nafai wanted to laugh. But then—maybe it was true. Maybe Elemak *hadn't* known—maybe Gaballufix had never taken him into his confidence on that subject. Of course he hadn't, Nafai realized. Elya might be Gaballufix's half-brother, but he was still Wetchik's son and heir. Gaballufix would never be absolutely sure whose side Elemak was really on. He could use Elya as a go-between, a messenger to Father—but he could never trust him with real knowledge.

That would explain Elemak's effort to keep Meb silent, too; he wanted to hide his involvement with Gaballufix, yes, but there was no murder plot to keep secret. How could Nafai have imagined it? Besides, if they were out in the desert as part of the Oversoul's plan, didn't that mean that Elemak and Mebbekew were *also* part of the plan? Here I am, filled with suspicion about them, harboring exactly the kind of malice that is going to destroy Basilica. How can I claim to be on the Oversoul's side, if I let myself behave like the kind of person who doesn't trust even his own brother?

"I'm sorry," said Nafai. "I shouldn't have said that."

Now they all looked at him in true startlement. It took a moment for Nafai to realize that it was the first time in his life that he had ever actually apologized for some nasty thing he said to one of his brothers, without first being wrestled into submission and locked in some painful grip.

"That's all right," said Mebbekew. His voice was full of wonder—his eyes, though, radiated with triumphant contempt.

You think my apology means I'm weak, Nafai said silently to him. But it doesn't. It means I'm trying to learn how to be strong.

It was then that Nafai told Father and Elemak and Mebbekew something of the visions the Oversoul showed him during the night. He didn't get far into his account, though.

"I'm tired," said Elemak. "I don't have time for this."

Nafai looked at him in astonishment. Didn't have time to hear the plan of the Oversoul? Didn't have time to learn about the hope of humankind returning to Earth?

Mebbekew also yawned pointedly.

"You mean you don't even care?" asked Issib.

Elemak smiled at his crippled brother. "You're too trusting, Issya," he said. "Can't you see what's happening here? Nafai can't stand not to be the center of attention. He can't prove himself by being useful or even marginally competent—so he starts having visions. Next thing you know, Nyef's going to be giving us the Oversoul's orders and bossing us all around."

"No I'm not," said Nafai. "I saw the visions."

"Right," said Mebbekew. "I saw visions last night, too. Girls that you don't even have the gonads to dream of, Nafai. I'll believe in your dreams of the Oversoul as soon as you're willing to marry one of the girls from my dreams. I'll even give you one of the prettiest ones."

Elemak was laughing, and even Father smiled a little. But Mebbekew's taunts only filled Nafai with rage. "I'm telling you the truth," he insisted. "I'm telling you what the Oversoul is trying to accomplish!"

"I'd rather think about what the girls in my dreams were trying to accomplish," said Meb.

"That's enough of such vulgarity," said Father. But he was chuckling. It was the cruelest blow, that Father plainly believed Elemak about Nafai making up his visions.

So when Elemak and Mebbekew left to see to the animals, Nafai remained behind with Father and Issib.

"Why aren't you going?" said Father. "Issib can't help with chores like that, here where his floats don't work. But *you* can help."

"Father," said Nafai, "I thought that *you* would believe me."

"I do," said Father. "I believe you honestly want to be part of the work of the Oversoul. I honor you for it, and maybe some of your dreams *did* come from the Oversoul.

But don't try to tell such things to your older brothers. They won't take it from you." He chuckled bitterly. "They barely endure it coming from me."

"I believe Nafai," said Issib. "They weren't dreams, either. He was awake, by the stream. I saw him come back to the tent, wet and cold."

Nafai had never been so grateful to anyone, to have Issib back him up. He didn't have to do it, either. Nafai had half expected Issib to *stop* believing him, if Father wasn't taking him seriously.

"I believe him, too," said Father. "But the things you were saying were far more specific than anything the Oversoul tells us in visions. So I'm just saying that there's probably a kernel of truth in what you're saying. But most of it must have come from your own imagination, and I for one am not going to try to sort it out, not tonight."

"I believed *you*," said Nafai.

"Not at first," said Father. "And we don't trade belief like favors. We give belief and trust where they are earned. Don't expect me to be any quicker to believe *you* than you were to believe *me*."

Abashed, Nafai got up from the rug. Father's tent was so large that he didn't have to duck when he stood upright. "I was blind at first, when you told me what you saw. But now I see that you're deaf, so you can't possibly hear the things I've heard."

"Help your brother back into his chair," said Father. "And watch how you speak to your father."

That night, in their tent, Issib tried to console Nafai. "Father's the *father*, Nafai. It can't be good news to him, to have his youngest son getting so much more information from the Oversoul than *he's* ever received."

"Maybe I'm more attuned to it or something," said

Nafai. "I can't help it. But what difference does it make, who the Oversoul talks to? Wasn't Gaballufix supposed to believe Father, even though Father is below his station in the Palwashantu clan?"

"Below his office, maybe," said Issib, "but not below his *station*. If Father had wanted to be clan leader, he would have been chosen—he's the Wetchik by birth, isn't he? That's why Gaballufix has always hated him—because he knows that if Father hadn't despised politics, he could have wiped out Gaballufix's power and influence easily, right from the start."

But Nafai didn't want to talk about Basilican politics now. He fell silent, and in the silence spoke again to the Oversoul. You have to make Father believe me, he said. You have to show Father what's really happening. You can't show me a vision and then not help me persuade Father.

"*I* believe you, Nyef," Issib whispered. "And I believe in what the Oversoul is trying to do. Maybe that's all the Oversoul needs, did you think of that? Maybe the Oversoul doesn't need Father to believe you right now. So just accept it. Trust the Oversoul."

Nafai looked at Issib, but in the darkness of night inside the tent couldn't tell whether his brother's eyes were open or not. Had it really been Issib speaking, or was Issib asleep, and had Nafai heard the words of the Oversoul in Issib's voice?

"Someday, Nyef, it may come down to what Elemak said. You may have to give orders to your brothers. Even to Father. Do you think the Oversoul will leave you to yourself then?"

No, it couldn't be Issib. He was hearing the Oversoul in Issib's voice, saying things that Issib could never say. And now that he realized that he had his answer, he could sleep again. But before he slept, questions formed in his mind:

What if the Oversoul is telling me more than Father, not because it's part of a plan, but simply because I'm the only one who can hear and understand?

What if the Oversoul is counting on me to be able to figure out a way to persuade the others, because the Oversoul hasn't the power to convince them anymore?

What if I'm truly alone, except for this one brother who believes me—the one brother who is crippled, and therefore can do nothing?

Belief is not *nothing*, said the voice whispering in Nafai's mind. Issib's belief in you is the only reason you haven't yet started doubting it yourself.

Tell Father, Nafai pleaded as he drifted off to sleep. Speak to Father, so he'll believe me.

The Oversoul spoke to Father in the night, but not with any vision that Nafai had hoped for.

"I saw the four of you going back to Basilica," said Father.

"About time," said Mebbekew.

"Going back, but for a single purpose," said Father. "To get the Index and bring it back to me."

"The Index?" asked Elemak.

"It's been with the Palwashantu clan from the beginning. I believe that it might have been the reason the clan has preserved its identity for all these years. We were once called the Keepers of the Index, and my father told me that it was the right of the Wetchiks to use it."

"Use it for what?" asked Mebbekew.

"I'm not sure," said Father. "I've only seen it a few times. My grandfather left it with the clan council when he began traveling, and my father never made any serious effort to get it back after Grandfather died. Now it's in

Gaballufix's house. But from the name of it, I'd guess it's a guide to a library."

"How useful," said Elemak. "And for *this* you're sending us back to Basilica? To get an object whose purpose you don't understand."

"To get it and bring it back to me. No matter the cost."

"Do you mean that?" said Elemak. "No matter the cost?"

"It's what the Oversoul wanted. I knew it—even though I—it's not my personal feeling. I want you back here, safe."

"Right," said Mebbekew. "It's as good as done. No problem."

"Should we bring back more supplies?" asked Nafai.

"There won't be more supplies," said Father. "I told Rashgallivak to sell all the caravaning supplies."

Nafai could see Elemak's face turn red under its dark tan. "So when our exile is over, Father, how do you propose we restore our business?"

It was a cusp of decision, Nafai could see that: Elemak was facing the fact that Father's actions were intended to be irrevocable. If Elya was going to rebel, it would be over this, which he could only see as the squandering of his inheritance. So Father spoke plainly in giving his reply.

"I don't propose to restore anything," said Father. "Do what I say, Elemak, or it won't matter to *you* what the Wetchik fortune is or is not."

There it was. It couldn't be more clear. If Elemak was ever to be Wetchik himself, he'd better obey the present Wetchik's commands.

Mebbekew cackled. "I never liked all those smelly animals anyway," said Mebbekew. "Who needs them?" His message was just as clear: I'll gladly become Wetchik in your place, Elemak—so please go ahead and get Father really really angry.

"I'll bring you your Index, Father," said Elemak. "But why send these others? Let me go alone. Or let me take Mebbekew, and keep the younger boys with you. Neither of them will be any use to me."

"The Oversoul showed me all four of you going," said Father. "So all four of you will go to Basilica, and all four of you will return. Do you understand me?"

"Perfectly," said Elemak.

"Last night you made fun of Nafai, because he claimed to be having visions," said Father. "But I tell you that you could learn a great deal from Nafai and Issib. *They*, at least, are making an effort to help. All I hear from my two elder sons is complaint."

Mebbekew glared pointedly at Nafai, but Nafai was more afraid of Elemak, who simply gazed steadily at Father through heavy-lidded eyes. Last night you wouldn't believe me, Father, Nafai said silently. Now today you make my brothers hate me even more than before.

"You know much, Elemak, Mebbekew," said Father, "but in all your learning you never seem to have mastered the concept of loyalty and obedience. Learn it from your younger brothers, and then you'll be worthy of the wealth and honors you aspire to."

That's it, Nafai said silently. I'm dead now. I might as well be a worm in their bread, the way they'll treat me on this whole trip. I'd rather stay home than go under these conditions, Father, thank you kindly.

"Father, I'll do all that you ask," said Elemak. But his voice was quiet and cold, and it made Nafai sick at heart to hear it.

Elemak sullenly set about preparing for the trip. As Nafai expected, Elya ignored him completely when he asked what he should do to help. And Mebbekew shot him such a look that Nafai felt a thrill of fear run through him. He wants me dead, he thought. Meb wants me to die.

Since he wasn't permitted to help, and since it would obviously be wiser for him to be as inconspicuous as possible for the next while, Nafai went back to the tent he shared with Issib and helped his brother pack up, which mostly consisted of wrapping his floats and stowing them in a bag. He could see in Issib's eyes as he looked hungrily at the floats that it didn't matter to Issib what Elemak or Mebbekew thought of him—he wanted to be back where his body was usable again, where he was free and didn't have to be dressed or taken outside to void himself like an infant or a pet. Such a prisoner he is, trapped in that body, thought Nafai. And then the job was done and Issib was in his chair, hovering over the ground looking like some ill-tempered monarch on his throne. He was impatient to go, impatient to return to Basilica.

All of them are, thought Nafai. But none for the right reason. None is eager to get there because of a desire to help with the Oversoul's plan.

Nafai found himself by the water's edge, gripping a bough that was ten centimeters thick, bending it between his hands, bending it like a horseshoe. It fought him, but it also gave under the strength of his grip.

"Don't break that," said Father.

Nafai turned, startled. He let go of the branch, and it whipped upward, out of control; some leaves slapped him in the face.

"It took so long for it to grow," said Father.

"I wasn't going to break it."

"It was on the verge," said Father. "I know plants. You don't. You were on the verge of breaking it."

"I'm not that strong."

"Stronger than you know." Father sized him up. "Fourteen." He laughed a little. "Your mother's genes, not mine, I fear. I look at you and I see—"

"Mother?"

"What Issib might have been, body as well as mind. Poor boy."

Poor boy. Why don't you look at me sometime, Father, and see *me*. Instead of some imaginary child. Instead of a little boy who makes up visions, why don't you see what I am: a man who heard the voice of the Oversoul, even more clearly than you.

"I'm afraid," said Father.

Nafai looked his father in the eye. Is he teasing me?

"I'm sending you into something more dangerous than I think your brothers understand. But *you* understand, don't you, Nafai."

"I think."

"After what you've seen," said Father. But it was as much a question as an answer. What was he asking, whether Nafai knew the truth about Elya and Meb? It couldn't be that, because Father didn't know about them himself. No, Father was asking whether Nafai really saw visions.

Nafai's first reaction was to be furious—hurt, offended. But then he realized that he was wrong to feel that way. Because Father had a right to ask, a right to let it take time to believe in his visions, just as Issib had said. He was *trying* to accept the idea of Nafai as a fellow servant of the Oversoul.

"Yes," said Nafai. "I've seen. But nothing about the Index."

"Gaballufix won't let it go," said Father. "In the vision he did, but the Oversoul can't see everything. The Index isn't just something you borrow. It's very powerful."

"Why? What can it do?"

"I don't know what it can do, of itself. But I know that it means power. I know that among the Palwashantu, the one who keeps the Index is the one who has the trust of the clan. The greatest honor. Gabya won't give it up. He'll kill first. And that's where I'm sending my sons."

The look on Father's face was angry. Nafai realized: He's furious at the Oversoul for requiring him to do this.

And then, as Nafai watched, Father mastered his rage, and his face grew calm. "I hope," said Father quietly, "I hope the Oversoul has really thought all this through."

"Father," Nafai said, "I'll go and do whatever the Oversoul has asked us to do. Because I know that the Oversoul wouldn't ask us to do it without preparing some way for it to be accomplished."

Father studied his face for the longest time. Then he smiled. Nafai had never seen such a smile on his father's face. The relief in it, the trust. "Not an act, is it," said Father. "You're not just saying what you think I want to hear."

"When have any of your sons said anything that they thought you wanted to hear?" asked Nafai.

Now Father laughed, tossed his head back and roared. "Never!" he cried. And then, just as suddenly, the laughter stopped. Father took Nafai's head between his hands, his large hands, callused and wiry and horned and rough from years of handling bark and leather harnesses and raw stone, and holding those great palms on either side of Nafai's face, he leaned forward and kissed him on the mouth. "My son," he whispered. "My son."

For a moment they stood there together, beside the tree, beside the water, until they heard footsteps and turned. It was Elemak, his face still sour and angry. "Time to go," he said. "If we're going to make any kind of progress today, anyway."

"By all means go," said Father. "I wouldn't delay you for a moment."

In a few minutes they were on their camels again, heading back to the city.

ELEVEN

BROTHERS

Basilica was not in sight yet, but Elemak knew the road. Knew it as well as he knew the skin of his own face in the mirror, every mole of the surface, every peak or declivity that snatched at the razor and bled. He knew the shadows of every hour of the day, where water might be waiting after a rain, where robbers might hide.

It was to one of those places that Elemak now led his brothers. They had not been on the road itself for some time, but till now had always kept it in sight. Now they left it behind, and soon the ground grew rough enough that he made them stop, dismount.

"Why are we stopping here?" asked Mebbekew.

"The floats are working," said Issib. "That's how close we are, I can move without the damn chair."

Elemak eyed his crippled brother and shook his head. "Not reliably. We'll dismount the chair—you'll have to use it."

Issib was usually so compliant, but not now. "Use it yourself, if you think it's so comfy."

"Look at you," said Elemak. "It's intermittent at best, with the float. You'll start losing it and fall over and we can't have that. Use the chair."

"It'll get better as we get closer."

"We aren't getting closer," said Elemak.

"Then what are we doing?" demanded Mebbekew.

"We're going down into this arroyo, where the magnetics of Basilica certainly do *not* reach, and there we're going to wait until nightfall."

"And then?" asked Mebbekew. "Since you seem to think you're in command here, I thought perhaps I'd ask."

Elemak had faced this kind of thing many times before from fellow travelers on the road, even sometimes from hired men. He knew how to handle it—brutal suppression, instant and public, so no doubt was left in anyone's mind of who was in charge. So instead of answering Mebbekew he took him by the arms—thin, womanly arms, an *actor,* by the Oversoul!—and slammed him back against a wall of rock. The sudden movement spooked one of the camels. It stamped, spat, blatted out a protest. For a moment Elemak was afraid he would have to go calm the animal—but no, Nafai had it, was calming it. The boy was actually useful for something besides sucking up to Father. Not like Mebbekew, who was reliable only in his unreliability. Why Gaballufix ever confided in him, Elemak never knew. Surely Gabya knew that Mebbekew would let something slip. Even if he didn't tell Father directly about the plot, he surely told *someone*—how else could Father have known?

There was raw panic in Meb's eyes, and pain, too—his head had smacked sharply against the stone. Well, good, thought Elemak. Think about pain a little bit. Think hard before you question my authority on the road.

"I *am* in command here," Elemak whispered.

Meb nodded.

"And I say that we'll wait until dark."

"I was joking," Meb whined. "You don't have to be so *serious* about everything, do you?"

Elemak almost hit him for that. Serious? Don't you realize that there inside Basilica, the most powerful, dangerous man in the city is almost certainly convinced that we betrayed him and warned Father to flee? To Mebbekew, Basilica was a city of pleasure and excitement. Well, there might be excitement indeed inside those walls, but of pleasure not a speck.

But Elemak did not hit Meb, because that would be excessive, and provoke resentment instead of respect among the others. Elemak knew how to lead men, and knew how to control his own feelings and not let them interfere with his judgment. He eased his grip on Mebbekew and then turned his back on him, to show his absolute confidence in his own leadership, and his contempt for Mebbekew. Meb would not dare attack him, even with his back turned.

"At nightfall, what will happen is simple enough. I will go inside the city, and I'll speak to Gaballufix, and I'll bring out the Index."

"No," said Issib. "Father said we should all go."

Another insubordination—but not a serious one, and it was Issib, the cripple, so a show of force was completely out of the question. "And we all *have* come. But *I* *know* Gaballufix. He's my half-brother—as much my brother as any of you. I have the best chance of talking him into giving us the Index."

"You mean we came all this way," said Issib, "and

you're going to make me stay here, in this metal coffin of mine, and never get any closer to the city than this?"

"Better your chair than a real coffin," said Elemak. "I tell you that if you think going into the city will be fun, you're a fool. Gaballufix is dangerous."

"He *is*," said Nafai. "Elya is right. If we all go in together, then a failure might mean all of us killed—or imprisoned—or anything. If only one goes, then even if he fails the rest of us might still be able to accomplish something."

"If I fail, then go back to Father," said Elemak.

"Right," said Meb. "I'm sure we've all memorized the road."

"It can't be you," said Issib. "Of all of us, you're the only one necessary to lead us home."

"I'll go," said Nafai.

"Right," said Elemak, laughing. "*You*, the one who looks most like Lady Rasa. I don't think you get the picture, Nyef—one look at you and Gaballufix is reminded of the one humiliation he's never been able to avenge—Lady Rasa lapsing his contract after two daughters and within a week making a new contract with Father—which she hasn't broken yet. Walk into Gaballufix's house alone, with no one in the city even knowing you're there, Nyef, and your life is over."

"Me, then," said Mebbekew.

"You'd only go get drunk or find some woman," said Elemak, "and then come back and lie and say you spoke to Gaballufix and he said no."

Mebbekew seemed to toy with the idea of getting angry, but then thought better of it. "Possibly," said Mebbekew. "But it's a better plan than I've heard from anyone else."

"What about mine?" said Issib. "*I* go and ask. What is Gaballufix going to do to a cripple?"

Elemak shook his head. "Break you in half with his bare hands, if he feels like it."

"And you were *friends* with him?" asked Mebbekew.

"Brothers. We're brothers. We don't get to choose our brothers, you know," said Elemak. "We just make do with what we get."

"He wouldn't hurt a cripple," Issib said again. "It would shame him in front of his own men."

Elemak knew that Issib was right. The cripple might be the best one to get into and out of an interview with Gaballufix alive. The trouble was that Elemak *couldn't* let Issib or Nafai talk to the man. Gaballufix might say something that would compromise Elemak. No, it had to be Elemak himself, so he could talk to Gabya alone, maybe smooth things over, persuade his brother that it wasn't him that warned Father of the plan to kill Roptat under circumstances that would implicate and discredit Wetchik. If they ever learned of this, Meb and Issya and Nyef wouldn't understand that in the long run it was the best plan for Father's own sake. If they didn't neutralize Father this way, then eventually it might be Father who died under mysterious circumstances.

"I'll tell you what," said Elemak. "Since we all disagree about who should go, let's let the Oversoul decide. A time-honored tradition—we draw lots."

He reached down and scooped up a handful of pebbles from the ground. "Three light ones, one dark one." But as he spoke, Elemak made sure a fourth light-colored stone was tucked out of sight between two of his fingers. "Dark stone goes into the city."

"All right," said Meb, and the others nodded.

"I'll hold the stones," said Nafai.

"Nobody holds the stones, my dear little boy," said Elemak. "Too much chance of cheating, yes?" Elemak reached up to a shelf in the rock, out of sight where they were standing. There he again made a show of mixing up the four stones. "When I'm through mixing them, though, you can mix them yourself, Nafai," he said. "That way we know that nobody knows which stone is which."

Nafai immediately strode forward, reached up to the shelf of stone, and mixed the stones. Four of them, of course—Elemak knew he would feel four stones and be satisfied. What he couldn't possibly know was that the dark stone was now between Elemak's fingers, and the four stones on the shelf were all light.

"While you've got your hand up there, Nyef, go ahead and choose a stone."

Nafai, poor fool, came away with a light-colored stone and frowned at it. What did he expect? He was playing at a man's game. None of these boys seemed to realize that a man with Elemak's responsibilities would never have lasted on the open road if he didn't know how to make sure that drawing lots always turned out the way he wanted.

"Me now," said Issib.

"No," said Elemak. "My draw." That was another rule of the game—Elemak had to draw early, or somebody might grow suspicious and check the rocks and see that there was no dark one there. He reached up, made a show of fumbling with the rocks, and then came away with the dark one, of course—but with the extra light one also tucked between his fingers. When they checked, they'd find only two stones left there on the shelf.

"You knew by the feel of it," said Mebbekew.

"Don't be a bad sport," said Elemak. "If all goes well, maybe we can all go into the city. It all depends on how Gaballufix reacts, yes? And he's my brother—if anyone can persuade him, I can."

"I'm going inside no matter what," said Issib. "I'll wait

until you come back, but I'm not leaving here without going inside."

"Issya," said Elemak, "I can't promise that I'll let you go inside the walls of the city. But I *can* promise that before you leave here, you'll get close enough that you can use the floats. All right?"

Sullenly Issib nodded.

"Your word, though, that no one leaves this spot until I come back."

"What do we do if Gaballufix kills you?" asked Meb.

"He won't."

"What do we do," Meb insisted, "if you don't come back?"

"If I'm not back by dawn," said Elemak, "then I'm either dead or incapacitated. At that point, my dear brotherlets, I won't be in charge anymore and so I don't really care what you do. Go home, go back to Father, or go into the city and get laid or killed or lost, it will make not a speck of difference to me. But don't worry—I'll be back."

That gave them plenty to think about as he led them down the arroyo into a clear area where no one was likely to find them. "But look," said Elemak. "You can see the city walls from here. You can see High Gate."

"Is that the gate you'll be using?" asked Nafai.

"On the way in," said Elemak. "On the way out, I'll use any gate I can get to."

With that he left them, striding boldly away, wishing that he felt half as bold as the show he was putting on for them.

Entering the city through High Gate was nowhere near as difficult as it would have been at Market Gate—after all, there was no Gold Market to protect. Still, Elemak had to have his thumb scanned to prove his citizenship, and thus the city computer knew he had entered. Elemak had no doubt that even if Gabya's house computer wasn't tied directly to the city computers—which would be, of course, illegal—he certainly had informants in the city government, and if Gabya cared whether Elemak entered Basilica, he would know the information within moments.

Elemak was actually quite relieved not to be detained by the guard at the gate; it meant that Gaballufix had not put out his name for immediate arrest. Or else it meant that Gabya didn't yet have quite as much power in the city as he boasted about to his friends and supporters. Maybe it was still beyond his reach to issue orders to the gate guards to detain his personal enemies.

Am I his enemy? thought Elemak. His brother, yes. His friend, no. An ally of convenience for a while, yes. We both saw ways to get benefit from a closer relationship. But now will he see me as an old business deal gone sour, as a possibly useful friend, or as a traitor to be punished?

Elemak meant to go straight to Gaballufix's house, but once he was inside the city he couldn't bring himself to do it. He jogged from High Funnel up Library Street, then took Temple to Wing. Either Temple or Wing would have carried him near to Gabya's house, but by now Elemak was becoming more and more alarmed by the soldiers he was passing, or that were passing him. There were more of them, for one thing, than in the days before Father led them out into the desert, and even though he carefully avoided looking directly at them, he began to feel more and more uneasy about them. Finally, when he saw a group of a dozen turning onto Wing Street, he ducked into a doorway and then allowed himself to look at them directly as they passed.

Immediately he realized what was wrong. They were

all identical—the faces, the clothing, the weaponry, everything. "Impossible," he whispered. There could not be so many identical people in the world at the same time. The ancient stories of cloning flashed through his mind—witches and wizards who tried to rule the world by creating genetically identical copies of themselves, which inevitably (in the stories, at least) turned on their creators and killed them. But this was the real world, and these were Gabya's soldiers; he had no more notion how to clone than how to fly, and if he *could* make clones, he could certainly have chosen a better model than this nondescript, stupid-looking hulk that was going up and down the streets by dozens.

"It's all fakery," said a woman.

No one stood in the doorway with Elemak. Only when he stepped out did he see the speaker, an ageless, filthy wilder, naked except for the layers of grime and dust that covered her. Elemak was not one of those who saw wilders as objects of desire, though some of his friends used them as casually as if they were urinals for lust. He would have ignored her, except she seemed to be answering his whispered comment, and besides, whom could he speak to more safely than to an anonymous holy woman from the desert?

"How do they do it?" he asked. "Look all alike, I mean."

"They say it's an old theatre costume technique, much in vogue a thousand years ago."

She didn't talk like a desert woman. "How does it work?"

"It's a fine netting, worn like a cloak. A control at the waist turns it on and off. It automatically adjusts itself to the surrounding light—it becomes very bright in sunlight, much more subtle in moonlight or shadow. A very clever device."

Her voice sounded more and more refined the more she talked.

"Who are you?" he asked.

She looked into his face. "I am the Oversoul," she said. "And who are you, Elemak? Are you my friend or my enemy?"

For a moment Elemak stood in terror. He had been so worried about Gaballufix, so fearful that a soldier would recognize him, call out his name, and carry him off or perhaps even kill him on the spot, that to now be recognized by a madwoman in the street left him completely empty-headed. How do you hide when even the street beggars know your name? Only when *she* moved, inserting her index finger into her navel and twiddling it around as if she were stirring some loathsome mixture there, did his disgust overcome his fear and send him out into the street, running blindly away from her.

Thus his plan of casual, unobtrusive movement through the streets was ruined. He did have enough presence of mind, however, not to go directly to Gabya's house, not in *this* state of mind. Where else could he go, though? Habit would lead him to his mother's house— old Hosni kept a fine old house in The Wells, near Back Gate, where she meddled in politics and made and broke reputations of rising young men and women of government. But desire triumphed over custom, and instead of taking refuge with his mother, he found himself on the porch of Rasa's house.

He had studied here as a boy, of course, even before Father first mated with her; indeed, it was because his mother had placed him with Rasa that his father and his teacher first met. It had been vaguely embarrassing to have the other students gossip about the liaison between their mistress and Elya's father, and from then on he had never been fully comfortable there until he gratefully left off his schooling at the age of thirteen. Now, though, he came to Rasa's house, not as a student, but as a suitor—and one whose suit had long been welcomed.

For a moment, hesitating at the door, Elemak realized that he was doing exactly what he had forbidden his young brothers to do—he was conducting personal business when he was supposed to be on Father's errand. But whatever qualms he felt, he immediately dispelled them. His wooing of Eiadh was far more than pursuit of an advantageous match. Sometime in the last few months he had fallen in love with her; he desired her more than he had ever thought he could desire a woman. Her voice was music to him, her body an infinitely variable sculpture that astonished him with every movement. But as his devotion for her grew, he had become increasingly fearful that in her there was no matching increase of love for him. For all he knew, she still desired him only as the heir of the great Wetchik, who could provide her with enormous fortune and prestige. And if that was all she saw in him, all she felt for him, then recent events would turn her against him. There might be no advantage to her in marrying the Wetchik's heir *now*, with so much of the business being closed down and sold off. How would she respond to him now?

He pulled the cord; the bell rang. It was an old-fashioned bell, a deepish gong rather than the musical chimes that were all the fashion now. To his surprise, it was none other than Rasa herself who answered the door.

"A man comes to my door," she said. "A strong young man, with the dirt and sweat of the desert on his face. What am I to make of you? Are you bringing me word from my mate? Are you bringing more threats from Gaballufix? Are you here to carry off my niece Eiadh? Or have you come with fear in your heart, back to the house of your childhood schooling, hoping for a bath and a meal and four stout walls to keep you safe?"

All was said with such humor that Elemak's fear was dispelled. It felt good to have Rasa address him almost as an equal, and with genuine affection, too. "Father is well," he answered, "I haven't seen Gabya since I returned to the city, I hope to see Eiadh but have no plans for abduction at the moment, and as for the bath and the meal—I would accept such hospitality gratefully, but I would never have asked for it."

"I'm sure you wouldn't have," said Rasa. "You would have bounded in and expected Eiadh to be glad of your embrace when you smell like a camel and you spread dust with every step you take. Come in, Elemak."

As he luxuriated in the bath he again felt some guilt, thinking of his brothers waiting for him in the rocks through the heat of the day—but then, bathing and cleansing himself before seeing Gaballufix was the most sensible of plans. It would make him look far less desperate and give the clear message that he had friends in the city—a much better bargaining position. Unless Gaballufix saw it as further proof that Elemak had played a double game against him. Never mind, never mind. His clothing, freshly washed and aired, was laid out for him in the secator, and he slipped it on gratefully when he arose from the bath, letting the secator dry him off as he dressed. He disdained the hair oils—keeping the hair oil-free was one of the ways the pro-Potokgavan party identified themselves, refusing to resemble the Wetheads in any way.

Eiadh met him in Rasa's own salon. She seemed timid, but he took that as a good sign—at least she did not seem haughty or angry. Still, did he dare to take the liberties she had granted him at his last wooing? Or would that be too presumptuous now, seeing how his circumstances had changed. He strode toward her, but instead of seating himself beside her on the couch, he sank to one knee before her and reached for her hand. She let him—and then reached out her other hand and touched his cheek. "Are we strangers now?" she asked. "Are you unwilling to sit beside me?"

She had understood his hesitation, and this was the reassurance that he needed. Immediately he sat beside her, kissed her, put his hand at her waist and felt how she breathed so passionately, how she yielded to him so eagerly. They said little at first, at least in words; in actions she told him that her feelings for him were undiminished.

"I thought you were gone forever," she whispered, after long silence.

"Not from you," he said. "But I don't know what the future holds for me. The turmoil in the city, Father's exile—"

"Some say that your brother was plotting to kill your father—"

"Never."

"And others that your father was plotting to kill your brother—"

"Nonsense. Laughable. They're both strong-minded men, that's all."

"That's not *all*," said Eiadh. "Your father never came here with soldiers, threatening that he could come in whenever he wanted the way Gaballufix did."

"He came *here*?" said Elemak, angry. "For what?"

"He was Aunt Rasa's mate once, remember—they have two daughters. . . ."

"Yes, I think I've met them."

"Of course," she said, laughing. "They're your nieces, I know. And they're Nyef's and Issya's sisters, too—aren't families so complicated? But what I meant was, Gaballufix's coming wasn't what was strange. It's the *way* he came, with those soldiers in their horrible costumes so they all look so—inhuman."

"I heard it was holography."

"A very old theatrical device. Now that I've seen it, I'm glad that our actors use paint or, at the most, masks. Holographs are disturbing. Unnatural." She put her hand inside his shirt, slid it along his skin. It tickled. He trembled. "You see?" she said. "How could a holograph ever feel like that? How could anyone bear to be so *unreal*."

"I imagine they're still real enough under the holograph. And they can make faces at you without your knowing it."

She laughed. "Imagine being an actor, though, with something like that. How would anyone ever know your facial expressions?"

"Maybe they only used them for non-speaking roles—so the same actors could play dozens of roles with instant costume changes."

Eiadh's eyes widened. "I didn't know you were so knowledgeable about the theatre."

"I once courted an actress," said Elemak. He did it deliberately, knowing how it bothered most women to hear about old loves. "I thought she was beautiful then. You see, I had never seen *you*. Now I wonder if she was anything but a holograph."

She kissed him as a reward for the pretty compliment.

Then the door opened and Rasa came in. She had allowed them the socially correct fifteen minutes—perhaps a little longer. "So nice of you to visit us, Elemak. Thank you, Eiadh, for conversing with our guest while I was detained." It was the delicate pretense of courting, this custom of acting as if the suitor had come to call on the lady of the house, while the young woman being wooed was merely helping the lady to entertain her guest.

"For all your hospitality, I am grateful beyond expression," said Elemak. "You have rescued a weary traveler, my lady Rasa; I didn't know how near death I must have been, until your kindness made me so alive."

Rasa turned to Eiadh. "He's really very good at this, isn't he."

Eiadh smiled sweetly.

"Lady Rasa," said Elemak, "I don't know what the future will hold. I have to meet with Gaballufix today, and I don't know how that will turn out."

"Then *don't* meet with him," said Rasa, her expression turning quite serious. "He's become very dangerous, I think. Roptat is convinced that there was a plot to kill him in that meeting at the coolhouse, the day that Wetchik left. If Wetchik had been there, as agreed, Roptat would have walked right into a trap. I believe him—I believe Gaballufix has murder in his heart."

Elemak *knew* he had; but he also had no idea what might come if he confirmed Rasa's suspicions. For one thing, Rasa and Eiadh might wonder how Elemak could have known of such a plot, and if he did, why he didn't give warning to Roptat himself. Women didn't understand that sometimes to avoid the thousands of casualties of a bloody war, it was kindest and most peaceable to prevent the conflict with a single timely death. Good strategy could so easily be misunderstood as murder by the unsophisticated.

"Perhaps," said Elemak. "Does anyone really know someone else's heart?"

"I know someone's heart," said Eiadh. "And mine holds no secrets from him."

"If it isn't Elemak that you're referring to," said Rasa,

"then poor Elemak might start contemplating some hot-blooded crime of passion himself."

"Of course I'm talking about Elya," said Eiadh. She took his hand and held it in her lap.

"Lady Rasa, I'm not going to Gaballufix unnecessarily. Father sent me. There's something he needs that only Gaballufix can give."

"There's something we *all* need that only Gaballufix can give," said Rasa, "and that is *peace*. You might mention that to him when you see him."

"I'll try," said Elemak, though of course they both knew he wouldn't.

"What is it that Wetchik wants? Did he send any message to me?"

"I don't think he expected me to see you," said Elemak. "It was a vision from the Oversoul that sent me. Actually, all four of us came—"

"Even Issib! Here!"

"No. I left them outside the city, in a safe place. No one but the two of you will know they're here, if I can help it. With any luck, I'll get the Index and be out of the city before night, and then I have no idea when we'll be back again."

"The Index," whispered Rasa. "Then he can never come back."

Elemak was disturbed to hear her say that. "Why? What *is* it?"

"Nothing," she said. "I mean, I don't know. Only that—let's just say that if the Palwashantu realize that it's gone . . ."

"How can it be that important? I never heard of it before Father sent us back for it."

"No, it's not much spoken of," said Rasa. "There hasn't been much need for it, I guess. Or perhaps the Oversoul didn't want it known."

"Why? There are lots of indexes—dozens in every library in the world, hundreds in Basilica alone. Why is this one *the* Index?"

"I'm not sure," said Rasa. "Really I'm not. I only know that it's the only artifact from the men's worship that is also mentioned in the women's lore."

"Worship? How is it used?"

"I don't know. It never *has* been used, to my knowledge. I've never seen it. I don't even know what it looks like."

"Oh, *that's* good news," said Elemak. "I assumed it would be like any other index, and now you're telling me that Gaballufix could hand me anything and call it the Index and I'd never even know if he was cheating me."

Rasa smiled. "Elemak, you must understand. Unless he wishes to lose his leadership of the Palwashantu, he will *never* give you the Index."

Elemak was worried, but not dismayed. She clearly meant what she was saying, but that did not necessarily mean that she was right. Nobody really knew what Gaballufix might do, and if he thought he could get some advantage out of it, he'd trade away anything. Even their mother, if Gabya ever thought old Hosni might have some value. No, the Index could be had, if the price was right.

And the more he realized how important this mysterious Index was, the more he wanted it, not just to humor Father, not just as part of the game he was playing to take possession of the future, but for the sake of having the Index himself. If so much power came to the one who had it, then why shouldn't it be Elemak's?

"Elemak," Rasa said, "if you do, somehow, get the Index, you must realize that Gaballufix won't let you keep it. Somehow he'll get it back. You'll be in terrible danger then. What I'm telling you is—if you or any of your brothers need refuge from Gabya, then trust no man. Do you understand? Trust no *man*."

Elemak was unsure how to answer. He *was* a man; how did she expect him to respond to such advice?

"There are few women in this city," said Rasa, "who would not rejoice to see Gabya deprived of much of his power and prestige. They would gladly help the taker of the Index to escape the grasp of Gaballufix—even if the Index had been obtained by some means that ordinarily might be viewed as . . ."

"Criminal," said Elemak.

"I hate the thought of it," said Rasa. "But your Father is certainly right that it would be a harsh blow against Gaballufix, to lose the Index."

"It wasn't Father's idea, really," said Elemak. "He said it came to him in a dream. From the Oversoul."

"Then it might happen," she said. "It might. Perhaps . . . who knows whether the Oversoul might still have enough influence over Gaballufix to make him—what, temporarily stupid?"

"Stupid enough to give it to me?"

"And stupid enough not to find you and strike you down once you have it."

Elemak felt Eiadh's hand in his, her body leaning against him. I came here for refuge, and out of desire for you, Eiadh—but it was Rasa whose help I really needed. Imagine if I had gone into Gabya's house, not realizing how important this Index really is! "Lady Rasa, how can I thank you for all you've done for me."

"I fear that I've encouraged you to risk your life in an impossible endeavor," said Rasa. "I hate to think Gaballufix might really harm you, but the stakes in this gamble are very high. The future of Basilica is the prize—but I fear that the getting of the prize might harm the city so much that it isn't worth the game."

"Whatever happens," Elemak said, "you can be sure that I will return for Eiadh if I can, and if she'll have me."

"Even if you're a pariah and a criminal?" said Rasa. "Would you expect her to go with you even then?"

"Especially then!" cried Eiadh. "I don't love Elya for his money or his position in the city, I love him for himself."

"My dear," said Rasa, "you've never *known* him without his money or his position. How do you know who he'll be when he doesn't have them anymore?"

It was a cruel thing for her to say; Elemak could not believe that she had even thought such a thought, let alone brought it to her lips. "If Eiadh were the sort of woman whose heart followed her coveting, Lady Rasa, then she would not be a woman I could love, or even trust. But I *do* love her, and no woman is worthier of my trust."

Rasa smiled at him. "Oh, Eiadh, your suitor has such a beautiful vision of you. Do try to be worthy of it."

"The way my Aunt Rasa talks, you'd think she was trying to talk you *out* of loving me," said Eiadh. "Maybe she's the teensiest bit jealous of me for having such a fine man courting me."

"You forget," said Rasa. "I already have the father. What would I want with the son?"

It was a tense moment; things were being said that should not—*could* not—be said in polite company. Unless it was as a joke.

At last Rasa laughed. At last. They joined in her laughter eagerly, in relief.

"May the Oversoul go with you," said Rasa.

"Come back for me soon," said Eiadh. She pressed herself against him so tightly that he could feel where every part of her body touched him, as if she were imprinting herself on his flesh. Or perhaps taking the imprint of his body on herself. He embraced her back; she would have no doubt of his desire *or* his devotion.

It was midafternoon when Elemak got to Gaballufix's house. By habit he almost slipped down the alleyway to the private side entrance. But then he realized that his relationship with Gaballufix had changed in unpredictable ways. If Gaballufix regarded him as a traitor, then a secret arrival, completely unobserved, would give Gabya a perfect opportunity to be rid of him with no one the wiser. Besides, to come in the back way implied that Elemak was of a lower station than Gaballufix. He had had enough of that. He would come in openly, obviously, through the front entrance, like a man of importance in the city, an honored guest—with plenty of witnesses.

To his pleasure, Gaballufix's servants were deferential, ushering him inside immediately, and there was very little waiting before Elemak was led to the library, where he had always met with Gaballufix. Nothing seemed changed—Gabya arose from his chair and greeted Elemak with an embrace. They spoke like brothers, gossiping for a few minutes about people they both knew in Gaballufix's circle of friends and supporters. The only hint of tension between them was the way Gabya referred to Elemak's "hasty midnight departure."

"It wasn't my idea," said Elemak. "I don't know which of your people talked, but Father woke us up hours before dawn, and we were out on the desert before the meeting was to have taken place."

"I didn't like being taken by surprise," said Gaballufix. "But I know that sometimes these things are out of one's control."

Gabya was being understanding. Relief swept over him, and Elemak sat back more comfortably in his chair.

"You can imagine how worried I was. I couldn't very well slip away and warn you what was happening—Father was on us the whole time, not to mention my little brothers."

"Mebbekew?"

"It was all I could do to keep him from loosing all his sphincters on the spot. You should never have brought him into the plan."

"Shouldn't I?"

"How do you know he wasn't the one who warned Father?"

"I don't know that," said Gaballufix. "All I know is that my dear cousin Wetchik left, and my brother Elemak with him."

"At least he's out of the city. He won't be interfering with you anymore."

"Won't he?"

"Of course not. What can he do from some secluded valley in the desert?"

"He sent *you* back," said Gaballufix.

"With a limited objective that has nothing to do with the whole debate over war wagons and Potokgavan and the Wetheads."

"The debate has moved far beyond those concerns anyway," said Gaballufix. "Or, perhaps I should say, it has moved far *closer* than those concerns. So tell me—what is your father's limited objective, and how can I thwart him?"

Elemak laughed, hoping that Gabya was joking. "The best way to thwart him, I think, is to give him what he wants—a simple thing, *nothing,* really—and then we'll go away and it'll be between you and Roptat, the way you wanted it."

"I never wanted it between me and anybody," said Gaballufix. "I'm a peaceable man. I want no conflict. I thought I had a plan whereby conflict could be avoided, but at the last moment the people I counted on fell through."

He was still smiling, but Elemak realized that things were not as steady between them as he had hoped.

"Now tell me, Elya, what is the little thing that you think I should do for your father, solely because your father asks for it?"

"There's some Index," said Elemak. "An old thing that's been in the family for generations."

"An Index? Why would I have one of Wetchik's family indexes?"

"I don't know. I assumed you'd know which one he meant. He just called it 'the Index' and so I thought you'd know."

"I have dozens of indexes. Dozens." Then, suddenly, Gaballufix raised an eyebrow, as if he had just realized something. Elemak had seen him put on that same performance before, however, so he knew he was being played with. "Unless you mean—but no, that's absurd, that's nothing that ever belonged to the Wetchik house."

Elemak dutifully played along. "What are you talking about?"

"The *Palwashantu* Index, of course," said Gaballufix. "The whole reason for the clan having been established in the first place, back at the dawn of time. The most precious artifact in all of Basilica."

Of course he would play up the value of it. Just like any merchant who was eager to sell. Pretend that what he's selling is the most valuable thing ever to exist on the planet, so you can set some absurdly high price, and then work your way down.

"That can't be the one, then," said Elemak. "Father certainly didn't think it had that much value. It was more of a sentimental thing. His grandfather owned it, and lent it to the clan council for safekeeping during his travels. Now Father wants to take it with him on his travels."

"Oh, that's the one, then. His grandfather had it, but only as a temporary guardian. It was delegated to the Wetchik by the Palwashantu clan; he wearied of the burden, and gave it back. Now another guardian has been appointed—me. And I'm not weary. So tell your father I'm grateful that he was willing to help me with my duties, but I'll struggle on without his help for another few years, I think."

It was time for the price to be mentioned. Elemak waited, but Gaballufix said nothing.

And then, when the silence had stretched on for several minutes, Gaballufix arose from behind his table. "Anyway, my dear brother, I'm glad to see you back in the city. I hope you'll be here for a long time—I can use your support. In fact, now that your father seems to have run off, I'll certainly use my influence to try to get you appointed Wetchik in his place."

This was not at all what Elemak had expected. It asserted a relationship between Elemak and his own inheritance that was completely intolerable. "Father is Wetchik," he said. "He hasn't died, and when he does, I'm Wetchik without any help from anyone."

"Hasn't died?" asked Gaballufix. "Then where is he? I don't see my old friend Wetchik—but I do see the son that stands to profit most from his death."

"My brothers will also witness that Father is alive."

"And where are *they*?"

Elemak almost blurted out the fact that they were hiding not very far from the city walls. Then he realized that this was almost certainly what Gaballufix wanted most to know—who Elemak's allies were, and where they were hiding. "You don't think I'd enter the city alone, do you, when my brothers are as eager to come back to Basilica as I am!"

Of course Gaballufix knew that Elemak was lying—or, at the least, he knew that Elemak's thumbprint was the only one that had shown up at any of the city gates. What Gabya couldn't know was whether Elemak was merely bluffing, and his brothers were all far away in the desert—or whether they had circumvented the guards at the gates and even now were in the city, plotting some mischief that Gaballufix would need to worry about. Yet Gaballufix couldn't say anything about the fact that he knew Elemak was the only one to enter the city legally—it would be as much as admitting that he had complete access to the city's computers.

"I'm glad they were able to return to the pleasures of the city," said Gabya. "I hope they're careful though. A rough element has been brought into the city—mostly by Roptat and his gang, I'm afraid—and even though I'm helping the city by letting a few of my employees put in extra duty hours patrolling the streets, it's still possible for young men wandering alone through the city to get involved in unfortunate incidents. Sometimes dangerous ones."

"I'll warn them to look out."

"And you, too, Elemak. I worry for you, my brother. There are those who think your father was involved in a plot against Roptat. What if they take out their resentment on *you*?"

At that moment Elemak realized that his mission had failed. Gabya clearly *did* believe that Elemak had betrayed him—or else had concluded that Elemak was no longer useful and might even be dangerous enough to be worth killing. There was no hope now of getting anything through a pretense of polite brotherliness. But it might be worth taking a different tack.

"Come now, Gabya," said Elemak, "you know that you're the one who's been putting out that story about Father plotting against Roptat. That was the plan, remember? For Father to be found in the coolhouse with Roptat's murdered corpse. He wouldn't be convicted, but he'd be implicated, discredited. Only Father didn't come, and therefore Roptat wouldn't get close enough for your thugs to kill him, and now you're trying to salvage as much of the plan as you can. We sat here and talked about it—why should we pretend now that we don't both know exactly what's going on?"

"But we *don't* both know what's going on," said Gaballufix. "I haven't the faintest idea what you're talking about."

Elemak looked at him with contempt. "And to think I once believed you were capable of leading Basilica to greatness. You couldn't even neutralize your opposition when you had the chance."

"I was betrayed by fools and cowards," said Gaballufix.

"That's the excuse that fools and cowards always give for their failures—and it's always true, as long as you realize that it's self-betrayal they're talking about."

"You call *me* a fool and a coward?" Gaballufix was angry now, losing control. Elemak had never seen him like this, except a flash of temper now and then. He wasn't sure that he could handle this, but at least it wasn't the suave indifference that Gabya had been showing him till now. "At least I didn't sneak off in the middle of the night," said Gaballufix. "At least I didn't believe every story I was told, no matter how idiotic it was."

"And I did?" asked Elemak. "You forget, Gabya, *you* were the only one telling me stories. So now, I'd like to know, which of the stories was I idiotic to believe? That you were only acting in the best interests of Basilica? I never believed that one—I knew you were out for your own profit and your own power. Or perhaps you think I believed the story that you really loved my father and were really trying to protect him from getting into the political situation over his head. Do you think I actually believed *that* one? You've hated him since Lady Rasa lapsed you and remated with him, and you've hated him more every year that they've stayed together."

"I never cared about that!" said Gaballufix. "She's nothing to me!"

"Even now she's the only audience you try to please—imagine, going to her house and strutting like some cockbird, showing off for her. You should hear how she laughs about you now." Elemak knew, of course, that saying such a thing put Rasa in great danger—but this was a game with high risks, and Elemak couldn't hope to win it unless he took some chances. Besides, Lady Rasa could handle Gaballufix.

"Laughs? She doesn't laugh. You haven't even spoken with her."

"Look at me—do you see any of the filth of travel on my clothing? I bathed in her house. I'm going to mate with her favorite niece. She told me that she would as soon have mated with a rabbit as to spend another night with you."

For a moment he thought Gaballufix would draw a weapon and kill him on the spot. Then Gabya's face relaxed a little, into something like a smile. "Now I *know* you're lying," he said. "Rasa would never say something so crude."

"Of course I made it up," said Elemak. "I just wanted you to see who was the fool, believing any story that he heard."

"It's one thing to believe for a moment," said Gaballufix. "It's another story to keep believing and believing in the stupidest ideas."

It was in that moment that it first dawned on Elemak what the lie was that Gaballufix was saying he still believed. And Gabya was right—Elemak was a fool ever to have believed it, and a worse fool to have kept on believing it until now. "You never meant to charge Father with killing Roptat, did you?"

"Of course I did," said Gabya.

"But not to bring him to trial."

"Oh, no, that would be silly—a waste of time. I told you that."

"You *said* it would be a waste of time because Father's prestige in the city meant he'd never be convicted. But the truth was he would never have come to trial because you meant people to discover both Roptat's *and* Father's bodies in the coolhouse."

"What a terrible accusation. I deny it all. You have such an evil imagination, *boy*."

"You were using me to betray my own father so you could *kill* him."

"For the longest time," said Gaballufix, "I assumed you knew that. I assumed you understood that we were simply not speaking directly about it because it was such an unpleasant subject. I thought you realized that the only way I could get you your inheritance early was by arranging your father's death."

Elemak's fury at having almost been a conspirator in father-killing overwhelmed all his self-control. He lunged toward Gaballufix—and found himself staring at the pulse in Gaballufix's hand.

"Yes, yes, I see that you have some idea of what a pulse can do to a man at close range. You killed a man with a weapon just like this, didn't you? In fact," said Gaballufix, "it might have *been* this weapon, mightn't it!"

Elemak looked at the pulse and recognized the wear marks on it, where it had been laid down on stone, where it had been nicked and marked, where the color had been faded by the sunlight as it rested at his hip during countless hours of travel in the desert. "I lent that pulse to Mebbekew the day I got home from my last caravan," he said stupidly.

"And Mebbekew lent it to me. I told him—speaking of fools—that I wanted it to surprise you with later, at a party, to honor you for drawing blood. I told him I was going to use your story to inspire my soldiers." Gaballufix laughed. And laughed.

"That's why you brought Meb in. To get my pulse." But why? Elemak imagined his father lying there, dead, and then someone discovering Elemak's pulse not far away, abandoned perhaps in his haste to flee. He imagined Gaballufix explaining to the city council, tears in his eyes. "This is where greed in the younger generation leads—my own half-brother, willing to murder his father in order to get his inheritance."

"You're right," said Elemak quietly. "I *was* a fool."

"You were and you are," said Gaballufix. "You were seen in the city today—all over the city. My men tracked you through several neighborhoods. There are many witnesses—and it will be so delicious to see Rasa forced to testify against her beloved Volemak's oldest boy. Because someone is going to die tonight, killed with this very pulse, which will be found near the body, and then everyone will know that it was Wetchik's son who was the assassin, probably at his father's orders. And the best part of it is, I can tell you this, and then I can let you know, I can put you out of the city *alive* and there's still nothing you can do about it. If you start telling people about *my* plot to kill somebody—whoever I decide it should be—they'll all assume that you were simply trying to cover up your own crime in advance. You *are* a fool, Elemak, just like your father. Even when you knew I wasn't afraid to kill to accomplish my purposes, you somehow thought that you and your family would be immune, that somehow I'd be more tender with you because the same weary old womb bore you and me during our nine months sucking life out of a placenta."

Elemak had never seen such fury, such hatred, such *evil* in a human face, had never imagined it was possible. Yet there he stood, looking at Gabya's glee in describing a crime he meant to commit. It frightened Elemak, but it also made him feel an insane kind of confidence. As if Gaballufix's having revealed his true inner smallness made Elemak realize how much larger he was himself, after all.

"Who's the fool, Gabya," said Elemak. "Who's the fool."

"I think there's no doubt of that now," said Gaballufix.

"True enough," said Elemak. "You'll make it impossible for Father and me to return to the city, for a while at least, but the death of Roptat won't open the road for you. Are you so stupid, really? Nobody will believe for a moment that Father would kill Roptat, or that I would either."

"I'll have the weapon!" said Gaballufix.

"The weapon, but no witness to the killing, just *your* story bruited about by *your* people. They aren't so stupid that they can't add one and one. Who stands to gain from Roptat's death and Father's exile? Only you, Gabya. This city will rise up in bloody rebellion against you. Your soldiers will die in the streets."

"You overestimate the will of my feeble-hearted enemies," said Gaballufix. But his voice didn't sound so certain anymore, and the glee was gone.

"Your enemies aren't feeble-hearted, just because they're unwilling to kill in order to get their way. They *are* willing to kill to stop a man like *you*. A weak-brained, jealous, spiteful, malicious little parasitic roach like you."

"Do you want so much to die?"

"Yes, kill me here, Gabya. Hundreds of people know I'm here. Hundreds are waiting to hear what I tell them. Your whole plan stands revealed, and none of it will work. Because you were so stupid that you had to brag."

Elemak's words were all bluff, of course, but Gaballufix believed him. At least enough to make him pause. To make him wonder. Then Gabya smiled. "Elya, my brother, I'm proud of you."

Elemak recognized surrender when he heard it. He said nothing in reply.

"You *are* my brother after all—the blood of Volemak didn't weaken you after all. It may even have made you stronger."

"Do you really think I'll swallow your flattery *now*?"

"Of course not," said Gaballufix. "Of course you'll disregard it—but that doesn't stop me from admiring you, does it? It just stops you from believing in my admiration! The loss is yours, dear Elya."

"I came for the Index, Gaballufix," said Elemak. "A simple thing. Give it to me, and I'm gone. Wetchik and his family will never bother you again, and you can play your little games until somebody puts a knife in your back just to stop that squealing noise you make whenever you think you've been especially clever."

Gaballufix cocked his head to one side.

He's going to give it to me, thought Elemak, triumphantly.

"No," said Gaballufix. "I'd like to, but I can't. The disappearance of the Index—that would be hard to explain to the clan council. A lot of trouble, that's what it would cause, and why should I put myself to all that trouble just to get rid of Wetchik? After all, I'm already rid of him."

Now, at last, Elemak was where he wanted to be: bargaining like a merchant. "What else would it take to make it worth your while?" asked Elemak.

"Make me an offer. Enough money that it'll make up for all the extra effort I have to go through."

"Give me the Index, and Father will release funds to you. Whatever you want."

"I'm supposed to *wait* for the funds? Wait for *Wetchik* to pay me later for an Index I give you now? Oh—I get it—I see what's happening!" Gaballufix laughed in derision. "You can't give me money *now* because you don't have any. Wetchik still hasn't released any of his fortune to you! He sent you on this errand and he didn't even give you access to his money!"

It *was* humiliating. Father should have realized that in dealing with Gaballufix it would eventually come down to money; he should have given him password that would have let him access the Wetchik family funds. Rashgallivak, the steward, had more control over the Wetchik fortune than Elemak did. He was filled with fury and resentment against his father for putting him in such a position of weakness. The stupid short-sighted old man, always tripping over his own feet when it came to business!

"Tell me, Elya," said Gaballufix, interrupting his own laughter. "If your own father doesn't trust you with his money, why should I trust you with the Index?"

With that, Gaballufix reached under his table and apparently triggered some kind of switch, for three doors opened at once and identical-looking soldiers burst into the room. They took hold of Elemak and roughly thrust him out into the hall, then out the front door.

Nor was that enough. They quick-marched him to the nearest gate, which happened to be the Back Gate—right past his mother's house—and threw him into the dirt in front of the guards.

"This one's leaving the city!" shouted one of the soldiers.

"And never coming back!" cried another.

The guards, however, did not seem terribly impressed. "Are you a citizen?" asked one.

"Yes," said Elemak, dusting himself off.

"Thumb please." They presented the thumbscreen, and Elemak held his thumb over it. "Citizen Elemak son of Hosni by the Wetchik. It is an honor to serve you." Whereupon the guards all stood at attention and saluted him.

It completely stunned him. Never, in all his passages into and out of the city of Basilica, had anyone done more than raise an eyebrow when the city computer reported his prestigious parentage. And now a salute!

Then Gaballufix's soldiers jeered again, boasting about what they'd do to him if he ever returned, and Elemak understood. The official city guards were letting him and everyone else near the gate see that *they* were not part of Gaballufix's little army. Furthermore, the very fact that the son of Wetchik was clearly the enemy of Gaballufix made city guards want to salute him. If Elemak could only figure out how to use this situation, he might very well be able to turn it to his advantage. What if I returned to the city as the deliverer, leading the guard and the militia in crushing Gabya and his hated army of costume clones. The city would then gladly give me all that Gabya is trying to win through trickery, intimidation, and murder. I'd have all the power Gaballufix ever imagined—and the city would love me for it.

TWELVE

FORTUNE

It was a miserable day in the desert, even allowing for the fact that except for about an hour and a half at noon, the canyon was in deep shade, with a steady breeze funneling through it. No place is comfortable, thought Nafai, when you're waiting for someone *else* to do a job you think of as your own. Worse than the heat, than the sweat dripping into his eyes, than the grit that got into his clothing and between his teeth, was the sick dread Nafai felt whenever he thought of *Elemak* being the one entrusted with the Oversoul's errand.

Nafai knew that Elemak had rigged the casting of lots, of course. He wasn't such a fool as to think Elemak would actually leave such a thing to chance. Even as he admired the deftness with which Elya handled it, Nafai was angry at him. Was he even *attempting* to get the Index? Or was he going into the city and meeting with Gaballufix in order to plan some further betrayal of

Father and of the city and, finally, of the Oversoul's guardianship of humanity?

Would he even return?

Then, at last, in mid-afternoon, there came the clatter and rattle of stones tumbling, and Elemak clambered noisily down into their hiding place. His hands were empty, but his eyes were bright. We have been betrayed, thought Nafai.

"He said no, of course," said Elemak. "This Index is more important than Father told us. Gaballufix doesn't want to give it up—at least not for nothing."

"For what, then?" asked Issib.

"He didn't say. But he has a price. He made it clear that he's willing to hear an offer. The trouble is—we have to go back to Father and get access to his finances."

Nafai didn't like this at all. How did they know what Elemak and Gaballufix had promised each other?

"All the way back, empty-handed," said Mebbekew. "Tell you what, Elya. *You* go back, and the rest of us will wait here till you come back with the password to Father's accounts."

"Right," said Issib. "I'm not going to spend the night out here in the desert, when I can go into the city and use my floats."

"How stupid are you, really?" said Elemak. "Don't you realize that things are different now? You can't go wandering anonymously through the city anymore. Gab-ya's troops are all over it. And Gaballufix is not Father's friend. Therefore he's not *our* friend, either."

"He's your brother," said Mebbekew.

"He's nobody's brother," said Elemak. "He's got both the morals and the surface properties of slime. I know him better than any of you, and I can promise you that he'd just as soon kill any of us as look at us."

Nafai was amazed to hear Elemak talking this way. "I thought you wanted him to lead Basilica."

"I thought his plan was the best hope for Basilica in the coming wars," said Elemak. "But I never thought Gaballufix was out to get anything except his own advantage. His soldiers are all over the city—wearing some kind of holographic costume that covers their whole bodies, so all his soldiers look absolutely identical."

"Whole-body masks!" cried Mebbekew. "What a great idea!"

"It means," said Elemak, "that even when somebody sees one of Gaballufix's soldiers committing a crime—like kidnapping or killing a stray son of old Wetchik—no one can possibly identify the individual who did it."

"Oh," said Mebbekew.

"So," said Nafai, "even if Father gives us access to his money, what then? What makes you think Gaballufix would sell it?"

"Think, Nafai. Even a fourteen-year-old should be able to grasp *something* of the affairs of men. Gaballufix is paying hundreds and hundreds of soldiers. His fortune is large, but not large enough to keep that up forever, not without getting control of the tax money of Basilica to support them all. Father's money could make a huge difference. At the moment, Gaballufix probably needs money more than he needs the prestige of possessing this Index, which hardly anybody has even heard of anymore."

Swallowing Elemak's condescension, Nafai realized that Elemak's analysis was right. "The Index *is* for sale, then."

"*Could* be," said Elemak. "So we go back to Father and see whether the Index is worth spending money for, and how *much* money. Then he gives us access to his finances and we go back and bargain—"

"And I say *you* go home and let me take my chances in the city," said Mebbekew.

"I want to get away from my chair tonight," said Issib.

"When we come back," said Elemak, "*then* you can get into the city."

"Like this time? You make us wait again, just like this time, and we'll never get in," said Issib.

"Fine," said Elemak. "I'll go back alone and tell Father that you've abandoned him and his cause, just so you can go into the city and float around and get laid."

"I'm not going in to get laid!" protested Issib.

"And I'm not going in to float," said Mebbekew, grinning.

"Wait a minute," said Nafai. "If we go back to Father and get permission, then what? It'll be almost a week. Who knows how things might have changed by then? There could already be civil war in Basilica. Or by then Gaballufix might have arranged other financing, so that our money wouldn't mean anything to him. The time to make an offer is *now*."

Elemak looked at him in surprise. "Well, yes, of course, that's true. But we don't have access to Father's money."

In answer, Nafai looked at Issib.

Issib rolled his eyes. "I promised Father," he said.

"You mean *you* have access to Father's password?" said Mebbekew.

"He said that somebody else ought to know it, in case of an emergency," said Issib. "How did *you* know about it, Nafai?"

"Come on," said Nafai, "I'm not an idiot. In your research you were getting access to city library files that they'd never let a kid like you get into without specific adult authorization. I didn't know Father had *given* it to you, though."

"Well," said Issib, "he only gave me the entry code. I kind of figured out the back half myself."

Mebbekew was livid. "All this time that I've been living like a beggar in the city, *you* had access to Father's entire fortune?"

"Think about it, Meb," said Elemak. "Who else could Father *trust* with his password? Nafai's a child, you're a spendthrift, and I was constantly disagreeing with him about where we ought to invest our money. Issib, though—what was *he* going to do with the money?"

"So because he doesn't *need* money, he gets all he wants?"

"If I had ever used his password to get money, he would have changed it and so of course I never used it," said Issib. "Maybe he has still another password for getting into the money—I never tried. And I'm not trying now, either, so you can forget it. Father didn't authorize us to go dipping into the family fortune."

"He told us that the Oversoul wanted us to bring him the Index," said Nafai. "Don't you see? The Index is so important that Father had to send us back to face his enemy, a man who planned to kill him—"

"Oh, come on, Nyef, that was Father's *dream*, not anything real," said Mebbekew. "Gaballufix wasn't planning to kill Father."

"Yes he was," said Elemak. "He was planning to kill Roptat *and* Father, and then put the blame on me."

Mebbekew's jaw hung open.

"He was going to arrange to have them find my pulse—the one I lent to *you*, Mebbekew—near Father's body. Clumsy of you to lose my pulse, Meb."

"How do you know all this?" asked Issib.

"Gaballufix told me," said Elemak. "While he was trying to impress me with my helplessness."

"Let's go to the council," said Issib. "If Gaballufix confessed—"

"He confessed—or rather *bragged*—to *me*, in a room alone. My word against his. There's no point in telling anybody. It wouldn't do any good."

"This is the opportunity," said Nafai. "Today, right now. We go down to the house, access Father's files through his own library, convert all the funds into liquid assets. We go to the gold market and pick it up as metal bars and negotiable bonds and jewels and what-not, and then we go to Gaballufix and—"

"And he steals it all from us and kills us and leaves the chopped-up bits of our bodies for the jackals to find in some ditch outside the city," said Elemak.

"Not so," said Nafai. "We take a witness with us—someone he won't dare to touch."

"Who?" said Issib.

"Rashgallivak," said Nafai. "He isn't just the steward of the house of Wetchik, you know. He's Palwashantu, and has a great deal of trust and prestige. We bring him along, he watches everything, he witnesses the exchange of Father's fortune for the Index, and we all walk out alive. Gaballufix might be able to kill *us*, because we're in hiding and Father's an exile, but he can't touch Rash."

"You mean all *four* of us go to Gaballufix?" asked Issib.

"Into the city?" asked Mebbekew.

"It's not a bad plan," said Elemak. "Risky, but you're right about this being the time to act."

"So let's go down to the house," said Nafai. "We can leave the animals here for the night, can't we? Issib and I can go to Father's library to do the funds transfer, while you and Meb find Rash and bring him there so we can go meet Gaballufix together."

"Will Rash go along with it?" asked Issib. "I mean, what if Gaballufix decides to kill us all anyway?"

"Yes," said Elemak. "He's a man of perfect loyalty. He will never swerve from his duty to the house of Wetchik."

It took only an hour or so. It was late afternoon when they walked into the Gold Market and began the final transactions. All of the funds that were not tied up in real property were all in spendable form in Issib's bank file—actually, like all the brothers' bank files, a mere subfile of Father's all-inclusive account. If anyone doubted that Issib was authorized to spend so much, there was Rashgallivak, silently observing. Everyone knew that if Rash was there, it had to be legitimate.

The amount involved was the largest single purchase of portable assets in the recent history of the Gold Market. No one broker had anything like enough ingots or jewels or bonds to handle even a large fraction of the buy. For more than an hour, until the sun was behind the red wall and the Gold Market was in shadow, the brokers scrambled among themselves until at last the whole amount was laid out on a single table. The funds were transferred; a staggering amount was moved from one column to another in all the computer displays—for all the brokers were watching now, in awe. The ingots then were rolled up in three cloth packages and tied, the jewels were rolled in cloth and bagged, and the bonds were folded into leather binders. Then all the parcels were distributed among the four sons of Wetchik.

One of the brokers had already arranged for a half-dozen of the city guards to accompany them wherever they were going, but Elemak sent them away. "If the guards are with us, then every thief in Basilica will see and take note of where we're going. Our lives will be worthless then," said Elemak. "We'll move swiftly and without guard, without notice."

Again the brokers looked at Rashgallivak, who nodded his approval.

Half an hour through the streets of the city, nervously aware of everyone who glanced at them, and then at last they were at the doors of Gaballufix's house. Nafai saw at once that both Elemak and Mebbekew were recognized here. So, too, was Rashgallivak—but Rash was widely known in the Palwashantu clan, so it would have been a surprise if he had *not* been recognized. Only Nafai and Issib had to be introduced as they stood before Gaballufix in the great salon of his—no, not *his*, but his *wife's* house.

"So you're the one who flies," said Gaballufix, looking at Issib.

"I float," said Issib.

"So I see," said Gaballufix. "Rasa's sons, the two of you." He looked Nafai in the eye. "Very large for one so young."

Nafai said nothing. He was too busy studying Gaballufix's face. So ordinary, really. A little soft, perhaps. Not young anymore, though younger than Father, who had, after all, slept with Gaballufix's mother—enough to produce Elemak. There was some slight resemblance between Elya and Gaballufix, but not very much, only in the darkness of the hair, and the way the eyes were perhaps a little close together under heavy-ridged brows.

It was in the eyes that they were alike, but also in the eyes that they differed most, for there was a rheuminess, a scarlet-rimmed look in Gaballufix's eyes that was the opposite of Elya's sharpness. Elemak was a man of action and strength, a man of the desert, who could face strangers and unknown places with courage and confidence and vigor. Gaballufix, by contrast, was a man who went nowhere and did nothing; rather he denned himself here and let others do his work for him. Elemak went out and penetrated the world, changing it where he would; Gaballufix stayed in one place and sucked the world dry, emptying it in order to fill himself.

"So the young one is speechless," said Gaballufix.

"For the first time in his life," said Meb. There was some nervous laughter.

"Why do the sons and the steward of Wetchik honor me with this visit?"

"Father wanted us to trade gifts with you," said Elemak. "We're living in a place where we need little in the way of money, yet Father has taken it into his heart—no, the Oversoul has commanded him—to bring the Index with him. While you, Gaballufix, have little use for the Index—have you even looked at it in all your years as leader of the clan council?—and might be able to turn some portion of the Wetchik estate to better advantage than Father ever could, being far from the city."

It was an eloquent, truthful, and completely deceptive speech, and Nafai admired it. There was no doubt in anyone's mind that a purchase was being attempted here, and yet it was delicately disguised as an exchange of gifts, so that no one could openly accuse Gaballufix of having sold the Index, or Father of having bought it.

"I'm sure my kinsman Wetchik is far too generous to me," said Gaballufix. "I can't imagine that I would be of much help to him, managing some trifling portion of his great fortune."

In answer, Elemak stepped forward and unrolled a heavy parcel of platinum ingots. Gaballufix picked up one ingot and hefted it in his hands. "This is a thing of beauty," he said. "And yet I know this is such a tiny part of the Wetchik fortune that I could not feel right about doing such a small favor for my kinsman, when he would bear in exchange the heavy burden of guarding the Palwashantu Index."

"This is only a sample," said Elemak.

"If I'm to be trusted with this, shouldn't I see the extent of my guardianship?"

Elemak removed all the rest of the treasure that he carried on his person, and laid it on the table. "Surely that is all that Father would dare ask you to be burdened with," he said.

"Such a slight burden," said Gaballufix. "I would be ashamed to have this be all the help I gave my kinsman." Yet Nafai could see that Gaballufix's eyes were shining at the sight of so much wealth all in one place. "I assume that it's only a quarter of what you carry." Gaballufix looked from Nafai to Issib and Mebbekew.

"I think that's enough," said Elemak.

"Then I couldn't agree to lay the burden of the Index on my kinsman," said Gaballufix.

"Very well," said Elemak. He reached out and started rolling up the ingots.

Is that all? thought Nafai. Do we give up so easily? Am I the only one who can see that Gaballufix hungers for the money? That if we offer just a little more, he'll sell?

"Wait," said Nafai. "We can add what I carry to this."

Nafai was aware that Elemak was glaring at him, but it was unthinkable to come so close and leave empty-handed. Didn't Elemak realize that the Index was *important*? More important than mere money, that was certain. "And if that isn't enough, Issib has more," Nafai said. "Show him, Issib. Let me show him."

In moments, they had tripled the offer.

"I fear," said Elemak, his voice icy, "that my younger brother has inconsiderately offered to burden you with far more than I ever intended you to have to deal with."

"On the contrary," said Gaballufix. "It is your younger brother who has more correctly estimated how much of a burden I'm willing to bear. Indeed, I think that if the last quarter of what you carried into my house were upon this table, I'd feel right about weighing down my dear kinsman with the heavy responsibility of the Palwashantu Index."

"I say it's too much," said Elemak.

"Then you hurt my feelings," said Gaballufix, "and I can't see any reason for further discussion."

"We came for the Index," said Nafai. "We came because the Oversoul demands it."

"Your father is famous for his holiness and his visions," said Gaballufix.

"If you're willing to accept all that we have," said Nafai, "we'll gladly lay it before you in order to fulfil the will of the Oversoul."

"Such obedience will long be remembered in the Temple," said Gaballufix. He looked at Mebbekew. "Or is Nafai's holiness not matched by that of his brother Mebbekew?"

Anguished with indecision, Mebbekew looked back and forth between Elemak and Gaballufix.

But it was Elemak who acted. He reached down and again rolled up ingots into the cloth.

"No!" cried Nafai. "We won't turn back now!" He held out his hand to Mebbekew. "You know what Father would want you to do."

"I see that only the youngest has true understanding," said Gaballufix.

Mebbekew stepped forward and began laying parcels on the table. As he did, Nafai could feel Elemak grip his shoulder, the fingers biting deep, and Elemak whispered in his ear, "I told you to leave this to me. You've given him four times what we needed to pay, you little fool. You've left us with nothing."

Nothing but the Index, thought Nafai. But still, he vaguely realized that Elemak might in fact have known better how to handle the bargaining, and perhaps he should have kept his mouth shut and let Elya handle things. But at the time he acted, Nafai was so *sure* that he had to speak or they would never get the Index.

All the Wetchik fortune except the land and buildings themselves was on Gaballufix's table.

"Is *that* enough?" asked Elemak dryly.

"Exactly enough," said Gaballufix. "Exactly enough to prove to me that Volemak the Wetchik has completely betrayed the Palwashantu. This great fortune has been put into the hands of children, who have, with childish stupidity, resolved to waste it all on the purchase of that which every true Palwashantu knows can *never* be sold. The Index, the sacred, holy trust of the Palwashantu— did Volemak think it could be bought? No, impossible, it could not be! I can only conclude that he has either lost his mind or you have killed him and hidden his body somewhere."

"No!" cried Nafai.

"Your lies are obscene," said Elemak, "and we won't tolerate them." He stepped forward and reached out for a third time to gather up the treasure.

"Thief!" shouted Gaballufix.

Suddenly the doors opened, and a dozen soldiers entered the room.

"Do you think you can do this in the presence of Rashgallivak?" demanded Elemak.

"I *insist* on doing it in his presence," said Gaballufix. "Who do you think first came to me with the news that Volemak was betraying the trust of the Wetchiks? That Volemak's sons were gutting the Wetchik fortune for some mad whim?"

"I serve the house of Wetchik," said Rashgallivak. He looked at each of the brothers, his face a mask of sadness. "It could not possibly be in the interest of that great house to let the fortune be destroyed by one madman who thinks he sees visions. Gaballufix could hardly believe what I told him, but he agreed with me that the fortune of Wetchik had to be shifted into the care of another branch of the family."

"As chief of the Palwashantu clan," Gaballufix intoned, "I hereby declare that Volemak and his sons, having proven themselves unfit and unreliable as guardians of the greatest house in the clan, are therefore removed as heirs and possessors of the house of Wetchik for all time. And in recognition of years of loyal service, by himself and his ancestors for many centuries, I grant temporary guardianship of the Wetchik fortune, and the use of the name of Wetchik, to Rashgallivak, to care for all aspects of the Wetchik house until such time as the clan council shall dispose of them otherwise. As for Volemak and his sons, if they make any effort to protest or dispute this action, they will be regarded as blood-enemies of the Palwashantu, and shall be dealt with by laws more ancient than those of the city of Basilica." Gaballufix leaned forward across the table, smiling at Elemak. "Did you understand all that, Elya?"

Elemak looked at Rashgallivak. "I understand that the most loyal man in Basilica is now the worst traitor."

"You were the traitors," said Rash. "This sudden madness of visions, a completely unprofitable journey into the desert, selling off all the animals, dismissing all the workers, and now this—as steward of the house of Wetchik, I had no choice but to involve the clan council."

"Gaballufix isn't the clan council," said Elemak. "He's a common thief, and you've put our fortune in his hands."

"You were putting the fortune in his hands," said Rashgallivak. "Don't you see that I did this for you? For all four of you? The council will leave me as guardian for a few years, until all this blows over, and in that time if one of you proves himself to be a sober and completely reliable man, worthy of the responsibility, the Wetchik name and fortune will be returned to you."

"There'll be no fortune left," said Elemak. "Gabya will spend it on his armies before the year is out."

"Not at all," said Gaballufix. "I'm turning it all over to Rash, to continue as steward."

Elemak laughed bitterly. "As steward, required to use it as the council directs. And how will the council direct? You'll see, Rash. Very quickly indeed—because the council has incurred some pretty heavy expenses with all these soldiers they're paying."

Rashgallivak looked quite uncomfortable. "Gaballufix did mention that some small part of this might need to be deducted to meet present expenses, but your father would have contributed to clan expenses anyway, if he were still in his right mind."

"He's played you for the fool," said Elemak, "and me too. All of us."

Rash looked at Gaballufix, clearly concerned. "Maybe we ought to call in the council on this," he said.

"The council has already met," said Gaballufix.

"How heavy *are* the clan expenses?" asked Rashgallivak.

"A trifle," said Gaballufix. "Don't waste time worrying about it. Or are you going to prove yourself as unreliable as Volemak and his sons?"

"See?" said Elemak. "Already it begins—do as Gabya wants, or you won't be steward of the Wetchik fortune anymore."

"The law is the law," said Gaballufix. "And now it's time for these worthless young spendthrifts to leave my house before I charge them with the murder of their father."

"Before we say anything more to help Rash see the truth, you mean," said Elemak.

"We'll go," said Mebbekew. "But all this talk about the Palwashantu clan council and making Rashgallivak the Wetchik is rat piss. You're a thief, Gabya, a lying murdering thief who would have killed Roptat *and* Father if we hadn't left the city the day we did, and we're not leaving our family fortune in your bloody hands!"

With that Mebbekew lunged forward and seized a bag of jewels.

Immediately the soldiers were upon them, all four of them. The jewels were out of Meb's hands in a moment, and with no particular gentleness all four of them were out of the salon, out of the front doors, and thrown into the street.

"Away from here!" cried the soldiers. "Thieves! Murderers!"

Nafai hardly had a chance to think before Mebbekew was at his throat. "*You're* the one who had to lay all the treasure on the table!"

"He meant to have it all anyway," Nafai protested.

"Shut up, fools," said Elemak. "This isn't over. Our lives aren't worth dust—he probably has men waiting to kill us not fifty meters off. Our only hope is to split up and *run*. Don't stop for anything. And remember—something Rasa told me today—*trust no man*." He said it again, changing the emphasis a little. "Trust no *man*. We'll meet tonight where the camels are. Anyone who isn't there by dawn we'll assume is dead. Now run—and *not* for any place that they'd expect you to go."

With that Elemak began to stride off toward the north. After only a few steps he turned back. "Now, fools! See—they're already signaling the assassins!"

Sure enough Nafai could see that one of the soldiers on Gaballufix's porch had raised one arm and was pointing at them with the other. "How fast can you go with those floats?" Nafai asked Issib.

"Faster than you," he answered. "But not faster than a pulse."

"The Oversoul will protect us," said Nafai.

"Right," said Issib. "Now move, you fool."

Nafai ducked his head and plunged into the thickest part of the crowd. He had run a hundred meters south along Fountain Street when he turned back and saw why people were shouting behind him: Issib had risen some twenty meters into the air, and was just disappearing over the roof of the house directly across from Gaballufix's. I never knew he could do that, thought Nafai.

Then, as he turned to run again, it occurred to him that Issib probably hadn't known it, either.

"There's one," said a harsh voice. Suddenly a man appeared in front of him, a charged-wire blade in his hand. A woman gasped; people shied away. But almost without knowing that he knew it, Nafai could feel the presence of a man directly behind him. If he backed away from the blade in front, he would walk into the real assassin behind him.

So instead Nafai lunged forward. His enemy had not expected this unarmed boy to be aggressive—his swipe with the blade came nowhere near. Nafai put his knee sharply into the man's groin, lifting him off the ground. The man screamed. Then Nafai shoved him out of his way and ran in earnest now, not looking back, barely looking ahead except to dodge people and watch for the shimmering red glow of another blade, or the hot white beam of a pulse.

THIRTEEN

FLIGHT

Issya had never tried to climb so high with his floats. He knew that they responded to his muscle tension, that whichever float he pressed down on the hardest remained fixed in its position in the air. But he had always thought that the position was somehow relative to the ground directly under the float. He was not entirely wrong—the higher he got, the more the floats tended to "slip" downward—but by and large he found that he could climb the air like a ladder until he was at roof height.

Naturally, everyone looked at him—but that's what he wanted. *Everybody* watch me, and talk about the young crippled boy who "flew" up to the roof. Gaballufix's goons wouldn't dare shoot him with so many witnesses, at least not directly in front of their leader's own house.

There was no one on the roofs, he saw that at once, and so he used them as a sort of highway, drifting low between vents and chimneys, cupolas and elevator housings, roofline ridges and the trees in rooftop gardens.

Once he did surprise an old fellow who was repairing the masonry on the low wall around a widow's walk; the clattering sound of a broken tile worried Issib for a moment; when he turned, though, he saw that the man had not fallen, but rather stared gape-mouthed at Issib. Will there be a story tonight, Issib wondered, about a young demigod seen drifting through the air over Basilica, perhaps on some errand of love with a mortal girl of surpassing beauty?

It was an exceptionally long block of houses, since several roads had been built over in this area. He was able to get more than halfway to Back Gate without descending to street level, and certainly he had made better time than any possible pursuers could have. There was always the chance, of course, that Gaballufix had assassins posted at all the city gates; certainly if he had an ambush at any gate it would be at Back Gate, the one nearest to his house. So Issib couldn't afford to be careless, once he was down at street level.

Before he left the roofs, though, he cast a longing gaze at the red wall of the city. High as he was, the sun was still up, split in half by the wall line. If only I could just fly over that. But he knew that the wall was loaded with complicated electronics, including the nodes that created the magnetic field that powered his floats. There was no crossing there—the tiny computer at his belt could never equalize the violently conflicting forces at the top of the wall.

He reached the end of a roof and drifted down into the crowd. This was the upper end of Holy Road, where men *were* allowed to go. Many noticed his descent, of course, but once he reached street level he immediately lowered himself to sitting position and scooted through the traffic at child-height. Let an assassin try to shoot me *now*, he thought. In minutes he was at the gate. The guards recognized his name the moment the thumb-scanner brought it up, and they clapped him on the back and wished him well.

It was not desert here at Back Gate, of course, but rather the fringes of Trackless Wood. To the right was the dense forest that made the north side of Basilica impassable; to the left, complicated arroyos, choked with trees and vines, led down from the well-watered hills into the first barren rocks of the desert. For a normal man, it would be a nightmare journey, unless he knew the way—as, he was sure, Elemak did. For Issib, of course, it was a matter of avoiding the tallest obstacles and floating easily down until the city was completely out of sight. He used the sun to steer by until he was down onto the desert plateau; then he bore south, crossing the roads named Dry and Desert, until, just at sunset, he reached the place where they had hidden his chair.

His floats were at the fringes of the magnetic field of the city now, and it was awkward maneuvering himself into the chair. But then everything to do with the chair was awkward and limiting. Still, it did have some advantages. Designed to be an all-purpose cripple's chair, it had a built-in computer display tied to the city's main public library when he was within range, with several different interfaces for people with different disabilities. He could even speak certain key words and it would understand them, and it could also produce a fair-sounding approximation of the commoner words in several dozen languages. If there were no such things as floats, the chair would probably be the most precious thing in his life. But there *were* floats. When he wore them, he was almost a regular human being, plus a few advantages. When he could not use them, he was a cripple with no advantages at all.

The camels were waiting outside the dependable influence of the city's magnetics, however, so use the chair he must. He got in, switched off the floats, and then guided the chair in its slow, hovering flight through narrow back canyons until at last he smelled, then heard the camels.

No one else was there; he was the first. He settled the chair onto its legs, leveled it, and then sat there alternately listening for anyone who might be approaching while scanning the library's news reports for word of any unexplained killings or other violent incidents. None yet. But then it might take time for word to reach the newswriters and the gossips. His brothers might be dying right now, or already dead, or captured and imprisoned and held for some sort of ransom. What would he do then? How could he hope to get home? The chair might carry him, though it was unlikely—it wasn't meant for long distance travel. He knew from experience that the chair could only move continuously for an hour or so before it needed several hours of solar recharging.

Mother will help me, thought Issib. If they don't come back tonight, Mother will help me. If I can get to her.

Mebbekew dodged through the crowd. He had seen several men trying to make their way toward him, but his experience as an actor—especially one who had to go through the audience collecting money—had given him a good sense of crowds, and he worked the traffic expertly against the men who were following him, heading always where the crowd was thickest, dodging through gaps that were about to be plugged by approaching groups of people. Soon the assassins—if that's what they were—were hopelessly far behind him. That was when Mebbekew began to *move*, a lazy, loping run that didn't give the impression of great haste but covered the ground very rapidly. It looked like he was running for the sheer joy of it, and in fact he was—but he never stopped watching. Whenever he saw soldiers, he headed straight for them, on the theory that Gaballufix wouldn't dare use men clearly identified as his own to conduct a public murder in the clear light of afternoon.

Within half an hour he had worked himself all the way east to Dolltown, the district that he knew best. The soldiers were rarer here, and while there were plenty of criminals for hire here, they were the sort who didn't stay bought for long. Meb also knew people who knew this part of town better than the city computer itself.

Trust no *man*, Elemak had said. Well, that was easy enough. Meb knew plenty of men, but his *friends* were all women. That had been an easy choice for him, from the time he was old enough to know the practical applications of the difference between men and women. He had almost laughed when Father got an auntie for him at the age of sixteen—he had enjoyed pretending to be new at lovemaking when he went to her, but within a few days she sent him away, laughingly saying that if he came back any more he'd be teaching *her* things that she had never particularly wanted to learn. Meb was good with women. They loved him, and they kept loving him, not because he was good at giving pleasure, though he was, but rather because he knew how to listen to women so they knew that he heard; he knew how to talk to them so they felt needed and protected, all at once. Not all women liked him, of course, but the ones that did liked him very much, and forever.

So it took only a few minutes in Dolltown before Mebbekew was in the room of a zither player on Music Street, and a few minutes more before he was in her arms, and a few minutes more before he was in her; then they talked for an hour, she went out and enlisted the help of some actresses they both knew, who were more than a little fond of Mebbekew themselves. Shortly after nightfall Mebbekew, in wig and gown and makeup, in voice and walk a woman, passed through Music Gate with a group of laughing, singing women. Only when he laid his thumb on the screen was his disguise revealed, and the guard, reading his name, merely winked at him and wished him a good night.

Mebbekew stayed in costume until he got to the rendezvous, and his only regret was that it was Issib who stared at him and didn't know him until he spoke, and not Elemak. It would have been nice to let his older brother see the joke. But then, given the fact that their entire fortune and Father's title as well had just been stolen from them, Elemak probably wouldn't have been in the mood for a joke anyway.

Elemak's passage from the city was the least eventful. He never saw an assassin, and had no problem getting to Hosni's house near the Back Gate. Fearing that perhaps the assassins were waiting at the gate itself, he ducked in to visit with his mother. She fed him a wonderful meal—she always hired the best cooks in Basilica—listened sympathetically to his story, agreed with him that if she had miscarried when pregnant with Gaballufix the world would be a better place, and finally sent him on his way several hours after dark with a bit of gold in his pocket, a sturdy metal-bladed knife at his belt, and a kiss. He knew that if Gaballufix came later that night, bragging about how he had tricked a fortune out of Volemak's sons, including Wetchik, Mother would laugh and praise him. She loved anything that was amusing, and was amused by almost anything. A cheerful woman, but utterly empty. Elemak was sure that Gaballufix got his morals from her, but certainly not his intelligence. Though, truth to tell, his teacher Rasa had told him once that his mother was actually very intelligent—much too intelligent to let others know how intelligent she was. "It's like being among dangerous foreigners," said Rasa. "It's much better to let them think you don't understand their language, so that they'll speak freely in front of you. That's how dear Hosni is when she's among those who fancy themselves very bright and well educated. She mocks them all unmercifully when they're gone."

Will she mock me to Gaballufix, as she mocked Gaballufix to me? Or ridicule us both to her woman-friends when we're gone?

At the gate, the guards recognized him at once, saluted him again, and offered to help him in any way they could. He thanked them, then plunged out into the night. Even by starlight he knew his way through the tangled paths leading down from Trackless Wood into the desert. Through all the dark journey he could think of nothing but his fury at Gaballufix, at the way he had outmaneuvered him by getting Rash on his side. He could hear in his mind their mother's laughter, as if it were all aimed at him. He felt so helpless, so utterly humiliated.

And then he remembered the most terrible moment of all, when Nafai had so stupidly interfered with his bargaining and given away Father's entire fortune. If he hadn't done that, Rashgallivak might not have concluded that they were unworthy to have the Wetchik fortune. Then he wouldn't have acted against them, and they could have walked out with the treasure *and* Father's title intact. It was Nafai, really, who had lost the contest for them. If it had been up to Elemak alone, he might have done it. Gaballufix might have come through with the Index and settled for a quarter of Father's fortune—it was more money even so than Gaballufix could lay hands on any other way. Nafai, the stupid young jackass who could never keep his mouth shut, the one who pretended to have visions of his own so that Father would like him best, the one who, by the sheer act of being born, had made Gaballufix into Father's permanent enemy.

If I had him in my hands right now I'd kill him, thought Elemak. He has cost me my fortune and my honor and therefore my whole future. Easy for him to give away the Wetchik fortune—it would never have been his anyway. It would have been mine. I was born for it. I trained for it. I would have doubled it and doubled it again, and again and again, because I'm a far better man of business than Father ever was or ever could be. But now I'm an exile and an outcast, accused of theft and stripped of fortune, without even the respect of the man who should have been at my right hand, Rashgallivak.

All because of Nafai. All his fault.

Nafai ran in blind panic, with no thought of destination. It was not until he broke away from the crowds and found himself in an open space that he began to calm enough to think of where he was and what he ought to do next. He was in the Old Dance, once as large a dancing space as the Orchestra in Dolltown, which replaced it many centuries ago. Now, though, the buildings encroached the dance on every side. It had lost its roundness, and even the bowl shape of the amphitheatre was lost among the houses and shops. But an open space *did* remain, and that was where Nafai stood, looking at the sky, pink-tinged in the west, graying to black in the east. It was nearly full dark, and he had no idea whether assassins were still following him. One thing was certain—in the dark, in this part of town, the crowds would thin out, and murder would be much easier to accomplish unobserved. All his running had got him farther from safety than ever, and he had no idea what to do next.

"Nafai," said a girl's voice.

He turned. It was Luet.

"Hi," he greeted her. But he didn't have time to chat. He had to *think*.

"Quick," she said.

"Quick what?"

"Come with me."

"I can't," he said. "I have to do something."

"Yes," she said. "You have to come with me."

"I have to get out of the city."

She grabbed him by the front of his shirt and stood on tip-toe, which she no doubt intended to bring her eye-to-eye with him, but which succeeded only in making her hang from his shirt like a puppet. He laughed, but she didn't join him. "Listen, O thou busiest of men," she said, "have you forgotten that I'm a seer of the Oversoul?"

He *had* forgotten. Had forgotten even that it was her coming in the middle of the night that had saved Father from Gaballufix's plot. There were things she still didn't know about that, he realized. For some reason he thought he ought to explain. "Elemak and Mebbekew *were* involved in the plot," he said. "But I think Gaballufix lied to them about what he meant to do."

She had no patience for his confused babbling. "Do you think I care now? They're looking for you, Nafai. I saw it in a dream—a soldier with bloody hands stalking the streets. I knew that I had to find you. To save you."

"How can *you* save *me*?"

"Come with me," she said. "I know the way."

He had no better idea. In fact, when he tried to think of any alternative to following her, his mind went blank. He couldn't hold the thought. Finally it dawned on him that this was a message from the Oversoul. It wanted him to go with her. It had sent her to him, and so he must go with her, wherever she led him.

She took his hand and pulled him from the Old Dance

down the street with the same name, until they reached the place where it narrowed, and then they took a fork to the left. "Our fortune is gone," said Nafai. "It was my fault, too. Except Rashgallivak betrayed us."

"Shut up," she said. "This isn't a good neighborhood."

She was right. It was dark here, and the road ran between old houses, dilapidated and dirty. There were few people there, and none of them seemed willing to look them in the eye.

They wound through a couple of sharp bends in the road, and then suddenly found themselves in Spring Street, near where it ran out into the holy wood. At that moment, Nafai saw ahead of him a group of soldiers, standing watch as if they had known he would emerge there. At once he turned to run, and then saw coming up the road they had just taken a couple of men with their charged-wire blades glowing slightly in the darkness.

"Good job, Nyef," Luet said contemptuously. "They probably wouldn't have noticed us. *Now* we look suspicious."

"*They* already know who we are," he said, pointing to the men approaching out of the dark street.

"Oh well," she said. "I had hoped to take the easy way in, but this one will have to do."

She grabbed his hand and half-dragged him the wrong way on Spring Street, away from the city and *toward* the holy forest. Nafai knew it was the stupidest thing she could possibly do. In the edges of the forest there'd be no witnesses at all. The assassins would have their way. If she imagined that Nafai had some particular skill at fighting and could somehow save them by disarming or killing the assassins, she would quickly discover the sad truth that he had never been interested in fighting and had no training along those lines at all. He couldn't even remember having hit someone in anger in his life, not even his older brothers, since fighting back against Meb or Elemak only made things worse in the end. Nafai might be large for his age, the tallest of Wetchik's sons, but it meant nothing when it came to battle.

As they moved into the darkness at the end of Spring Street, the assassins became bolder.

"That's right," one of them called out—softly, but audible enough to Nafai and Luet. "Into the shadows. That's where we'll have our conversation."

"We have nothing for you to steal." Luet's voice sounded panicked, trembling—but Nafai knew from her hand's steady grip that she was not trembling at all.

Nafai was trembling, however.

"Into the shadows," said the man again.

So they obeyed him. Plunged into the darkness under the trees. But to Nafai's surprise, they didn't stop, nor did they turn south, to skirt the forest and perhaps reenter the city at the next road. She led him almost straight east. Deeper into the forbidden country.

"I can't go here," he said.

"Shut up," she said. "Neither can they, unless they hear us talking and follow the sound."

He held his tongue, and followed her. After a while the ground began to fall away, not a slope anymore as much as a cliff, and it became very difficult to pick his way. The sky was fully dark now, and even though many leaves had fallen here, the shade of the trees was still quite deep. "I can't see," he whispered.

"Neither can I," she answered.

"Stop," he said. "Listen. Maybe they've stopped following us."

"They have," she said. "But we can't stop."

"Why not?"

"I've got to take you out of the city."

"If I'm caught here, the punishment is terrible."

"I know," she said. "As bad for me, though, for bringing you."

"Then take me back."

"No," she said. "This is where the Oversoul wants us to go."

It was too hard, however, to hold hands anymore—they both needed both hands to make their way down the ragged face of the cliff. It wouldn't have been that dangerous a climb in daylight, but in the darkness they might not see a drop-off that would kill them, so every step had to be tested. At least on this slope the trees were rarer, so the starlight could do a better job of helping them to see. At least, that's how it was until they reached the fog.

"Now we *have* to stop," he said.

"Keep climbing."

"In the fog? We'll get lost on the cliff face and fall and die."

"It's a good sign," said Luet. "It means that we're at least halfway down to the lake."

"You're not taking me to the lake!"

"Hush."

"Why don't I just throw myself down the quick way, then, and save them the effort of killing me?"

"Hush, you stupid man. The Oversoul will protect us."

"The Oversoul is a computer link with satellites orbiting Harmony. It doesn't have any magical machines to reach down and catch us if we fall."

"She is making us alert," said Luet. "Or she's helping *me*, at least, to find the way. If you'd only stop talking and let me listen to her."

They were hours climbing down through the fog, or so it seemed to Nafai, but at last they reached the bottom. Grass on a level plain, giving way to mud.

Warm mud. No, *hot* mud.

"Here we are," she said. "We can't go into the water here—it comes up from a rift deep in the crust of the world, where it's so hot that it boils and gives off steam.

The water would cook the meat from our bones if we stayed in it for any length of time, even near the shore."

"Then how do women ever—"

"We do our worship nearer to the other end, where the lake is fed by ice-cold mountain streams. Some go into the coldest water. But the visions come to most of us when we float in the water at the place where the cold and hot waters meet. A turbulent place, the water endlessly rocking and swirling, freezing and searing us by turns. The place where the heart of the world and its coldest surface come together. A place where the two hearts of every woman are made one."

"I don't belong here," said Nafai.

"I know," said Luet. "But here is where the Oversoul led us, so here we'll stay."

And then what Nafai feared most. A woman, speaking not far off. "I *told* you I heard a man's voice. It came from *there.*"

Lanterns came near, and many women. Their feet made splatting noises with each step in the hot mud, then sucking noises as they pulled them out again. How far have *I* sunk into the mud? wondered Nafai. Will they have trouble pulling me out? Or will they simply bury me alive right here, letting the mud decide whether to cook me or suffocate me?

"I brought him," said Luet.

"It's Luet," said an old woman. The name was picked up in a whisper and carried back through the gathering crowd.

"The Oversoul led me here. This man isn't like other men. The Oversoul has chosen him."

"The law is the law," said the old woman. "You have taken the responsibility on yourself, but that only moves the punishment from him to you."

Nafai saw how tense Luet looked. He realized: She doesn't understand the Oversoul any better than I do.

For all she knows, the Oversoul doesn't care whether she lives or dies, and may be perfectly content to let her pay with her life for my safe passage here tonight.

"Very well," said Luet. "But you must take him to the Private Gate, and help him through the wood."

"You can't tell us what we *must* do, lawbreaker!" cried one woman. But others shushed her. Luet was held in great reverence, Nafai could see, even when she had committed an outrage.

Then the crowd parted, just a little, to let a woman pass, appearing like a ghost from the fog. She was naked, and because she was clean Nafai didn't realize for a moment that she must be a wilder. It was only when she came very close, plucking at Luet's sleeve, that Nafai could see how weathered and dry her skin was, how wrinkled and how gaunt her face.

"You," whispered Luet.

"You," echoed the wilder.

Then the holy woman from the desert turned to the old woman who seemed to be the leader of this band of justicers. "I have already punished her," she said.

"What do you mean?" asked the old woman.

"I am the Oversoul, and I say she has already borne my punishment."

The old woman looked at Luet, full of uncertainty. "Is this true speech, Luet?"

Nafai was amazed. Was their trust in Luet so complete that they would ask her to confirm or deny testimony that might cost her life or save it, depending on her own answer?

Their trust was justified, for Luet's answer contained no special pleading for herself. "This holy woman only slapped my face. How could it be punishment enough for this?"

"I brought her here," said the wilder. "I made her bring this boy. I have shown him great visions, and I will show him more. I will put honor in his seed, and a great nation shall arise. Let no one hinder him in his path through the water and the wood, and as for her, she has borne the mark of my hand upon her face. Who can touch her after I have done with her?"

"Truly this is the voice of the Mother," said the old woman.

"The Mother," whispered some.

"The Oversoul," whispered others.

The holy woman turned to face Luet again, and reached up and touched one finger to the girl's lips. Luet kissed that finger, gently, and for a moment Nafai ached for the sweetness of it. Then the wilder's expression changed. It was as if some brighter soul had been inside her face, and now it was gone; she looked distracted, vaguely confused. She looked around, recognizing nothing, and then wandered off into the fog.

"Was that your mother?" whispered Nafai.

"No," said Luet. "The mother of my body isn't holy anymore. But in my heart, all such women are my mother."

"Well spoken," said the old woman. "What a fairspoken child she is."

Luet bowed her head. When she lifted her face again, Nafai could see tears on her cheeks. He had no idea what was happening here, or what it meant to Luet; he only knew that for a while his life had been in danger, and then hers, and now the danger had passed. That was enough for him.

The wilder had said that no one should hinder him in his path through the water and the wood. After brief discussion, the women decided that this meant he had to traverse the lake from this point to the other end, from the hot to the cold; he had no idea how they discerned that from the holy woman's few words, but then he had often marveled at how many meanings the priests could wrest from the holy writings of the men's religion, too. They waited a few minutes until several women called out from the water. Only then did Luet lead him near enough for him to see the lake. Now it was clear where the fog came from—it rose as sheets of steam from the water, or so it appeared to him. Two women in a long low boat were bringing it to shore, the one rowing, the other at the tiller. The bow of the boat was square and low, but since there were no waves upon the lake, and the rowing was smooth, there seemed no danger of the boat taking water at the bow. They drew close, closer to shore, until at last they had run aground. Still there were several meters of water to cross between the boat and the mud flats where Nafai and Luet stood. The mud was painfully hot now, so that Nafai had to move his feet rather often to keep from burning them. What would it be like to walk through the water?

"Walk steadily," Luet whispered. "The less you splash, the better, so you mustn't run. You'll see that if you just keep going, you're in the boat soon, and the pain passes quickly."

So she had done this before. Very well, if Luet could bear it, so could he. He took a step toward the water. The women gasped.

"No," she said quickly. "In this place, where you're a child and a stranger, you must be led."

Me, a child? Compared to *you*? But then he realized that of course she was right. Whatever their ages might be, this was her place, not his; she was the adult and he the infant here.

She set the pace, brisk but not hurried. The water burned his feet, but it was shallow, and he didn't splash very much, though he was not as graceful and smooth in his movements as Luet. In moments they were at the boat, but it seemed like forever, like a thousand agonizing steps, especially the hesitation as she stepped into the boat. At last she was in, and her hand drew him in after her, and he walked on feet that stung so deep within the skin that he was afraid to look down at them for fear the flesh had been cooked off them. But then he *did* look, and the skin looked normal. Luet used the hem of her skirt to wipe his feet. The oarsman jammed the blade of an oar into the mud under the water and pushed them back, her muscles of her massive arms rippling with the exertion. Nafai faced Luet and clung to her hands as they glided through the water.

It was the strangest journey of Nafai's life, though not a long one. The fog made everything seem magic and unreal. Huge rocks loomed out of the water, they slipped silently between them, and then the stones were swallowed up as if they had ceased to be. The water grew hotter, and there were places where it bubbled; they steered around those spots. The boat itself was never hot, but the air around them was so hot and wet that soon they were drenched, their clothing clinging to their bodies. Nafai could see for the first time that Luet did, in fact, have a womanly shape to her; not much, but enough that he would never again be able to think of her as nothing but a child. Suddenly he was shy to be sitting there holding her hands, and yet he was more afraid to let go. He needed to be touching her, like a child holding his mother's hand in the darkness.

They drifted on. The air cooled. They passed through narrows, with steep cliffs on either hand, seeming to lean closer together the higher they went, until they were lost in the fog. Nafai wondered if perhaps this was a cave, or, if it wasn't, whether sunlight ever reached the base of this deep rift. Then the cliff walls receded, and the fog thinned just a little. At the same time, the water grew more turbulent. There were waves now, and currents caught the boat and made it want to spin, to yaw from side to side.

The oarsman lifted her oars; the steersman took her hand from the tiller. Luet leaned forward and whispered,

"This is the place where the visions come. I told you—where the hot and the cold meet. Here is where we pass through the water in the flesh."

In the flesh apparently meant exactly that. Feeling even more shy to watch Luet undressing than to undress himself, he watched his own hands unfasten his clothing and fold it as Luet did hers and lay the pile in the boat. Trying to somehow watch her without seeing her, Nafai couldn't quite grasp how she managed to slip so noiselessly into the water, then lie motionless on her back. He could see that she made no move to swim, so when he—noisily—dropped himself into the water, he also lay still. The water was surprisingly buoyant. There was no danger of sinking. The silence was deep and powerful; only once did he speak, when he could see that she was drifting away from him.

"No matter," she answered quietly. "Hush."

He hushed. Now he was alone in the fog. The currents turned him—or perhaps they didn't, for in the fog he couldn't tell east from west or anything else having to do with location, except for up and down, and even *that* seemed to matter very little. It was peaceful here, a place where his eyes could see and yet not see, where his ears could hear and yet hear nothing. The current did not let him sleep, however. He could feel the hot and cold wash under him, sometimes very hot, sometimes very cold, so that sometimes he thought, I can't bear this another moment, I'll have to swim or I might die here—and then the current changed again.

He saw no vision. The Oversoul said nothing to him. He listened. He even spoke to the Oversoul, begging to know how he might somehow manage to get the Index that Father had sent him for. If the Oversoul heard him, it gave no sign.

He drifted on the lake forever. Or perhaps it was only a few minutes before he heard the soft touch of the oars in the water. A hand touched his hair, his face, his shoulder, then caught at his arm. He remembered how to turn his head and then he did it, and saw the boat, with Luet, now fully dressed, reaching out to him. It did not occur to him to be shy now; he was only glad to see her, and yet sad to think that he had to rise out of the water. He was not deft at climbing into the boat. He rocked it badly, and spilled water into it.

"Roll in," whispered Luet.

He lay on his side in the water, reached a leg and an arm into the boat, and rolled in. It was easy, almost silent. Luet handed him his clothing, still wet, but now very cold. He drew it on and shivered as the women propelled the boat on into the bone-chilling fog. Luet also shivered, but seemed undisturbed even so.

At last they came to a shoreline, where again a group of women were waiting. Perhaps another boat had gone directly across the lake, not waiting for the ritual of passing through the water in the flesh, or perhaps there was some road for runners bearing messages; whatever the reason, the women waiting for them already knew who they were. There was no need for explanations. Luet again led the way, this time through icy water that made Nafai's bones ache. They reached dry land—a grassy bank this time, instead of mud flats—and women's hands wrapped a dry blanket around him. He saw that Luet also was being warmed.

"The first man to pass through the water," said a woman.

"The man who passes through the waters of women," said another.

Luet explained to him, seeming a little embarrassed. "Famous prophecies," she said. "There are so many of them, it's hard not to fulfil one now and then."

He smiled. He knew that she took the prophecies much more seriously than she pretended. And so did he.

He noticed that no one asked her what had happened on the water; no one asked whether she had seen a vision. But they lingered, waiting, until finally she said, "The Oversoul gave me comfort, and it was enough." They drifted away then, most of them, though a few looked at Nafai until he shook his head.

"We're through the easy part now," she said.

He thought she was joking, but then she led him through the Private Gate, a legendary gap in the red wall that he had only half-believed was real. It was a curving passageway between a pair of massive towers, and instead of city guards, there were only women, watching. On the other side, he knew, lay Trackless Wood. Quickly he learned that it had earned its name. His face was streaked with cuts, and so was hers, and their arms and legs as well, by the time they emerged onto Forest Road.

"That way is Back Gate," said Luet. "And down any of these canyons you'll reach the desert. I don't know where you're going from there."

"That's good enough," said Nafai. "I can find my way."

"Then I've done what the Oversoul sent me to do."

Nafai didn't know what to say. He didn't even know the name for what he was feeling. "I think that I don't know you," said Nafai.

She looked at him, a little perplexed.

"No, that's wrong," Nafai said. "I think that I didn't know you before, even though I thought I knew you, and now that I finally know you, I don't really know you at all."

She smiled. "Those crossing currents do it to you every time," she said. "Tell no one, man or woman, what you did tonight."

"I'm not sure, when I remember it, whether I'll believe that it really happened myself."

"Will we see you again, at Aunt Rasa's house?"

"I don't know," said Nafai. "I only know this: that I

don't know how I can get the Index without getting killed, and yet I have to get it."

"Wait until the Oversoul tells you what to do," said Luet, "and then do it."

He nodded. "That's fine, if the Oversoul actually tells me something."

"She will," said Luet. "When there's something to do, she'll tell you."

Then, impulsively, Luet reached out her hand and grasped his again, for just a moment. He remembered again, like an echo in his flesh, how it felt to cling to her on the lake. He was a little embarrassed now, though, and drew his hand away. She had seen him being weak. She had seen him naked.

"See?" she said. "You're forgetting already how it really was."

"No I'm not," he said.

She turned away and headed down the road toward Back Gate. He wanted to call out to her and say, You were right, I *was* forgetting how it really was, I was remembering it through common ordinary eyes, I was remembering it as the boy I was before, but now I remember that it wasn't me being weak or me being naked, or anything else that I should be ashamed of. It was me riding like a great hero out of prophecy across the magical lake, with you as my guide and teacher, and when we shed our clothing it wasn't a man and woman naked together, it was rather two gods out of ancient stories from faraway lands, stripping away their mortal disguises and standing revealed in their glorious immortality, ready to float over the sea of death and emerge unscathed on the other side.

But by the time he thought of all the things he wanted to say, she had disappeared around a bend.

FOURTEEN

ISSIB'S CHAIR

Nafai didn't know what to expect when he got to the rendezvous. All the way across the desert in the starlight, he kept imagining terrible things. What if none of his brothers escaped? *They* didn't have the help of Luet and the women of Basilica. Or what if they *did* escape, but the soldiers followed one of them to their hiding place, and then slaughtered them? When he got there, would he find their mutilated bodies? Or would there be soldiers lying in wait for him, to take him as he made his way down the canyon?

He paused at the top of the canyon, the place where they had stopped to cast lots early that same morning. Oversoul, he said silently, should I go down there?

The answer he got was a picture in his mind—one of Gaballufix's inhuman soldiers walking through the empty nighttime streets of Basilica. He didn't know what sense to make of this. Was the Oversoul telling him that the soldiers were all in the city? Or was Nafai seeing this vision because the Oversoul was telling him that soldiers were waiting for him in the arroyo, and his brain had simply added irrelevant details of the city to the vision?

One thing was inescapable—the sense of urgency he was getting from the Oversoul. As if there was an opportunity he could not afford to miss. Or a danger he had to avoid.

When the message is so unclear, Nafai said silently, what can I go on except for my own judgment? If my brothers are in trouble I need to know it. I can't abandon them, even if there might be danger to myself. If I'm wrong, take this thought from me.

Then he started down the arroyo. There came no stupor, no distraction. Whatever else the Oversoul was trying to tell him, it certainly didn't mind him going down to the rendezvous with his brothers.

Or else it had given up on him. But no—it had just gone to so much trouble to bring him out of the city, through the Lake of Women, the Oversoul could hardly plan to abandon him now.

It was so dark in the canyon that he ended up stumbling, sliding down, until he finally came to rest on the gravelly shelf where his brothers were supposed to be waiting.

"Nafai."

It was Issib's voice. But Nafai hardly had time to hear it before he felt a harsh blow. Someone's sandal against his face, shoving him down into the rocks.

"Fool!" shouted Elemak. "I wish they'd caught you and killed you, you little bastard!"

Another foot, from the other side, smashing into his nose. And now Mebbekew's voice. "All gone, the whole fortune, everything, because of you!"

"He didn't take it, you fools!" cried Issib. "Gaballufix stole it!"

"You shut up!" shouted Mebbekew, advancing on Issib. Nafai was at last able to see what was happening. Though his face stung from the tiny rocks embedded in the bottoms of their sandals, they really hadn't hurt him seriously. Now, though, he could see that they truly were raging. But why at *Nafai*?

"Rash was the one who betrayed us," said Nafai.

Immediately they turned back to him. "Is that so?" said Elemak. "Didn't I tell you that *I* was going to do all the talking? I could have had the Index for a quarter of what we had, but no, *you* had to—"

"You were giving up!" cried Nafai. "You were walking out!"

Elemak roared in fury, pulled Nafai up by the shirt, lifting him partway from the ground. "Half of bargaining *is* walking out, you fool! Do you think I didn't know what I was doing? I, who have bargained in foreign lands and made great profit on few goods—why couldn't you trust me to know what I was doing? All you've ever bargained for is a few stupid myachiks in the market, little boy."

"I didn't know," said Nafai.

Elemak threw him down onto the ground. Nafai's elbows were scraped, and his head struck the stones hard enough that it hurt him. Without meaning to, he cried out.

"Leave him alone, you coward," said Issib.

"Calling me a coward?" said Elemak.

"Gaballufix was going to have our money no matter what we did. He already had Rash on his side."

"So now you're the expert on what *would* have happened," said Elemak.

"Sitting on your throne, judging us!" cried Mebbekew. "You think Nafai's so innocent, what about *you*! You're the one who got the money out of Father's accounts!"

Nafai stood up. He didn't like the way they were menacing Issib. It was one thing for them to take out their fury on him, but something else again when they seemed about to hurt Issya. "I'm sorry," said Nafai. There was nothing for it but to take the blame, and their anger. "I didn't understand, and I should have kept my mouth shut. I'm sorry."

"What is *sorry*?" said Elemak. "How many times have you said *sorry* when it was too late to undo the consequences? You never learn anything, Nafai. Father never taught you. His little baby, precious Rasa's little boy, who could do no wrong. Well, it's time you learned the lessons that Father should have taught you years ago."

Elemak pulled one of the rods out of a pack frame leaning against the canyon wall. It was designed to carry heavy loads on the back of a camel; it had some flex to it, and it wasn't terribly heavy, but it was sturdy and long. Nafai knew at once what Elemak intended. "You have no right to touch me," said Nafai.

"No, nobody has the right to touch you," said Mebbekew. "Sacred Nafai, Father's jewel-eyed boy, no one can touch him. He can touch *us*, of course. He can lose our inheritance for us, but no one can touch *him*."

"It would never have been *your* inheritance, anyway," Nafai said to Mebbekew. "It was always for Elemak." Another thought came into Nafai's mind, thinking of who would have received the inheritance. He knew before he said it that it wasn't the wisest thing to say, when Elemak and Mebbekew were already in a fury. But he said it anyway. "When it comes to what you *lost*, you both deserved to be disinherited anyway, plotting against Father."

"That is a lie," said Mebbekew.

"How stupid do you think I am?" said Nafai. "You might not have known Gaballufix meant to kill Father that morning, but you knew he meant to kill *somebody*. What did Gaballufix promise you, Elemak? The same thing he promised Rash—the Wetchik name and fortune, after Father was discredited and forced out of his place?"

Elemak roared and rushed at him, laying on with the rod. He was so angry that few of the blows actually landed true, but when they did, they were brutal. Nafai had never felt such pain, not even when he prayed, not even when his feet were in the scalding water of the lake. He ended up sprawled face-down in the gravel, with Elemak poised above him, ready to hit him—where, on his back? On his head?

"Please!" Nafai shouted.

"Liar!" roared Elemak.

"Traitor!" Nafai shouted back. He started to get to his knees, to his feet.

The rod fell, knocking him back down to the ground. He's broken my back, thought Nafai. I'll be paralyzed. I'll be like Issib, crippled in a chair for the rest of my life.

It was as if the thought of Issib brought him into action. For as Elemak raised the rod again, Issib's chair swung across in front of him. The chair was turning as it went—it couldn't have been completely under control—and the rod caught Issib across one arm. He screamed in pain, and the chair lost control completely, spinning crazily and reeling back and forth. Its collision avoidance system kept it from banging into the stone walls of the arroyo, but it did bump into Mebbekew as he tried to run out of the way, knocking him down.

"Stay out of the way, Issib!" shouted Elemak.

"You coward!" cried Nafai. "You were *nothing* in front of Gaballufix, but now you can beat a cripple and a fourteen-year-old boy! Very brave!"

Again Elemak turned away from Issib to face Nafai. "You've said too much this time, boy," he said. He wasn't shouting this time. It was a colder, deeper anger. "I'm never going to hear that voice again, do you understand me?"

"That's right, Elya," said Nafai. "You couldn't get Gaballufix to kill Father for you, but at least you can kill *me*. Come ahead, prove what a man you are by killing your little brother."

Nafai had been hoping to shame Elemak into backing off, but he miscalculated. Instead Elemak lost all self-control. As Issib spun by in front of him, Elemak seized an outflung arm and dragged Issib from the chair, throwing him to the ground like a broken toy.

"No!" screamed Nafai.

He rushed for Issib, to help him, but Mebbekew was between them, and when Nafai got near enough, Mebbekew shoved him to the ground. Nafai sprawled at Elemak's feet.

Elemak had dropped his rod. As he reached for it, Mebbekew ran to the pack frame and drew out another one. "Let's have done with him now. And if Issib can't keep his mouth shut, both of them."

Whether Elemak heard or not, Nafai couldn't tell. He only knew that the rod came whistling down, smashing into his shoulder. Elemak's aim still wasn't good, but this much was clear: He was striking high on Nafai's body. He was trying for the head. He meant Nafai to die.

Suddenly there was a blinding light in the canyon. Nafai lifted his head in time to see Elemak whirl around, trying to follow the source of the light. It was Issib's chair.

Only it couldn't be. Issib's chair had a passive switching system. When it was not being told explicitly what to do, it settled down, leveled itself on its legs, and waited for instructions. It had done just that the moment Elemak dragged Issib to the ground.

"What's happening?" asked Mebbekew.

"What's happening?" said a mechanical voice from the chair.

"You must have broken it," said Mebbekew.

"I am not the one who is broken," said the chair. "Faith and trust are broken. Brotherhood is broken. Honor and law and decency are broken. Compassion is broken. But I am not broken."

"Make it stop, Issya," said Mebbekew.

Nafai noticed that Elemak said nothing. He was eyeing the chair steadily, the rod still in his hands. Then, with a grunt, Elemak rushed forward and swung at the chair with the rod.

Lightning flashed, or so it seemed. Elemak screamed and fell back, as the rod flew into the air. It was burning, the whole length of it.

Carefully, slowly, Mebbekew slid his own rod back down into the pack frame.

"Why were you beating your younger brother with a rod, Elemak?" said the chair. "Why did you plan his death, Mebbekew?"

"Who's doing this?" Mebbekew said.

"Can't you guess, fool?" Issib spoke feebly, from where he lay in the rocks. "Who sent us on this errand in the first place?"

"Father," said Mebbekew.

"The Oversoul," said Elemak.

"Don't you understand yet, that because your younger brother Nafai was willing to hear my voice, I have chosen him to lead you?"

That silenced them both. But Nafai knew that in their hearts, their hatred of him had passed from hot anger to cold hard resentment that would never die. The Oversoul had chosen Nafai to lead them. Nafai, who couldn't even get through negotiations with Gaballufix without messing everything up. Oversoul, why are you doing this to me?

"If you had not betrayed your father, if you had believed in him and obeyed him, I would not have had to choose Nafai ahead of you," said the chair—said the Oversoul. "Now go up into Basilica again, and I will deliver Gaballufix into your hands."

With that, the chair's lights dimmed, and it settled slowly to the ground.

They all waited, dumbly, for a few silent moments. Then Elemak turned to Issib and gently, carefully lifted him back and put him into the chair. "I'm sorry, Issya," he said gently. "I was not in my right mind. I would never hurt you for the world."

Issib said nothing.

"It was Nafai we were angry at," said Mebbekew.

Issib turned to him and, in a whisper, repeated Meb's own words back to him. "Let's have done with him now. And if Issib can't keep his mouth shut, both of them."

Mebbekew was stung. "So I guess you're going to hold that against me forever."

"Shut up, Meb," said Elemak. "Let's think."

"Good idea," said Mebbekew. "Thinking has done us *so* much good up to now."

"It's one thing to see the Oversoul move a chair around," said Elemak. "But Gaballufix has hundreds of soldiers. He can kill each of us fifty times over—where are the soldiers of the Oversoul? What army is going to protect us now?"

Nafai was standing now, listening to them. He could hardly believe what he was hearing. "The Oversoul has just shown you some of its power, and you're still afraid of Gaballufix's soldiers? The Oversoul is stronger than these soldiers. If it doesn't want them to kill us, the soldiers won't kill us."

Elemak and Mebbekew regarded him in silence.

"You were willing to kill me because you didn't like my words," said Nafai. "Are you willing to follow me now, in obeying the words of the Oversoul?"

"How do we know you didn't rig the chair yourself?" said Mebbekew.

"That's right," said Nafai. "I knew before we ever went into the city today that you were going to blame me for everything and try to kill me, and so Issya and I rigged the chair to deliver exactly that speech."

"Don't be stupid, Meb," said Elemak. "We're going to get killed, but since we've lost everything else, it doesn't really make that much difference to me."

"Just because you're a fatalist doesn't mean *I* want to die," said Mebbekew.

Issib swung his chair forward. "Let's go," he said to Nafai. "It's the Oversoul I'm following, and you as his servant. Let's go."

Nafai nodded, then led the way up the canyon. For a while he heard only the sound of his own footfalls, and the faint whirring of Issib's chair. Then, at last, came the clatter of Elemak and Mebbekew, following him up the arroyo.

FIFTEEN

MURDER

If we are to have any hope at all, thought Nafai, we have to stop trying to come up with our own plans. Gaballufix outmaneuvers us every time.

And now there was even less hope, since Elemak and Mebbekew were deliberately being uncooperative. Why did the Oversoul have to say what it did about Nafai leading them? How could he possibly take command over his own older brothers, who would be far gladder to see him fail than to help him succeed? Issib would be no problem, of course, but it was hard to see how he would be much help, either, even wearing his floats again. He was too conspicuous, too fragile, and too slow, all at once.

Gradually, as they made their way through the desert—Nafai leading, not because he wanted to, but because Elemak refused to help him pick out a path— Nafai came to an inescapable conclusion: He would have a much better chance alone than with his brothers.

Not that he thought his chances were very good on his own. But he would have the Oversoul to help him. And the Oversoul *had* got him out of Basilica before.

But when the Oversoul got him out of Basilica, it was because Luet held his hand. Who would be his Luet now? She was the seer, as familiar with the Oversoul as Nafai was with his own mother. Luet could feel the Oversoul showing her every step; Nafai only felt the guidance of the Oversoul now and then, so rarely, so confusingly. What was his vision of a bloody-handed soldier walking the streets of Basilica? Was this an enemy he would have to fight? Was it his death? Or his guide? He was so confused, how could he possibly come up with a plan?

He stopped.

The others stopped behind him.

"What now?" asked Mebbekew. "Enlighten us, O great leader anointed by the Oversoul."

Nafai didn't answer. Instead he tried to empty his mind. To relax the knot of fear in his stomach. The Oversoul didn't speak to him the way it spoke to Luet because Luet didn't *expect* herself to come up with a plan. Luet listened. Listened *first*, understood *first*. If Nafai was serious about trying to help the Oversoul, trying to be its hands and feet here on the surface of this world, then he had to stop trying to make up his own foolish plans and give the Oversoul a chance to talk to him.

They were near Dogtown, which stretched along the roads leading out from the gate known as the Funnel. Till now, he had assumed that he should go around Dogtown and pick his way through some canyon back up to Forest Road and enter Basilica through Back Gate. Now, though, he waited, tested the ideas. He thought of going on, around Dogtown, and his thoughts drifted aimlessly.

Then he turned toward the Funnel, and at once felt a rush of confidence. Yes, he thought. The Oversoul is trying to lead me, if I'll just shut up and listen. The way I should have shut up and listened while Elemak was bargaining with Gaballufix this afternoon.

"Oh, good," said Mebbekew. "Let's go up to the second most closely watched gate. Let's go through the ugliest slum, where Gaballufix owns everybody that's for sale, which is everybody that's alive."

"Hush," said Issib.

"Let him talk," said Nafai. "It'll bring Gaballufix's men down on us and get us all killed right now, which is exactly what Mebbekew wants, because as we all die Meb can say, 'See, Nyef, you got us killed!' which will let him die happy."

Mebbekew started toward Nafai, but Elemak stopped him. "We'll be quiet," said Elemak.

Nafai led them on until they came to High Road, which ran from Gate Town to Dogtown. It was lined with houses much of the way, but at this time of night it wasn't too safe, and few people would be abroad on it. Nafai led them to the widest gap between houses on both sides of the road, scanned to the left and right, and then ducked down and scurried across. Then he waited in a dry ditch on the far side of the road, watching for the others.

They didn't come.

They didn't come.

They've decided to abandon me now, thought Nafai. Well, fine.

Then they appeared. Not scurrying, as Nafai had done, but walking. All three of them. Of course, thought Nafai. They had waited to get Issib out of his chair. I should have thought of that.

As they walked across the road, Nafai realized that

instead of Issib floating, he was being helped by the other two, his arms flung across their shoulders, his feet being half-dragged. To anyone who didn't know the truth, Issib would look like a drunk being helped home by his friends.

Nor did they walk straight across the road. Rather they angled across, as if they were really going *with* the road, but losing their way in the dark, or being tipped in one direction by the drunk they were helping. Finally they were across, and slipped off into the bushes.

Nafai caught up with them as they were untangling Issib, helping him adjust his floats. "That was so good," he whispered. "A thousand people could have seen you and nobody would have thought twice about it."

"Elemak thought of it," said Issib.

"You should be leading," said Nafai.

"Not according to the Oversoul," said Elemak.

"Issib's chair, you mean," said Mebbekew.

"It was just as well, Nyef, you going across first," said Elemak. "The guards will be looking for four men, one of them floating. Instead they saw three, one of them drunk."

"Where now?" said Issib.

Nafai shrugged. "This way, I guess." He led the way, angling through the empty ground between High Road and the Funnel.

He got distracted. He couldn't think of what to do next. He couldn't think of anything.

"Stop," he said. He thought of leading them onward, and it felt wrong. What felt right was for him to go on alone. "Wait here," he said. "I'm going into the city alone."

"Brilliant," said Mebbekew. "We could have waited back with the camels."

"No," said Nafai. "Please. I need you *here*. I need to be sure I can come out of the gate and find you here."

"How long will you be?" asked Issib.

"I don't know," said Nafai.

"Well, what are you planning to *do*?"

He couldn't very well tell them that he hadn't the faintest idea. "Elemak didn't tell us what *he* was planning," said Nafai.

"Right," said Mebbekew. "Play at being the big man."

"We'll wait," said Elemak. "But if the sun rises with us here, we're out in the open and we'll be caught for sure. You understand that."

"At the first lightening of the sky, if I'm not back, get Issib's chair and head for the camels," said Nafai.

"We'll do it," said Elemak.

"If we feel like it," said Mebbekew.

"We'll feel like it," said Elemak. "Meb will be here, just like the rest of us."

Nafai knew that Elemak still hated him, still felt contempt for him—but he also knew that Elemak would do what he said. That even though Elemak was expecting him to fail, he was also giving him a reasonable chance to succeed. "Thank you," said Nafai.

"Get the Index," said Elemak. "You're the Oversoul's boy, get the Index."

Nafai left them then, walking toward the Funnel. As he got nearer, he could hear the guards talking. There were too many of them—six or seven, not the usual two. Why? He moved to the wall and then slipped closer, to where he could hear fairly well what they were saying.

"It's Gaballufix himself, *I* say," said one guard. "Probably killed Wetchik's boy first, so he couldn't leave the city, and then killed Roptat and put the blame where nobody could answer."

"Sounds like Gaballufix," another answered him. "Pure slime, him and all his men."

Roptat was dead. Nafai felt a thrill of fear. After all the failed plots, it had finally happened—Gaballufix had finally committed a murder. And blamed it on one of Wetchik's boys.

Me, Nafai realized. He blamed it on me. I'm the only one who didn't leave the city through a monitored gate. So as far as the city computer knows, I'm still inside. Of course Gaballufix would know that. So he seized the chance, had Roptat killed, and put out the word that it was the youngest son of Wetchik who did it.

But the women know. The women know he's lying. He doesn't realize it yet, but by tomorrow every woman in Basilica will know the truth—that when Roptat was being killed I was at the lake with Luet. I don't even have to go inside tonight. Gaballufix will be destroyed by his own stupidity, and we can wait outside the walls and laugh!

Only he couldn't think of waiting outside. The Oversoul didn't want that. The Oversoul didn't care about Gaballufix getting caught in his lies. The Oversoul cared about the Index, and the fall of Gaballufix wouldn't put the Index into Father's hands.

How do I get past the guards? Nafai asked.

In answer, all he felt was his own fear. He knew *that* didn't come from the Oversoul.

So he waited. After a while, the guards' conversation lagged. "Let's do a walk through Dogtown," said one of them. Five of them walked out of the gate, into the darkness of the Dogtown streets. If they had turned back to look at the gate, they would have seen Nafai standing there, leaning against the wall not two meters from the opening. But they didn't look back.

It was time, he knew that; his fear was undiminished,

but now there was also a hunger to act, to get moving. The Oversoul? It was hard to know, but he had to do *something*. So, holding his breath, Nafai stepped out into the light falling through the gate.

One guard sat on a stool, leaning against the gate. Asleep, or nearly so. The other was relieving himself against the opposite wall, his back to the opening. Nafai walked quietly through. Neither one stirred from his position until Nafai was away from the gatelight. Then he heard their voices behind him, talking—but not about him, not raising an alarm. This must be how it was for Luet, he thought, the night she came to give us warning. The Oversoul making the guards stupid enough to let her pass as if she were invisible. The way I passed through.

The moon was rising now. The night was more than half spent. The city was asleep, except probably Dolltown and the Inner Market, and even those were bound to be a bit subdued in these days of tension and turmoil, with soldiers patrolling the streets. In this district, though, a fairly safe one, with no night life at all, there was no one out and about. Nafai wasn't sure whether the emptiness of the streets was good or bad. It was good because there'd be fewer people to see him; bad because if he *was* seen, he'd be noticed for sure.

Except tonight the Oversoul was helping him *not* to be noticed. He kept to the shadows, not tempting fate, and once when a troop of soldiers did come by, he ducked into a doorway and they passed him without notice.

This must be the limit to the power of the Oversoul, thought Nafai. With Luet and Father and me, the Oversoul can communicate real ideas. And through a machine—through Issib's chair—but who can guess how much that cost the Oversoul? Reaching directly into the minds of these other people, it can't do much more than distract them, the way it steers people away from forbidden ideas. It can't turn the soldiers out of the road, but it *can* discourage them from noticing the fellow standing in the shadowed doorway, it *can* distract them from wanting to investigate, to see what he's doing. It can't keep the guards at the gate from doing their duty, but it *can* help the dozing guard to dream, so that the sound of Nafai's footsteps are part of the story of the dream, and he doesn't look up.

And even to do that much, the Oversoul must have its whole attention focused on this street tonight, thought Nafai. On this very place. On me.

Where am I going?

Doesn't matter. Turn off my mind and wander, that's what I have to do. Let the Oversoul lead me by the hand, the way Luet did.

It was hard, though, to empty his mind, to keep himself from recognizing each street he came to, keep himself from thinking of all the people or shops he knew of on that street, and how they might relate to getting the Index. His mind was too involved even now.

And why shouldn't it be? he thought. What am I supposed to do, stop being a sentient being? Become infinitely stupid so that the Oversoul can control me? Is my highest ambition in life to be a *puppet*?

No, came the answer. It was as clear as that night by the stream, in the desert. You're no puppet. You're here because you chose to be here. But now, to hear my voice, you have to empty your mind. Not because I want you to be stupid, but because you have to be able to hear me. Soon enough you'll need all your wits about you again. Fools are no good to me.

Nafai found himself leaning against a wall, gasping for breath, when the voice faded. It was no joke, to have the Oversoul *push* into his thoughts like that. What did our ancestors do to their children, when they changed us so that a computer could put things into our minds like this? In those early days, did all the children hear the voice of the Oversoul as I hear it now? Or was it always a rare thing, to be a hearer of that voice?

Move on. He felt it like a hunger. And he moved. Moved the way he had twice before in the last few weeks—going from street to street almost in a trance, uncertain of where he was, not caring. The way he had been only this afternoon, running from the assassins.

I don't even have a weapon.

The thought brought him up short. Pulled him out of his walking trance. He wasn't sure where he was. But there, half in shadow, there was a man lying in the street. Nafai came closer, curious. Some drunk, perhaps. Or it might be a victim of tolchocks, or soldiers, or assassins. A victim of Gaballufix.

No. Not a victim at all. It was one of Gaballufix's identical soldiers lying there, and from the stench of piss and alcohol, it wasn't any injury that put him on the ground.

Nafai almost walked away, until it dawned on him that here was the best disguise he could possibly hope for. It would be much simpler to get near Gaballufix if he was wearing one of the holographic soldier costumes—and here lay just such a costume, a gift that was his for the taking.

He knelt beside the man and rolled him over onto his back. It was impossible to *see* the box that controlled the holograph, but by running his hands through the image, he found it by touch, on a belt near the waist. He unfastened it, but even then it wouldn't come away from the man more than a few centimeters.

Oh, that's right, thought Nafai. Elemak said it was a kind of cloak, and the box was just a part of that.

Sure enough, when he pulled the box up the man's

body, it slid easily. By half-rolling the man this way and that, he was finally able to get the holographic costume off his arms, out from under his body, and then off the man's head.

Only then did Nafai realize that the Oversoul had provided him with more than a costume. This wasn't a hired thug with a soldier suit. It was Gaballufix himself.

Drunk out of his mind, lying in his own urine and vomit, but nevertheless, without any doubt, it was Gaballufix.

But what could Nafai *do* with this drunk? He certainly didn't have the Index with him. And Nafai harbored no delusion that by dragging him home he could win Gaballufix's undying gratitude.

The bastard must have been out celebrating the death of Roptat. A murderer lying here in the street, only he'll never be punished for it. In fact, he's trying to get *me* blamed for it. Nafai was filled with anger. He thought of putting his foot on Gaballufix's head and grinding his face down into the vomit-covered street. It would feel so good, so—

Kill him.

The thought was as clear as if someone behind him had spoken it.

No, thought Nafai. I can't do that. I can't kill a man.

Why do you think I brought you here? He's a killer. The law decrees his death.

The law decreed *my* death for seeing the Lake of Women, Nafai answered silently. Yet I was shown mercy.

I brought you to the lake, Nafai. As I brought you here. To do what must be done. You'll never get the Index while he's alive.

I can't kill a man. A helpless man like this—it would be murder.

It would be simple justice.

Not if it came from my hand. I hate him too much. I want him dead. For the humiliation of my family. For stealing my father's title. For taking our fortune. For the beating I got at my brother's hands. For the soldiers and the tolchocks, for the way he has blotted the light of hope out of my city. For the way he turned Rashgallivak, that good man, into a weak and foolish tool. For all those things I want him to die, I want to crush him under my foot. If I kill him now I'm a coward and an assassin, not a justicer.

He tried to kill you. His assassins had you marked for death.

I know it. So it would be private vengeance if I killed him now.

Think of what you're doing, Nafai. Think.

I'm not going to be a murderer.

That's right. You're going to *save* lives. There's only one hope of saving this world from the slaughter that destroyed Earth forty million years ago, and leaving this man alive will obliterate that hope. Should the billion souls of the planet Harmony all die, so that you can keep your hands clean? I tell you that this is not murder, not assassination, but justice. I have tried him and found him guilty. He ordered the death of Roptat, and your death, and your brothers' death, and the death of your father. He plots a war that will kill thousands and bring this city under subjugation. You aren't sparing him out of mercy, Nafai, because only his death will be merciful to the city and the people that you love, only his death will show mercy to the world. You're sparing him out of pure vanity. So that you can look at your hands and find them unstained with blood. I tell you that if you don't kill this man, the blood of millions will be on your head.

No!

Nafai's cry was all the more anguished for being silent, for being contained inside his mind.

The voice inside his head did not relent: The Index opens the deepest library in the world, Nafai. With it, all things are possible to my servants. Without it, I have no clearer voice than the one you hear now, constantly constantly changed and distorted by your own fears and hopes and expectations. Without the Index, I can't help you and you can't help me. My powers will continue to fade, and my law will dwindle among the people, until at last the fires come again, and another world is laid waste. The Index, Nafai. Take from this man what the law requires, and then go and get the Index.

Nafai reached down and took the charged-wire blade that was hooked to Gaballufix's belt.

I don't know how to kill a man with this. It doesn't stab. I can't stab the heart with this.

His head. Take off his head.

I can't. I can't, I can't, I can't.

But Nafai was wrong. He could.

He took Gaballufix by the hair, and stretched out his neck. Gaballufix stirred—was he waking up? Nafai almost let go of his hair then, but Gaballufix quickly dropped back into unconsciousness. Nafai switched on the blade and then laid it lightly against the throat. The blade hummed. A line of blood appeared. Nafai pressed harder, and the line became an open wound, with blood spouting over the blade, sizzling loudly. Too late to stop now, too late. He pressed harder, harder. The blade bit deeper. It resisted at the bone, but Nafai twisted the head away and opened a gap between the vertebrae, and now the blade cut through easily, and the head came free.

Nafai's pants and shirt were covered with blood, as were his hands and face, spattered with it, dripping with it. I have killed a man, and this is his head that I'm holding in my hands. What am I now? Who am I now? How am I better than the man who lies here, torn apart by my hands?

The Index.

He couldn't bear to wear his blood-soaked clothes. Almost in a panic to be rid of them, he tore them off, then wiped his face and hands on the unbloodied back of his shirt. These were the clothes that Luet handed to me when I climbed back into the boat in the beautiful, peaceful place, and now see what I've done with them.

Now, kneeling beside the body, his own clothes cast down into the blood, he realized that because of the downhill slope of the street and the fact that the blood mostly poured upward out of the neck, away from the body, Gaballufix's own clothing was unstained with blood. Vomit and urine, yes, but not blood. Nafai had to wear something. The costume wouldn't be enough— underneath it he'd be cold and barefoot.

When he thought of putting on Gaballufix's clothing, it was abhorrent to him, yes, but he also knew that he had to do it. He dragged the body up away from the blood a little, then undressed it carefully, keeping the blood off. He almost gagged as he pulled the cold wet trousers on, but then he thought contemptuously that a man who could kill the way he had just killed should hardly feel squeamish about wearing another man's piss on his legs. The same with the stench of stomach acid in the shirt and the body armor that Gaballufix had been wearing underneath. Nothing is too horrible for me to do it now, thought Nafai. I'm already lost.

The only thing he could *not* bring himself to do was put the blade at his waist, the way Gaballufix had done. Instead he wiped his fingerprints from the handle and tossed it down near where the head was lying. Then he laughed. There are my clothes, which countless witnesses saw me wearing today. Why should I have tried to conceal myself, if I'm leaving those behind?

And I *am* leaving those behind, thought Nafai. Like my own dead body I'm leaving those. The costume of a child. I'm wearing a man's clothes now. And not just any man. The most vile, monstrous man I know. They fit me.

He pulled the cloak of the soldier costume over his head. He felt no different, but he assumed that the look was there. He stepped away from the body. He could not think of where to go now. He could not think of anything.

He turned back to the body. He had left something behind, he knew that. But all that was left was his old clothing, and the blade. So he picked up the blade again after all, wiped the blood from it with his old clothes, and put it on his belt.

Now he could go on. To Gaballufix's house, of course. He knew that now, very clearly. He could think very clearly now. The trousers froze on his legs, and chafed. The body armor was heavy. It was awkward walking with the charged-wire blade. This is how it felt to be Gaballufix, thought Nafai. Tonight I am Gaballufix.

I have to hurry. Before the body is found.

No. The Oversoul will keep them from noticing the body, for a while at least. Until they are so many people out in the morning that the Oversoul can't influence them all at once. So I do have time.

He came up Fountain Street, but then thought better of it. Instead he walked over to Long Street and came up to Gaballufix's house from behind. In the alley he found the door that he had seen Elemak use, so many—so few—days before. Would it be locked?

It was. What now? Inside there would be someone waiting. Keeping guard. How could he, in the guise of a common soldier, demand entrance at this hour? What if they made him switch off the costume once he got inside? They'd recognize him at once. Worse, they'd recognize Gaballufix's clothing and they'd know that there was only one way he could come in wearing their master's clothes.

No, *two* ways.

Gaballufix must have come home drunk before.

Nafai tried, silently at first, to think of how Gaballufix's voice sounded. Husky and coarse. Rasping in the throat. Nafai could get it generally right, he was sure—and it didn't have to be too perfect, because Gaballufix was *drunk*, of course—he reeked of it—and so his voice could be slurred and out of control, and he could stagger and fall and—

"Open up, open the door!" he bawled.

That was awful, that didn't sound like Gaballufix at all. "Open the door you idiots, it's me!"

Better. Better. And besides, the Oversoul will nudge them a little, will encourage them to think of other things besides the fact that Gaballufix isn't really sounding like himself tonight.

The door opened a crack. Nafai immediately shoved it open and pushed his way through. "Locking me out of my own house, ought to send you home in a box, ought to send you back to your papa in pieces." Nafai had no idea how Gaballufix usually talked, but he guessed at general surliness and threats, especially when he was drunk. Nafai hadn't seen many drunks. Only a few times on the street, and then fairly often in the theatres, but those were actors *playing* drunk.

He thought: I'm an actor, after all. I thought that was what I might end up being, and here I am.

"Let me help you, sir," said the man. Nafai didn't look at him. Instead he deliberately stumbled and fell to his knees, then doubled over. "Going to puke, I think," he rasped. Then he touched the box at his belt and turned off the costume. Just for a moment. Just long enough that whoever else was in the room could see Gaballufix's clothing, while Nafai's face and hair were out of sight as he bent over. Then he turned the costume back on. He tried to produce the sound of dry heaves, and was so successful that he gagged and some bile and acid *did* come into his throat.

"What do you want, sir?" said the man.

"Who keeps the Index!" Nafai bawled. "Everybody wants the Index today—well now *I* want it."

"Zdorab," said the man.

"Get him."

"He's asleep, he . . ."

Nafai lurched to his feet. "When I'm off my ass in this house, *nobody* sleeps!"

"I'll get him, sir, I'm sorry, I just thought . . ."

Nafai swung clumsily at him. The man shied away, looking horrified. Am I carrying this too far? There was no way to guess. The man sidled along the wall and then ducked through a door. Nafai had no idea whether he would come back with soldiers to arrest him.

He came back with Zdorab. Or at least Nafai assumed it was Zdorab. But he had to be sure, didn't he? So he leaned close to the man and breathed nastily in his face. "Are you Zdorab?" Let the man imagine that Gaballufix was so drunk he couldn't see straight.

"Yes, sir," said the man. He seemed frightened. Good.

"My Index. Where is it?"

"Which one?"

"The one those bastards wanted—Wetchik's boys—*the* Index, by the Oversoul!"

"The *Palwashantu* Index?"

"Where did you put it, you rogue?"

"In the vault," said Zdorab. "I didn't know you wanted

it accessible. You've never used it before, and so I thought—"

"I can look at it if I want!"

Stop talking so much, he told himself. The more you say, the harder it will be for the Oversoul to keep this man from doubting my voice.

Zdorab led the way down a corridor. Nafai made it a point to bump into a wall now and then. When he did it on the side where Elemak's rod had fallen most heavily, it sent a stab of pain through his side, from shoulder to hip. He grunted with the pain—but figured that it would only make his performance more believable.

As they moved on through the lowest floor of the house, fear began to overtake him again. What if he had to provide a positive identification to open the vault? A retina scan? A thumbprint?

But the vault door stood open. Had the Oversoul influenced someone to forget to close it? Or had it all come down to chance? Am I fortune's fool, Nafai wondered, or merely the Oversoul's puppet? Or, by some slim chance, am I freely choosing at least some portion of my own path through this night's work?

He didn't even know which answer he wanted. If he was freely choosing for himself, then he had freely chosen to kill a man lying helpless in the street. Much better to believe that the Oversoul had compelled him or tricked him into doing it. Or that something in his genes or his upbringing had forced him to that action. Much better to believe that there was no other possible choice, rather than to torment himself with wondering whether it might not have been enough to steal Gaballufix's clothing, without having to kill him first. Being responsible for what he did with his opportunities was more of a burden than Nafai really wanted to bear.

Zdorab walked into the vault. Nafai followed, then

stopped when he saw a large table where the entire fortune that Gaballufix had stolen from them that afternoon was arranged in neat stacks.

"As you can see, sir, the assay is nearly done," said Zdorab as he wandered off among the shelves. "I have kept everything clean and organized there. It's very kind of you to visit."

Is he stalling me here in the vault, Nafai wondered, waiting till help can arrive?

Zdorab emerged from the shelves at the back of the room. He was a smallish man, considerably shorter than Nafai, and he was already losing his hair though he couldn't have been more than thirty. A comical man, really—yet if he guessed at what was really happening, he might cost Nafai his life.

"Is this it?" asked Zdorab.

Nafai hadn't the faintest idea what it was *supposed* to look like, of course. He had seen many indexes, but most of them were small freestanding computers with wireless access to a major library. This one had nothing that Nafai could recognize as a display. What Zdorab held was a brass-colored metal ball, about twenty-five centimeters in diameter, flattened a little at the top and the bottom. "Let me see," Nafai growled.

Zdorab seemed reluctant to part with it. For a moment, Nafai felt a wave of panic sweep over him. He doesn't want to give it to me because he knows who I really am.

Then Zdorab revealed his true concern. "Sir, you said we must always keep it very clean."

He was worried about how dirty Gaballufix might have got himself under his soldier costume. After all, he seemed falling-down drunk and smelled of liquor and worse. His hands could be covered with anything.

"You're right," said Nafai. "*You* carry it."

"If you wish, sir," said Zdorab.

"That's the one, isn't it?" said Nafai. He had to be sure—he could only hope that the drunk act was convincing enough that stupid questions wouldn't arouse suspicion.

"It's the Palwashantu Index, if that's what you mean. I just wondered if that's the one you really wanted. You've never asked for it before."

So Gaballufix hadn't even brought it out of the vault—he never, not for one moment, intended to give it to them, no matter how Elemak bargained or what they paid. It made Nafai feel a little better. There had been no missed opportunity. Every script would have led to the same ending.

"Where are we taking it?" asked Zdorab.

Excellent question, thought Nafai. I can't very well tell him that we're giving it to Wetchik's sons, who are waiting in the darkness outside the Funnel.

"Got to show it to the clan council."

"At this time of night?"

"Yes at this time of night! Interrupted me, the bastards. Having a party and they had to see the *Index* because they got some whim that maybe it got itself stolen by Wetchik's murdering lying thieving sons."

Zdorab coughed, ducked his head, and hurried on, leading Nafai down the corridor.

So Zdorab didn't like hearing Gaballufix lay such epithets on Wetchik's sons. Very interesting. But not so interesting that Nafai intended to take Zdorab into his confidence. "Slow down, you miserable little dwarf!" called Nafai.

"Yes sir," said Zdorab. He slowed down, and Nafai lurched after him.

They came to the door, where the same man stood on guard. The man looked at Zdorab, a question in his eyes.

Here's the moment, thought Nafai. A signal passing between them.

"Please open the door for Master Gaballufix," said Zdorab. "We're going out again."

The only signal, Nafai realized, was that the door-keeper was asking if this man in holographic soldier costume was Gaballufix, and Zdorab had answered by assuring him that the drunken lout inside the costume was the same one who had come in only a few moments before.

"Making merry, sir?" asked the doorkeeper.

"The council seems to be asserting itself tonight," said Zdorab.

"Want any escort?" asked the doorkeeper. "We've only got a couple of dozen close enough to lay hands on, but we can get some in from Dogtown in a few minutes, if you want them."

"No," barked Nafai.

"I just thought—the council might need a reminder, like last time—"

"They remember!" said Nafai. He wondered what "last time" was.

Zdorab led the way through the door. Nafai stumbled outside. The door latched behind them.

As they walked along the near-empty streets of Basilica, it began to dawn on Nafai what he had just accomplished. After all the day's failures, he had just come out of Gaballufix's house *with* the Index. Or at least with a man who was carrying the Index.

"The air is very invigorating, isn't it, sir," said Zdorab.

"Mm," said Nafai.

"I mean—your head seems to have cleared considerably."

It dawned on Nafai that he had forgotten to continue his drunk act. Too late to put it on again *now*, though—it would be stupid to stumble immediately after Zdorab had commented on how much less drunk he seemed. So instead, Nafai stopped, turned toward Zdorab, and glared. Not that Zdorab could see his facial expression. No, instead the man would have to imagine it.

Apparently Zdorab had a very good imagination. He immediately seemed to cower inside himself. "Not that your head wasn't clear to begin with. I mean, all along. That is, you're head is *always* clear, sir. And you've got a meeting with the clan council tonight, so that's a good thing, isn't it!"

Wonderful, thought Nafai.

"Where *are* they meeting tonight?" asked Zdorab.

Nafai hadn't the faintest idea. He only knew that he had to meet his brothers outside the Funnel. "Where do you *think!*" he growled.

"Well, I mean, it's just—you seemed to be headed toward the Funnel, and . . . which isn't to say they couldn't hold a meeting out in Dogtown, it's just that usually they . . . not that anybody ever brings me along. I mean, for all I know you might hold the meetings in a different place every night, I just heard somebody talk about the clan council meeting at your mother's house near Back Gate, but that was just—it could have been just the once."

Nafai walked on, letting Zdorab talk himself into ever greater dread.

"Oh no!" cried Zdorab.

Nafai stopped. If I take the Index and run for the gate, can I make it before he can raise an alarm?

"I left the vault open," said Zdorab. "I was so concerned about the Index . . . Please forgive me, sir. I know that the door is supposed to be open only when I'm there, and I . . . goodness, I just realized that I left it open before, too, when I came to meet you at the back door. What's got into me? I'll understand if I lose my job over this, sir. I've never left the vault door unattended. Should I go back and lock it? All that treasure there—how can you be sure that none of the servants will . . . Sir, I can rush back and still rejoin you here in only a few minutes, I'm very fleet of foot, I assure you."

This was the perfect opportunity to rid himself of Zdorab—take the Index, let the man go, and then be out the Funnel before he can return. But what if this was just a subterfuge? What if Zdorab was trying to break free of him in order to give warning to Gaballufix's soldiers that an impostor in a holographic costume was making off with the Index? He couldn't afford to let Zdorab go, not now. Not until he was safely outside the gate.

"Stay with me," said Nafai. He winced at how little his voice sounded like Gaballufix's now. Had Zdorab's eyebrows risen in surprise when Nafai spoke? Could he be wondering even now about the voice? Move on, thought Nafai. Keep moving, and say nothing. He hurried the pace. Zdorab, with his shorter legs, was jogging now to keep up.

"I've never been to a meeting like this, sir," said Zdorab. He was panting with the exertion now. "I won't have to say anything, will I? I mean, I'm not a member of the council. Oh, what am I saying! They probably won't let me into the actual meeting, anyway. I'll just wait for you outside. Please forgive me for being so nervous, I've just never . . . I spend my time in the vault and the library, of course, doing accounts and so on, you've got to realize that I just don't get out and about much, and since I live alone there's not much conversation, so most of what I know about politics is what I overhear. I know that *you're* very much involved, of course. All the people in the house are very proud to be working for such a famous man. Dangerous, though, isn't it—with Roptat murdered tonight. Aren't you just the tiniest bit afraid for yourself?"

Is he really such a fool as this? thought Nafai. Or is he, in fact, suspicious that Gaballufix might be Roptat's murderer, and this is his clumsy way of trying to extract information?

In any event, Nafai doubted Gaballufix would answer such questions, so he held his tongue. And there, at last, was the gate.

The guards were very much alert. Of course—Zdorab would be too curious if they were so strangely inattentive this time. Nafai cursed himself for having brought Zdorab along. He should have got rid of the man when he had a chance.

The guards got into position, holding out the thumb-screens. They looked belligerent, too—Nafai's soldier costume made him an enemy, or at least a rival. The thumbscreen would silently reveal his true identity, of course, but since Nafai was now under suspicion of having murdered Roptat, it wouldn't be much help.

As he stood there, frozen in indecision, Zdorab inter-vened. "You aren't actually going to insist that my master lay his thumb on your petty little screen, are you!" he blustered. Then he pressed his own thumb onto the scanner. "There, does that tell you who I am? The treasurer of Lord Gaballufix!"

"The law is, everybody lays his thumb here," said the guard. But he now looked a great deal less certain of himself. It was one thing to trade snubs with Gaballufix's soldiers, and quite another to face down the man himself. "Sorry, sir, but it's my job if I don't require it."

Nafai still didn't move.

"This is harassment," said Zdorab. "That's what it is." He kept glancing at Nafai, but of course he could read no approval or disapproval in the emotionless holographic mask.

"There's murderers out tonight," said the guard, apologetically. "You yourself reported the Wetchik's youngest son killed Roptat, and so we have to check everybody."

Nafai strode forward and reached out his hand toward the thumbscreen. As he did, however, he leaned his head close to the guard and said, quietly, "And what if the man who reported such an absurd lie was the murderer himself?"

The guard recoiled, surprised at the voice and hardly making sense of the words. Then he looked down at the screen and saw the name that the city computer showed there. He paused a moment, thinking.

Oversoul, give this man wit. Let him understand the truth, and act on it.

"Thank you for submitting to the law, Lord Gaballufix," said the guard. He pressed the clear button, and Nafai saw his name disappear. No one else could have seen it.

Without a backward glance, Nafai strode out through the gate. He heard Zdorab pattering along behind him. "Did I do right, sir?" asked Zdorab. "I mean, it seemed as though you were reluctant to give your thumb to it, and so I . . . Where are we going? Isn't it a little dark to be cutting through the brush here? Couldn't we stick to the road, Lord Gaballufix? Of course, there's a moon, so it's not *that* dark, but—"

With Zdorab's babbling, it was impossible to be subtle as they moved straight toward the spot where Nafai had left his brothers to wait for him. And now Zdorab had loudly called him by the name Gaballufix. It was hardly a surprise when Nafai saw a flurry of movement and heard footsteps, running away. Of course—they thought Nafai had been caught, that he had betrayed them, that Gaballufix had come to kill them. What could they see, except the costume?

Nafai fumbled with the controls. How could he tell whether it was off or not? Finally he yanked the costume off over his head, and then called out as loudly as he dared, and in his own voice. "Elemak! Issya! Meb! It's me—don't run!"

They stopped running.

"Nafai!" said Meb.

"In Gaballufix's clothing!" said Elemak.

"You did it!" cried Issib, laughing.

A tiny screech just behind him reminded Nafai that this sweet reunion scene would seem just a little less than happy to poor Zdorab, who had just discovered that he had been following the very man accused of murdering Roptat only a few hours before, and who had almost certainly done something quite similar to Gaballufix.

Nafai turned in time to see Zdorab turning tail and starting to run. "I'm very fleet of foot," Zdorab had said earlier, but now Nafai learned that it wasn't true. He outran the man in half a dozen steps, knocked him down, and wrestled with him on the stony ground for only a few moments before he had him pinned, with his hand over the poor man's mouth. The guards were no more than fifty meters away. No doubt the Oversoul had kept them from paying attention to the shouting that had just gone on, but there were limits to the Oversoul's ability to make people stupid.

"Listen to me," Nafai whispered fiercely. "If you do what I say, Zdorab, I won't kill you. Do you understand?"

Under his hand, Nafai felt the head nod up and down.

"I give you my oath by the Oversoul that I did not murder Roptat. Your master Gaballufix caused Roptat's death and gave orders for me and my brothers to be killed. *He* was the murderer, but now I've killed Gaballufix and that was justice. Do you understand me? I'm not one who kills for pleasure. I don't want to kill *you*. Will you be silent if I uncover your mouth?"

Again the nod. Nafai uncovered his mouth.

"I'm glad you don't want to kill me," Zdorab whispered. "I don't want to be dead."

"Do you believe my words?" Nafai asked.

"Would you believe my answer?" asked Zdorab. "I think we're in one of those situations where people will say pretty much whatever they think the other person wants to hear, wouldn't you say?"

He had a point. "Zdorab, I can't let you go back into the city, do you understand me? I guess what it comes down to is this—if you really are one of Gaballufix's men, one of the louts that he hires to do his dirty work in Basilica, then I can't trust anything you say and I might as well kill you now and have done. But I don't think that's who you are. I think you're a librarian, a record-keeper, a *clerk* who had no idea what working for Gaballufix entailed."

"I kept seeing things but nobody else seemed to think they were strange and no one would ever answer my questions so I kept to myself and held my tongue. Mostly."

"We're going out into the desert. If you go with us, and stay with us—if you give me your word by the Oversoul—then you'll be a free man, part of our household, the equal of any other. We don't want you for a servant; we'll only have you as a friend."

"Of course I'll give my oath. But how will you know whether to believe me?"

"Swear by the Oversoul, my friend Zdorab, and I'll know."

"By the Oversoul, then, I swear to stay with you and be

your loyal friend forever. On the condition that you don't kill me. Though I guess if you killed me then the rest of it would be moot, wouldn't it."

Nafai could see that his brothers were now gathered around. They had heard the oath, of course, and had their own opinions. "Kill him," Meb said. "He's one of Gaballufix's men, you can't believe them."

"I'll do it, if it must be done," said Elemak.

"How can we know?" asked Issib.

But Nafai didn't hear them. He was listening for the Oversoul, and the answer was clear. Trust the man.

"I accept your oath," said Nafai. "And I swear by the Oversoul that neither I nor anyone in my family will harm you, as long as you keep your oath. All of you—swear it."

"This is absurd!" said Mebbekew. "You're putting us all at risk."

"For this night the Oversoul gave me the command," said Nafai, "and you promised to obey. I came out of the city with the Index, didn't I? And Gaballufix is dead. Swear to this man!"

They took the oath, all of them.

"Now," said Nafai to Zdorab, "give me the Index."

"I can't," said Zdorab.

"See?" said Meb.

"I mean—when you knocked me down, I dropped it."

"Wonderful," said Elemak. "All this way to get this precious Index, and now we're going to be picking up pieces of it all over the desert."

Issib found it, though, only a meter away, and when Elemak picked it up, it seemed unharmed. By moonlight, at least, there didn't seem to be even a scratch.

Mebbekew also took a close look at it, handled it, hefted it. "Just a ball. A metal ball."

"It doesn't even *look* like an index," said Issib.

Nafai reached out his hands and took the thing from Mebbekew. Immediately it began to glow. Lights appeared under it.

"You've got it upside down, I think," said Zdorab.

Nafai turned it over. In the air over the ball, a holographic arrow pointed southwest. Above the arrow were several words, but in a language Nafai didn't understand.

"That's ancient Puckyi," said Issib. "Nobody speaks it now."

The letters changed. It was a single word. *Chair.*

"The arrow," said Issib. "It's pointing toward where I left my chair."

"Let me see that," said Elemak.

Nafai handed him the Index. The moment it left Nafai's hands, the display disappeared.

Nafai reached out to take the Index back. Elemak looked at him steadily, his eyes like ice, and then he handed Nafai the metal ball. When Nafai touched it again, the display reappeared. Nafai turned to Zdorab. "What does this mean?"

"I don't know," said Zdorab. "It never did anything before. I thought it was broken."

"Let me try," said Issib.

"Please, no," said Nafai. "Let's wrap it up and carry it home to Father without looking at it again. Elemak knows the way. He should lead us."

"Right," said Mebbekew.

"Whatever," said Issib.

"Which one's Elemak?" asked Zdorab.

Elemak strode away toward High Road, toward the place where Issib's chair was waiting for them. By the time they got back to the camels, the sky was just beginning to lighten in the east. Nafai wrapped the Index and gave it to Elemak to stow it on a pack frame.

"*You* should give it to Father," Nafai said.

Elemak reached out and took a pinch of Nafai's—no, Gaballufix's—shirt between his thumb and forefinger. He leaned close and spoke softly. "Don't patronize me, Nafai. I see the way of things, and I'll tell you now. I won't be given power or honor or anything as a gift from *you*. Whatever I have I'll have because it's mine by right. Do you understand me?"

Nafai nodded. Elemak let go of his shirt and walked away. Only then did Nafai understand that there would be no healing this breach between him and his eldest brother. The Index had come to life under Nafai's hands. It had lain inert in Elemak's. The Oversoul had spoken, and Elemak would never forgive the message that it gave.

SIXTEEN

THE INDEX OF
THE OVERSOUL

Nafai and Father sat and Issib lay on a rug in Father's tent. The Index rested on the rug between them. Nafai touched the Index with his fingers. Father also reached out and touched it with one hand. Then, with the other, he lifted Issib's arm and brought his hand near, until it touched. With the three of them in contact with it at the same time, the Index spoke.

"Awake, after all this time," said the Index. It was a whisper. Nafai wasn't altogether sure whether he was hearing it with his ears, or whether his mind was transforming the ambient noises—the desert breeze, their own breathing—into a voice.

"You came to us at great cost," said Father.

"I waited for a long time to have this voice again," answered the Index.

It wasn't the Index speaking. Nafai knew that now. "This is the voice of the Oversoul."

"Yes," said the whisper.

"If this contains your voice," said Father, "why is it called an index?"

The answer came only after a long hesitation. "This is the index to *me*," it finally said.

The Index of the Oversoul. An index was a tool created to make it easier for people to find their way through the labyrinthine memory of a complex computer. The Oversoul was the greatest of all computers, and this was the tool that would let Nafai and Issib and Father begin, at last, to understand it. "Now that we have the Index," said Nafai, "can you explain to us who you—*what* you are?" Nafai asked.

Again the pause, and then the whispering: "I am the Memory of Earth. I was never meant to last so long. I am weakening, and must return to the one who is wiser than I, who will tell me what to do to save this unharmonious world called Harmony. I have chosen your family to carry me back to the Keeper of Earth."

"*That* is where you're leading us?"

"The world that was buried in ice and hidden in smoke is surely alive and awake now. The Keeper who drove humankind from the planet they destroyed will surely not turn his face away from you now. Follow me, children of Earth, and I will take you back to your ancient home."

Nafai looked from Father to Issib and back again. "Do you realize what that means?" he said.

"A long journey," said Father, wearily.

"Long!" cried Nafai. "So long that it takes *light* a hundred years to reach us!"

"What are you talking about?" said Issib. "You'd think the Oversoul had promised to take us to another planet."

Issib's words hung in the air like music out of tune. Nafai sat there, stunned. Of *course* the Oversoul had promised to take them to another planet. Those were its plain words. Except that this wasn't what Issib had heard.

Or Father. Obviously, then, the Index did not make literal sounds, and they were in fact hearing with their minds, not their ears.

"What did *you* think the Oversoul said?" Nafai asked.

"That he was going to lead us to a beautiful land," said Father. "A good place, where crops would grow, and orchards thrive. A place where our children could be free and good, without the evils of Basilica."

"But *where?*" asked Nafai. "Where did it say that this beautiful land would be?"

"Nafai, you must learn to be more patient and trusting," said Father. "The Oversoul will lead us one step at a time, and then, one day, one of those steps will be the last one in our journey, and we'll be home."

"It won't be a city," said Issib, "but it will be a place where I can use my floats again."

Nafai was deeply disappointed. He knew what he had heard, but he also knew that Father and Issib had not heard it. Why not? Either it meant that they simply couldn't comprehend the voice of the Oversoul as clearly as he could, or it meant that the Oversoul had given them a different message. Either way, he couldn't force his own understanding on them.

"What did *you* hear?" asked Father. "Was there more?"

"Nothing important for now," said Nafai. "What really matters is knowing that we're not going to wait around for Basilica to take us back. We're not exiles now, we're expatriates. Emigrants. Basilica is not our city anymore."

Father sighed. "And to think I was just about to retire and turn the business over to Elya. I didn't want to journey anymore! Now I'm about to take the longest journey of my life, I fear."

Nafai reached out and took the Index between his hands and drew it close. It trembled in his grasp. "As for you, my strange little Index, I hope you turn out to be worth all the trouble that was taken to get you. The price that was paid."

"Such a fortune," said Issib. "I never knew we were so rich until the day we weren't."

"We're richer than ever now," said Father. "We have a whole land promised to us, with no city or clan or enemy to take it away. And the Index to the Oversoul is here to lead the way."

Nafai hardly heard them. He was thinking of the blood that he had shed, of how it stained his clothing and his skin. I didn't want to do it, he thought, and it was simple justice, to take the life of a murderer. When Elemak thought he might have killed a man, from far off, with a pulse, he bragged about it. But I killed him close, under my own hand, as he lay drunken and helpless on the street. I did it, not in fear for my own life, and not to protect a caravan, but in cold blood, without anger. Because the Oversoul told me that it was right. And because I believed in my own heart that it was necessary.

But I also hated him. Will I ever be sure that I didn't do it because of that hatred, that longing for vengeance? I fear that I will always suspect that I am an assassin in my heart.

I can live with that, though. I can sleep tonight. With time I'm sure that the pain of it will even fade. It's the price of the thing that I agreed to be: a servant of the Oversoul. I'm not my own man anymore. I'm the man the Oversoul has chosen to make of me. I hope I like at least a small part of what I've become, when at last the Oversoul is through with me.

He slept that night and dreamed. Not of murder. Not of Gaballufix's head, nor of the blood on his own clothes. Instead he dreamed of drifting on a sea whose currents ran hot and cold, as fog drifted endlessly in front of his face. And then, out of this lost and mysterious and peaceful place, hands searched across his face, his shoulder, and then took hold of his arm and pulled him close.

I'm not the first one here, he realized as he woke from the dream. I'm not alone in this place, this kingdom of the Oversoul. Others have been here before me, and are with me now, and *will* be with me through all that is to come.

GUIDE TO PRONUNCIATION OF NAMES

For the purpose of reading this story silently to yourself, it hardly matters whether the reader pronounces the names of the characters correctly. But for those who might be interested, here is some information concerning the pronunciation of names.

The rules of vowel formation in the language of Basilica require that in most nouns, including names, at least one vowel be pronounced with a leading *y* sound. With names, it can be almost any vowel, and it can legitimately be changed at the speaker's preference. Thus the name Gaballufix could be pronounced *Gyah*-BAH-loo-fix or Gah-BAH-*lyoo*-fix; it happens that Gaballufix himself preferred to pronounce it Gah-B*YAH*-loo-fix, and of course most people followed that usage.

Dhelembuvex [thel-EM-byoo-vex]

Dol [DYOHL]

Drotik [DROHT-yik]

Eiadh [AY-yahth]

Elemak [EL-yeh-mahk]

Hosni [HYOZ-nee]
Hushidh [HYOO-sheeth]
Issib [IS-yib]
Kokor [KYOH-kor]
Luet [LYOO-et]
Mebbekew [MEB-bek-kyoo]
Nafai [NYAH-fie]
Obring [OB-rying]
Rasa [RAHZ-yah]
Rashgallivak [rahsh-GYAH-lih-vahk]

Roptat [ROPE-tyaht]
Sevet [SEV-yet]
Shedemei [SHYED-eh-may]
Truzhnisha [troozh-NYEE-shah]
Vas [VYAHS]
Volemak [VOHL-yeh-mak]
Wetchik [WET-chyick]
Zdorab [ZDOR-yab]